"*A Poisoned Season* is a rollicking romp through Victorian London's high society, encompassing romance, scandal, thievery, and murder most foul. It all comes right at the end, and is loads of fun to read."

—Judith Koll Healey, author of *The Canterbury Papers*

"Tasha Alexander's exciting and cleverly plotted new novel transports us to late nineteenth-century London and a world of hansom cabs, glittering society balls, brazen theft, and murder. Emily Ashton is undoubtedly one of the most spirited and fascinating heroines to appear in years, and we cannot help but cheer her on as she cleverly unravels the twists and turns of a bold and determined killer. Romance, suspense, and remarkable historical detail add to the richness of Alexander's tale. *A Poisoned Season* is pure delight!"   —Shirley Tallman, author of
Murder on Nob Hill and *The Russian Hill Murders*

"A delightful Victorian cozy with a charming heroine that devotees of the genre will want to meet again."

—C. S. Harris, author of *When Gods Die*

"Sometimes touching, sometimes funny, and always absorbing, this Victorian-era mystery hits all the right notes."   —*Romantic Times*

"Lady Emily Ashton is clever, lovely, and thoroughly entertaining. . . . I couldn't put down *A Poisoned Season* and look forward to many more of Lady Emily's adventures."

—Sujata Massey, award-winning author of *Girl in a Box*

"*A Poisoned Season* draws the reader into the glittering Victorian age with its society balls, Worth gowns, hansom cabs, and proper manners. Throw in a complex mystery with several intriguing twists, and you have the ingredients for a charming historical cozy with a clever heroine readers won't soon forget."   —*BookPage*

"One first-rate history mystery, *A Poisoned Season* mixes spot-on dialogue, manners, and mores, with a splash of erotic friction in a lively, delightful tale. Alexander's sweetly choreographed plot dances between her wonderfully drawn sleuth, Lady Emily Ashton, and Victorian high society."   —Julia Spencer-Fleming, Edgar Award finalist
and author of *All Mortal Flesh*

Wolf Hoffman

About the Author

TASHA ALEXANDER is a graduate of Notre Dame, where she signed on as an English major in order to have a legitimate excuse for spending all her time reading. Following graduation, she played nomad for several years, eventually settling with her family in Tennessee. When not reading, she can be found hard at work on her next book featuring Lady Emily Ashton.

A POISONED SEASON

Also by Tasha Alexander

AND ONLY TO DECEIVE

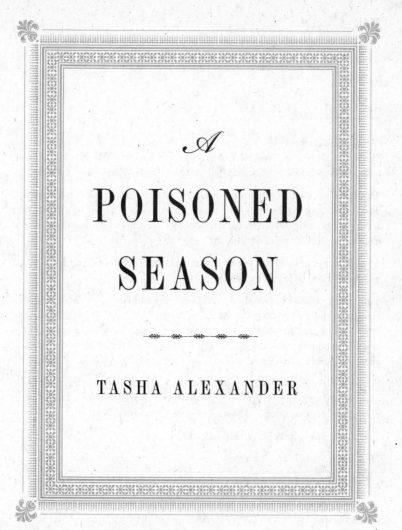

A

POISONED
SEASON

TASHA ALEXANDER

HARPER

NEW YORK · LONDON · TORONTO · SYDNEY

HARPER

A hardcover edition of this book was published in 2007 by William Morrow, an imprint of HarperCollins Publishers.

A POISONED SEASON. Copyright © 2007 by Anastasia Tyska. All rights reserved. Printed in the United States of America. No part of this book may be used or reproduced in any manner whatsoever without written permission except in the case of brief quotations embodied in critical articles and reviews. For information address HarperCollins Publishers, 10 East 53rd Street, New York, NY 10022.

HarperCollins books may be purchased for educational, business, or sales promotional use. For information please write: Special Markets Department, HarperCollins Publishers, 10 East 53rd Street, New York, NY 10022.

FIRST HARPER PAPERBACK PUBLISHED 2008.

Designed by Susan Yang

The Library of Congress has catalogued the hardcover edition as follows:

Alexander, Tasha.
    A poisoned season / Tasha Alexander. — 1st ed.
    p. cm.
    ISBN: 978-0-06-117414-8
    ISBN-10: 0-06-117414-9
    1. Jewelry theft—Fiction. 2. England—Social life and customs—19th century—Fiction. I. Title.

PS3601.L3565P65   2007
813'.6—dc22   2006046758

ISBN: 978-0-06-117421-6 (pbk.)

    10 11 12 ID/RRD 10 9 8 7 6

For Xander, who prefers
his books read aloud

AT LAST THE SECRET IS OUT

At last the secret is out, as it always must come
  in the end,
The delicious story is ripe to tell to the intimate friend;
Over the tea-cups and in the square the tongue has its
  desire;
Still waters run deep, my dear, there's never smoke
  without fire.

Behind the corpse in the reservoir, behind the ghost on
  the links,
Behind the lady who dances and the man who madly
  drinks,
Under the look of fatigue, the attack of migraine and the
  sigh
There is always another story, there is more than meets
  the eye.

For the clear voice suddenly singing, high up in the
  convent wall,
The scent of elder bushes, the sporting prints in the hall,
The croquet matches in summer, the handshake, the
  cough, the kiss,
There is always a wicked secret, a private reason for this.

—W. H. Auden

CAST OF CHARACTERS

LADY EMILY ASHTON ("KALLISTA")—Daughter of Earl Bromley, widow of the Viscount Ashton (Philip), and a scholar of Greek language and art

COLIN HARGREAVES—A gentleman of independent means who is frequently called upon by Buckingham Palace to investigate matters requiring discretion

CÉCILE DU LAC—A French woman of a certain age, an iconoclast and patron of the arts

IVY BRANDON—Emily's childhood friend, a perfect English rose

ROBERT BRANDON—Ivy's husband, an up-and-coming politician and very traditional gentleman

MARGARET SEWARD—Daughter of an American railroad tycoon, a Bryn Mawr–educated Latinist with little tolerance for society's rules

LADY CATHERINE BROMLEY—Emily's mother, wife of Earl Bromley, former lady-in-waiting to Queen Victoria

CHARLES BERRY—A gentleman newly arrived in London who claims to be a direct descendant of Marie Antoinette and Louis XVI

JEREMY SHEFFIELD, DUKE OF BAINBRIDGE—Childhood friend of Emily's whose twin goals are to avoid marriage and to be the most useless man in England

DAVID FRANCIS—A gentleman and patron of the arts

BEATRICE FRANCIS—David Francis's wife

LADY FRIDESWIDE—A terrifying society matron bent on seeing her daughter married to the Duke of Bainbridge

LETTICE FRIDESWIDE—Lady Frideswide's daughter, who is not in the least interested in marrying the Duke of Bainbridge

LORD BASIL FORTESCUE—Queen Victoria's most trusted political adviser, widely considered the most powerful man in the Empire

MRS. REYNOLD-PLYMPTON—A lady who takes great interest in politics

LADY ELINOR ROUTLEDGE—Longtime friend of Emily's family, widow of the Chancellor of the Exchequer

ISABELLE ROUTLEDGE—Lady Elinor's extremely romantic daughter

LORD THOMAS PEMBROKE ("TOMMY")—the Viscount Langley, eldest son of the Earl of Westbrook

LADY ELLIOTT—A devoted friend of Lady Bromley's and one of London's most fiercely judgmental society ladies

MICHAEL BARBER—A sculptor

JANE STILLEMAN—Beatrice Francis's maid

MOLLY, BRIDGET, AND GABBY—Maids at the Savoy hotel

MEG—Emily's maid

DAVIS—Emily's incomparable butler

A POISONED SEASON

1

THERE ARE SEVERAL THINGS ONE CAN DEPEND UPON DURING THE
London Season: an overwhelming barrage of invitations, friends
whose loyalties turn suspect, and at least one overzealous suitor. This
year was to prove no exception.

Having recently come out of mourning for my late husband, Philip,
the Viscount Ashton, I was determined to adopt a hedonistic approach
to society, something that I imagined would involve refusing all but
the most enticing invitations and being forced to cull disloyal acquaintances. This would allow me to enjoy the summer months instead of
trudging from party to party, feeling like one of the exhausted dead,
finding myself the subject of the gossip that fuels young barbarians at
play.

However, it became clear almost immediately that my theory was
flawed. Declining to attend parties proved not to have the desired
effect. Instead of dropping me from their guest lists, people assumed I
was in such demand that I was choosing to attend events even more exclusive than their own, and there are few better ways to increase one's
volume of invitations than by the appearance of popularity. So for a
short while—a very short while—my peers held me in high esteem.

It was during this time that I found myself at the home of Lady Elinor Routledge, one of the finest hostesses in England and a long-standing friend of my mother's. By definition, therefore, she was more concerned with a person's societal standing than with anything else. Despite this, I had decided to attend her garden party for two reasons. First, I wanted to see her roses, whose equal, according to rumor, could not be found in all of England. Second, I hoped to meet Mr. Charles Berry, a young man whose presence in town had caused a stir amongst all the aristocracy. The roses surpassed all of my expectations; unfortunately, the gentleman did not.

When stepping into the garden at Meadowdown, one was transported from the gritty heat of London's streets to a sumptuous oasis. For the party, lovely peaked tents were scattered between hedgerows, trees, and beds of flowers, ensuring that guests would never be more than a few paces from refreshment, and the sounds of a small orchestra wafted through the grounds. Young ladies flitted about, their brightly colored dresses competing with the flowers for attention and rarely losing the battle. The gentlemen, turned out in dark frock coats, were elegant, too, keeping their companions well supplied with ices, strawberries, or whatever delicacies might catch their fancy. *Et in Arcadia ego.* It would take little effort for one to imagine in this scene an eligible prince, all courtesy and ease, graciously bestowing his favor on those around him. But there was no such gentleman at Lady Elinor's that day. The only prince present—if he could be called that—was a grave disappointment.

The romantic ideals swirling around the heir to a throne are seldom capable of surviving close scrutiny. In the case of Charles Berry, these ideals hardly stood observation from afar. His appearance was not unpleasant, but his manners were dreadful, and to say that he was prone to drink more than he ought would be a very diplomatic statement indeed. The young ladies who followed his every move with admiration happily ignored all of this; they were captivated by the notion of marrying into a royal family. The situation was rendered all the more ridiculous when one considered the fact that the throne to which Mr. Berry aspired no longer existed.

"I hoped he would be more handsome." Cécile du Lac formed opinions of people quickly and rarely changed them. We had known each other for less than a year, but she had become one of my closest confidantes almost from the moment I'd met her, despite the fact that she was nearer in age to my mother than to me. She watched him as she continued. "And he lacks completely the generous spirit one likes to find in a monarch. If he could not claim a direct relation to Louis XVI and Marie Antoinette, society would hold him in much less regard."

Almost from the moment Louis XVI's son and heir had died in a French prison during the revolution, rumors that the boy had escaped began to circulate. Now, nearly a century later, gentlemen were still coming forward, insisting that they were descended from Louis Charles. Charles Berry was the most recent to make the claim, and his story was filled with enough details to convince the surviving members of the Bourbon family to accept him as the dauphin's great-grandson.

"Don't judge him too harshly," Lady Elinor said, moving her hands gracefully in a gesture designed not to emphasize her words, but to show off the spectacular ruby ring on her right hand. "He's led a difficult life."

"Do you know him well?" I asked her.

"He was at Oxford with my son, George, although they didn't move in the same crowd. George has always been very serious. He takes after his father." Lady Elinor's husband, Mr. John Routledge, had been a steady if somewhat humorless man, who served in the government as chancellor of the exchequer until his death some years ago. George, who was much older than his sister, had taken a position in the diplomatic corps and had been stationed in India for so long that I could hardly recall what he looked like. "Let me introduce you. I think you'll find Mr. Berry most charming."

The gentleman in question stood not far from us, surrounded by several very eligible heiresses whose mothers watched, hawklike, from a safe distance, eagerly trying to gauge which girl garnered the most attention from the purported heir to the House of Bourbon. I wondered if any of them gave even momentary consideration to what it might be like to actually be the wife of such a man. None of the mothers tried to hide her irritation when Lady Elinor pulled him away.

"How do you find London?" I asked after the introductions had been made.

"A wonderful city. But I must admit that I long for Paris. I have great hopes, you know, that my throne will be restored."

"Really, Monsieur Berry?" Cécile asked, incredulous. "I had no idea the Third Republic was in danger of being replaced by a monarchy."

"France would be lucky to have you," Lady Elinor said.

"It is not impossible. I, of course, would never presume to seek such a thing, but if it proves to be the will of the people ..." He let his voice trail off and looked at me as if appraising my value. "You, Lady Ashton, would be an ornament in any court."

"You flatter me." I saw a look of dissatisfaction pass quickly across Lady Elinor's face and realized that she, too, had fallen victim to wanting a royal husband for her daughter. Isabelle was a sweet girl, out for her second season. She was not pretty, not in the classical way, but possessed bright eyes and an eager smile that more than made up for any imperfections in her features. I confess to being surprised by how much she had matured in the past year; gone completely was the child I remembered following me around after my own debut, begging for stories of balls and parties. If she still harbored any of the romantic ideas she'd had as a girl, she was headed for disappointment unless she could convince her mother that Mr. Berry was not a desirable suitor. I decided to direct the subject away from the gentleman altogether and turned to my hostess. "Have you seen Mr. Bingham this afternoon?"

"He arrived not half an hour ago," Lady Elinor replied. "Though I must warn you that he's not one for genteel conversation."

"I know it all too well. He owns a silver libation bowl—the sort the ancient Greeks used to hold offerings to the gods. The decoration on it is exquisite—Athena, Hermes, Dionysus, and Ares riding in chariots driven by winged Nikes."

"What is a Nike?" Lady Elinor asked.

"Victory. Perhaps you've seen the Nike Samothrace in the Louvre?"

"Ah, yes. How…interesting that you know about such things."

"I've been trying to convince Mr. Bingham to sell me the piece for the past three months and have barely had a civil word from him."

"Are you a collector?" Mr. Berry asked.

"My late husband was, but he also made many donations to the British Museum. I've continued this practice, though I admit it's not always easy for me to part with what I've acquired. But in this case, I want the *phiale* for the museum. It's too significant to be left languishing in a private home. I had hoped I could persuade Mr. Bingham to donate it himself, but he will not be convinced."

"Aren't you clever!" Lady Elinor said, then turned to Mr. Berry. "Lady Ashton is quite a scholar."

"Surely you've put aside all thoughts of studying during the Season?" he asked.

"Studying Greek, Mr. Berry, is what will get me through the Season." He made a dissatisfied-sounding grunt, and Lady Elinor smiled, confident that branding me a scholar would be enough to keep the gentleman from growing *too* interested in me. I hoped she was correct.

"You speak almost like an Englishman, Monsieur Berry," Cécile said. "I expected to find you more French."

"I spent much of my youth in the United States. We did not speak French, even at home. My father sent me to Oxford for university, and I've lived in England ever since. He was a very private man, never wanted the public to know his true identity. I respected this position while he was alive, but now that he is dead, I believe it is time to reclaim my heritage." He stepped close to Cécile and continued in a low voice. "I am moved more than you can imagine by the sight of your earrings. I understand that they belonged to my twice *arrière-grand-mère*."

"They did, monsieur, and I thought it appropriate to wear them when I met the pretender to the Bourbon throne. Marie Antoinette had them on when she was arrested during the revolution."

"How I wish I could touch them." He moved even closer to her, and for a moment I thought he would reach out for them.

Isabelle, who had been summoned to her mother's side, frowned. "She was arrested wearing them?" she asked. "Aren't you afraid they'll bring you bad luck?"

"Not at all," Cécile replied.

"They're just the sort of thing that would carry a curse, the tragic fate of a previous owner haunting everyone else who possesses them," Isabelle said with a dramatic flair.

"I assure you, mademoiselle, that I am not concerned in the least," Cécile said, shrugging.

"Where did you get them, Cécile?" I asked.

"My brother purchased them for his fiancée. Unfortunately, she died before they were married, and he gave them to me."

"Died before they were married?" I asked. "Clearly the poor woman was cursed."

"Not in the least. Claudette had a sickly constitution long before Paul gave her the earrings."

Although I counted Cécile among my dearest friends, this story of her brother, along with vague rumors that her ancestors had been sympathetic to the monarchy during the revolution, was nearly all the information I'd heard about her family. Like me, she was a widow, though her husband had died almost thirty years ago. It was this that first drew us together—not simply that we had lost husbands, but that we had lost husbands we did not mourn.

"I would hesitate to wear them," Isabelle said. "You're very brave."

"It would take more than a curse to stop Madame du Lac," Colin Hargreaves said, striding confidently towards us, a broad smile on his face. "Do my eyes deceive me? Or is it true that the delights of the Season are enough to entice Lady Ashton to abandon the pleasures of Greece?"

"Colin!" I cried, feeling an unmistakable rush of pleasure as he brushed his lips over my gloved hand, the color rising in my cheeks as our eyes met. "Your letter said you would be in Berlin until next week."

"My business finished more quickly than expected. I called on you at Berkeley Square not an hour ago, and your butler told me I could find you here. Lady Elinor was kind enough to allow me in without an invitation." His face was already tanned from riding in the summer sun.

"You are always welcome in my home, Mr. Hargreaves," our hostess said, clearly relieved to find a gentleman other than Mr. Berry paying attention to me. "Have you met Mr. Berry?"

"Yes, we spent some time together on the Continent this spring." This surprised me. In all the letters he'd sent to me in the past months, Colin had never once mentioned Mr. Berry, and Mr. Berry did not strike me as the sort of man with whom Colin would have much interest in spending time.

"Lady Elinor, would you show me where to find your claret cup?" Cécile asked, a sly smile forming on her lips.

"May I get some for you, Madame du Lac?" Colin asked.

"Non, merci, Monsieur Hargreaves. That would defeat my purpose entirely." She tapped his arm with her fan as she spoke before turning to Mr. Berry. "And you, sir, come with us. I'd like to hear more about your plans for France." Isabelle hung back for a moment, but a sharp glance from her mother spurred her to follow the group.

"I shall never be able to adequately thank Cécile for her continuing interest in leaving me alone with you," Colin said, kissing my hand again as soon as they had left us, "although I'd prefer a more private setting altogether. I should like nothing better than to take you in my arms."

"You wouldn't dare," I replied, half wishing that he would, my hand still warm where his lips had lingered. "But I suppose it's best not to cause a scandal this early in the Season. Are you free for dinner this evening?"

"Unfortunately not. I've a prior engagement."

"A prior engagement?"

"I am a very eligible bachelor, Emily. You must expect that my calendar will be very full in the coming months."

"Well, before you begin proposing to any of the debutantes who are sure to throw themselves at your feet, I do hope you'll consider my feelings. I'd be quite lost if you refused to help me with my Greek."

"How kind of you to find some use for me." He squeezed my hand. "It's work, actually, that will keep me from you tonight."

"Anything that might interest me?" I asked. Colin was frequently called upon by Buckingham Palace to assist in matters that, as he explained it, required more than a modicum of discretion.

"Definitely not." Without another word, he led me, rather forcefully, to a quiet corner of the garden, where, though we did not have the privacy my library would have afforded, we were able to greet each other in a much more satisfactory manner.

❀ ❀ ❀

That night, though I wished I could have seen Colin, I applied my-self to translating passages from Homer's *Odyssey*. I brought my work to bed, where I continued to read until I drifted off to sleep, only to be awakened long before morning, disturbed by the hard cover of the book, which had wedged itself against my back. Sitting up, I gath-ered my now wrinkled papers and placed them on the bedside table. As I laid the volume of Homer on top of them, something moved near the wall across from me. I hesitated for only a moment before quietly slipping out of bed to investigate, but I was too late. There was noth-ing there. I might have dismissed it as a dream had I not noticed the curtains begin to sway. Flinging them aside, I half expected to find someone standing before me. Instead, all I saw was the window, which had been closed when I went to bed, now wide open, rain blowing into my chamber.

I quickly lit every lamp in the room, and the flitting shadows that followed me startled me whenever they caught my eye. It was summer, but I felt a chill that I could not shake. My silk curtains were soaked and ruined, but other than that, everything looked as it had when I'd fallen asleep. Nonetheless, I rang for my butler and crossed the hallway to the room where Cécile slept. It appeared that I had overre-acted until she inspected her jewelry cases. The locks on each of them had been picked, but of all the exquisite pieces that they contained, only one was missing: Marie Antoinette's teardrop-shaped diamond earrings, the ones Cécile had worn that afternoon.

Davis, my butler, sent for the police at once, and their thorough search of my house proved what I had suspected after seeing Cécile's cases: Nothing was missing except the earrings. The priceless antiqui-ties displayed in my library, the old masters' paintings that could be found throughout the house, and my own jewelry were untouched. Not even the two-hundred-carat emerald-and-diamond necklace that sat next to the earrings was disturbed. Our thief had known what he wanted.

"It is difficult to be angry with a man who shows such refined taste," Cécile said the next morning as we sat at the breakfast table. "Clearly he is not motivated by greed."

"It's a pity your dogs did not bark to warn us of the intruder." Cécile refused to leave her home in Paris without her pets and would not come to visit me unless I agreed to let her bring them. Caesar and Brutus were tiny things, more likely to cower at the sight of a cat than to bark at a burglar. "If I had woken up earlier, I might have seen him," I said, frowning. The police had found footprints in the garden beneath my room, and although the rain had washed away any identifying features, they were able to determine that the intruder had entered the house through my window. This revelation had deeply disturbed Davis, who reprimanded the entire staff and assured me that he would personally check the locks in the house every evening. I did not hold anyone responsible. Had it not been raining, I would have directed my maid to leave the window open, and I said as much to Colin when he arrived to find Cécile and me still at breakfast.

"Best to keep the windows closed and locked in the future. I am most relieved to see both of you unharmed after your ordeal. I wouldn't have called at such a beastly hour if I weren't concerned about you."

Cécile smiled. "I've always wanted to breakfast with you, Monsieur Hargreaves. Let me assure you we are quite fine, though I suspect that had you been here last night, my earrings would not have vanished. How unfortunate that you had other plans."

"Even if I had called last night, I would not have been here so late."

Cécile looked at me pointedly. "That, of course, is not for me to say," she said.

"How did you learn of the theft?" I asked.

"A friend in Scotland Yard alerted me."

"And will you investigate?"

"No, Emily. I'm not a detective."

"Such is our misfortune, Monsieur Hargreaves," Cécile said.

"It is a strange case, though," Colin said. "Lord Grantham's house was broken into three weeks ago, and the only object taken was a Limoges box. The following week, a gilt inkwell disappeared from the home of Mrs. Blanche Wilmot. Both items belonged to Marie Antoinette."

"I have great hopes for our thief, Monsieur Hargreaves," Cécile said. "It is rare to find a man with such focus."

"There is no reason to think that he will come here again, unless one of you is hiding another of the ill-fated queen's possessions."

"We aren't, so I suppose we're safe," I said, rubbing my temples and suddenly feeling very tired. "I admit that it's unnerving to have been so violated."

"I shall have Inspector Manning, who has been assigned to the case, step up patrols near your house. You needn't worry."

"I don't know the inspector, but you, Monsieur Hargreaves, inspire absolute confidence," Cécile said. "I will quite depend upon you." She patted his arm as she walked past him. "Do not keep Kallista too long." Cécile had not abandoned her habit of calling me by the name my late husband had used for me.

"Excitement seems to follow you," Colin said, accepting the cup of tea I poured for him.

"It's following Cécile. I've never owned anything of Marie Antoinette's."

"I'm glad of it." His dark eyes flashed. "I cannot stand thinking of that criminal in your room. I should have come to you last night."

"Cécile's remark was not meant as a rebuke. She merely wanted me to ponder the idea of having you here so late at night. She's quite a corrupting influence."

"Then I am forever indebted to her."

"As you should be."

"And *did* you ponder the idea of having me here so late at night?"

"I did. It was most pleasant." Our eyes met. At once my fatigue dissipated as the feeling of violation was replaced with a lovely warmth. "Perhaps after the Season you should come to Greece with me." I had spent much of the spring exploring Greece, using as my base the villa that had become mine after Philip's death.

"Hardly appropriate for us to travel together."

"I thought you approved of my corruption?"

"I wholeheartedly do, but I don't want to see you *that* corrupt." He stood up, walked around the table to me, and took my hands. I closed my eyes, anticipating his kiss when Davis entered the room, carrying the morning mail on a small silver tray. Colin contented himself with quickly kissing my hand and went back to his seat. Doing my best to show no disappointment, I turned my attention to the envelopes before me. With invitations to two or three balls every evening, and as many dinner parties, not to mention teas, garden parties, and luncheons, one could easily be overwhelmed during the Season. And that was before considering the Derby, Ascot, the Royal Academy's Summer Exhibition, or any of the numerous other events not to be missed. I sifted through the pile before me, checking for personal correspondence.

"Anything interesting?" Colin asked.

"That's unlikely, unless you've sent me something." I tossed aside a note from my mother, knowing full well that it contained an admonishment for my turning down an invitation to her friend Lady Elliott's reception for Charles Berry. Although my mother had been content to see me married to a viscount—particularly as Philip's family had connections to royalty going back to the reign of Elizabeth—she had taken a renewed interest in my status since I'd come out of mourning and had returned to her hope that I might yet marry royalty.

Another envelope caught my attention. It bore no stamp so must have been hand-delivered. Inside was a short passage, written in ancient Greek:

Ἅδιον οὐδὲν ἔρωτος ἃ δ' ὄλβια δεύτερα πάντα
ἐστίν

"Is this from you?" I asked, passing it to Colin.

"Unfortunately not, though I wish it were. I agree heartily with the sentiment."

"Could you translate for me? I'm afraid I couldn't do it without my lexicon."

"Nothing is sweeter than love, and all delicious things are second to it." It's from *The Greek Anthology*. Perhaps your tutor has succumbed to your charms."

"Mr. Moore?" I laughed. "Not likely. If anything, he's infuriated by my insistence on reading only Homer. Though perhaps I should reconsider that position now that I know how…inspiring…*The Greek Anthology* is."

"You could focus on its religious epigrams."

"Mr. Moore would like that very much."

"Have you any idea who it might be from?"

"Not the slightest."

"Should I be jealous?"

"Of course not. If I'm not certain that even *you* could convince me to marry again, then this anonymous admirer, whoever he may be, has not the remotest chance."

"Oh, I'll convince you, Emily. Never doubt it. By this time next year, we'll be breakfasting together daily, and it won't be downstairs."

2

W HAT A BIZARRE INCIDENT," DAVID FRANCIS SAID AFTER LISTENING
to my spirited account of the burglary. Cécile had met him the
previous week at the studio of Michael Barber, a sculptor, and tonight
we brought both gentlemen to my house in Berkeley Square following a trip to the theater to see Mr. Ibsen's controversial new play,
Hedda Gabler. Like Cécile, Mr. Francis was a patron of the arts, and
the pair had become fast friends the moment they began discussing
their mutual admiration of French impressionism.

"Even more bizarre when you consider the fact that there have
been three such thefts," I said, and told them what had occurred at the
houses of Lord Grantham and Mrs. Wilmot.

"How strange to find a thief with such specific purpose," Mr.
Barber said. "Why this interest in the French queen?"

"It's hard to avoid the House of Bourbon since Mr. Berry arrived in
London," I said. "Society is consumed with all things French."

"*C'est vrai*," Cécile said. "But I will not believe for a moment that
Monsieur Berry is behind the crimes. He's not clever enough by
half."

"And even if he were, he drinks far too much to pull off such a scheme," Mr. Barber said.

"Do you think he truly is who he says? Surely Marie Antoinette wouldn't have produced a great-great-grandson of such dubious merit." I swirled the port in my glass as I spoke.

"Marie Antoinette is not often viewed as a sympathetic character," Mr. Francis said.

"And history, Mr. Francis, is recorded by the victor. I'd wager that the poor queen wasn't nearly as bad as we're led to believe. I've always felt she was treated badly in the matter of the diamond necklace."

"It was a most convoluted business," Cécile said. "And very likely the queen's enemies were all too willing to encourage anything that might harm her reputation."

"Wasn't there evidence that she was having an affair with a cardinal and had asked him to acquire the jewels for her?" Mr. Barber asked.

"Gossip, Mr. Barber, is hardly reliable evidence," I replied. "A jeweler made the necklace, which was absurdly expensive, and Marie Antoinette refused to buy it. One of her enemies convinced the cardinal, who was hoping to become the queen's lover, that she wanted it, and he gave this woman the money to buy it, believing she would give it to the queen."

"The woman—the Comtesse de la Motte—disappeared with both the necklace and the cardinal's money," Cécile continued. "And the queen was presented with a very large bill by the jewelers. Eventually the cardinal and the *comtesse* were brought to trial, but it was the queen's reputation that suffered. People were quick to believe she was behind the scheme, and it brought to light the idea that her morals were not what they ought to be."

"The cardinal, perhaps, should not have been brought to trial, but the queen insisted," I said. "He was charged with insulting her dignity."

"I should very much like to own the diamonds from that necklace," Cécile said, her eyes sparkling. "I wonder how difficult it would be to persuade the current owner to part with them."

"Don't even consider such a thing until our intrepid thief is caught," I said.

"I find the nature of these burglaries particularly intriguing," said Mr. Francis, dragging deeply on his cigar as he walked to the table on which stood a decanter of port. He slowly refilled his glass, offering no further explanation of his comment. "Your port, Lady Ashton, is worthy of its reputation."

"I wasn't aware that it had a reputation."

"Oh, yes. Your scandalous habit of taking it after dinner is a favorite topic of conversation at my club. The members are divided on how a gentleman should react when a lady refuses to retire to the drawing room. Many insist that it would be better to forsake the beverage entirely than to encourage the corruption of a viscount's widow. However, when faced with your most excellent cellar, it's difficult for a fellow to stand by his principles."

"There are few things I enjoy more than a nice port, and I think it's outrageous that ladies are sent away right as the conversation starts to get interesting," I said.

Mr. Francis smiled. "Gentlemen don't want ladies hearing the sorts of conversation that are interesting, and they would be quick to point out that there are many lovely sherries that you could drink." He returned to his seat.

I noticed that he had done a neat job of directing the conversation away from his comment about the thefts. "If I may return to our previous subject, why is it that you are particularly intrigued by the burglaries we were discussing?"

"A pink diamond from the French queen's personal collection was taken from my safe no less than a fortnight ago."

"I had no idea!" Mr. Barber exclaimed. "Why didn't you tell me?"

"I didn't consider the matter to be of any consequence to you," Mr. Francis said.

"You are my friend. Of course a theft at your house is of consequence to me."

"What did the police say?" I asked. "Were they able to find any clues?"

"I didn't bother to contact them. There's little hope they would recover the stone, and I prefer to keep my affairs private."

"Have you hired an investigator to pursue the matter?" I asked.

"No. I can't imagine there would be any point in doing so."

"You can't let such a thing go unreported," I said.

Mr. Francis was nonplussed. "When was the last time you heard of jewelry stolen by a cat burglar being returned to the rightful owner? It's a hopeless business."

"But Mr. Francis, it's imperative that the crime be investigated," I said. "Even if it goes unsolved, one must *try* to uncover the truth."

"I'd rather not upset my wife," he said. "She's exceedingly shy and suffers greatly when forced to talk to strangers."

"But surely she's noticed that the diamond is missing?" Cécile asked.

"It's not the sort of thing she would want to wear." He studied the ashes on the end of his cigar thoughtfully for a moment, then changed the subject. "Have you ladies been to the Royal Academy exhibition? Barber's got several good pieces in it this year."

"I've been twice," I said. "There is one sculpture that I remember in particular. A woman holding a basket of flowers. I believe it is yours, Mr. Barber."

"I'm pleased that you noticed it," Mr. Barber replied. "It's one of my favorites."

"I very much enjoyed it. You did a magnificent job capturing a sense of movement. I almost believed she would bend over and pick one of the blossoms at her feet."

"Thank you, Lady Ashton."

"Do you have an extensive collection of art, Mr. Francis?" I asked.

"Not so extensive as I would like."

"Francis spends as much money subsidizing studio rentals for artists as he does on their work," Mr. Barber said.

"No wonder you and Cécile get along so famously," I said. "I should love to see your collection."

"I'm afraid you would find it rather underwhelming."

"I consider that an insult, Francis," Mr. Barber said, grinning. "You've got some of my best pieces."

"I meant only that, given her own holdings, Lady Ashton would be disappointed in the scope and quantity of what I have."

"Quantity is a poor measure of the artistic merits of a collection, Mr. Francis. I'm fortunate that my husband possessed such exquisite taste," I said. "I've let his standards for acquisition guide me, although I confess that I'm guilty of keeping for myself some pieces he would argue belong in a museum." I twisted the gold ring with its image of the Trojan horse that I wore on my right hand. I'd been given it in Paris last year after trapping the man who had murdered Philip.

"But I understand that you've made many significant donations yourself," Mr. Francis said.

"Yes, but there are times when I'm quite overwhelmed with sentiment and find that I can't donate things that I ought."

"*Peut-être* Monsieur Bingham is attached to this dish you are trying to get from him," Cécile said.

"No, he's keeping it for himself simply out of spite. He's made no secret of the fact that he doesn't care for it." My gaze fell on Mr. Francis, and I felt compelled once again to return to the topic of the thefts, despite a worry that I was being too forward. "I really must implore you to report the loss of your diamond to the police. It is not something that affects only you. Surely you can't believe that there is more than one burglar in England seeking objects that belonged to Marie Antoinette?"

"Of course not," he replied.

"The police need to have as complete a picture as possible of this man's activities. Perhaps there is something at your house that may assist them in their investigation. Or a pattern of behavior that would be revealed by adding your location to the list of the crime scenes."

"She is right," Cécile said. "If you were the sole victim of this intruder, you could choose to keep quiet about it. But you are not."

"I suppose it would be wrong of me to do anything that might keep you from getting your earrings back," Mr. Francis said, smiling good-naturedly.

"It's not simply about recovering the earrings," I said.

"*Je ne sais pas*," Cécile said. "I would very much like to get my earrings back. They're a favorite pair."

"Of course," I said. "But isn't catching the thief and preventing further thefts of primary importance?" Cécile shrugged but did not answer. "If nothing else, I call on you, as a gentleman, to see to it that you do all you can to keep the name of poor Marie Antoinette from being subject to more intrigue and scandal."

"You are most persistent, Lady Ashton. I will talk to the police in the morning if you insist that it is the right thing to do. In the meantime, tell me what you thought of the play we saw tonight."

"I adored it," I said. "Hedda's plight is fascinating. She's incapable of taking pleasure in those things it is assumed will bring a woman happiness."

"So miserable, yet she seems the perfect wife," Mr. Barber said.

"It's rarely wise to accept at face value the image presented by a society wife," I said.

"Or a husband," said Mr. Francis.

"Quite." I smiled, all the while wondering what layers could be found beneath my guest's polished façade.

Mr. Francis was true to his word and spoke to the police about the pink diamond the very next morning. Within two days, the newspapers were filled with sensationalised stories about the thefts. All of society was buzzing about it, and Charles Berry made a great show of issuing a plea to the burglar through the *Times*, asking that all the objects that belonged to his great-great-grandmother be returned to their rightful owners. Those in possession of such items were thrown into a frenzy, desperate to protect themselves from the thief. Lady Middleton, who owned a chair purported to have been in the queen's bedroom at Versailles, caused a scene when she sent it to her bank and insisted that it be stored in the vault.

"The president of the bank tried to dissuade her, but she refused," Margaret Seward told me as we sat in the Elgin Room of the British Museum that afternoon. "I wish I could have witnessed their exchange."

"Who would dare cross Lady Middleton? I wonder that he even tried." I was sketching a piece of the east pediment of the Parthenon, which depicted the birth of the goddess Athena. Margaret, who read classics at Bryn Mawr, had brought a volume of Ovid with her, and she alternately read and chatted with me while I worked. Occasionally, she would meander through the museum, ready with amusing reports upon her return.

"I have just spotted a man nearly as handsome as Colin," she said after one such journey.

"Really?" This caught my attention.

"Well, not quite. I don't suppose there is another man as handsome as Colin. But this one comes close. He's walking with a terrified-looking young lady and her mother—a real dragon."

"Did you recognize any of them?"

"The girl is called 'Lettice.'"

"Ah," I said. "Lettice Frideswide. The man must be Jeremy."

"You know him?"

"Oh yes, quite well. He's the Duke of Bainbridge. Inherited last year. His estate is near my father's."

"Emily, I will never forgive you for hiding him from me. You know my parents have me here to look for a husband. My father won't settle for anyone without a title—it's crass, but that's the truth of it." Mr. Seward was a wealthy railroad man who, like so many other Americans, longed to see his daughter part of England's aristocracy. Margaret had agreed to do the Season only in exchange for her parents' promise that she could study at Oxford in the fall. "Tell me, is dear Jeremy engaged to the lovely Lettice?"

"I don't think so. He's quite in demand and doesn't seem inclined to settle down."

"He is perfect," she sighed.

"Margaret, I am all astonishment. I thought you'd no intention of marrying."

"I don't want to marry him, but I am desperate for someone to flirt with. Perhaps the good duke and I can come to some sort of understanding that can see me through the rest of the Season. He pays court, which keeps my parents happy, but is safe in the knowledge that I've no desire to marry him. When he hasn't proposed and it's time for me to go to Oxford, they'll return to America, armed with stories about the English lord who let their daughter slip away."

"Lady Frideswide would never forgive you. She's been trying to catch Jeremy for her daughter almost since the girl was born."

"And what does the daughter think?"

"I've not the slightest idea."

"She's awfully young. It won't harm her to wait another Season. Will you introduce me?"

"I suppose so. Were they coming this way?"

"They're upstairs looking at mummies." Margaret looked at me expectantly.

"Are you suggesting that you want me to rush over there and non-chalantly introduce you to the Duke of Bainbridge? Won't it look a bit obvious?" I turned back to my sketch. "No one comes to the museum without visiting the Elgin Room. Be patient, Margaret, and your duke will come to you."

I was right. Not half an hour passed before Jeremy and his party, which had expanded to include Lady Elinor and Isabelle, appeared. The ladies were dressed with such violent elegance that I almost regretted having chosen to abandon the tight lacing of corsets. To stave off the feeling, I took a breath far deeper than any of them could hope to draw and smiled broadly, giving my hand to the duke. Greetings were exchanged and introductions made, following which there was little conversation of substance. Lady Elinor complimented my drawing, and I her pin, a striking bird of paradise fashioned out of gold, its feathers covered with sapphires, rubies, and emeralds. Margaret was politeness itself, eager to impress Jeremy, who clearly felt no discomfort at finding himself the only gentleman in such a large group of ladies. The younger members of the party remained silent, posed prettily behind their mothers, until Lettice stepped towards me, squinting as she looked at the sculptures in front of us.

"Where's the baby?" she asked. "The sign says this shows the birth of Athena."

"There is no baby," I said, smiling. "Athena sprang fully grown from Zeus's head."

"Really?" She looked at me, then at Isabelle. "I don't know the story."

"Athena's mother was Metis, Zeus's first wife—"

"Yes, thank you, Lady Ashton." Lady Frideswide took Lettice's arm and steered her back to Isabelle. I was stunned by her rudeness and decided there was no reason now for me not to act boldly on Margaret's behalf.

"Have you plans for luncheon, Your Grace?" I asked, turning to Jeremy.

"Really, *Lady Ashton*," he replied, stressing each syllable of my name. "There's no need for such formality. We've known each other since we were babies. I'm lunching at my club."

"What a disappointment," I said. "I should so like to visit with you." Lady Frideswide flashed a look of disbelief. "Leave your club for tomorrow and join Miss Seward and me today."

"Is there a man in Britain able to resist you, Lady Ashton? What time do you want me?" Jeremy's acceptance of this invitation would be viewed as a social coup. Luncheon was typically a ladies' meal; gentlemen preferred their clubs. My mother would certainly pay me a visit the moment she heard of this. I turned to Margaret as the duke and ladies left us.

"You are going to be forever indebted to me for this."

"Oh, he's perfectly agreeable. You didn't have to work on him at all. I love him already."

"The gossips will say that I've set my cap for the Duke of Bainbridge."

"Not once he turns his attentions to me."

"How, precisely, do you plan to manage that? Are you going to speak to him directly about what you want?"

"I was hoping you could broker it for me, Emily. Then I truly will be forever indebted to you."

Margaret excused herself soon after we had retired to the sitting room following the luncheon. Jeremy squirmed uncomfortably, clearly surprised at having been left alone with me.

"Have you contrived this meeting, Em?" he asked, addressing me as he had since he was five years old. "What's going on?"

"Don't worry, Jeremy, you're quite safe from me. I've no interest in marrying you."

He slumped in his chair. "That's a relief. Although I will say candidly that when at last I accept the inevitable and marry, I won't be able to find a more charming wife than you."

"Don't waste your flattery on me."

"Let me flatter you. Doing it to anyone else will set tongues wagging across town and lead to rumors of imminent marriage."

"I know your plight only too well."

"I suppose you do. But I thought you and Hargreaves…" He stopped.

"Colin and I are not engaged," I said. "What about you and Lettice Frideswide?"

"There is no affection between us. Lettice seems more terrified of me than anything, and there has never been any talk of an engagement except by our mothers. You and I are similar creatures. Each with perfect opportunity before us yet unwilling to take it. Perhaps we should join forces. If all of society believes we have an understanding, they'll leave us alone."

"An interesting proposition, Jeremy, and very similar to the one I was about to make to you, but not for myself."

"For whom, then?"

"Margaret." I quickly described her situation. "If her parents think she's got a duke, they'll let her do whatever she wants."

Jeremy laughed loudly. "This is priceless. What a lark. Tell her I'll do it," he said, continuing to laugh. "I'd never have expected such a devious plan from you."

"All credit goes to Margaret."

"And, Emily"—he grew serious—"if you ever...if Hargreaves doesn't...if you do need someone...I think you and I could come to a mutually satisfactory understanding."

"Really, Jeremy, that has to be one of the most romantic proposals in all of English history. May I record it in my diary?"

"I mean it, Em."

"I shall keep that in mind, Your Grace."

3

To say that my mother was gratified by the attentions bestowed on me by the Duke of Bainbridge would be a grotesque understatement. Although our families were close, her friendship with Lady Frideswide had precluded her considering him as a potential husband for me. Now, however, she was convinced that the duke had strayed from Lettice of his own accord, and if her daughter was now the object of his affections, who was she to protest? I insisted to her that Margaret, not I, was in his sights, but she refused to accept this. No one could make her believe that a duke would choose an American over the daughter of an English peer.

"I'll listen to none of this nonsense," she said, after she had accosted me on the banks of the Thames at the Henley Regatta. "Between the Duke and Colin Hargreaves, you're sure to make an excellent match before the end of the Season. Neither will be willing to let you wait knowing that the other is competing for your favor." She looked at me and frowned. "Where is your parasol?"

"I didn't feel like dragging it along with me."

"My child, I fear for you. You are mere days away from completely destroying your complexion." She tugged at my hat, trying to make it better shade my face. "I've had a lovely day. His Grace was kind enough to offer me a spot on Temple Island. How I wish you could have joined us!"

"I didn't realize Jeremy was a member of the Leander Club." The island, which was for Leander members, not only provided an excellent vantage point, but also was the most exclusive area from which to view the race. Of its two merits, I knew it was the latter that most impressed my mother.

"Don't play coy, Emily. You're perfectly aware of all of Bainbridge's attributes. I'm just glad to see that he's beginning to take notice of yours."

"Mother—"

"And this is as good a time as any to point out that your odd reading habits are beginning to disconcert people."

"My reading habits are not—"

"We all understand that it was terribly shocking for you to lose your husband. Mourning is a dreadful time. But now it is over and there is no need to persist in this morbid habit of reading tedious books. Lady Elliott told me that she saw you with a copy of the *Odyssey* in the park."

"Do you have a particular objection to Homer, or are you against all ancient texts?"

"There is no need to speak to me like that, Emily. I cannot imagine what possessed you to bring a book to the park."

"The weather was fine and I wanted to sit outside. A shocking concept, I agree."

"Well, open a window, or if you must be outdoors, stay on your own property. There's no need to flaunt your eccentricities in front of all of London." She removed a pair of spectacles from her reticule, put them on, and peered at my face. "I do believe you are getting freckles." She thrust her parasol over me.

"Thank you, Mother. As always, your support overwhelms me."

"Don't take a snide tone with me. You are the widow of a viscount and need to start acting like one."

"Acting like a viscount?" I bestowed on her my most charming smile. "Perhaps that's what I'm doing when I'm reading Homer."

"Your behavior is intolerable. You should take better care or you'll find yourself isolated from all the decent people in England." With that, she marched away.

I left the river not long afterwards and returned home, exhausted, my cheeks and nose a distressingly bright shade of pink. On this count, at least, my mother had been correct. My hat, though very elegant, had not provided enough protection from the sun. I longed for a cool bath, but as soon as I had asked Meg to draw one, Davis announced a visitor. I looked at the card he handed me and walked, puzzled, to my drawing room, where I faced a woman I had never before seen. She was dressed in the unrelenting black of a new widow and darted towards me the moment I entered the room.

"I shall not apologize for coming to you like this, Lady Ashton. You cannot be surprised to see me."

"I'm so sorry, I've not the slightest idea to what you refer." I glanced again at her calling card. "Mrs. Francis? Is your husband David Francis?"

"There's no need to play naïve with me, young lady. I know all about—" She stopped, her eyes brimming with tears.

"Please sit down." I ushered her to a chair and rang for tea, growing more confused with each passing moment. "Have we met before?"

This made her laugh, with a deep, nervous sound. "I am quite aware that you were my husband's mistress. Now that he is dead—"

"Dead? Mr. Francis is dead?" I pictured him sitting in my library not two weeks ago and, though I had not known him well, was consumed with the horrible, sinking sensation that is the faithful spouse of all dreadful news.

"He died two days ago."

"I am more sorry than I can say. Was he ill?"

"You know that he was not." Above their red rims, her eyes blazed with acrimony. The heat in my house was suffocating. I crossed the room and began flinging open windows. A parlormaid entered with a tea tray.

"No, take it away," I said. "Bring us something cold."

Mrs. Francis did not speak again until the girl had left the room. "His last words were about you."

"How can that be? I only met him once."

"I'll thank you not to pretend innocence. If it was only once—" She had started to cry again, and I could not bear seeing the pain etched on her face.

"Please, let me comfort you." I took her hand, and though she would not look at me, she did not pull it away. "I know not how such a misunderstanding has come to pass. I was never your husband's mistress, nor was I romantically linked with him in any way. He was one of a group of my friends at the theater a week or so ago, and we all came here afterwards. Nothing of significance transpired between us."

"Why, then, was it your name that he uttered with his last breath?"

"I've no idea. You must know his friend, Mr. Michael Barber? He was here with us, and I'm sure he could put your mind to rest."

"Michael was here?" Her shoulders relaxed slightly.

"What did your husband say about me?"

"He asked that I bring his snuffbox to you."

"His snuffbox?"

"It's a pretty silver thing that once belonged to Marie Antoinette. I assumed that he had promised it to you."

This gave me a better sense of why he had wanted me to have the box. "Did he know he was dying?"

"Yes." She raised her eyes to meet mine.

"I can well understand why you suspect what you do. But I think,

Mrs. Francis, that your husband was simply trying to protect you."
I recounted for her our conversation about the thefts and the pink
diamond, leaving out the bits in which he had described his wife. Any
lady capable of confronting her husband's suspected paramour so soon
after his death had far too much spirit to be painfully shy.

"Now it is I who am confused. What is this pink diamond?"

"The one that was stolen from your home. Your husband saw no
point in upsetting you with the news of the theft, although I suppose
once it was in the papers he had to come clean. Men do so like to think
they're protecting ladies, don't they?"

"We've never owned a pink diamond."

"You're certain?" I asked, not terribly surprised. I remembered
that Mr. Francis said that it wasn't the sort of thing his wife would
have liked.

"Without a doubt. I've always admired colored diamonds—the
white ones seem to me altogether lacking in soul. David knows that
better than anyone." She held out her hand to show me her wedding
ring, a gold band with a large blue diamond set in it. "You say the
newspapers reported this? We don't take them at the house, so I never
see them. David prefers to read them at his club."

"The thefts have been the biggest news of the Season." I frowned,
wondering why Mr. Francis would have hidden the diamond from his
wife. "Could your husband have only recently bought the diamond,
intending it as a gift for you?"

"He could not have afforded such a thing. Not anymore." The
tears began again.

"I'm sorry. I've done nothing but upset you."

"No." She managed a smile. "I believe you when you say you were
not David's mistress. Finding that he was unfaithful to me would be
far more troubling than this pink diamond ever could be."

"May I ask how he died? You said he was not ill. Was there an accident?"

"No, Lady Ashton. My husband was murdered. His valet fell victim to the same poison yesterday morning." The air rushed out of my lungs and I could scarcely draw breath. Murdered. My heart felt torn in two for this woman, who, like me, had lost a spouse to violence.

"I must tell you a story," I said, and, taking her hands in mine, recounted for her the story of my own husband's demise, along with my role in uncovering his killer. Soon we were both weeping, and when at last the maid returned with cold lemonade, neither of us touched the glasses she set in front of us.

"You are good to share this with me after I barged into your home making dreadful accusations," Mrs. Francis said. "I'm so sorry."

"When I learned that Philip had been murdered, I accused innocent parties of far worse than adulterous affairs." I remembered well the implacable calm with which Colin had faced my erroneous charges. I may not have been bold enough at the time to denounce him directly, but he knew full well that I suspected him of killing his best friend. "You and I are bound together by a bitter kinship. Please do not feel that you ever need apologize to me for transgressions brought on by your grief."

We sat together some time longer, saying very little. Before she left, I promised to come to her in Richmond after the funeral was over. I knew she would need friends then, when the rest of society would abandon her, another lonely widow left for dead. I felt deeply unsettled when she was gone, all the memories of Philip stirring in me again. I had not thought about him—not really—in months, and realizing this brought back that most unwelcome of companions, guilt. My present happiness in life—my independence, my fortune, even Colin—all stemmed from my husband's death. Had he lived, I would not find myself so pleasantly situated.

My melancholy solitude was soon interrupted. Davis announced Colin and handed me a letter at the same time. Despite the heat, my friend managed to look more cool and crisp than was strictly fair, particularly given the marked contrast of my own appearance. "You've not changed your dress since the regatta," he said, and sat next to me on the silk-covered settee.

"No," I said, dropping the letter on the table next to my lemonade as I told him of my meeting with Mrs. Francis.

"A terrible tragedy," he said. "I read about it in the papers this morning. You're sweating." He caught a drip of water that was falling down my glass of still-untouched lemonade and traced his cool, wet finger around my face, then down my neck. And though my skin responded as it always did to Colin's touch, I was too distracted to really enjoy the sensation.

"What color were Philip's eyes? They were light, that much I remember, but were they blue or gray?"

He pulled back from me. "Blue. What brings this on?"

"Mrs. Francis, I suppose. Speaking with her made me realize that I owe all my current joy to him. It's an odd sort of feeling."

"One of which I'm all too aware. Had I not lost my best friend, I might never have found a woman who could captivate me the way you do. There will always be a touch of the bittersweet in our love, Emily." He stood up, walked across the room, and stared out the window.

I did not feel much like pursuing the subject and fidgeted uncomfortably for a moment before finally picking up my lemonade. "Would you like some?"

"No, thank you. Are you going to open your letter or are you bent on wallowing all afternoon?"

"Why the sudden interest in my mail?"

"Because it was I who found it sitting on your doorstep. Quite mysterious, I thought."

This piqued my curiosity, and I picked up the envelope, examining it carefully before opening it. "I really must spend more time on my Greek," I said once I had unfolded the note. "My skills at sight-reading are woefully lacking. Will you?" I handed it to him:

Λίσσμ', Ερως, τὸν ἄγρυπνον ἐμοὶ πόθον
κοίμισον

"*I beseech thee, Love, charm asleep the wakeful longing in me.*" He
frowned. "*The Greek Anthology* again."

"Would you read it in Greek?" He obliged me immediately, and
the seductive lilt of the ancient language drove from me any lingering
melancholy.

"That certainly brightened your eyes," he said. "Who is sending
you these messages?"

"I've not the slightest idea."

"I wish you would find out. I should very much like to know my
competition."

"I wouldn't know how to begin."

"Try," he said. "I'll wager that you can figure it out."

This made me laugh. "A bet? What will I win?"

"Identify your admirer before the end of the Season, and I shall
travel with you through Greece this fall."

"Scandalous! I thought you weren't willing to see me *that* corrupt?"

"I'd prefer not to." He took my hand in both of his, and the feel
of his skin on mine thrilled me more than I ought to admit. "But the
temptation is hard to resist."

"And if I lose?"

"You agree to marry me." His gaze held steady on mine.

"Sounds like a risky proposition for me either way."

"It is."

"I'll take your wager, Colin. It shall bring an added interest to
what might otherwise be a vapid Season. And who knows what gentlemen I might encounter during my search. An admirer who courts
his lady in Greek is not to be lightly discarded. Perhaps you ought to
be jealous."

"Not at all. I'm confident that no one you find can do for you what I would." Our eyes met and we leaned towards one another. My lips parted, and I waited for his kiss. It did not come. "No, I'd better not kiss you," he said, keeping his gaze steady and not pulling back from me. "I must accept the possibility that you could turn down my proposal. And, should you eventually marry someone else, I would not want your husband to hold against me the fact that I had taken such a liberty with his future wife."

"You've kissed me before."

"And it was most ungentlemanly of me to have done so. I shall be more careful in the future." With that, he kissed my hand, lingering over it deliciously, and left, turning to smile at me one more time before he closed the door.

Not two minutes later, my maid appeared, asking me if I still wanted a bath.

"Yes, Meg. Cold. I want it painfully cold."

Three days later I received a note from Mrs. Francis. Her house had been burgled again. This time, the only thing taken was her husband's silver snuffbox. The newspapers had been filled with stories about Mr. Francis's death from the moment they learned of it, and each of them had mentioned that he died clutching the object. They attributed his death to Marie Antoinette's curse and warned the citizens of London to take heed, suggesting that those whose property was stolen were lucky to have escaped with their lives.

4

AFTER PENNING A HASTY REPLY TO MRS. FRANCIS, I CHANGED INTO a well-cut riding habit and made my way to Rotten Row, needing desperately to clear my head. It was late in the afternoon, so most people were parading in their carriages, but I wanted my horse. The exercise was refreshing but did little to rid me of the searing feeling that I was responsible for having brought Mr. Francis to the attention of his murderer. I did my best to rally my spirits when I came upon my dearest childhood friend, Ivy, who was in her carriage with her husband and Lord Fortescue, a gentleman whom I avoided whenever possible. Our contrary views on seemingly every topic made conversation uncomfortable at best.

"I'm so glad to see you!" Ivy said, smiling brightly at me before turning to her companions. "Emily has been keeping herself hidden far too much lately."

"Strange time of day to be riding, Lady Ashton." Lord Fortescue looked at me closely, making no attempt to hide the fact that he found fault only with my behavior, not my ensemble, with its smart, double-breasted jacket and red vest.

"I've adopted a strictly self-indulgent approach to the Season.

Why should one be limited to riding in the morning?" Robert shifted uncomfortably in his seat, and I realized that this was not, perhaps, a wise thing to have said in front of Lord Fortescue.

Poor Ivy! Ever since her husband had determined to enter politics, she had found herself much in the company of Lord Fortescue. He had the queen's ear and was considered to be the most powerful man in the government, although he occupied no formal position beyond the seat in the House of Lords that his title brought him. All aspiring politicians were at his mercy, and he delighted in exercising any control he could over them.

"What drivel," Lord Fortescue said. "Shouldn't want any wife of mine to think like that." It was all I could do to keep from wondering aloud if he would want any wife of his to think at all. "Which reminds me, Lady Ashton, that Aloysius Bingham tells me you've been harassing him over some gaudy bowl. Leave him alone. It's no business of yours if he wants to keep the thing for himself. This rot you've been spewing to him about it belonging in the museum suggests to me that you are in desperate need of a husband with a very firm hand." The sound of a horse stopping next to mine saved me from having to respond to this inane comment, and I turned to see Charles Berry tipping his hat.

"Ah! Berry! Still enjoying London?" Lord Fortescue asked, then continued without waiting for an answer. "I've been meaning to have someone throw a party for you. I'm sure Mrs. Brandon is up to the task. What do you say? Will you give a ball? Thursday next would be convenient, I think."

"I—" Ivy hesitated. She would barely have time to come up with a menu, let alone arrange for an orchestra, flowers, and all the rest of the planning a ball required. Robert stepped in.

"Give her more time, Lord Fortescue, and she'll prepare the greatest masquerade ball London has ever seen."

"Very well, then. I will count on you, Mrs. Brandon." Ivy managed a weak smile. "Send me your guest list. I want to make sure you haven't forgot anyone."

Lord Fortescue was a clear example of why no man should have too much power. Small things, like checking over a guest list, were meant to remind a gentleman in Robert's position where his allegiance had better lie. Mr. Berry showed little interest in any of this. He was looking me over very carefully, evidently pleased with what he saw.

"I want to ride with you, Lady Ashton. Will you join me?" I quickly assessed the situation and decided that, of the two, Mr. Berry was preferable to Lord Fortescue. We walked our horses slowly and had not gone more than a hundred feet before I began to regret my choice.

"There is something about you that brings to mind Madame de Pompadour," he said. "I find myself most drawn to you."

"I warn you, Mr. Berry, that I am not susceptible to flattery." I pushed a stray curl back up into my hat.

"Your modesty does not fool me. Do you know that I may have a court of my own before long?"

"In England?" I wondered how he could afford such a thing. From what I understood, he had very little fortune.

"Initially, yes. But later—" He stopped. "I say too much. Suffice it to say that I shall count on your coming to me there. I don't think you will be disappointed."

I wondered if I ought to be affronted that he never dangled the queenship in front of me, the way he did with so many other young ladies. He had suggested even to Margaret that she might find herself in the happy position of wearing a crown. Perhaps he was familiar with my views on marriage. This thought made me smile.

"Lady Ashton! Mr. Berry!" Lady Elinor called. "What a surprise to find you here together!" Our horses, whose speed had increased gradually during our conversation, were about to overtake the carriage she shared with her daughter. She immediately focused on Mr. Berry and, good mother that she was, did all she could to draw him into conversation with Isabelle. The girl gave him a halfhearted smile, then sat quietly, scanning the park.

"Where is Mr. Hargreaves this afternoon?" Lady Elinor asked. "You remember Mr. Hargreaves, of course, Mr. Berry? Such an excellent gentleman! And quite devoted to our Lady Ashton."

"Hargreaves is a capital fellow. I was out far too late with him last night," Mr. Berry said, and I wondered what they had been doing. "It's easy to see why he's taken with my riding companion." Lady Elinor was quick to move the discussion in another direction, and once she had succeeded in commanding Mr. Berry's attention, I excused myself, hoping that Isabelle hadn't been searching the park for another gentleman. Her mother's intentions for her were all too clear.

I saw Isabelle again two days later. Cécile and I were in the library, waiting for Margaret to join us, when the girl appeared, making no attempt to hide the fact that she had been crying. Given the amount of time our families had spent together over the years, it did not surprise me that she would come to me when she was upset. Before her father's death, her parents had traveled a great deal, and Isabelle often stayed with us while they were gone. The difference in our ages, which had seemed so great just a few years ago, was less noticeable now, but I still pictured her as a little girl, butting in when Ivy and I wanted to trade private observations regarding the gentlemen of our acquaintance. Nonetheless, I had no desire to shun her when she was so distressed; if anything, this was an opportunity to make up for all the times when I'd shooed her away. I sat her next to Cécile on the settee and gave her a glass of port, figuring that I might as well take the opportunity to convert her to my view that the beverage should not be reserved for gentlemen alone.

"What is troubling you?" I asked. She took a sip of her drink before answering.

"Oh! That's quite good!" she exclaimed. She paused for a moment, as if trying to gather her courage. "I'm being forced to marry Mr. Berry." The tears began to flow again. "Mother has agreed to all the details, and I've nothing to say in the matter. She won't even let me tell Tommy myself."

"Tommy?" I asked gently.

"Lord Pembroke." More sobs. "She has sent him a letter."

"Did you have an understanding with him?"

"Nothing official, of course. But I love him so dearly." As eldest son of the Earl of Westbrook, Pembroke stood to inherit one of the finest estates in the north of England as well as a respectable fortune. He was the sort of man mothers ordinarily longed for their daughters to catch.

"*Je suis très désolée, chérie,*" Cécile said, putting her arm around Isabelle's heaving shoulders.

"Does your mother know that you're here?" I asked.

"No." She dabbed at her eyes with a handkerchief. "You were always kind to me when I was little, though I know I was a terrible bother. I so admire you, Emily. I know we haven't seen each other much since your marriage and…well…since the viscount died. I'm sorry." She sobbed again. "I'm making a dreadful mess of this. Everyone says that you believe ladies shouldn't be forced to marry against their wishes. My friend Clara wasn't allowed to go to Mrs. Brandon's luncheon last week because you were to be there. Her parents were afraid you'd convince her to break her engagement."

I had no idea who Clara was, or why she would want to break her engagement, but I hated to think that someone had refused an invitation of Ivy's simply to avoid me. "I shall write your mother a brief note, telling her that you are with me. You may stay here tonight if you wish. But then—" I stopped, knowing that there was little more I could do for her. Davis sent one of the footmen to deliver the note and wait for a reply. Lady Elinor was relieved to learn where her daughter was, but her words revealed little sympathy for the girl:

> *I will send a carriage for her in the morning and expect to find that she is willing to accept the arrangements that I have made for her.*

Margaret, who had arrived in the midst of all the excitement, was outraged. "I can't believe you would entertain the notion of supporting her mother in this," she said, pulling me to a quiet corner of the room.

"What can I do, Margaret?"

"Send for Pembroke."

"And then what?"

"They could go to Scotland."

"You can't be serious," I said. "I have no idea what Lord Pembroke's intentions are."

Although she had not heard us, Isabelle echoed Margaret's request. "Emily, I must see Tommy. Can you help me?"

Much as I hated to see her forced into a marriage, especially to Charles Berry, I did not want to be party to her ruin. How unfair of her mother not to let her tell Lord Pembroke herself, to say good-bye to him. I thought how incensed I would be if my own mother had done such a thing. Then I thought of Colin. If someone forced me away from him I would want—need—to see him one last time.

"All right, Isabelle," I said with a sigh. "We will bring Lord Pembroke to you, but you will have to be patient while I arrange it." I sent a maid to draw a hot bath while Cécile led Isabelle upstairs.

"What will you do?" Margaret asked. "Can Colin help?"

"He's at his brother's in Richmond. We'll send for Jeremy instead and ask him to collect Lord Pembroke. You should write to him, Margaret. No one will think anything of his receiving a summons from you, and it will add nicely to the rumor of your growing attachment to each other. Don't say anything specific about why you want to see him. It will be best to have as little of this as possible in writing."

Davis dispatched the footman again, and in short order Jeremy was standing before us. "Brilliant!" he said when I told him our plan. "Pembroke will be eternally grateful. He's quite taken with the girl, you know."

After Jeremy departed to collect Lord Pembroke, Isabelle and Cécile returned to the library. Isabelle, dressed in one of my lacy tea gowns, looked much better composed after her bath and could hardly stop talking about the merits of the man she loved. Soon after we had eaten a light supper, the gentlemen arrived. Isabelle rushed to Lord Pembroke, who looked pleased, though a bit embarrassed, at this public display.

"Em," Jeremy began, taking my arm. "I understand you have a collection of Greek vases in your library. Would you be so good as to show them to me?"

"I suppose so," I said, noting that Cécile and Margaret had already fled the room and feeling not altogether comfortable with the notion of leaving the couple entirely alone. Jeremy gave Pembroke a jaunty salute and pulled me out the door.

"Having second thoughts about your role in the corruption of the youth of England?"

"Not exactly. I just don't want to leave her in a situation that could cause her more harm than good."

"Don't worry, darling. Pembroke's half-terrified and is not about to do anything improper. They'll have a kiss, and a good cry and all will be forgotten in the morning."

"Is he quite in love with her?" I asked.

"As much as any gentleman might be."

"Will he ask her to go to Gretna Green?"

"I don't think so. He made it clear to me that he's not interested in courting scandal."

"Then perhaps Isabelle is better off marrying Charles Berry. Pembroke can't be much devoted to her if he's willing to stand by and watch her marry another man."

"You are a romantic, aren't you?" He paused before the door to the library. "It's quite fetching." We entered the room, where Margaret and Cécile were in the thick of a game of chess. Jeremy sat beside Margaret, commenting on her every move. I pulled *She* by H. Rider Haggard off a shelf. With effort, I forced myself to follow the adventures of Ludwig Horace Holly and the exotic queen, Ayesha, She Who Must Be Obeyed, though all the while I was wondering if Lord Pembroke loved Isabelle enough to take her to Scotland. When an hour had passed, I put down the book, marched back to the drawing room and knocked loudly on the door, waiting a few moments before opening it. Pembroke, who looked very rumpled, was pacing furiously in front of the fireplace. Isabelle was crying harder than ever.

"I'm so sorry to interrupt you, but I think that it's best if—"

I did not need to finish my sentence. Pembroke grabbed Isabelle's hand, kissed it with great emotion, and ran from the room. Isabelle looked as if her heart was shattered. She buried her face in a pillow she found on the settee and continued to sob. I sat next to her, gently rubbing her back. Cécile came in and said nothing for several minutes. At last, she pulled Isabelle from her supine position and began to speak in a very serious tone.

"What did Lord Pembroke say to you?"

"He told me I should marry Mr. Berry. I thought he loved me. How could he ask me to marry someone else?"

"He wants to protect you from scandal," I said, knowing full well that he was at least as concerned for himself as he was for her.

"I feel like such a fool. I thought he would beg me to go to Gretna Green."

"And would you have?"

"Of course I would." She stopped crying. "So Mr. Berry is forced upon me, and dreadful though that is, I know there is only worse to come, for someday my dear Tommy will have to marry, too. Would that I might die before having to see that." The tears began to flow again.

"It may not be for some time," I said, trying to encourage her. "Young gentlemen are rarely eager to settle down. When at last it happens, you may find that you've quite forgotten Lord Pembroke."

"I shall never forget him, and for that my husband will suffer. He will never have my affection."

"There are many such marriages, Isabelle," Cécile said. "You do not have to let yourself be miserable. Give yourself over to grief tonight, but no longer. After that, you will have to make your own happiness." I remembered Jeremy's comment about us being able to reach a mutually agreeable understanding. What a dreadful way that would be to live.

5

⟡──⟡──⟡──⟡──⟡──⟡──⟡──⟡──⟡

I'M SO SORRY, MADAM," THE MAID SAID, WIPING UP THE TEA SHE HAD
spilled on the table.

"Don't think on it another moment, Lizzie." The girl, newly hired
by my housekeeper, seemed a bit nervous at finding herself part of
such a large household. "I spill it myself more often than not and
wonder why people insist upon serving hot tea in a heavy silver pot. It
seems to me that whoever pours is doomed to fail." Ivy watched the
maid, waiting to speak until she had left us alone.

"You are far too nice to your servants," she said.

"Lizzie's only been here a week or so. She's constantly going to the
wrong rooms, showing up where she's not wanted, bringing me things
that I haven't asked for, pouring tea when I ought to do it myself. I
haven't the heart to scold her, though. She's so very young, and Mrs.
Ockley is convinced that she'll do well once she's settled."

"She must learn to be competent as quickly as possible," Ivy said as
she fiddled with the cup in front of her. She raised it to her lips, then
returned it to the saucer without taking a sip. "I hardly know how to
bring this up. Of course it is only a false rumor, but I fear..." Her
pretty cheeks flushed pink when her eyes met mine.

"Oh, dear. What have I done now?"

"Have you and Colin quarreled?"

"Of course not. If we had, I would have ranted to you about it immediately. You know that."

"Well...Lady Elliott told my mother she has heard that you and Jeremy have been spending a considerable amount of time together."

"Jeremy is here quite often, but only to give the appearance of courting Margaret."

"Rumor has it that their relationship is intended only to hide that which he has with you."

"That is ridiculous," I said.

"I know it is. But several people have noticed that Colin has not been seen with you often lately, something that seems to add veracity to the story."

"Colin is immersed in his work. Furthermore—"

"Yes, but Emily, you are gaining a reputation as an eccentric who would prefer to spend her time buried in the library instead of on more...er...feminine pursuits."

"Excellent. I long to be eccentric."

"You know that I fully support your studies, but I do wish you would, perhaps, temper your approach to the Season. Would it be so awful to play the society game, just for a few months?"

"I never thought I would hear such criticism from you," I said. Ivy looked as if she would crumple. "Don't be upset, dear. I'm not angry." I was unable to continue, as Davis opened the door and announced Jeremy.

"I'm to meet Margaret here," he said, dropping into a chair after greeting the two of us with perfect politeness. "It's exhausting arranging these clandestine meetings for public consumption."

"You seem to be enjoying yourself," I said. "I saw the two of you riding yesterday."

"Capital girl, Margaret. Loads of fun." He rested his chin on the gold handle of his walking stick. "I can think of plenty worse ways to spend a Season."

Ivy frowned but did not comment. The door opened and Davis reappeared, this time bringing Colin with him.

"What did you think of that dinner last night, Hargreaves?" Jeremy asked as I handed Colin a cup of tea. "I can't remember when I've had such awful soup."

Colin laughed. "Lady Cranley would be horrified to hear you say that."

"Fear not. I told her that I'd never had its equal, and she took it as a compliment."

"You men are dreadful," Ivy said. "I hate to abandon you to them, Emily, but I must go see to the invitations for my ball."

"When do you expect Margaret?" I asked Jeremy when Ivy had left.

"I thought she'd be here by now," he replied, refusing another cup of tea.

"It's not like her to be late," I said. "I wish I had known she was meeting you here. I would have asked her to come early so that she could help me with my Greek."

"Ah, Emily and her Greek," Jeremy said, smiling. "I'm glad someone can be entertained by such pursuits."

"I adore it and will not tolerate your teasing me about it."

"I'm not teasing," he protested. "You know that I have been one of your greatest admirers ever since you proved you could run faster than me."

"It was a necessary skill, or I wouldn't have been able to escape you when you chased me with—what was it—frogs?"

"Mmmm, yes, frogs. Not one of my finer moments."

"I suppose I can forgive you your youthful exuberance."

"You are as generous now as you were when you were five," Jeremy said.

"What is troubling you with your Greek, Emily?" Colin asked, giving Jeremy a brief but pointed look. "Perhaps I can be of some use."

"Beware, Em. A Cambridge man is rarely of any use," Jeremy said.

"Mr. Moore has left me with a difficult passage, and I don't quite understand the grammar," I said.

"Why don't you show me?" Colin asked. I walked to my desk and pulled out a pile of papers and books.

"Oh, dear," Jeremy said. "Not the lexicon. That's my cue to leave."

"But what about Margaret?" I asked.

"She can't expect me to wait all afternoon," he said. "Tell her that she has wounded my heart and that I am unlikely to recover."

"I'll pass along the message," I said with a laugh, giving him my hand to kiss before he departed.

"Margaret was never going to come," Colin said when we were alone. "He's using her as an excuse to see you."

"What gives you that idea? Have you been listening to idle gossip?"

"Gossip? It takes nothing beyond ordinary powers of observation to notice that Bainbridge is captivated by you."

"Don't be ridiculous. He's more expert at avoiding romantic entanglements than even I am."

"You're not back to avoiding romantic entanglements, are you?" he asked.

"Not when they involve you." How easy it was to lose myself in his eyes.

"Show me your Greek," he said. We bent over the text, and Colin carefully explained the grammar to me. His arm brushed against mine, and my heart quickened. He squeezed my hand and returned to the book before us. "*The Greek Anthology* is marvelous. One can find a passage appropriate for nearly any situation in it. This is one of my favorites." He flipped through the pages and then read aloud, first in English, then in Greek. "'I know that I am mortal and ephemeral; but when I scan the multitudinous circling spirals of the stars, no longer do I touch earth with my feet, but sit with Zeus himself, and take my fill of the ambrosial food of gods.'" The rhythmic sound of the ancient language always moved me, and I watched him closely as he spoke. When he finished he gently touched my face. "I think, Emily, that you are my ambrosia," he said, almost in a whisper. I dropped my pencil.

"I could grow rather fond of this method of study. Perhaps we should make a habit of it," I said.

"What would Mr. Moore say?"

"If you would tutor me yourself, I'd have no need for Mr. Moore."

"There is much I long to teach you," he murmured against my neck. "But I fear we are far too easily distracted for you to learn much Greek with me as your guide."

"Such is my misfortune," I said, turning my head towards him. Before I could bring my lips to his, he pulled away, straightened his jacket, and brushed his hair back from his forehead.

"You'll notice that Margaret has never arrived," he said, tugging at a curl that had escaped from my pompadour. "Watch out for Bainbridge."

I stayed home that night, happy for a quiet evening with Homer. Cécile was at a ball, and knowing that she would be out extremely late, I took my book to bed and soon fell asleep reading. Once again, something disturbed me while I slept, and I awoke around four in the morning, stunned by what I saw. My copy of the *Odyssey* still lay on my bed, but in it had been placed a single long-stemmed pink rose.

Resting on top of the book was a small package and a note. I felt a strong breeze and watched the curtains, which I'd replaced since the burglary, billow. The window had been locked when I went to bed; now it was open.

All at once the darkness of my room was terrifying. Was I alone? Or was the intruder hiding, watching me? Summoning all the courage I could, I lit the lamp beside my bed. The light revealed nothing immediately, and I was too afraid to do a thorough search. I tapped on Cécile's door, but she did not answer. She had not yet returned home. I started to reach for the bell but did not want to wait alone for my maid. Rushing upstairs to the servants' quarters, I pounded on Davis's door.

"Get Mr. Hargreaves at once," I commanded. My butler did not hesitate, closed the door so he could dress, and was ready to leave the house in fewer than three minutes. My appearance in the servants' hall had caused quite a commotion. Lizzie poked her head out her door and shrieked when she saw me; soon the entire household was awake. I followed Davis downstairs where I sat on the staircase, clutching my knees to my chest, my back pressed hard against the railing as I accepted, but did not drink, the glass of brandy my maid had handed me. Meg was at least as upset as I was, and I considered offering her some brandy of her own.

Sooner than I could have hoped, Colin burst through the door, Davis right behind him. "What has happened? Where is Cécile?" The moment I'd explained the situation to him, he raced up the stairs, two at a time. Davis organized the footmen, who began to methodically search the house. I knew they would find nothing; the intruder was sure to be long gone. I returned to my bedroom, where I found Colin staring at the note, the rose flung carelessly on the bed.

"Have you read it?" he asked.

"No." I glanced at the text as he read:

Εἴθε ῥόδον γενόμην ὑποπόρφυρον, ὄφρα με
χερσὶν ἀρσαμένη χαρίση στήθεσι χιονέοις.

"Would I were a pink rose, that fastening me with thine hands thou mightest grant me grace of thy snowy breast. Bloody hell." He looked at me. "Forgive me."

I smiled weakly. "What's in the package?" He opened it carefully, revealing a small box and another note.

"'A pink for you and a pink for another. Please return this to the rightful owner.'" Inside the box was a pink gemstone.

"It must be Mr. Francis's Marie Antoinette diamond," I said.

"I think you're right."

"So my admirer is the cat burglar."

"He cut a circle of glass from your window and unlocked it. Have you sent for the police?"

"No. I only wanted you."

He took me in his arms. "You're trembling."

"This isn't like when he broke in before, Colin. He came for me this time," I said, making no effort to stop the tears flowing down my cheeks. "He could have returned the diamond to Mrs. Francis himself. I cannot believe there is no connection between this stone and the murder. And if there is a connection, it is I who am culpable—" I stopped at the sound of a forced cough from my butler as he entered the room. Colin stepped away from me.

"It doesn't appear that anything in the house has been disturbed," Davis said.

"I'm not surprised," Colin said.

"Is there anything else I can do for you, madam? Shall I summon the police?"

"Must we?" I asked Colin.

"You will have to talk to them in the morning, but there's nothing they can do now that I can't take care of myself."

"I'm quite all right, Davis. Thank you for your assistance." The butler left, leaving the door partly open behind him. Colin opened it the rest of the way.

"I don't want to compromise your reputation." He looked at the letter again. "Have you received any other similar notes?"

"Just the one you saw me open some weeks ago." I was suddenly aware that I was wearing nothing but my nightgown and a flimsy lace robe, and that Colin, who had dressed in a great hurry, had only partly buttoned the wrinkled shirt that he had neglected to tuck into his trousers. "I am most grateful that you came so quickly," I said quietly, tears filling my eyes. "I want to believe that I could face any situation head-on, with no assistance, but find myself more vulnerable than I expected."

"No one should have to face every situation alone, Emily."

"Having you here is an enormous comfort."

"I am loath to leave you at all tonight," he said. "But you know I cannot stay." He picked me up and carried me across the room, placing me gently on the bed. "Try to sleep." Tracing my lips with a finger, he smiled. "I suppose this is inappropriate, but I can't resist pointing out that, were we married, you would not have to spend this night alone."

And then he was gone, but he did not return to his house on Park Lane. Davis informed me the next morning that, after conducting a thorough search of the house and grounds, Colin had stayed in the garden, pacing beneath my window, for the remainder of the night.

6

I NSPECTOR MANNING ARRIVED AT MY HOUSE EARLY THE NEXT MORN-
ing, just as Cécile and I were sitting down at the breakfast table.
The cheerful room, filled with sunshine and freshly cut flowers, belied
the sullen mood of its occupants. The inspector questioned me about
the events of the previous evening but admitted to having no leads as
to the identity of the intruder. There seemed little hope that he would
ever be caught.

"Please eat something, Inspector," I said. "I really must insist.
There's no point letting all this food go to waste, and I've no appetite
this morning."

"Thank you, Lady Ashton." He hesitated for a moment, but the
temptation of the dishes on the sideboard was too great. He picked up
a plate and began to fill it.

"So this intruder left no clues?" Cécile asked.

"Not that we can find. He's a skilled thief." He dove into his eggs
and smiled gratefully when the maid gave him a steaming cup of coffee.
"I would like to assure you that we'll be able to keep news of this from
reaching the papers, but I'm afraid that would be a false promise."

I sighed. "I suppose it doesn't matter. Have you any objection to my returning the diamond to Mrs. Francis?"

"Not in the least. So far, the local constabulary has handled the case in Richmond, but I am hoping that now we may be able to transfer it to Scotland Yard."

"Do you think there's a connection between the thefts and the murders?"

"Not necessarily," the detective said. "But don't worry, we'll figure it out. Mr. Hargreaves has asked that I once again increase the patrols near your house, something I will do gladly. I've also arranged to have an undercover policeman stationed in Berkeley Square overnight."

"Thank you. I will rest easier knowing that."

"Do you think she is in danger?" Cécile asked.

"If the intruder had wanted to harm her, he had ample opportunity to do so last night. It seems that his interest in Lady Ashton is of a...er...romantic nature. Still, I wouldn't like to see you have another run-in with him. Difficult to guess what the criminal mind might try next."

"I think we ought to go to Richmond at once," I said, rising from the table. Inspector Manning pushed his plate away and stood up quickly, almost knocking over his coffee. "There's no need to stop eating, Inspector," I said. "You're welcome to stay here as long as you like."

"I couldn't, madam," he said, but I would have none of it. I rang for the maid and instructed her to see to it that he had whatever he wanted, and then I left him there, embarrassed but obviously pleased with his breakfast.

The drive to Richmond was a short one. Mrs. Francis herself opened the door for us, was delighted to meet Cécile, and welcomed us into her house, which, though modest, had been beautifully furnished by someone with excellent taste. We followed her into a small sitting room that was bathed in darkness and extremely hot, the curtains closed as demanded by the customs of mourning. Before I could launch into the story of my extraordinary night, Mrs. Francis announced her own surprising news.

"The police have just left—they've arrested my maid. She's poor Stilleman's widow. They'd been married less than a year."

"Stilleman?" I asked.

"David's valet."

"What evidence do they have against her?" I sat down and pulled off my gloves.

"Apparently she was having an affair with the gardener and David caught them."

"So why isn't the gardener arrested?" Cécile asked. "His motive would be as strong as hers."

"Thomkins was away visiting his sister when David died, so they don't consider him a suspect."

"Have they determined the cause of death?" I asked.

"Nicotine poisoning, but they don't yet know how it was administered."

"Is there no possibility that Thomkins planted it before leaving to visit his sister?"

"That I do not know. But I am convinced that Jane is being wrongly accused. I know this girl well—she would never have killed my husband, let alone hers. You must help me, Lady Ashton."

I frowned. "I don't know what I could do."

"Find the truth, as you did when your husband was killed. Please. I've no one else to turn to."

"I'm sure that the police—"

"As far as they are concerned, the case is closed as of this morning."

"We would never leave an innocent woman to sit in jail," Cécile said, giving me a pointed look. "Waiting to hang. *C'est horrible*. The guillotine is far less barbaric."

"Having one's head severed is *less* barbaric?" I asked, raising an eyebrow.

"It is quicker, *chérie*. Much quicker."

"This is all too awful. Please, Lady Ashton. I cannot bear to see her wrongly accused, or to think that the person who killed David will not be punished."

How could I deny her? "I shall try, Mrs. Francis."

"That is all I can ask. Where will you begin?"

"Before we go any further, I need to give you this." I handed her the box that contained the pink diamond.

"Is this David's?" I nodded. "But how—"

"Last night someone broke into my house and left it with a note asking that I return it to you."

"It is stunning, though I don't understand why it was returned to you." She fingered it carefully, then walked over to a window and opened the curtains to examine the stone in the light. Her pleasure was so evident that I could not help but wonder why her husband had not given it to her himself. Her smile disappeared as suddenly as it had come, and she started to cry. "I'm so glad you're both here. David didn't like to entertain and guarded his privacy fiercely. Now that he's gone, I find myself quite without friends."

Cécile took her by the arm and marched her back to a chair. "You have us. What is your Christian name, Madame Francis? I cannot abide formality."

"Beatrice," she said, drying her eyes. "Thank you, Mrs. du Lac." Cécile shook her head. "Cécile. Thank you. I never pictured myself without him, you know. Foolish, isn't it? Never to have considered what I was doing when I buried myself here? All I cared about was being with him, with no regret for all that I left behind."

"We will find out who killed him," I said, hoping my voice did not betray the lack of confidence I felt. "I'll need you to tell me everything the police have shared with you." This, unfortunately, turned out to be very little. From what I could gather, they had interviewed everyone in the household, and as soon as they discovered Jane's affair, their attention focused solely on her. Unable to provide an alibi, she had no defense against their charges.

There seemed little point in searching the house for clues; the police would have taken anything of note. Nonetheless, I wanted to look at Mr. Francis's study. I knew not how to best conduct a murder investigation, but it seemed sensible to assume that a careful look at the victim's personal possessions might reveal something about the crime. Beatrice led us through the dark house into a pleasant room with a series of French doors that opened into a garden. It would have been a lovely place in which to work. Neatly stacked books rested on the desk next to a mahogany box that held thick writing paper, wax, and a heavy seal.

I looked through the desk, scrutinized the bookshelves, even pulled down volume after volume to see if anything was hidden behind them, but found nothing of note. I paced the room, trying my best to look authoritative. At last, my eyes came to rest on a pile of unopened mail laid haphazardly on a table behind the desk.

"Is this recently delivered?" I asked, holding it up for Mrs. Francis to see.

"Yes. It's what has arrived since David's death. I haven't had the heart to open it. You may if you think it would be of some use."

Most of it was of little consequence—a bill from his tailor, a receipt for some books, several personal letters. But before I reached the bottom of the pile, my curiosity was rewarded as I opened a letter written on stationery from the Marlborough Club. I scanned it quickly, taken aback by its contents.

Dear Mr. Francis,

Many thanks for your kind letter. Unfortunately, my schedule at present does not allow for a visit to Richmond, so I'm afraid we will not be able to meet. I thank you for alerting me to the situation you mentioned, and assure you that I have the matter well in hand.

Yrs., etc.

C. Berry

7

I STOOD IMPATIENTLY ON THE STEPS OF THE MARLBOROUGH CLUB, twirling my parasol, wondering what could be delaying Mr. Berry. After leaving Richmond, where Cécile had stayed for tea with Beatrice, I had headed directly for the Savoy Hotel, carrying the letter with me. He was not in his room, but the man behind the desk said that, if the matter was of some importance, the gentleman could most likely be found at his club. I got the distinct impression that the staff at the Savoy were quite accustomed to unaccompanied ladies calling for Mr. Berry.

"Lady Ashton, I am astonished you have come here," he said, when at last he appeared before me.

"You've kept me waiting nearly half an hour."

"Apologies, of course. I was lunching with the Prince of Wales."

I was not impressed. "I'd like to speak with you."

"So I see," he said. "Shall we go to the Savoy? My rooms are quite comfortable."

"Really, Mr. Berry, I'm in no mood to be trifled with. Let's go to the park." The dress I was wearing was one of Mr. Worth's creations, expertly cut from a lovely floral fabric. The neck was high, the sleeves slightly puffed, and lace wrapped tightly around the lower section of the bodice, making my waist look impossibly small with only a moderately laced corset. It flattered my figure and was elegant in a subtle, alluring way. I had selected it that morning in an attempt to improve my mood. It was not, however, a good choice when calling on a man like Mr. Berry, who was looking at me with a rather lecherous intensity.

"Where is your carriage, Lady Ashton?"

"I walked."

"Walked! How industrious you are. At Versailles, you know—"

"No Versailles today, Mr. Berry." I ignored the arm he offered, and we headed across the Mall into St. James's Park. "I would like to talk to you about Mr. David Francis. I believe you have corresponded with him?"

"The name is vaguely familiar."

"I imagine it would be," I said, giving him the note. "Why did he want you to come to Richmond?"

"Impossible to say. I've never actually met him, you know. I believe he had asked if I would dine with him."

"Strange to be invited to dine by a man you've never met, don't you think?"

"I find that my position generates many such invitations. People are likely to overlook formality in an attempt to meet me."

"You do know that he is dead, don't you?"

"Francis? How dreadful. I recall reading something about it in the papers."

"He was murdered, Mr. Berry."

"I'm sorry to hear it, but I don't see how it's any concern of mine." We came to a bench that stood between two groves of trees and provided a fine view of the canal. Mr. Berry sat down, not bothering to first offer me a seat.

"What was the situation about which you thanked him for alerting you?"

"The best I can remember is that Mr. Francis wanted me to buy something from him. He had a number of objects that belonged to my twice *arrière-grand-mère*. Said I shouldn't allow my family heirlooms to slip away and would offer me a good price for anything I wanted. He invited me to dine with him and look over his collection."

"Do you still have the letter he sent you?"

"Heavens, no. If I kept all the inconsequential notes I receive, I'd be overwhelmed with paper."

"Do you own anything that belonged to Marie Antoinette?"

"No." He scowled. "But I expect that to change soon enough." He grabbed my hand and pulled me down next to him on the bench. "Why have you really come to me, Lady Ashton? Were you distressed by the news of my engagement?"

I am certain that I bristled visibly at this comment and immediately removed my hand from his. "Not in the least."

"It's all right. Isabelle's most understanding."

I was not about to let this nonsense go any further. "Mr. Berry, I am here only because I hoped that you might be able to tell me something of use regarding Mr. Francis. As it appears that you cannot, I must beg your leave." I started to stand, but he yanked me back down and leaned close to me.

"Please don't think you've embarrassed yourself by coming to me like this. I find it surprisingly alluring. I've heard all about your illicit assignations and probably should have suspected that you would approach me so directly. My official position is going to change very soon, and when it does"—he began to massage my hand—"I expect I shall see much more of you."

I pulled my hand away. "You cannot think that I would—"

"I will, of course, need you to be more discreet once I am king, but until then, you may amuse yourself as you see fit. Do you plan to marry Bainbridge, or are the two of you just playing? I imagine he'd be as understanding a spouse as Isabelle."

"You have no right to ask me such a question," I said, furious, and stormed out of the park without uttering another word.

When I arrived at Berkeley Square, Cécile had not yet returned from Richmond. Eager though I was to tell her what had transpired since I left her, I was happy for the opportunity to take a bath, a very long, very soapy bath, and wash any trace of Mr. Berry from my person. After I had dried off and put on a lace-covered dressing gown, I sat in my bedroom and was just starting to comb through my wet hair when my friend knocked on the door.

"It is intolerable that Isabelle should be forced to accept such a husband," she said after I had recounted my conversation with Mr. Berry. "We should have encouraged Pembroke to elope."

"You're right," I said, feeling acutely guilty that I had not done more for the girl. "She's the only person I know who spent most of her youth actively dreaming about romantic fairy tales. For such a girl to wind up with Mr. Berry is not to be borne."

"I'm afraid there is little that can be done about her engagement now."

"He's such an awful man!" I said. "What do you think he was referring to when he mentioned my *illicit assignations*?"

Cécile waved her hand dismissively. "The most foolish sort of gossip, Kallista. I heard it reported at a party several nights ago. The story is that the Duke of Bainbridge was seen leaving your house at five o'clock in the morning."

"Jeremy? Why on earth would he be here so late?"

"It became clear that the time in question was the second night the intruder broke into your room. Someone must have seen Monsieur Hargreaves and thought he was the duke."

"But they look nothing alike."

"*C'est vrai*. I cannot imagine anyone would mistake one for the other."

"Colin's being here wasn't inappropriate in the least," I said. "The police came the next morning, and the story was in all the papers."

"That is precisely what I said to correct the story."

"Have you any idea who is the source of the rumor?"

"No one ever owns up to starting such a thing. I wouldn't let it trouble you—soon enough they'll find someone else to gossip about."

"I suppose you're right," I said. "I'm much more interested in Berry's connection to Mr. Francis. Berry's story doesn't sit right with me. If Mr. Francis had wanted to sell him something, why wouldn't Berry have referred to the object in his reply?"

"And why would Monsieur Francis have tried to sell something to a man whom everyone in London knows is at the mercy of his creditors?"

"I should very much like to find Mr. Francis's letter."

"But Monsieur Berry did not keep it."

"Do you think we can trust him to tell the truth? I wonder…" I thought for a moment. "If only there were some way to know Berry's plans for the evening."

"Lady Londonderry is giving a dinner party in his honor."

"How do you know that?"

"I received an invitation." She looked at the watch pinned to her bodice. "If I do not dress soon, I'll be late."

"She didn't invite me," I said. "How odd. She's thick as thieves with my mother."

"I'll gladly cancel if you think she is slighting you."

"No. Go, Cécile, and make sure that Berry doesn't leave early."

"*Pourquoi?*"

"It would be best if I don't tell you. That way, should I be discovered, you won't have to feign ignorance of my plan."

"I do not like this, Kallista."

"Don't worry about me. So long as you keep Berry occupied, I'll be in no danger."

As soon as Cécile had left for dinner, I changed into a modest, dark blue dress and a veiled bonnet, careful to choose something that would not draw any attention to my presence. I waited until it was safe to assume Lady Londonderry's guests had been seated, then headed to the Savoy, having my driver leave me two blocks from the hotel lest anyone recognize my carriage. Once inside, I walked quickly past the desk. The lobby was relatively quiet, most of the guests already gone for the evening or dining in the restaurant. I slipped up the stairs to the fourth floor and knocked on Mr. Berry's door. There was no answer. Excellent. I went to the back stairs and descended to the lower level, where in short order I found three maids drinking tea in a small room.

"I'm so sorry to disturb you," I said as they all leapt to their feet. "I'm in the most terrible bind. I was visiting a…a gentleman this afternoon and am afraid that I lost a bracelet in his room. It's rather awkward, you see, as he's engaged to a friend of mine."

The maids, wide-eyed, watched me closely.

"There once, long ago, had been an attachment between us, and I only called on him to say good-bye. But if my friend were to discover that I'd seen him alone, she would be dreadfully upset."

"Who is the gentleman?" one of the maids asked.

"Mr. Charles Berry. He's in room 423," I replied. "Can you help me?"

"I don't see what we could possibly do," said the oldest of the three girls, who appeared to have taken on the role of spokesman.

"Couldn't you let me into the room? No one's there now. It would only take me a moment to find my bracelet."

"We could lose our jobs," the maid said.

"He's unlikely to return soon. No one will ever know."

One of the other girls laughed. She had pretty eyes and a pert smile. "From what I can tell, the gentleman in that room wouldn't object to finding you there anyway."

"Gabby!" the spokesman exclaimed.

"Oh, hush up, Bridget. We all know what sort of gentleman he is. I say we let her in and hope she steals something."

"Let me assure you that I would do no such thing," I said.

"I'll let you in," Gabby said. Bridget glared at her.

"I promise there will be no trouble for you."

At this, the third girl broke her silence. "I wish you could cause trouble for him," she said, bursting into tears.

"Has he hurt you?" I asked. She cried harder, and I found it not difficult in the least to believe the worst about Mr. Berry. "Did you tell anyone?"

"Who could she tell?" Bridget asked. "No one would believe her. And even if someone did, it wouldn't matter. He's practically the king of France, you know."

"Well, I believe you," I said, taking her hand. "For what little that's worth. I give you my word that I shall try to find a way to help you."

"Come with me, milady," Gabby said. "Let's get you into that room." Once upstairs, the girl unlocked the door. I thanked her and sent her back downstairs. "Promise you won't forget Molly," she said as she left.

I closed and locked the door, looking at the space before me. There was a sitting room and a bedroom, neither of which was particularly neat. Mr. Berry had left gloves, letters, and discarded papers scattered on every surface. I began to methodically sift through everything, careful to return each object to its place in the mess. The number of bills I found was staggering, and it was clear from the careless way they had been tossed about that paying them was of little concern to Mr. Berry. Most likely that would fall to Lady Elinor's solicitor as wedding plans with Isabelle were solidified.

I went into the bedroom, feeling more than a little uneasy to enter the space where this odious man slept. The wardrobe was full of clothing, all of it Savile Row's best and certainly acquired on credit. I begrudgingly admitted that the man's taste, at least in clothes, was excellent. The pockets of his coats contained nothing but cigarettes and still more bills. I was about to close the cabinet door when I noticed something leaning against the back wall of the armoire behind a row of shoes. It was an oversized book containing reproductions of paintings by Fragonard. If memory served, the artist was a favorite of Louis XIV's. It was the only book in Mr. Berry's suite. I opened it and flipped through the pages, hoping to uncover something between them. Luck was with me. Partway through the book I found a piece of paper folded in half. On it was a list of objects that had been owned by Marie Antoinette, each item followed by the name and address of the person to whom it currently belonged. Everything that had been stolen was marked with a small star. The last two entries were the pink diamond and something described as *Personal Correspondence*. Both were listed as being in the Francis house. There was no mention of the silver snuffbox.

I jumped at the sound of a key rattling in the lock. Would Gabby have returned to the room? Surely Mr. Berry was not back this early in the evening. Even if he had tried to leave the Londonderrys', Cécile would have found a way to detain him. Desperate, I looked around for somewhere to hide. Using the wardrobe for such a purpose would be too obvious, and if, for some reason, Berry had returned, he would almost certainly open it to change his clothes. Panic filled me, and seeing that I had few options, I clutched the book and ducked behind the heavy velvet curtains. The door opened, and I heard footsteps too heavy to belong to the maid. They circled the sitting room slowly. Drawers opened and shut. Papers shuffled. Eventually, the steps moved to the bedroom. I stood as still as possible, hardly breathing, hoping that I would not be discovered. Whoever it was stopped in front of the wardrobe. More rummaging.

As the footsteps moved back to the sitting room, I could not resist peeking out from behind the curtain. I moved it slowly, just enough to look through the door into the other room, careful not to draw attention to myself. Colin Hargreaves stood not thirty feet away from me, carefully examining a piece of paper before putting it into his pocket.

8

———————

MY HEART POUNDED AGAINST MY CHEST SO LOUDLY THAT I worried he might hear it. This was foolish, of course, but I couldn't help it. I pressed against the window in an attempt to make myself as flat as possible. He was still in the sitting room but wasn't making any noise. An eternity seemed to pass before I heard his footsteps again. He came back to the bedroom, and it sounded as if he was looking under the bed and the mattress. He wants the book, I thought, wishing I'd had the sense to return it to the wardrobe before hiding. What should I do? Reveal myself?

I never had the opportunity to decide. All at once, the curtain was snapped away from me. With effort, I forced myself to meet Colin's eyes. "I've not before seen you so flustered," I said, hoping to deflect his anger with a smile. He grabbed me roughly by the arms.

"This is no time to joke. What are you doing here?"

"Apparently the same thing you are, although I suppose that had *you* arrived first you wouldn't have felt it necessary to hide when I entered the room."

"Emily, this is outrageous." His eyes flashed. "Wait for me in the lobby."

"I've already found that which you seek," I said, and handed him the book. "There's a list inside."

"Go downstairs."

"Not without you."

"We don't have time for this."

"Have you found anything useful? What was the paper you put in your pocket?"

"Nothing of consequence." He scrutinized the list of Marie Antoinette objects, then pulled out a small notebook and began scribbling furiously on it. When he finished, he replaced the list in the book and handed it back to me.

"What should I do with it?" I asked.

"Put it back where you found it."

I did as he directed, not liking at all the feeling of his being so displeased with me. The moment I closed the wardrobe door, he steered me firmly into the hallway, locking Mr. Berry's room behind us.

"How did you get a key?"

"Say nothing further, Emily. You've already done more than enough." I wanted to tell Gabby that we'd locked the door, but Colin's tight grip on my arm indicated that he was in no mood to sanction a trip down the back stairs. As we approached the guests' stairway, he released me. "It will not do for us to be seen leaving a hotel together. Return to your house at once and wait for me there."

Nearly an hour passed before he turned up at Berkeley Square, an hour that I spent wondering if I had gone too far in my investigations. Perhaps I was not so capable as I believed. I was filled with melancholy thoughts of self-doubt when Colin closed the door to my library behind him, and though he looked better composed than he had at the Savoy, his calm demeanor did little to hide his aggravation once he began to speak.

"I cannot believe that you would be so foolish as to—"

"Did you go back to Mr. Berry's room?" I interrupted, my confidence returning in the face of his rebuke.

"That is none of your concern."

"It most certainly is!"

"Never in my life would I have thought to find you sequestered in another man's hotel room."

I could not help but smile at this. "Not in *another* man's room? Should I take that to mean you have entertained the notion of finding me in *yours*?"

"Don't flirt with me, Emily." His tone was cold, but I detected the slightest beginning of a thaw in his dark eyes.

"But surely you and I wouldn't require hotels for clandestine meetings. After all, we're each in possession of two perfectly good houses— I've got three if you count the villa, though I suppose—"

"Have you any idea of the danger in which you placed yourself tonight?"

"I would never have gone had I not known that Mr. Berry was out for the evening. There was almost no chance that I would be caught."

"What if someone other than me had found you?"

"What gave me away?" I asked.

"No curtain could hide that dress entirely. Your skirts are too full."

I sighed. "And I thought the demise of the bustle had given me such freedom. I suppose I shall have to order a new wardrobe designed specifically to allow me to skulk about hotel rooms in search of clues."

"I'd rather that you leave your wardrobe out of it and abandon the enterprise altogether."

"Spoken like a husband," I said. He ignored this.

"Furthermore, you dropped this." He passed me a handkerchief that bore my monogram.

"It must have been tucked in my sleeve," I said, mortified by my carelessness. "I didn't even know I had it with me."

"What were you doing in Mr. Berry's room?" he asked. I showed him the letter I had found at Mr. Francis's and recounted my conversation with Mr. Berry.

"I am convinced there is a connection between the two men," I said.

"You may be right. I promise that I shall do everything in my power to find out."

"I've made the same promise to Mrs. Francis." I continued without letting him reply. "Why are you so interested in Mr. Berry? Is this something to do with your work for Buckingham Palace?"

"Yes, it is. I'm not at liberty to divulge details, so you will have to content yourself with the knowledge that Berry's political position may be more important to Britain than anyone would suspect."

"Because there's a plan in place to restore the French monarchy?" I asked.

"You are a very smart girl," he said, all the warmth back in his voice. An unexpected feeling of relief rushed over me, and I realized that his approval meant more to me than I thought it did. He picked up my hand and kissed my palm.

"Have you lifted the embargo on kissing?"

"This doesn't really count. It's just your hand." So pleasant was the feeling of his lips on my skin that I completely forgot Mr. Berry. "I don't suppose you'd let this investigation to me?"

"Ah, is this display of affection designed to trick me into agreeing to that?"

"Not entirely." He turned his attention to my other hand. "I don't imagine you'd be so easily manipulated."

"I wouldn't." I slipped a hand into his pocket and removed the paper he had taken from the Savoy. "You're as readily distracted as I am," I said, holding it up before him.

"Probably more so. Were you ever to use all your feminine wiles on me, I wouldn't stand a chance."

"What do you take this to mean?" I asked, then read the letter aloud. "'Sir: As you did not respond to my first letter, I am forced to write again to beg you to reconsider your public actions. I should like to speak with you. Would you come to me Tuesday in Richmond?' It's signed D. Francis."

"I shall ask Berry about it."

"You're quite the friend of his these days."

"It's all official business, Emily. His idea of an entertaining evening could not be more different from mine."

"I've heard that you're spending inordinate amounts of time with the Marlborough Set. Dare I ask if the Prince of Wales and the would-be heir to the Bourbon throne are becoming close?"

"They have many similar"—he cleared his throat—"interests."

"Hmph." I knew all the rumors about Bertie and his *interests*, particularly those of the female persuasion. I did not much like the idea of Colin running with the Marlborough Set.

"You can imagine the delicate situations that might arise should Berry make any bad political moves."

"How lucky that he's got you to look after him." I looked at the letter again. "This makes me wonder if he had reason to want Mr. Francis eliminated."

"Don't let your imagination run wild, Emily. This situation is more precarious than you know. Investigate if you wish, but do not"—with a finger, he lifted my chin so that I was looking directly at him—"do not make accusations you cannot back up with irrefutable facts."

"The police seem perfectly willing to lock up Jane Stilleman without solid evidence."

"She had motive, she had opportunity. I know you dislike Berry. He is…not the gentleman he ought to be. But if you want to help Mrs. Francis, letting your dislike of him cloud your judgment will be an enormous mistake. Murder is not a crime limited to the obviously contemptible."

"I shall keep that in mind." I straightened his lapels. "I am most pleased that you are not trying to dissuade me from helping my friend."

"I wouldn't dream of it. First of all, you'd ignore me if I did, and you know how I deplore futile endeavors. Second, anything that distracts you from uncovering the identity of your admirer brings me closer to having you as my wife."

"You underestimate me. I'm perfectly capable of solving both puzzles and look forward to spending the fall with you in Greece. Shall we keep to Santorini? Or would you like to visit the mainland, too?"

"A question I shall not have to answer. Better that you, Emily, ponder options for our wedding trip. I thought Ephesus, and then Egypt."

"Someday, perhaps." I smiled, thinking that giving Colin permission to court me had been a very, very good idea.

I returned to Richmond the next morning and immediately told Beatrice about the list I had found at the Savoy as well as the letter Colin had discovered. While she searched for anything that could be considered "personal correspondence" of Marie Antoinette, I set about conducting interviews with the servants, hoping that I might discover something the police had missed. I started with Thomkins, whom I found working in the garden. He was less than forthcoming and clearly did not appreciate having to answer to a woman.

"How long have you been involved with Mrs. Stilleman?"

"Two years."

"If the affair began before she wed, why didn't she marry you?"

"I never asked," he said. "I always knew she'd do better with Stilleman. Marrying a gardener would have been a step down for her."

Truly, servants were worse about class distinction than their masters.

"But you loved her?"

"I suppose."

Faint praise, I thought. "When did Mr. Francis discover the two of you?"

"About two months ago."

"That long? Did he put you on notice?"

"He made it clear that he wouldn't tolerate that sort of thing in his household but said he would keep me on."

"And Jane?"

"I never talked to her after it happened."

"Not at all?"

"I need this work, milady."

"Do you think that Jane committed these crimes?"

"No." His voice was unsure.

"Why would Mr. Francis have threatened Jane's position but not yours?"

"I'm sure he wouldn't have told me. You'd have to ask Jane."

I returned to the house and sought out the housekeeper, an efficient sort of woman who confirmed what Thomkins had said and assured me that Jane would have been let go immediately if it were not for her husband.

"That's the tragedy of it, Lady Ashton. Mr. Francis quite depended upon Stilleman. If his wife were to lose her position and couldn't find something nearby, which she wouldn't—the entire county knows of her indiscretion—he might follow her. She was allowed to stay on a probationary basis."

"Then her position was not in jeopardy?" I asked.

"Not until she and Thomkins started carrying on again."

"What happened?"

"Stable boy caught them." So Thomkins had lied about not talking to Jane again.

"Had Jane been given her notice?"

"No. Mr. Francis died the next day."

"And what of Thomkins?"

"I was not privy to Mr. Francis's decision on that matter."

None of this information boded well for Jane, but when I said as much to Beatrice, she insisted that the maid was innocent. "Jane is like family to me. She is a good girl. I am disappointed that Thomkins was able to seduce her, but adultery is a far cry from murder."

"Quite right, Beatrice, but what if Stilleman had threatened her with divorce? That, coupled with the loss of her position, would have ruined her. Even good people can act badly when cornered."

"I am certain she is not guilty."

"I know you are," I said, taking her hand. "This is very difficult. I shall do all I can to uncover the truth, but please remember that it may not be what we hope it is. Did you have any luck with your search?"

"I did." She passed to me a bundle of letters tied with a red ribbon. "They were in a box where he kept theater programs."

I untied the ribbon, then, mindful of the fragile nature of the old paper, slowly unfolded the first sheet before me. It was written in French, a seemingly innocuous note to a friend, and would have meant very little were it not for Marie Antoinette's signature at the bottom of the page. "Oh! This"—I could not help but smile—"this is almost too easy. May I read the rest of them?"

"I wish you'd take them home with you. I'd rather not have anything here that might lure the thief back to my house."

Thinking of what I'd told Colin about there being nothing in my house that could lead to another break-in, I hesitated.

"Please take them, Emily," she said. "I can't stand the thought of them being here."

"All right." I folded the letter I was holding and returned it to the bundle, retying the ribbon. "I wonder why our intrepid thief did not steal them before."

"I've no idea. You will let me know if there is anything of significance in them?"

"Of course," I replied, and as my thoughts began to wander, I decided it was time to return home. Surely Charles Berry was not the thief. He could never pull off such a sophisticated series of crimes. Nor, however, could he afford to hire someone to do it for him. So why did he have the list I'd found in his room? And what had Mr. Francis wanted him to stop doing? Jane may have had reason to want both her husband and her employer dead, but a nagging instinct told me that Mr. Berry may have benefited from at least one of the murders, too. I was still contemplating these questions when, back at Berkeley Square, my driver, rather than one of the footmen, opened the carriage door.

"I thought you should know, Lady Ashton," he said, helping me down from my seat. "A coach followed us all the way from Richmond. It bore no markings and disappeared soon after we entered London. I did not get a good look at the driver. With the house having been broken into, we're all of us a mite worried about you."

9

JEREMY AND MARGARET DINED WITH CÉCILE AND ME THE FOLLOW-
ing night. I had hoped Colin might join us, but he was once again
playing chaperon to Charles Berry. Cécile missed him as much as I did.
"Such a terrible shame that he must waste his time with that man. I like
you very well, Bainbridge, but Monsieur Hargreaves..." She sighed.

"Say no more, Madame du Lac. I've yet to meet a lady immune to
Hargreaves. He's too bloody handsome."

"I wish he were around more so that the gossips would have less to
say about you and my darling Jeremy," Margaret said. "Do you know
that Lady Elliott asked me if I minded that she was going to invite
you to her ball? She was afraid that if I didn't come, Jeremy's mother
might not, and confided that she didn't want to do anything to draw
the dowager duchess's ire."

"Mother adores Emily," Jeremy said. "Lady Elliott is wasting her
time if she's trying to stir up controversy between them. Besides—and
I know you will take no offense at this, Margaret, darling—she would
die before seeing me marry an American. She's never forgiven the
colonists for leaving the empire."

"Ah!" Margaret cried. "Perfect! That is what will end our affair. I'm devastated already." She and Cécile stayed only another quarter of an hour before leaving for a ball. The fourth ball, I might point out, to which I had not been invited. Jeremy remained with me, something that did nothing but provide more fodder for London's gossiping matrons. At the time, however, I did not care, my feelings for society and its rigid rules being ambiguous at best.

"I cannot face another dance," Jeremy said, slouching in one of my library's most comfortable chairs. "Ballrooms are always too hot, and there are never enough seats. A chap can only stand so much dancing in a Season. I've already surpassed my limits."

"I shall consider the Season a success only if I can persuade Mr. Bingham to part with his silver *phiale*."

"Are you still pursuing that?"

"I've offered him an obscene amount of money for it and can't imagine that he'll refuse me this time."

"That depends on the state of his own fortune. If he's flush, he won't need the money and is likely to deny you out of spite."

"I'm afraid you're right," I said. "I should have begun the whole process differently. He's not the sort of man to respond to a willful lady. It would have been better for me to get an invitation to view his collection and then simper stupidly over the bowl. He probably would have given it to me on the spot."

Jeremy laughed. "You must be sure to keep at least some conventional behavior in your arsenal, Em. Ladies have more power than you might imagine."

"I suppose you're right." I sunk deeper into my chair. "You and Margaret are getting along famously. Your false courtship was a stroke of brilliance on her part. At the park the other day, I overheard two ladies, who shall remain nameless, lamenting the loss of one of Britain's most eligible peers."

"It's like a dream," he said, grinning. "But I'm afraid that the mothers of London will not leave me completely alone until I'm actually engaged."

"Poor man."

"It's a terrible bore."

"At least your position ensures that you'll be able to choose whatever wife you want."

"Does it?" He looked at me quizzically. "You turned me down easily enough."

"We both know that you only proposed to me because you were safe in the knowledge that I would refuse you."

"Point taken. But think on it, Emily. If we were married, we could agree to continue living as if we were single and everyone would leave us alone."

"I don't know that I'd like a husband who behaved as if he were a bachelor."

"You would if he were discreet, made no demands of you, and let you have your freedom."

"He would have to make some demands."

"Well, yes, but that needn't be unpleasant."

"Really, Jeremy! You are shocking!"

"So long as I amuse you."

"You've always done that. I'm beginning to think you should propose to Margaret. She'd appreciate your scheme."

Davis opened the door. "Mr. Berry is here to see you, Lady Ashton."

"Berry?" Jeremy was all amazement. "Emily, I'd no idea that you received gentleman callers this late in the evening."

"I can't imagine what he wants," I said. "Send him in, Davis, and bring us some port. His Grace is in desperate need of fortification."

"Perhaps the '51, then? That, I should think, would improve any gentleman's situation."

"Perfect. Whatever would I do without you, Davis?" When he returned a while later, I noted with some amusement that Mr. Berry had not passed muster with my butler, who, while he collected the port, had left the gentleman waiting in the hallway. Mr. Berry appeared agitated, his face flushed, and he did nothing to hide his surprise at finding me alone with Jeremy.

"Well," he said, a bit unsteady on his feet. "This is quite unusual, isn't it? Cozy evening at home with the duke?"

Jeremy stood. "You're intoxicated, sir."

"I'll be the judge of that."

"Why are you here, Mr. Berry?" I asked.

"I need to speak with you privately, Lady Ashton," Berry said.

"I'm not about to ask the duke to leave," I said. I eyed the decanter Davis had left on a table but decided it would be best not to pour any port. Mr. Berry needed no more to drink.

"I shouldn't think you'd want him to hear the sordid details of our private affairs."

"Forgive me, Mr. Berry, I was not aware that we have any private affairs."

Jeremy stepped closer to the other man. "Look here, Berry—"

"I didn't think you were vicious. Have I not offered you a position in my court? Looked on you with favor and made you the envy of half the girls in London? Surely you could not have expected that I would make you my queen. You're a widow, Lady Ashton."

"What on earth can you mean by all this?" I asked.

"Why are you trying to destroy me?"

"Destroy you?" My mind was racing.

"Have you any idea the difficulties I face? I suppose you're filled with jealousy for Isabelle and want her denied the things you could never have. Foolish woman! As if being mistress to a king isn't good enough for you."

"I'll not have you talk to her like that," Jeremy said.

"Mr. Berry," I said, keeping my voice calm. "Let me assure you that I have never entertained the idea of becoming your mistress."

"I know you've been to Richmond, and I know what you're doing. You are trying to keep me from my throne."

"I'm sorry to be unpleasant, but do try to remember, Mr. Berry, that there *is* no throne in France," I said.

"Stay out of my business, Lady Ashton, or you will live to regret it."

"That's quite enough," I said. "Your Grace, would you please escort Mr. Berry out?"

"What's going on here, Emily?" Jeremy asked when he returned. He poured two glasses of port and pressed one into my shaking hand.

"Charles Berry can't believe there is a woman in London not desperate for his attention." I forced a smile, not wanting to tell Jeremy about my involvement in the Francis investigation.

"And my darling Emily won't be satisfied as the next Madame de Pompadour. Devastating for Berry, of course, but hardly a threat to his position in general."

"I'd no idea I was so powerful politically. Perhaps I should turn my attention to Lord Fortescue next."

"I'd love to see you spar with him," Jeremy said, sipping his port. I hardly heard him speak, my thoughts remaining focused on more serious subjects. Was it Berry who had followed me from Richmond? My guest soon realized that I was hopelessly distracted and took his leave from me. Almost as soon as he was gone, Davis entered the library with an envelope.

"The duke noticed this on the doorstep when he left, madam," he said. I recognized the handwriting at once.

I did not reply but leapt from my seat, thrust my half-empty glass at the butler, and ran out the front door, calling for Jeremy, thinking he might still be in the vicinity. There was no reply. I would have to wait to ask him if he had seen anything else suspicious. I went back to the house, where I turned my attention to the note:

τί δ' ἔρωτι λογισμός; ἅπτε τάχος. ποῦ δ' ἡ
πρόσθε λόγων μελέτη; Ἐρρίφθω σοφίας ὁ πολὺς
πόνος· ἓν μόνον οἶδα τοῦθ', ὅτι καὶ Ζηνὸς λῆμα
καθεῖλεν Ἔρως.

It took me only a few moments with my lexicon to translate the passage: *And what is Reason to Love? Light up, quick! — And where is thy old study of philosophy? — Away with the long toil of wisdom; this one thing only I know, that Love took captive even the mind of Zeus.*

"Davis, did you see the note before the duke picked it up?"

"No, madam, I did not. I can assure you that it was not there when Mr. Berry departed. He dropped several cigarettes when His Grace removed him from the house. Molly swept the stairs immediately." I had hired Molly away from the Savoy the day after I learned about Charles Berry's treatment of her.

"Would you please go into the square and see if the undercover policeman Mr. Hargreaves has stationed there saw anyone?" I asked. Davis did so, but the man had noticed nothing out of the ordinary. Whoever had left this missive was skilled in the art of remaining hidden.

If I hadn't witnessed firsthand Jeremy's lack of interest in the ancient language, I might have suspected him of having left the message. As it was, I dismissed the thought almost at once. My admirer and the cat burglar were the same person, and there was no possibility that Jeremy was the thief. He'd never have the focus for such an endeavor. I would not be surprised to learn that he frequently found himself in the bedrooms of some of the best houses in London, but I doubted that he was ever reduced to using the window as his method of entrance.

The walk from Berkeley Square to Park Lane was a short one, past tree-lined rows of stately houses. It was a fine day, the heat having relented at last, and the improved weather had driven society outdoors. I passed no fewer than seven acquaintances before reaching the perfectly manicured park at Grosvenor Square, and until that moment, I had given no thought to the notion that my mission might be considered inappropriate. Being in close proximity to my parents' house, which stood on the north end of the square, made me more self-conscious, and I wondered if calling unescorted on a gentleman would further damage my already tender reputation. I steeled my resolve and continued on, feeling only the slightest tinge of apprehension when I reached my destination and knocked on the heavy door. The dignified butler who opened it confirmed that Mr. Hargreaves was at home and ushered me quickly into the magnificent house, doing nothing to disguise the fact that he was neither accustomed to nor approving of finding young ladies on his master's doorstep. He led me to an elegant salon, where rather than sit, I circled the room, examining the pictures that hung on the walls. So engrossed was I by a scene of the Thames painted by Turner that I did not notice Colin had entered the room until he stood next to me.

"Very daring of you, Lady Ashton," he murmured, "to come here quite unprotected."

I laughed. "I know that you're right, though I don't see how it is any different from your calling on me."

"At your house you are surrounded by your own servants. Here you are at my mercy."

"Your butler clearly does not approve of me and is certain to look after your own honor, so I feel confident I'm in no danger."

He stood very close but was careful not to touch me. "Fear not, Lady Ashton, your reputation is perfectly safe." He kissed both of my hands, then stepped away.

"You are taking this no-kissing business far too seriously," I said.

"It is quite serious." His eyes sparkled. "What brings you to me this afternoon?" I told him, as succinctly as possible, about the letters Beatrice had found.

"What do they say?" he asked.

"They were written when the queen was in jail and seem to contain nothing of consequence, just a friendly correspondence with a man called Léonard. Cécile says he was Marie Antoinette's hairdresser and a close confidant. She entrusted him with her personal jewels when it became clear the royal family was in danger. It was he who took them out of France and eventually brought them to her daughter after the revolution."

"Was the pink diamond one of those jewels?"

"Yes."

"That's most likely why Francis had the letters. They, in a sense, go with the stone."

"I am certain they are somehow more significant."

"Has Cécile read them? It's possible that a native speaker of the language might notice something you overlooked."

"I had not considered that. I'll give them to her when I get home."

"Is there something else, Emily?" he asked, looking at me closely. "What haven't you told me? Your brow creases right here"—he touched me lightly—"whenever you are not being candid with me."

"There's no need to accuse me of deception. I hadn't finished with my story."

"I see." He raised an eyebrow. "Do continue."

"I have been involved in a number of strange incidents."

"A number?"

"Three." I described the coach that followed me from Richmond, the note from my anonymous admirer, and last, Mr. Berry's visit to my house.

"Did he try to harm you?"

"No. Jeremy was with me."

"I see." He stood very still.

"Colin, you know that—"

"Was Cécile with you?"

"She was at a ball."

"Right." He cleared his throat. "Well, thank heavens you at least had Bainbridge." His demeanor had not changed, but I could sense an increasing tension in him.

"Colin, you know that Jeremy is nothing more than a friend to me."

"Of course." The tension did not dissipate. I took his hand in mine, wanting to reassure him. He continued to speak in a most businesslike manner. "I am most sorry that my work has taken me away from you so much lately."

"I understand."

"To make matters worse, I must go now. I'm to meet our friend Berry on Rotten Row."

"Are you free this evening?"

"I had planned to go to the Ellesmeres' ball. Will you be there?"

"No. I wasn't invited. I'm afraid that the combination of my intel-lectual pursuits and these ridiculous rumors about Jeremy is having a rather detrimental effect on my social life. Not that I particularly mind. It makes the mail much easier to manage."

"You should, perhaps, ask Miss Seward to use someone else as the front person for her false engagement. It's one thing for Bainbridge to embroil himself in scandal. He'll recover from it unscathed. It might not be so easy for you."

"What do I care about that? The fewer invitations I receive, the fewer excuses I have to make for not accepting them."

"You say that now, but I don't think you would enjoy being cut from society."

"I hardly think there's any danger of that happening," I said, adjusting my hat and preparing to leave. "Am I really to have no kiss good-bye?"

"Are you really accepting my proposal?"

"I might if it weren't such fun to tease you about not accepting it."

"Then I see we are at an impasse," he said with a most charming smile. He raised my hand to his lips but did not even brush my glove with them, then saw me out of the house.

I had not gone half a block down Park Lane when an open carriage pulled to the side of the road and stopped next to me.

"Emily, my dear, dear girl! How lovely to see you," my mother said, so forgetting herself that she reached out of the open carriage as if she would embrace me. What could I have done to gain such uncharacteristic approval? "You must be on your way to see me—I knew you would come today. I do wish your father were home, but he's at his club. He's been utterly silent on the subject, you know. Just like him, isn't it?"

I was thoroughly confused. "What subject?"

"Oh, child, don't bother to trifle with me now. I've heard everything."

"You have?" I asked, climbing in next to her. The driver urged the horses on, turning towards Grosvenor Square.

"You should be more careful about receiving gentlemen visitors late at night, my dear. It can lead to all sorts of gossip."

"What exactly have you heard?"

"All of London has heard tales of you and the Duke of Bainbridge.

I will admit to having been most distressed by your conduct until I heard about last night."

"Last night?" I was mystified.

"Have you and Jeremy settled all the details between you? I imagine he spoke to your father at his club."

"Mother—"

"I think you ought to be married from our house, Emily. Berkeley Square is too much the domain of your late husband, and a duchess should have a completely fresh start. I am so pleased that Jeremy does not object to your having been married before. Some men, you know—"

"Mother!"

"Do not interrupt me, Emily. Have you told Mr. Hargreaves? He is a dear man, and I hate to see him disappointed, but don't concern yourself with that too much. He'll recover nicely. He's so much in the company of the Marlborough Set that I can't help but think he knew his suit was hopeless. Oh, Emily, a duke! I'm so happy!"

"Jeremy and I are not engaged."

"What can you possibly mean by saying such a thing?" She gave me a sharp look.

"I don't know that I could speak more plainly."

"Of course you are engaged. Were you not chasing him through Berkeley Square, calling out for him? Odd behavior in any case, but I suppose young persons in love must be forgiven for such transgressions."

"How on earth do you know I did that?" I had not seen anyone in the square. Surely the undercover policeman sent by Inspector Manning would not have started such gossip.

"Everyone is talking about it."

"Hardly evidence of a betrothal, Mother."

"Well, if you are not engaged to him, you'd better remedy the situation quickly. Whatever were you thinking to send Mrs. du Lac and Miss Seward away in the middle of the night?"

"It was not the middle of the night, and I did not send anyone away. Jeremy dined with us. Cécile and Margaret went to a ball. I stayed home."

"No wonder Mr. Hargreaves has thrown you over. Who would want a wife with so little a sense of propriety?"

"Mr. Hargreaves has not thrown me over, and I can't believe that you are angry at *me* over this. Shouldn't your anger instead be directed to whoever is spreading this gossip?"

"There was nothing malicious in the story, Emily. People assume that the daughter of an earl would always act honorably, and, given your behavior, which is completely lacking in discretion, that would necessitate marrying the Duke of Bainbridge." There was a little too much satisfaction in her voice.

"Colin's called on me innumerable times in similar circumstances, and no one's ever raised an eyebrow over that. I'm a widow, and not subject to chaperones like an unmarried girl." She did not reply. "Have you orchestrated this, Mother?"

"How could you accuse me of such a thing?"

"It's not difficult in the least. You've made no secret of your desire to see me married again."

"I will not allow my own daughter to speak to me like this."

"Then I've nothing further to say on the subject." I rapped on the side of the carriage to signal for the driver to stop and climbed out, slamming the door behind me. "I do not appreciate being so brazenly manipulated and can assure you, Mother, that such tactics will never succeed."

"If you are not engaged to the Duke of Bainbridge, you'd better find a way to become so as soon as possible. I'll not have my daughter providing fodder for gossip." Much to my chagrin, tears filled my eyes, and I turned away before she could see them. Suddenly, the day felt oppressively hot.

10

⸺⸺⸺⸺⸺⸺⸺⸺⸺⸺

Lady Ashton! My dear child! Are you unwell?"
    I recognized the voice at once, and cringed at the thought of any of my acquaintances seeing me in my current condition. Unfortunately, I did not have the luxury of ignoring Lady Elinor's question; given my rank and the friendship between our families, deliberately slighting her would be a gross insult. I stopped walking and tipped my head back, trying to will the tears away. My eyes would not cooperate.

Lady Elinor caught up with me and took my arm. "Do forgive me for accosting you like this, but I could not help overhearing your argument with your mother. Will you walk with me?" Having at the ready no acceptable excuse to refuse, I consented, and we headed along Upper Grosvenor Street and crossed Park Lane. All this time, Lady Elinor said nothing. It was not until we had entered Hyde Park through the Grosvenor Gate that she broke her silence. "It is difficult to be at odds with one's own mother."

"I'm afraid that my mother and I have quite different ideas of what makes for a satisfactory life. She looks no further than a high-ranking husband."

"And you prefer intellectual pursuits?"

"Yes."

"The two need not be incompatible."

"No, of course not. But, invariably, no matter how enlightened one's spouse is, a woman loses much of her freedom when she agrees to marry."

"Theoretically, yes, but a good husband can broaden one's view of the world. I'd never left England before my marriage. In fact, my mother only rarely brought me to London. So far as I knew, the world hardly extended beyond Sevenoaks and Kent."

"It sounds as if you made an excellent choice for a husband. But for me, at this moment, I've so much that I want to do on my own. There is merit in discovering things independently." We were rapidly approaching the southern edge of the park and sat on a bench near a fountain decorated with stone portraits of Shakespeare, Chaucer, and Milton.

"A sentiment with which your mother cannot agree." She shook her head. "So unfortunate. I hate to see the spirit driven out of a young lady."

"There's no danger of that happening," I replied, closing my parasol and tipping back my head, savoring the feeling of the sun on my face as I contemplated Lady Elinor's comment. Had she not driven the spirit out of her own daughter by forcing her into an engagement with Mr. Berry?

My companion must have guessed my thoughts. "Isabelle's situation is entirely different. I abhor gossip so shan't recount the details, but suffice it to say that she is far better off away from Lord Pembroke. I hate to see her heartbroken, but she's already beginning to recover. Mr. Berry does, after all, have his charms. But I'm sure I need not tell you that. He's always held you in high regard." Her voice held the slightest note of question in it.

"No more so than any other lady he happens to encounter. There has never been any understanding between us." My words had the desired effect. The tiny wrinkles around Lady Elinor's mouth smoothed as she relaxed.

"Isabelle and I have been closer than the closest of friends ever since she was a tiny girl. If I had any doubt that marriage to Mr. Berry would bring her much happiness, I should never have agreed to the match. Now, in your situation, marrying the Duke of Bainbridge—"

"Would bring little lasting joy." I snapped my parasol back open.

"You have already made one brilliant marriage. You have both rank and fortune. It is only natural, though, that your mother would grow concerned when she finds your actions being scrutinized by gossips. I'm afraid it's due to your age, Lady Ashton. Were you an older widow, your romantic liaisons would be of far less interest."

"Society has such vacuous standards. Sometimes I think I ought to live in Greece year-round."

"Mr. Routledge took me there several times. Have you been to Delphi?"

"More magnificent views are not to be found on the earth. The crags are spectacular, and the way the fields of olive trees stretch all the way to the Itea Bay is mesmerizing."

"Their leaves seem to shimmer in the sun. Will you go back to Greece soon?"

"I drank from the Castalia Spring to ensure it."

"Ah, yes. Many poets have been inspired by those same waters."

"I had no idea you were so well informed about Greece," I said.

"I'm not, really. All I know is what anyone could pick up from Baedeker's."

"Where else have you visited?"

"All of the standard places in Europe, of course, as well as Egypt and India."

"And what is your favorite?"

"St. Petersburg in the summer, when the sun never sets." She rose from the bench. "I see, Lady Ashton, that I have succeeded in cheering you up."

"You have. I'm most grateful."

"And I owe you thanks, too. I must confess to having wondered if there was…something…between you and Mr. Berry."

"Let me assure you, Lady Elinor, that you will never have cause to worry on that front."

"Please do not think less of me for having mentioned it."

"Of course I don't."

"And know that you have a staunch supporter in me. I'm aware that you are suffering at the hands of gossips, and shall do all I can to counter their vicious stories. You won't be left off any guest list of mine."

Although Lady Elinor had succeeded in improving my mood, I had to admit that this latest quarrel with my mother left me deeply unsettled. To distract myself, instead of returning home, I headed towards the library at the British Museum, hoping to begin researching the letters of Marie Antoinette's confidant, Léonard. When I asked for assistance at the desk, I could not help remembering my first visit to the museum after my husband's death. On that occasion, the staff had responded to me immediately because of the generous donations Philip had made to the Greco-Roman collection. Now, however, I had a reputation of my own, not only because of my donations to the museum, but also because of my efforts to encourage others to return important pieces to scholarly institutions.

"We are delighted to see you, Lady Ashton," a short, ruddy-faced clerk said, snapping to attention the moment he saw me. "Is there anyone in particular with whom you would like to speak?" I briefly described for him the letters in which I was interested. His red cheeks took on an even darker color. "Then I am most pleased to offer my services. I specialize in eighteenth-century manuscripts."

"Do you know anything about Léonard's letters?"

"Only that they exist. If I recall..." He came out from behind the desk and motioned for me to follow him. "I read a story recently about someone looking for them." He led me through a maze of desks, each one piled with research material. A variety of gentlemen huddled over them, almost none glancing up as we passed. My guide stopped at a desk at the far end of the Reading Room and began to rummage through a stack of books heaped in a haphazard fashion.

"Is this your desk, Mr.—"

"Right. Most sorry. Adam Wainwright. This is my desk. I'm afraid I'm a tad disorganized. Ha! Here it is." He opened a thick notebook, hardly having to page through it before finding the passage he sought. "Yes...yes..."

I did my best to try to read over his shoulder, but the angle was such that all I accomplished was to strain my neck. "What does it say?" I asked.

"Léonard's letters were never located. I do wish I could be of more help."

"These are your own notes?" I asked, indicating the notebook.

"Yes. I'm working on a book about the fall of the House of Bourbon."

"And do you find that Marie Antoinette deserves her reputation?"

"She was naïve, undoubtedly, and perhaps not of more than average intelligence, but she was not cruel. She adored her children, and was, in the end, an extremely pious woman."

"I imagine a looming guillotine would make most of us keenly religious."

Mr. Wainwright grinned. "Quite right, madam. It was the queen's confessor, Father Garrard, who preserved the letters she received from Léonard. Had he not, her jailors almost certainly would have destroyed them after her execution." He dabbed a rather too gray handkerchief across his brow. "I am certain Léonard kept those she sent to him but have never been able to determine what became of them after his death."

I would have liked to tell him that the letters were at this moment in my own library but worried that admitting I had them might somehow bring danger to my household. I would, however, make a point of letting him read them once I'd solved all the puzzles before me. "Have you tried to find Léonard's letters?" I asked.

"Not really," he said. "When things like that disappear into private collections, they are often lost entirely to scholars. If one knows who possesses them, there's at least hope that the owner will allow them to be studied. But, often, it's impossible to figure out who owns what."

"This is precisely why I have been trying to convince collectors to donate significant pieces to the museum."

"Yes, I have heard about your efforts." He pulled a face. "It's unfortunate that it is so difficult to persuade your peers to part with their treasures."

"I know it all too well. I wonder if it would be feasible to at least catalog what people have tucked away in their homes."

"A daunting prospect, Lady Ashton. Have you any idea how long it would take to do that at just one aristocratic estate?" I thought about my husband's collection at Ashton Hall, the magnificent Derbyshire estate of the Viscounts Ashton. He had, in fact, kept his pieces cataloged, but I knew that was not common practice. "And aside from things that are displayed in houses, there are untold treasures, historical documents in particular, packed away in attics. To catalog those would be nearly impossible."

"You're undoubtedly correct."

"If you'd like, you may borrow my copy of Léonard's memoir. I don't know that it will be of much help." He handed a book to me. I thanked him and left the library, my thoughts scattering in more directions than I cared to count. I had an idea of how to begin my search for the letters but wondered if they really would provide any insight into the murders in Richmond. I thought of Jane in prison. I thought of Mrs. Francis, and I felt more than slightly guilty that a good portion of my brain was occupied with thoughts of how I might begin to catalog the treasures of England's country houses.

For the moment, the catalog would have to wait. I remembered the list I had found in Mr. Berry's room. He had known where to find Marie Antoinette's letters, something that, according to Mr. Wainwright, was not common knowledge. And our intrepid thief certainly had no difficulty figuring out who owned objects that had belonged to the French queen. If both of them could acquire this knowledge, certainly it was not beyond my reach.

Not feeling much like having another encounter with Mr. Berry, I decided to focus on the thief. That his identity remained a mystery did not deter me in the least. I would do what any lady would when trying to contact an unknown gentleman; I marched directly to the offices of the *Times* and placed an ad in the classifieds section. Tomorrow, buried in with pleas that *the lady in the pink dress near the Achilles statue* and that *the gentleman who so kindly bestowed upon me a rose at so-and-so's ball* would come forward and identify themselves, my own request would appear:

> *To the gentleman who delivered the two pinks: You may find me in front of the Rosetta Stone at two o'clock Thursday.*

Pleased with myself, I returned to Berkeley Square. I hardly realized how exhausted I was until I'd dropped into the most comfortable chair in my library, where Cécile woke me three quarters of an hour later.

"Beatrice has just arrived."

Still groggy, I dragged myself to my feet, and Cécile took my arm. "I am worried about her, Kallista. She is extremely upset."

Lizzie was standing in the hallway outside the drawing room and opened the door for us. "Will you want tea for Mrs. Francis, madam?"

"Yes, please," I replied, thinking it was odd that Lizzie knew the identity of my caller. Surely Davis would not have sent her to hover outside the room. This thought was entirely forgotten, however, when I saw Beatrice's tear-streaked face.

"The police have proof that Jane Stilleman delivered the poison to David's room," she said, pulling on her black-hemmed handkerchief with such force that I thought it would rip.

"My dear friend, sit," I said, ushering her to a chair. "You must try to calm down."

"This is too awful to bear," she said, sobbing. "They will hang her, you know."

"What is their evidence?" I asked.

"One of the housemaids was changing the bed linens the day before David died. While she was in the room, Jane came in with a bottle of shaving lotion. The maid remembers this, because the valet—"

"Stilleman?"

"Yes. He was also in the room and told Jane that it was not the proper kind of lotion. David always used Penhaligon's, and this was from Floris. She insisted that it had been delivered for Mr. Francis and persuaded her husband to set it with the other toiletries."

"Has this maid any reason to want Jane found guilty?" Cécile asked.

"Of course not. I've told you, Jane is a sweet girl. No one would want to harm her."

"I know you're distressed," I said. "But we must look at the facts before us with as little bias as possible. Jane was having an affair. There may be persons other than her husband who were upset by this. I shall come to Richmond tomorrow and see what I can uncover."

"I don't know what I would do if I couldn't turn to you."

Davis opened the door. "Mrs. Brandon to see you, madam." Ivy came in, looking more drawn and fatigued than I had ever before seen her. As soon as she saw Beatrice, however, she forced a bright smile and acted delighted to make the acquaintance. Beatrice, too, pulled herself together with remarkable speed. They conversed effortlessly, breezing through society's favorite banal subjects, neither of them paying any real attention to what the other said. It was as if the exchange were perfectly choreographed.

I was unnerved to see how well Ivy had slid into the role of society lady, hiding her emotions, concerned only with putting on a polite appearance. And as for Beatrice, although I did not know her so well as I did Ivy, it was an extraordinary thing to watch her bury emotions that only moments before had completely overwhelmed her. I tried to catch Cécile's eye, but she was busy removing Brutus from a battle with my velvet curtain. I'm sorry to say that the curtain appeared to have lost the struggle.

"Emily and Cécile, I've no desire to keep you from your charming friend," Beatrice said. "Forgive my intrusion, and please accept my thanks for your assistance." She took her leave just as Lizzie entered with a tea tray.

"Are you well, Ivy?" Cécile asked.

"Everything is lovely, thank you, Madame du Lac," Ivy replied, watching the maid pour. "Those are beautiful teacups, Emily. Have you always had them?"

"I never took you for a connoisseur of china," I said. Brutus, not pleased with being pulled off the drapes, turned his attention to Lizzie's skirts. I picked up the dog, dropped him into Cécile's lap, and dismissed the maid. "Come now, what is troubling you?"

"I'm perfectly fine," Ivy said, her pretty brow furrowed.

"There are no servants here. You are free to say anything you wish."

She cringed. "Am I so obvious?"

"*Oui*," Cécile replied. "And I think you will speak more frankly if I leave you to Kallista."

"Oh, madame, I wouldn't want to drive you from your tea."

"Do not trouble yourself. I've no interest in tea and only drink it when Kallista forces it upon me." She collected her dogs—Caesar, never as bad-mannered as Brutus, was sitting quietly under his own-er's chair—and sailed out of the room, giving Ivy a reassuring pat on the arm as she passed her.

"I'm afraid I've had a rather brutal day," Ivy said. "Robert's mother and I have been working together to rearrange the paintings in the family portrait gallery." Ivy's mother-in-law had a tendency to meddle, but Ivy, brilliant in her ability to manage people, had quickly figured out how to make the former mistress of her house feel useful, even necessary, without bowing to her every wish.

"Surely you've made her think that your ideas are her own, and the pictures are precisely where you'd like them."

"Not quite. I couldn't bear to spend another moment surrounded by Robert's ghastly ancestors all looking as if they're sitting in judg-ment on me, and had a footman remove a picture of some woman with her thirteen hideous children. Mrs. Brandon was rather affronted."

"I can well imagine. What brings on this sudden animosity?" I had my suspicions, but instead of saying so, put my arm around my friend and drew her head onto my shoulder.

"Do you ever speak with Philip's mother?" she asked.

"Not often. She calls on me occasionally if she's in town."

"I suppose you would see her more often if you and Philip had a child."

"Is Robert's mother beginning to prod you about producing an heir?"

"She would never bring up such a delicate subject."

"But she can't help applying subtle pressure," I said.

"It's not just her." I poured her more tea, and she emptied the cup in one gulp. "Robert and I have been married for almost a year. Every person to whom I speak inquires pointedly after my health."

"That's common courtesy, Ivy."

"I don't think so." She filled her cup and drained it quickly again. "They *look* at me. To see if I'm tired. Or flushed. It's intolerable."

"My poor dear. Has Robert commented on the situation?"

"He dances around the issue, asking me every few weeks if I have any news."

"Well, I suppose—"

"When he knows perfectly well that...that...he would have to...that with him gone so frequently..." She poured still another cup of tea but this time did not drink it, just stirred and stirred the contents with a small silver spoon.

"Is he neglecting you?"

"Of course not! But entering politics is awfully time-consuming, and he winds up going to his club most evenings after we come home."

"And he doesn't want to wake you when he returns?"

"He almost never comes to me," she said in a voice hardly above a whisper.

My heart broke for her. The most obvious explanation for her husband's behavior would be a mistress, though I found it hard to believe he would have strayed so early in their marriage. "Are things between you well otherwise?"

"You know Robert. He's a consummate gentleman. Attentive, kind, generous."

"But not quite attentive enough."

Ivy turned red to her fingertips. "How was it with you and Philip?"

"Oh, Ivy, you can't compare that. We were hardly together beyond our wedding trip."

"I'm probably overreacting," she said. "When he needs my comfort, he'll find me. I have to learn to be more patient."

I stopped her stirring her tea. "Ivy, marriage is a partnership. Your need for comfort is as important as his, and it's obvious that you need more than he is giving you. Can't you talk to him? Tell him your feelings?"

"I would never want to be a source of worry to him."

"Surely a man who loves you would not want you to feel so unhappy?" I wondered if Robert did love her and continued quickly. "Perhaps this is nothing more than a miscommunication. Why don't you tell him that you'd like to see him after he gets home?"

"I couldn't do that!"

"Why on earth not?"

"It would be as if I were...really, Emily, I could never say that!"

"That is most unfortunate."

"Not everyone is as comfortable with unconventional behavior as you are."

"Ivy! Are you reprimanding me?"

She burst into tears. "No, no, of course not. But your life, Emily, is not at all like mine anymore. You're happy to be on your own. I'm not. All I want is to be a good wife and bring Robert happiness."

"There's nothing wrong with that." I embraced her.

"I know you don't believe that," she said.

She was right, and I felt terrible. We had been inseparable since we were girls, learning to embroider side by side, picking out our first ball gowns together, swapping sensational novels. We had even been presented at court on the same day. But ever since her marriage and my realization that I wanted to pursue an intellectual life, our lives had veered in different directions. "Just because I haven't followed the same path as you doesn't mean that I condemn your choices," I said.

"You think your choices are better."

"Better for me, not for you." A silence hung between us. "You know that I respect your decisions. I just don't want to see society engulf you and churn out another perfect matron."

"There's no danger of that happening."

"There is if your only purpose in life is to keep Robert comfortable. When is the last time you brought me a book to read?"

She wouldn't meet my eyes. "Robert does not much like popular fiction."

It outraged me that she would alter her reading habits at the whim of her husband, but I decided that, for once, I ought not say what I was thinking. "You are not giving Robert the credit he deserves. He does drink port with you, does he not?"

"Yes, when we dine alone."

"And it's been what? Five? Six months since you started drinking port? You've given him plenty of time to get used to modern thinking. It's undoubtedly safe to introduce literature to the household."

This brought the beginnings of a smile to Ivy's face. "I'd hardly call the novels we read literature."

11

I VY LEFT WITH MY COPY OF MARY ELIZABETH BRADDON'S *MOUNT Royal*. Mrs. Braddon had for years been one of our favorite guilty pleasures. I had brought another of her books, *Lady Audley's Secret*, on my honeymoon, and had no doubt that the author's retelling of the story of Tristran and Iseult would give my friend relief from her marital woes. Eventually, however, she would need more than simple distraction. I was determined to find a way to gently persuade her to take a more active role in her relationship with her husband. This might prove more difficult than uncovering the identity of my mysterious admirer.

I went to Richmond as early as possible the next morning, eager to see what Jane Stilleman's peers thought of her. The response was underwhelming. While no one expressed animosity towards her, she did not seem to have any particular friends amongst the staff. Beatrice was waiting for me in her sitting room, pacing nervously, desperate for new information.

"There must be something we've overlooked," she said.

"It will perhaps be easier to prove someone else's guilt than to prove Jane's innocence. I'm very curious about the snuffbox that was stolen from you. Have you any idea how your husband acquired it?"

"It was a gift from one of the Sinclairs' servants. They're our nearest neighbors."

"Isn't that a bit odd? A servant giving a gift to a gentleman?"

"Not for David. He was generosity itself, always doing what he could for those less fortunate. It was not uncommon at all for those he had helped to offer him some sort of thanks, however humble it might be."

A silver box that had belonged to Marie Antoinette could hardly be described as humble. "Do you know the servant's name?"

"Dunston, I believe. Jeanne Dunston. I've no idea what David did for her."

I set off at once to call on the Sinclairs. Beatrice's house stood on a small piece of land that backed into her neighbors' magnificent park, and a walk was just what I needed to gather my thoughts before descending upon them unannounced. I took solace in the knowledge that my rank would allow me to get away with this sort of thing.

Mrs. Sinclair received me without the slightest indication that she found my arrival out of the ordinary. She was gracious and elegant, plied me with tea and cakes, and happily answered my questions about her servant.

"Jeanne was a treasure, an absolute treasure. Her father worked in the stable when my husband was a boy, and her grandmother was with the family before that."

"But Jeanne is no longer with you?"

"No. She died some months ago. She was quite old."

"I understand that she gave a silver snuffbox to your neighbor, David Francis. Were you aware of that?"

"Yes. He had helped her with some family matter. I don't know the details, but imagine that it had something to do with her son, who turned out very wicked. It was he who should have been given the box—it had been in their family for ages. But he disappeared years ago."

"Did she have no idea where he went?"

"My husband tried to locate him when Jeanne fell ill, but to no avail. He had notices of her death printed in the papers, but Joseph didn't come to the funeral."

"His name is Joseph?"

"His mother called him that, but it appears that he took a different name after he left our house."

"I am sorry that he never reconciled with his mother," I said automatically, though the sentiment was not entirely heartfelt. Unless I heard proof of Joseph's guilt, I would withhold judgment against him. "Have you any idea how the box came to be in the Dunstons' possession?"

"Not in the slightest. Jeanne's grandmother fled France during the revolution. I suppose she picked it up before she left."

"Perhaps it was a gift from her previous employer?"

"Highly unlikely. Who would give a servant such a valuable item? I imagine it was one of the many objects looted from Versailles. Not, mind you, that I am suggesting she stole it."

"Of course not," I replied.

"And now the box has been stolen from poor Mrs. Francis. She must be devastated."

"Do you know her well?"

"I can't say that I do. The Francises are good neighbors but not much interested in society."

When we had finished our tea, Mrs. Sinclair was kind enough to allow me to question her servants. None of them knew where Joseph Dunston might be found, and only one admitted to knowing about the silver snuffbox. The girl, a young maid, had walked into Jeanne's room while the woman was looking at the box.

"She snapped it shut the second she saw me and scolded me something fierce for coming in without knocking."

This snuffbox grew more interesting with every passing moment. I was still wondering what Jeanne Dunston might have hidden in it when, on my way out of the house, I noticed a striking sculpture in their foyer: Greek, from the Archaic Period. I looked at it carefully, trying to memorize its details and wondered if the Sinclairs could be convinced that it belonged in the British Museum.

Colin's hat and walking stick were in the hallway when I returned home, and, thrilled at the thought of him waiting for me, I started for the library, only to be stopped by Davis.

"Mr. Hargreaves and Mrs. du Lac are in the blue drawing room, madam. Mr. Hargreaves asked most emphatically that they not be disturbed, though I am certain he would not include you in a list of potential disturbers. Also, while you were gone, four cases of champagne arrived from Berry Bros. and Rudd."

"Did Madame du Lac order them?"

"Apparently not. The deliveryman said they were sent as a gift but didn't know from whom. Perhaps Mr. Hargreaves?"

"I've always considered him more of a port man, don't you, Davis?"

"If I may, Lady Ashton, I believe Mr. Hargreaves was always exceedingly fond of the viscount's whiskey."

"I had not realized, Davis. Thank you." My butler looked immensely pleased with himself.

When I reached the sitting room, I opened the door slowly. Colin and Cécile sat next to each other at a game table, papers strewn all over its inlaid surface. Colin snapped to attention the moment I cracked the door but relaxed when he saw me and continued his conversation.

"I am indebted to you, Madame du Lac," he said, hardly pausing to acknowledge me.

Cécile shrugged. "I have little concern for the Prince of Wales and his reputation but admire the loyalty you feel for your country. For you, I will offer my help."

"While I am grateful for the compliment, I suspect you are as concerned about the welfare of France as I am for that of the British Empire."

"What, may I ask, are you two scheming so secretly?" I sat at the table across from Colin.

"Monsieur Hargreaves needs me to return to Paris."

"Paris? Oh, Cécile—"

"There is to be no argument. You cannot expect me to resist the will of a man as handsome as he."

Colin smiled. "There is a political scandal brewing that threatens both of our countries. I need Madame du Lac's assistance with a particular gentleman in Paris."

I raised an eyebrow. "What sort of assistance?"

"Whatever sort it might take," Cécile replied.

"Has this to do with Charles Berry?"

"Yes," Colin said. "It appears that his talk of gaining a crown has not sprung wholly out of his imagination. There are plans under way to topple the Third Republic and restore the monarchy to France."

"How does that threaten England?"

"We are more secure if our neighbor has a stable government."

"And how is the Prince of Wales involved?"

"He and Berry have become fast friends."

"Two kings, as it were?"

"So Berry would like. But should this coup fail—and I am confident that it will"—he looked at Cécile as he said this—"it will not benefit the prince to be viewed as someone who supported an attempt to overthrow a foreign government."

"Can't you just tell him to stop letting Berry hang about?" I asked.

"Staggering though the thought is, you, Emily, are not the most stubborn person in the empire. His Royal Highness prefers not to be told who makes an acceptable friend."

At that instant I felt a newfound respect for the future king of England. "Well, it may be that I've been too harsh in my assessments of the prince. I shall try to make a fresh start with him."

"I shouldn't bother, Kallista," Cécile said. Colin began to gather up the papers from the table.

"Have I given you all the information you require?" he asked my friend.

"*Oui*. I am eager to meet Monsieur Garnier. He is certain to be a man of great possibility."

"Garnier?" I asked.

"The power behind the throne, as it were," Cécile said. "It will be most interesting to meet a man who considers himself Richelieu's equal." I expected that she would excuse herself and leave me alone with Colin, but instead she challenged him to a game of chess. I watched them, an uneasy tension hovering in the air, and wondered what dangers my friend had agreed to face for the good of someone else's crown and country. Unsettled, I turned my attention to the *Odyssey*. Neither of my friends spoke until the match was over.

"Checkmate," Colin said, trapping Cécile's king with his queen.

"*Magnifique*. I would have been most disappointed had you let me win."

"I should not dream of insulting you so." He kissed her hand, then crossed the room and pulled me from my chair so that I was standing mere inches from him. "As for you, my dear," he said, almost under his breath. "I'm pleased to see that you're spending more time with

Homer than *The Greek Anthology*. Makes me quite confident that my proposal will be accepted. You'll not find the identity of your admirer in the *Odyssey*. How soon could your trousseau be assembled? I'd love to take to you the carnival in Vienna."

"And I should love to go. The Viennese have lifted the waltz to new heights of glory. But do not think you will win our wager. I'm well on my way to identifying our mysterious friend."

"Hmmmm," he said, holding his fingers up to my lips but not touching them. "We shall see." He squeezed my hand, said good-bye to Cécile, and left.

"I am not happy about leaving you alone," Cécile said.

"I'll be perfectly all right," I said, though I felt a pang at the thought of her going. I had grown used to her constant companionship and would miss even Caesar and Brutus.

"You could come with me."

"No, I promised I'd help Beatrice."

"I do worry, Kallista, about you here with that man paying such close attention to you."

"Inspector Manning has so many officers watching this house that I fear more for my privacy than my safety." I glanced through the papers Colin had left on the table for Cécile. "What exactly are you to do in Paris?"

"Befriend this man, Garnier. He's an obscenely popular politician who's constantly preaching against government corruption. The bourgeois adore him. Monsieur Hargreaves suspects that he is going to complete what General Boulanger left unfinished."

"Boulanger? Didn't his attempt to take over the government fail? I remember reading in the papers that it descended into a farce."

"Boulanger had not the character to lead a nation."

"From what I heard, he was overly attached to his mistress," I said. "Didn't he stay with her instead of going to the Elysées Palace at the appointed hour?"

"He did. Left the garrisons of Paris waiting for him. Imagine having that kind of power over a man."

"Do you really think she had anything to do with it? Most likely he was scared and found staying with her easier than taking the reins of the country."

Cécile shrugged. "It is dangerous to discount the power of a woman's influence."

"So is that what you're to do? Influence Monsieur Garnier?"

"Not at all. I will find out when he plans to stage his coup."

"Surely he can't think he will succeed so soon after Boulanger's failure?"

"Garnier has what Boulanger did not: Charles Berry. Many people in France question the value of our democracy. The government is too corrupt."

"And Charles Berry would somehow be an improvement?"

"*Pas de tout*. But imagine taking France back to the days of the Sun King. That is the mood Garnier is trying to capture. He has the backing of all the members of the exiled Bourbon and Orléans royal families as well as the support of other monarchies, and he is viewed as a man who wants what is best for his country. He is not, after all, suggesting that he should be on the throne, only that France should be returned to its former glory."

"And this is common knowledge?"

"*Mais non*. Only his closest confidants know his plans."

"The Prince of Wales?"

"The prince is friends with Berry, not Garnier."

"Surely Berry knows the plan."

"Monsieur Hargreaves does not think so."

"Garnier knows Berry well enough not to trust him," I said. "Yet he would make him king of France?"

"Fascinating, *n'est-ce pas?* You will have your part in the excitement, Kallista. I am to send all correspondence to you. Monsieur Hargreaves thought you would like that." She patted my arm. "And it will be *très intéressant* to see how you like being alone in this house again. You may find you want to keep him with you."

"Cécile, I will never forgive you if you try to get me married. It's bad enough that Ivy has defected to my mother."

"Your mother wants to see you make a good society match. Ivy only wants one that would bring you happiness. There is very little similarity between the two positions."

"I know you're right, but it doesn't always feel that way."

"Someday, Kallista, you will learn to stop resisting things only because they are sanctioned by others."

"I don't do that, Cécile."

"I am not saying that you should marry Monsieur Hargreaves to appease these society ladies. But he is too much the gentleman to take you as anything but his wife. And if that is the only way to get such a man, well...marriage might not be so awful. I can think of many things more disappointing than waking up next to him every morning."

"You are terrible."

She shrugged. "To turn away something you want simply because it is de rigueur is as foolish as blindly following society's rules. You must make your own decisions, Kallista, but do not become an iconoclast at the expense of your own happiness."

"I hope I'm not that foolish. I adore Colin, but more than I want him I want to find something in life that is mine alone. An identity beyond that of wife. Something that I love, that edifies, that inspires me."

"You are already on your way to finding it, *chérie*. How many objects have you secured for the British Museum?"

"Not enough. Did I tell you about the statue I saw in Richmond?" As I began to describe it to her, all other thoughts rushed out of my head. When Cécile went upstairs to direct the packing of her belongings, I wrote an impassioned note to Mr. Sinclair about the piece and sent it immediately. No sooner was that done than I penned a second, this one to Mr. Bingham. Lord Fortescue might reprimand me for harassing the poor man, but I did not care. The silver libation bowl needed to be in a museum, and I had no husband with political aspirations whose career was at the mercy of Lord Fortescue.

12

THURSDAY WAS CÉCILE'S LAST DAY IN LONDON, AND HER IMPENDING departure had a deleterious effect on my household. Caesar and Brutus, who had become inexplicably fond of Berkeley Square, recoiled at the sight of their travel boxes and crawled beneath a large cabinet in the red drawing room from which they could not be coaxed, even with scraps from the previous evening's roast beef. Cook took this as a personal insult and stalked about belowstairs all morning in a state of high dudgeon. As a result, our luncheon was delayed, and I had no time at all to eat before leaving for the British Museum, where I hoped to meet my anonymous admirer.

As I walked towards Great Russell Street, it started to rain, but the drops amounted to little more than a mist that would do nothing to alleviate the claustrophobic humidity enveloping the city. I did not open my umbrella, using it instead as a walking stick, its metal point echoing the rhythm of my feet. My claim to Colin that I was near to unmasking my would-be *innamorato* had not been quite accurate. Other than placing the ad in the *Times*, I had done almost nothing to find him. Initially, I had thought I might ferret him out by baiting young gentlemen of my acquaintance, but that had been when I believed him to be nothing more than a creative suitor keen to take advantage of my interest in Greek. Now, however, knowing that he was responsible for the Marie Antoinette thefts, I believed it would take a great deal of persuasion to get him to reveal himself. My only real hope came from his romantic designs on me. Surely a gentleman in love would not wish to remain eternally incognito.

Once inside the museum, I left my umbrella in the hall and ducked through the rooms leading to the Southern Egyptian Gallery, which housed the Rosetta Stone. I meandered about, patiently reading the cards describing each object while I watched for any solitary gentlemen who lingered too long in front of the famous basalt tablet. No one came. I studied the sarcophagus of the queen of Amasis II, admired a statue of the god of the Nile, and pondered figures of the goddesses Bast and Sekhet. I watched a young man whisper something that made a young lady blush while her chaperone scrutinized an obelisk through spectacles that pinched her nose. I enjoyed a brief moment of anticipation when a well-dressed gentleman entered the room, pursued by a docent telling him that he must deposit his walking stick in the hall. He gave me a jaunty smile as he surrendered the stick, then left the room without so much as glancing at the Rosetta Stone.

The stone itself provided ample distraction for another quarter of an hour. After doing my best to read the Greek inscription on it, I turned my attention to the hieroglyphs and was entirely seduced by their elegant beauty. My fingers ached to try to draw them, and as I was longing for my sketchbook, a man approached me. My eyebrows shot up, then fell immediately as soon as I recognized him as the docent who had taken the gentleman's stick.

"Lady Ashton?" he asked. I nodded. "Forgive me for disturbing your reverie. This was left for you at the desk." He handed me a too-familiar envelope.

"Can you describe the gentleman who delivered it?"

"It was a young boy, madam, not a gentleman." I thanked him and crossed through the Central Egyptian Saloon to the Refreshment Room, notorious for its dreadful food, and sat down to a pot of tea no better than the café's reputation. The note, as I expected, began in Greek:

Αὐτὰ γὰρ μί᾽ ἐμοὶ γράφεται θεός, ἅς τὸ ποθεινὸν
οὔνομ᾽ ἐν ἀκρήτῳ συγκεράσας πίομαι.

She is enrolled as my one goddess, whose beloved name I will mix and drink in unmixed wine. I could not help but smile. If nothing else, receiving these letters had done wonders for my sight-reading skills. He continued in English:

Do hope you will enjoy the champagne. Accept it along with my thanks for returning Marie Antoinette's pink. I don't imagine you really expected to meet me today—and you know I wouldn't dream of disappointing you, Kallista, darling. Fear not— you will see me soon enough.

His use of Kallista, Philip's name for me, was unnerving. Who was this presumptuous man? I considered the gentleman with the walking stick. Certainly it was odd for him to have come into the gallery and not look at the Rosetta Stone. Unless he had come only to see if I was there. I abandoned my tea and went to the main desk in the vestibule.

"Good afternoon, Lady Ashton. How may we help you today?"

"A docent just delivered a note that was left here for me. I was hoping that I could talk to him."

"A docent? Do you know who it was? I've been here all afternoon, and no one brought a note for you."

"I don't know his name. He was rather tall. Had bright blue eyes and a dark beard, very bushy."

"I'm so sorry, I've not the slightest idea who it could have been." He called over one of his colleagues who confirmed that no one had left anything for me at the desk but suggested that perhaps the envelope had been left elsewhere, and rushed off to inquire in the Reading Room, where the clerks knew nothing about a note addressed to me. I was weighing the merits of searching the museum for the docent when I noticed Colin standing next to a statue of Shakespeare near the entrance to the library. He tipped his hat and came to me.

"Are you spying on me?" I asked.

"Far from it. I read your advertisement in the *Times* and thought that, on the odd chance your admirer would show his face, I'd like to be here to personally confirm that I'd lost our bet."

"I never thought he would come."

"Is that so?" His dark eyes danced. "I think, Emily, that you harbored hopes that your multitudinous charms would lure the poor boy out of hiding. Admit it. You're not used to being disappointed."

"Remind me why it is that I'm so fond of you."

"I can't say that I have the slightest idea."

"I suppose that since you're here you may as well walk with me," I said, letting him take my arm and doing my best not to thrill at his touch. I was not particularly successful. For two hours we combed through every room in the museum looking for either the docent or the gentleman with the walking stick, but to no avail. Not only did we find neither man, we could not locate a single employee who recognized my description of the docent.

"It's very likely that one of them is the thief," Colin said, when at last we abandoned our search. "Whom do you suspect?"

"I hope it was the gentleman. I didn't like the docent's beard."

"Really?"

"Too scruffy."

"Is that so? I was thinking of growing one. It might look fashionable." He rubbed his smooth chin.

"Since when are you concerned with fashion?"

"A wife, Emily, might be able to influence matters concerning her husband's appearance. As it is, I have no one to answer to but myself. I'd look quite distinguished with a beard."

"I shan't dignify that with a response," I said. We had left the museum and were nearly halfway back to Berkeley Square when the rain began to fall in earnest, the wind blowing it in sheets parallel to the street. Despite our two umbrellas, we were well on our way to getting soaked, so Colin hailed the first available cab and sat next to me on its narrow bench. "I'm beginning to despise my no-kissing policy," he said, leaning so close to me that our heads nearly touched.

"Only beginning to despise it? I've deplored it from the moment you adopted it."

"You always did have a keen eye for the absurd."

Now I leaned closer to him and lifted his hand to my lips. "You could abandon the policy."

He almost did. Not taking his eyes off mine, he took my face in his hands and brought his lips near enough that I could feel his breath. But then he stopped. "The temptation is great, my dear, but I will remain strong. I think, however, that in the future, I shall avoid sharing hansom cabs with you."

The following day it became clear that I was not the only one lamenting the loss of Cécile, or, to be more precise, the loss of her maid. Davis saw to every detail of their trip personally, organizing their luggage, ensuring that the carriage was ready to take them to the station. He even directed Cook to prepare a picnic luncheon for the journey. And though he did all of this in his usual exacting manner, it was obvious to anyone who knew him well that he took no pleasure in any of it. His eyelids drooped ever so slightly, and he held his mouth more firmly than ever in a stiff, straight line. I even caught him starting to slouch when he thought no one was looking.

"I understand that Odette will be sorely missed by the staff," I said as we watched the coach pull away from the house.

"She is a most capable woman, madam, and provided a great deal of help in the aftermath of the robbery."

"Cécile is lucky to have her." We watched until the carriage had passed out of Berkeley Square. "I believe Odette is quite fond of walking around the Serpentine in Hyde Park."

"Yes."

I smiled. My own maid, Meg, never could resist keeping me on the qui vive when it came to gossip from the servants' quarters. Last month Davis had requested Wednesday rather than Sunday as his weekly day off. Odette always took Wednesdays, and from the time Davis altered his schedule, she never walked alone.

"Well, I do hope that you'll be able to rally your spirits. If not, I'll simply have to relocate the entire household to Paris. I cannot have a sullen butler." It gratified me no end to see that this made him smile. I bade him farewell and set off for Mr. Barber's studio, not eager in the least to go back into my own house, which was certain to feel empty without Cécile. I hoped that Mr. Barber would be able to offer me some insight into his friend David Francis.

The sculptor had just started chipping away at a large block of marble when I interrupted him. He insisted on making me a cup of tea, which I accepted gratefully.

"Mint," I said, as I took a sip from the rough ceramic mug. "Delicious."

"Wonderful, isn't it?" He poured some for himself and sat on the edge of the marble. "I've been taken with mint tea ever after I first had it in Constantinople."

"I should love to go there."

"But you have not come here to discuss my travels."

"No. Beatrice Francis has asked for my help, so I am trying to figure out who would have wanted her husband dead."

Mr. Barber frowned. "David was not the sort of man who collected enemies. He was very gracious, very...well, it might sound silly, but he was very noble."

"Nobility attracts as many enemies as it does friends."

"David wasn't close to many people, but he was thought of kindly by everyone he met. He was a perfect casual acquaintance. Only rarely did he open himself up enough to form true friend-ships."

"I am told that he did his best to help those in need."

"I am proof of that. I wouldn't have this studio if it weren't for him."

"And now that he is gone?"

"I'm fortunate. I've sold enough of my work to keep myself afloat for the next few months."

"And after that?"

"We'll see," he said, smiling. I did not want to cause him any embarrassment, so did not offer assistance but decided at once that I would purchase his statue of the woman gathering flowers from the Royal Academy Summer Exhibition.

"Why did Mr. Francis tell me that his wife was so shy?"

"David was always fiercely protective of Beatrice."

"She's a perfectly capable woman. Why did he hide her away in Richmond?"

"I can't say that I know. He liked to keep his life in London separate from his life at home."

"Did he spend much time in town?"

"Not a lot."

"So why the secrecy?"

"Well." He cleared his throat. "It's difficult to say."

"He had a mistress, didn't he?"

"Please, Lady Ashton, do not ask me to impugn the character of my friend."

"Had he a recent falling-out with this woman?"

"I don't know, but it's unlikely. She was distraught when she learned of his death."

"How do you know that?"

"I'm the one who told her what happened. It would have been awful for her to have seen it in the papers."

"Does Beatrice know?" I asked.

"No, no, of course not. David was discreet to a fault."

"What is this mistress like?"

"Liza? I don't know her well."

"Yet you are already familiar enough with her to use her Christian name?"

"Not at all. I apologize."

"Did he speak of her often?"

"No. He never mentioned her. I only learned of her existence after his death." He picked up his hammer and chisel and began working on the marble. "David gave me a letter years ago and asked me to promise not to read it unless he died. I laughed about it, because he was always a picture of health, but he assured me it concerned a matter of great importance."

"But he gave you no idea what it said?"

"None."

"And you never looked at the letter while he was alive?"

"Of course not. I promised him I wouldn't."

I admired Mr. Barber's will, wondering if I would have been able to stave off my curiosity for such a long time. "What did the letter say?"

"He asked that I personally inform Mrs. Liza White of his death. That was all."

"Was she his mistress?"

"I believe so, Lady Ashton. She grieved like a wife."

I felt sorry for her, but my sympathy was tempered by my allegiance to Beatrice. Once I had assured Mr. Barber that I would not reveal his friend's secret to his widow, he gave me Mrs. White's address. She did not live terribly far from the studio, but the directions were confusing enough that I let my driver take me in the carriage. We stopped in front of a decent, middle-class house, nothing at all like I had expected. I must confess that my reaction horrified me. For all that I thought I was enlightened, liberated, free from the ignorant biases of society, I had judged this woman from the moment I knew she was having an affair with someone else's husband. I expected to find her low, common, no better than she ought to be. In fact, it was I who should have been better. I knew nothing of this woman, her heart, her love, her reasons for the affair. I had no right to criticize her.

A broad, sturdy woman in a gray dress and crisp white apron trimmed in black answered the door. I handed her my card and asked to see the lady of the house, only to be informed that she was indisposed. Over the maid's shoulder I saw a small boy, who couldn't have been older than six, pulling a wooden train through the hallway. Although I had met David Francis only once, there could be no question that this was his son. The boy was the image of his father.

"It's urgent that I speak with Mrs. White," I said. "Do you know when might be a good time for me to return?"

"The house is in mourning, madam. I will give Mrs. White your card." My mother would never have stood for such a response. I could picture her walking past the maid, telling her to announce the Countess Bromley. This, however, was not something I was prepared to do. I would give Mrs. White a few more days to mourn in peace, then call again.

Frustrated, I returned to my carriage. I stood frozen as the footman opened the door for me. Inside, on the seat, was a large bouquet of wilted roses.

13

‡‡‡ ‡‡‡ ‡‡‡ ‡‡‡ ‡‡‡ ‡‡‡ ‡‡‡ ‡‡‡

D ID YOU PUT THESE HERE?" I ASKED MY FOOTMAN, WHO IMMEDIATELY denied all knowledge of the flowers. He removed them from the seat and held them out to me; I did not take them but ripped open the note tied to the bouquet. "These are from the man who broke into my house. Did you see him put them in the carriage?"

"No, madam," the footman replied, looking distressed. "I was sitting up with Waters." My driver, recognizing that something was amiss, came down from his perch. His face went pale when I told him what had happened.

"I saw nothing unusual. We should have paid better attention. It won't happen again." I had no reason to doubt my servants but was surprised that such a thing could have happened under their watch. Waters in particular had been exceedingly cautious since the burglary, and it was he who had noticed the coach following me from Richmond. I tried to shrug off the incident; it was, after all, harmless, but I did not like the knowledge that this unknown man could have such ready access to me. More disturbing was the fact that he was following me.

How I wished that Cécile was still in London. Not wanting to go back to my empty house, I directed Waters to take me to the Taylor residence, where Margaret was staying with her parents. Here, as at Mrs. White's, I was rebuffed. The butler took my card, made me wait a considerable time, and when he returned, told me that Miss Seward was not at home. I could tell from his cool expression that this was not true. Had I done something to offend Margaret?

I returned to Berkeley Square rather depressed. Refusing to submit to this unwelcome emotion, I sat down at my desk in the library and took out a blank notebook; it was time to organize the information I had gathered so far about the death of Mr. Francis. First I cataloged facts: the date he had died, that he was killed by nicotine, that Jane had put the poisoned lotion in his room, that the murder occurred after the papers reported the theft of the pink diamond. Then I started a list of questions. Who benefited from his death? Who had access to the lotion once it was in his room? Who knew he was having an affair? And, perhaps more important, who knew he had an illegitimate child?

Heeding Colin's advice, I made a careful effort not to phrase my questions in a manner that would necessarily implicate Charles Berry. Colin's wisdom in this matter was apparent. There didn't seem to be much evidence against Mr. Berry. Still, I was troubled by the correspondence between him and Mr. Francis. Intuition told me that something not quite aboveboard had taken place; I had to find out what it was.

I was about to pull out the Marie Antoinette letters when Margaret burst into the room, Davis trailing on her heels.

"This is absolutely outrageous!" she said, thrusting her parasol into my butler's hands. "Sorry, Davis, couldn't wait for you to announce me."

"No apology necessary, Miss Seward. It is the ongoing drama of this household that keeps me young." He bowed and left the room.

"Margaret, I was just at—"

"I know. They wouldn't let me see you! Can you believe it?"

"Well, I confess that is a relief. I was worried that I had done something to offend you."

This made her laugh. "Oh, really, Emily, you've been in London too long if you could have thought such a thing. Society is making your brain go soft. I want a drink, and not tea." It was too early for port, but Davis brought us a lovely German wine, and as Margaret drank, she continued her rant. "So, here's how you rank in the Taylor house. My mother, who is generally a reasonable woman, is so taken with aristocrat fever that she's turned against you. She's convinced that the only reason Jeremy hasn't proposed to me is that he is carrying on with you."

"But surely you—"

She continued without letting me speak. "Mrs. Taylor has never been a friend of mine. She was scandalized that my parents let me go to college. I think the only reason she ever lets me stay with her is a misguided belief that exposure to her and her insipid daughters will put me back on track to becoming a dear, sweet thing."

Now it was my turn to laugh. "I don't think there's any danger of that happening."

"Of course there's not. I let her believe what she wants, though. It makes her happy. But now she is counseling my mother, warning her that our friendship may compromise my own reputation with the *right* sort of people."

"Oh, Margaret—"

"This should be funny. I'm ten times the radical you are, Emily. I should be corrupting you, not vice versa. I'm offended, actually, that Mrs. Taylor doesn't find my own self shocking enough."

"What exactly am I doing that is so outrageous?"

"Let's see...well, your academic interests are inappropriate for a young lady. That's why so many mothers have cautioned their daughters against speaking to you. They're afraid you'll make them want to read obscene Greek myths."

"Well, we can't have ladies reading mythology. Education starts women on a dangerous path. The next thing you know, they'll be fighting for rational dress and the right to vote."

"Exactly." She smiled and picked up the bottle of wine. "Have some more to drink. But it is not just your academic sins that have condemned you. I'm as guilty as you on that count. Added to that is your flagrantly inappropriate relationship with Jeremy, the disgraceful way you lead on poor Colin—" Here, she interrupted herself. "*Poor Mr. Hargreaves*. It's ridiculous. He's the last sort of man who would ever let himself be led on. He knows exactly what he's doing."

"I don't like that he's being spoken about in such a way."

"Neither do I."

"What I don't understand is these rumors about Jeremy. Where do they come from?"

"The best I can tell, they're all loosely based on fact. A gentleman *did* once leave your house at five o'clock in the morning. That it was Colin assisting you after a break-in is not interesting. Much more fun to think you were cavorting with Jeremy."

"But mothers love Jeremy."

"They do, but they want him to marry their daughters, not to carry on with a widow who shows no inclination towards remarriage." She poured more wine. "You ran through Berkeley Square calling for him. Fine, fine, there was a reasonable explanation. The story goes that you were wearing a dressing gown at the time."

"I would never—"

"Wait," she said. "That particular detail comes from Charles Berry's retelling of the story."

"Is that so?"

"He has been telling anyone who will listen that he came upon you and Jeremy in a most compromising position that same evening. Says you were both mortified and that Jeremy threw him out of the house in a wasted effort to save your reputation."

"Why does he despise me so?"

"You've had the bad taste to refuse to be his mistress."

"It must be more than that. I've never publicly rebuffed him. But I have confronted him about his relationship with David Francis. What about that might lead him to drown me with vitriol?"

"Could he have killed Francis?"

"I think he knows something about the murder, and I'm convinced there's a connection of some sort between the Marie Antoinette thefts and Mr. Francis's death."

"Those are beautiful flowers," Margaret said, indicating the sorry-looking bouquet from my carriage.

"They're from the man who undoubtedly knows more about both of these crimes than either of us." I showed her the note that had been tied to the roses.

> *Don't you think it was disloyal, Kallista darling, to have left the museum with him when you were waiting for me? I don't like being disappointed. Your flowers wouldn't be in such dreadful condition had you allowed me the opportunity to present them yesterday.*

I told Margaret what had happened at the museum. "There was no indication in the note the docent gave me that I would see my friend, if I may use the word loosely, later that day."

"I don't like that he's following you."

"Nor do I. But let's consider the situation from his point of view. He gave me a stolen diamond, so he knows that I must think he's the one who took it. Although he is enamored of me, he's not so foolish that he would trust me blindly. I could have had the police ready to arrest him at the Rosetta Stone. So, he stood back, watched to see if I had come alone, and maybe was going to approach me as I left the museum. Enter Colin—"

"Does he know Colin is an agent for the Crown?"

"I've no idea. But even if he doesn't, he's hardly going to speak to me when I'm with another gentleman."

"So he follows you the next day?"

"He can't deliver things to my house anymore—it's too well guarded. What options has he left?"

"There is something oddly romantic about it. If I didn't wonder at his involvement in the murder, I'd probably suggest that you consider his suit. What an adventure to be married to such an exclusive thief."

"Really, Margaret. No good could come of associating oneself with a person of such ambiguous morals."

"There's nothing ambiguous about them. He's bad through and through. Very appealing. I bet that if you married him, you could get him to steal Helen of Troy's jewelry for you."

"We'd have to live in the villa. The police would be less likely to track us down in Santorini than in England." I looked at the note again. "I wonder if it's significant that he didn't write anything in Greek this time."

"This is a rebuke, not a love note. You've had your first spat."

"You're very amusing," I said. "But it's all rather unsettling. Can any good come of disappointing a criminal?"

"We'll just have to hope that his crimes are limited to stealing, not murder."

Lady Elinor called on me the next day, and she brought with her a postcard album. "I collected these on the trips my husband and I took," she said. "Looking at them is the nearest thing to traveling without leaving England, so I thought you would enjoy them."

"How thoughtful," I said, paging through the book, which was filled with images of Pompeii, the Great Pyramids, Luxor, Rome—all places I longed to visit.

"Have you considered traveling, Lady Ashton? There's no reason you shouldn't. I'm sure you'd have no trouble finding a companion. Thomas Cook and Son offer tours that are perfectly suitable for ladies."

"I think I should prefer to find local guides, explore archaeological sites, learn local customs. I'm not well suited for a planned tour."

"So much the better. What adventures you could have!" She pulled an envelope out of her reticule and handed it to me. "This is an invitation to a ball I'm giving to celebrate Isabelle's engagement. I do hope you'll come."

This was the first ball to which I'd been invited in weeks. "Thank you, Lady Elinor. I shouldn't dream of missing it. How is Isabelle?"

"She's managing well enough, becoming used to the idea of getting married. She and Mr. Berry are spending a great deal of time together, and she is beginning, I think, to welcome his affections."

"Then I am happy for her," I said, wondering how on earth Isabelle could welcome anything from Mr. Berry.

"I never did properly thank you for taking care of her when she threw herself on your mercy. It was very wrong of her to leave the house, but I'm glad that she had the sense to come to you."

"I'm afraid there are not many mothers in London who would agree with that sentiment."

"Your views on marriage are, perhaps, not traditional. But I am an excellent judge of character. You're not the sort of person who would sanction ruinous behavior. I know that Isabelle was quite safe with you."

I wondered if her opinion of me would change should she discover that I had allowed her daughter to be alone with Lord Pembroke.

"And, really, I'm most grateful to you. Because of your...unconventional ways "—she smiled—"Isabelle was more willing to listen to what you had to say. Had she looked to any of her other friends for solace, they would have told her to abandon Pembroke, and she knew that. Hearing the same advice when she did not expect to was more powerful than fifty ladies telling her the same thing."

"So long as Isabelle is happy, I am glad."

"I've told you before, I would never press my daughter into a situation that would not bring her joy. She is everything to me, Lady Ashton."

"She is a lucky girl," I said. Lady Elinor stayed some while longer, but I found myself too distracted to take much notice of what she said. I did not like the idea that I was somehow responsible for Isabelle's acceptance of her impending nuptials, particularly given the grave concerns I had about the character of her fiancé.

14

$\cdot\!\!\!\ast\!\!\!\cdot\;\ast\!\!\!\cdot\;\ast\!\!\!\cdot\;\ast\!\!\!\cdot\;\ast\!\!\!\cdot\;\ast\!\!\!\cdot\;\ast\!\!\!\cdot\;\ast\!\!\!\cdot$

B EFORE I RETURNED TO MY INVESTIGATION OF MR. BERRY, I HEADED
back to the offices of the *Times*, where I placed another message
for my disappointed admirer. Ivy thought that it was perhaps not wise
to further engage him, but I saw no other way to draw him out of
hiding. Maybe, if he thought I was willing to communicate with him,
he would eventually reveal himself. This time I did not ask him to
meet me; I merely admonished him for sending me dying flowers.

When I had finished placing my notice, I went to Oxford Street
to visit a shop that sold rare prints, books, and some historical documents. I hoped the clerks there would be able to help me in my search
for Léonard's letters to Marie Antoinette. I like to think that I have
reasonable expectations; I knew it would be too much to hope for
specific information, but I thought it likely that they would be able to
tell me in general terms how best to begin my quest. But even this, it
seemed, was too much to expect. Aside from taking note of my interest in the letters, and promising to inform me should they ever come
up for sale, there was little they could do. Private correspondence
changing hands in private sales could not be readily tracked.

Undaunted, I walked to the park. It was a fine day, the heat not having bothered to return after the rain stopped, and the crisp air inspired clear thinking. I found a bench near the Serpentine, pulled out the notebook in which I was recording details of my investigations, and looked over what I had written down.

"Slumming, Lady Ashton?" Charles Berry leaned over from behind the bench. "This isn't the most fashionable section of the park."

"I was hoping for some solitude."

His eyes narrowed as he looked over my shoulder at the notebook on my lap. "Why are you so interested in David Francis? Is his wife a particular friend of yours?"

How could he possibly know what was written in my notebook? I slammed it shut. "I am most sympathetic to Mrs. Francis's situation."

"That's no reason to be muddling about in her husband's affairs."

I raised an eyebrow. "His affairs?"

"Some things are best left forgotten. You'd be wise to let the dead rest."

"I'm curious to know why you're so concerned with Mr. Francis."

"Some gentlemen might be amused by your insistence on being viewed as a thinking woman. I am not one of them."

"A fact, Mr. Berry, that does not disappoint me in the least."

He put his hands firmly on my shoulders, too near my neck. "Yet I cannot help being drawn to you. I wonder if a king could tame you."

Much though I would have liked to throttle him for this comment, I managed to restrain myself, determined to pry something worthwhile from this otherwise useless man. "For someone who claims not to have known Mr. Francis, you're awfully concerned about him now that he's dead. Why the sudden interest? Does it pertain to the objects you say he wanted to sell you?"

"I don't even know what they were." His hands were still pressing down on my shoulders. I wrenched myself away, stood up, and turned to face him, glad to have the bench between us.

"He didn't mention the letters?" I smiled fetchingly. "What a surprise!"

"What letters?"

"Oh, I shouldn't fret about them. I've read them and they're deadly dull."

"Which letters are these?"

I thought for a moment before answering. "Léonard's, of course."

A cold pallor overtook the ordinary ruddiness of his face, and his features turned unnaturally hard. "Léonard's letters?"

"What letters did you think I meant?"

"He didn't say he had—"

"So, you did talk to him?" I closed my parasol and leveled it towards him. "I'm tired of your lies, Mr. Berry."

"I don't like people interfering in my business. This is none of your concern."

"So you admit to having been involved with Mr. Francis?"

"I knew he possessed things that by right should be legacies of my family. That's not the same as being involved with him."

"Did you discuss the letters with him?" I asked.

"You despise me." His narrow eyes met mine. "And you have no right to. I won't continue this conversation." He stalked away, turning to leer at me after he had gone some distance. If only Cécile was still in London! I longed to rush home to report the fascinating details of this conversation, even if it meant sacrificing the trim on my skirt to Caesar and Brutus. Without having consciously decided to do so, I found myself walking towards Park Lane, and a few minutes later was waiting for Colin in his library.

This was a room that was used, not meant for show. Books lined the walls from floor to ceiling, and tall ladders ensured that none of them was out of reach. Every surface had at least one book on it. One table was covered with atlases and travel books, another held three of Shakespeare's plays, each binding well worn, no crispness left in the pages. In front of an enormous marble mantelpiece stood a table that held a chess set carved from some sort of exotic wood, the pieces representing figures from Arthurian legend. Next to the game board was John Thursby's *Seventy-Five Chess Problems*, held open with a book weight.

"White's to mate in three moves," Colin said, entering the room. "I'm afraid I haven't got beyond setting up the board." His lips brushed my hand. "How do you like the room? I finally realized that if I'm to have any hope of marrying you, I'd have to show you my library first."

"It's magnificent."

"My collection of ancient texts is no rival to your own, but you'll find I've a better selection of fiction." As he said this, I considered something that had not before occurred to me. The books to which he referred weren't mine at all; they belonged to the Ashton family. Nothing in my house, save my clothing, personal items, and the handful of antiquities I had purchased since Philip's death, was truly mine. Someday the new viscount would want to take possession of his house. Because the boy was barely four years old, it was unlikely this would happen for some time, but the fact remained that I did not have a home of my own. "Is something wrong?"

"No, not precisely." I forced a smile. "I'll simply have to expand my own fiction holdings."

"Have you already heard from Cécile?"

"Am I not allowed to call on you except in an official capacity?"

"I am, of course, delighted to see you, but I fear for the health of my butler. Poor Hoskins is not accustomed to unescorted young ladies calling."

"I'd be distressed if he were. It would call into question your very character." I sat in a large, extremely comfortable leather chair. "I've just seen Charles Berry. He was so abominable I longed for a friendly face." Colin frowned as I told him about my encounter with the dreadful man in the park.

"He's not foolish enough to hurt you, but I do not like this, Emily."

"Have you any idea of how he was involved with Mr. Francis?"

"I don't, but when I see him tonight, I shall find out what I can."

"Are you going to Lady Elinor's ball?"

"Yes. You?"

"She's the one person aside from Ivy who still considers me worthy of her guest list."

"Will you waltz with me?"

"We could waltz now," I said, meeting his steady gaze.

"Too dangerous. From experience I'm keenly aware of the ruinous effect dancing with you in private has on my self-control."

"Lovely though it is to contemplate you losing your self-control, I shan't tempt you further, though I reserve the right to do so in the future. But I've more to tell you. When we left the British Museum the other day, my friend followed us. He left me a note hidden in some half-dead flowers the next day."

"I was careful to check that no one was tailing us, and I didn't see anyone. He must be very good at this game." He ran his hand through his hair, stood up, and leaned against the mantel, his elbow resting on the marble top. "Do you feel threatened by this man?"

"I don't think he's dangerous," I said, hesitating slightly.

"I'll be perfectly frank with you, my dear. There's nothing I would like better than to lock you up somewhere, preferably at my country house, while I uncover this...person...and determine whether he means you harm. He's a criminal, not an ordinary admirer. We've no idea the lengths to which he would be willing to go to reach you." His eyes met mine, his expression all seriousness. "But I shall not undermine you by trying to rescue you. Know, Emily, that if you truly need me, I am here."

I think had he the presence of mind to propose at that moment, I would have accepted. The combination of hearing him speak in such an enlightened manner and the perfect setting of his library would have been too much to resist.

"Colin, I—"

He knelt in front of me and took my hands in his, squeezing them. "My dear, dear girl. I could not go on if something were to happen to you. I have enough trust in your abilities to know that you'll be able to find out who he is. But promise me that you will not put yourself in danger. Do not take risks. You have a tendency to—"

"That's quite enough." How I wished he would take me in his arms. "I shall be careful."

"I would not love you so well if you were less headstrong. Please do not make me regret it."

"Regret loving me or regret that I am headstrong?"

"I shall never regret loving you, Emily. Not even if, once you've unmasked this admirer of yours, you decide to run off with him and pursue a life of crime."

"You're not the first to suggest such an outcome. Are my morals really so questionable?"

"It's not your morals; it's your attraction to adventure."

"Well, I shall have to work at controlling myself. Perhaps one day I'll be able to match your strength." I placed two fingers on his lips but knew better than to hope he would kiss me. "Though I will confess that I've no desire to have such self-restraint when it comes to you."

"That, my dear, is the luxury of being a lady. You're perfectly safe with me, and you know it. So long as I exercise some control, you've no need to."

"Someday, I'm sure, I'll want to thank you for that. At the moment, however, my views on the subject are rather conflicted."

I was more excited than I had expected to be about Lady Elinor's ball. It had been too long since I had danced, and I felt no small measure of irritation at the thought of holier-than-thou society matrons keeping me from their guest lists and, in turn, from waltzing. The entrance hall to the Routledges' house was filled with enormous masses of flowers, providing a perfect backdrop for the legions of ladies in their stylish gowns and brightening the patches of black where gentlemen congregated in their elegant black jackets and white ties.

Isabelle was less miserable than I would have guessed. She stood next to her fiancé on the stairway that led to the ballroom, a charming smile on her face, but there was no brightness in her eyes as she welcomed her guests. Although Mr. Berry deliberately took as little notice of me as possible, I could feel his eyes linger unpleasantly on me after I had passed him, and I shuddered at the thought of his attention. I hurried away from him, eager to find a friendly face at the party; instead, my mother headed me off the instant I entered the room.

"You must behave yourself," she whispered with such force that it was clear she had every intention of being overheard. "Otherwise there's no chance that you will be able to reclaim your place in decent society."

It was unfair of her to accost me in public, where she knew I could not respond to her as I wished. "There's no need to worry, Mother. I'm always perfectly appropriate."

"You are not to speak to Bainbridge tonight unless you plan to marry him. I won't let you ruin yourself with flirting."

"I'll thank you to stop telling me what to do."

She looked at me with such satisfaction that it was obvious this performance was for her own benefit. She wanted to make sure that society knew that she was doing all she could to control me, so that, should I be ruined, she would have their sympathy rather than their censure.

"I'll not stand by and watch you drag the reputation of our family through the gutter, Emily." She may have objected to watching that, but she certainly did not object to watching me, closely, for the entire evening. The only time I was able to escape her was when I danced. Happily, although the ladies of society seemed bent on cutting me, the gentlemen did not share their scruples, and I had no shortage of partners. But other than my mother, Lady Elinor, Isabelle, and dear Ivy were the only ladies who spoke to me.

I did, at last, get to waltz with Colin. Feeling his arm at my waist was more intoxicating than our hostess's champagne, and he guided me across the floor with expert grace.

"Holding you like this makes me realize how wise I was to avoid dancing with you in private," he said. "It could have led to nothing good. You're lovelier than ever tonight." I had spent a small fortune on my gown, cut from silk of the palest shade of rose, embroidered with silver thread and crystal beads. The neckline was daringly low, and the sleeves puffed subtly at the shoulder, tapering to fit tightly at the elbow. Mr. Worth himself had beamed with pleasure when he saw me in it at my final fitting.

When the music ended, Colin handed me off to my next partner, Jeremy, whom I had accepted as much to irritate my mother as I had because I wanted to dance with him. He and Colin nodded sharply at one another but said very little. It did not occur to me at the time that one might be jealous of the other. Almost before the dance had ended, my mother was stalking us on the edge of the crowd.

"Your Grace, it is a pleasure, as always, to see you."

"The pleasure is all mine, Lady Bromley."

"I do hope Emily is being kind to you."

Jeremy flashed a smile but did not reply. My father, who had early in the evening abandoned my mother to talk politics with a group of his friends, returned to collect her, and not a moment too soon. Given more time, she would have brokered a marriage contract between the two of us right there on the dance floor. I was about to seek out a glass of champagne when Lord Fortescue appeared in front of me.

"I think we ought to dance, Lady Ashton."

"If you insist, Lord Fortescue," I said, hating the feel of his arm on mine. He was not a bad partner; that much I will give him. But his manner was in every other way deplorable.

"You'd do well with Bainbridge," he said, leading me across the floor. "You're both in dire need of settling down. I know you've had your eye on Hargreaves, but he's not a good match for you."

"I'm sure it's none of your concern," I said, doing my best to keep a smile on my face.

"It's very much my concern, as it is the concern of anyone with a sense of loyalty to the empire."

"Really? I'm all astonishment."

"Do not play ignorant with me. Hargreaves's work for the Crown is invaluable. You've proven to be nothing but a distraction to him."

"His work has suffered on my account? Not only do I find that unbelievable, but it's also insulting to Mr. Hargreaves. He would never allow personal concerns to interfere with his work. How dare you suggest such a thing?"

"I know your type, Lady Ashton. Always wanting to be involved, meddling where you should not. If you care for him, leave him alone. He does not deserve the trouble you are certain to heap upon him."

Clearly, my only options were to ignore my partner entirely or to engage him in a discussion of the weather. I chose the former. When the music stopped, we stood next to Robert and a woman whom I did not recognize. Her age fell somewhere between mine and that of my mother, and she was dressed in an extremely expensive, though ostentatious, gown.

"Have you met Mrs. Reynold-Plympton?" Robert asked. I shook my head, and the introduction was made. I was about to ask her how long she'd been in London when the music began again, and she turned to my friend's husband.

"Shall we dance again? I can't remember when I've had such a pleasant partner." Robert mumbled something unintelligible and led her back to the floor, leaving me stranded with Lord Fortescue.

"Will you excuse me?" I asked before he had the chance to claim another dance. As I made my way across the room, a servant approached me.

"Lady Ashton, a gentleman asked that I give this to you." He handed me a large ivory envelope.

"Lord Fortescue?"

"I don't believe it was he, madam."

I looked around the room, searching for Colin, but did not see him. Ivy was not far from me, and I pulled her into the garden, wanting someone with me when I opened the parcel. She was appropriately horrified when I told her what had been going on.

"Oh dear," she said. "Perhaps I should get Robert."

"We can open an envelope without him, Ivy." I pulled a pin out of my hair, which was piled high on my head in a simple pompadour, and carefully slit the paper.

"Who left it for you? Is he still here?" She looked around, then relaxed as much as her corset would allow, apparently satisfied that there was no one stalking us in the garden.

"Highly unlikely." Within the envelope was a note wrapped around another letter. *I can help more than you know, Kallista darling* was scrawled in now-familiar handwriting. Inside this was a letter, folded, with the remains of a wax seal on the back. Excitement filled me; the letter was addressed to Marie Antoinette. Careful not to harm the fragile paper, I unfolded the page, eager to see who had written the letter. "It's from Léonard." He gave a terse description of his daily activities, referred briefly to some of the queen's acquaintances, and closed with an account of an altercation he'd had with a merchant in a butcher's shop. He wished the queen well, said he was praying for her soul, and promised to write again soon.

I handed it to Ivy. "How tragic," she said after she had read it. "To think, the poor woman was waiting to be executed, and this is the sort of correspondence from which she was to take consolation."

"I'm sure everything was read by her jailors. Hardly circumstances in which someone would be willing to divulge personal details. But you're right. It is sad." I touched the fading ink on the page. "I had hoped for something else, something that would reveal the significance of the queen's letters."

"Could he have more of Léonard's letters?"

"That, Ivy, is an excellent question. He must have been following me when I went off in search of the letters. How else would he know I was looking for them?"

"I wonder…" she began, but was interrupted by Robert.

"What are you two discussing? I thought Hargreaves was with you."

"No, darling, Emily and I were talking about another of her admirers," Ivy said, standing and giving her husband her arm.

"Hmmm. Dangerous topic these days, eh, Emily?" Robert was quite handsome when he smiled.

"It wouldn't be a dangerous topic if people would limit themselves to the discourse of facts."

"Until reality becomes as interesting as fiction, I'm afraid that's unlikely," he said.

"That reminds me," I began. "How are you enjoying the book I lent you, Ivy?"

"Oh, it's…well…I thought—"

"What book is this?" Robert asked.

"*Mount Royal,*" I said. "Are you familiar with it?"

"It's not the sort of thing that Robert—"

"Not more trash by that Braddon woman, I hope," Robert said. "A dreadful waste of time."

"I prefer to think of it as an entertaining escape," I said. "Have you any concept of the amount of effort it takes to run a large household well? Ivy's overdue for some relaxation."

Robert looked at me, then at Ivy, then at his shoes, then back at me. "There are plenty of methods of relaxation that are not so utterly without merit." His smile softened the remark, but not enough.

"I didn't mean—" I said, but Ivy interrupted me.

"Oh, it's perfectly all right, both of you. Robert has arranged for me to assist the Duchess of Petherwick with her charity work, so I've no time at all for reading."

"What are you doing for her?"

"Sewing baby clothes for orphans."

"Sewing? And this is meant to be relaxing?" I looked at Robert.

"Ivy enjoys handwork." I could see there was no use arguing. With effort, I managed a smile. Robert pulled a heavy gold watch from his pocket. "It's getting late. You should go home, darling. I'm to meet Fortescue and some others at my club." Even Ivy's curls seemed to droop, and though Robert didn't look closely enough to notice, she could hardly keep her eyes from filling with tears. "I'll get the carriage for you."

"No, Robert," I said. "Let Ivy come home with me." I stopped myself almost at once, disgusted to find that I was talking about my friend as if she were not there. "Would you come with me, Ivy? It's so lonely at my house without Cécile."

"I wouldn't want to leave you alone, Emily, but Robert—"

I hoped he would protest. "Of course you shall go with Emily. I'll be dreadfully late—you may as well stay the night." He looked more pleased than he ought to with this arrangement. "I can't imagine you'll have finished analyzing the events of the evening before morning."

And I couldn't imagine that, if he knew what sort of events we would be analyzing, he would approve of his wife spending the night with me. But as I gave the matter more thought, I decided that Ivy and I would not sit up until all hours discussing my investigations. Instead, we would read out loud to each other favorite passages from Mary Elizabeth Braddon's books.

15

⁕⁕⁕ ⁕⁕⁕ ⁕⁕⁕ ⁕⁕⁕ ⁕⁕⁕ ⁕⁕⁕ ⁕⁕⁕ ⁕⁕⁕ ⁕⁕⁕

THE DAY AFTER THE BALL I CALLED AGAIN AT THE WHITE RESIDENCE, and again the housekeeper rebuffed me. "I don't think the lady of the house needs to be bothered by the likes of you," the housekeeper said, glaring at me.

"Excuse me?"

"A lady in mourning should be left alone. This is a house of decent people. I won't have you harassing my mistress."

That a servant would speak to me in such a tone was astonishing, and I could hardly find my voice to reply. "That is a decision to be made by Mrs. White, not you. You give her this note. I shall come back in an hour and expect a reply." I had thought it likely that Mrs. White would refuse to see me and in preparation for this possibility had brought with me a letter explaining that I needed to discuss with her some information about David Francis at the earliest possible moment. After an hour had passed, I returned to the house. This time the housekeeper admitted me, though she made no effort to make me feel welcome.

I began to understand her behavior the moment I met Mrs. White. She was younger than I had expected but extremely frail, and looked on the verge of falling apart. She came into her drawing room, cling-ing to furniture as she walked, so slowly it was painful to watch. At last she lowered herself into a straight-backed wooden chair.

"Forgive me, Lady Ashton, for not admitting you when you came before," she said, her voice so soft that it was difficult to hear. "I've never been fond of society and find it worse than ever now that Mr. Francis—" She pressed a hand to her forehead.

"I am most sorry to disturb you during such a difficult time." I wished there was something I could say to make this conversation easier. "I have promised to assist in the investigation of Mr. Francis's death and am hoping that you might be able to help me."

"Are the police not capable of handling the matter themselves?"

"Yes, of course they are, but there is some concern that they made an arrest too quickly."

"Who is concerned?"

"Mrs. Francis."

"I see." She had not looked at me directly since she entered the room. "I have not met her, of course. I understand she was quite de-voted to Mr. Francis."

I had no answer for this. Mrs. White sat in silence, but she was not at ease, tugging at her cuticles while she held her hands in her lap. She couldn't have been more than twenty-five, but there was a tiredness in her eyes that made her look far older. I waited as long as I could bear to before speaking.

"I have offered to help Mrs. Francis, but please know that I am not here to sit in judgment of you. I just thought that, given your...closeness...to Mr. Francis, you might have an idea of who would have wanted to harm him."

"Mr. Francis was a complicated man."

"Did he have enemies?"

"I wouldn't know, Lady Ashton. As you may have guessed, the part of his life that he shared with me was very limited."

"Did you see him often?"

"He came to me every Sunday. He felt it was important that he see the boy at regular intervals."

"His son?"

"Yes. He visited more often before Edward was born. Things change after a child comes."

"But surely he wanted to see Edward?"

"He wanted a child, and until he was certain I had provided one, it was necessary for him to spend a great deal of time with me."

"And you did not object to this?"

"Why should I?" She did not appear to have the energy to object to anything.

"Has he provided for the two of you?"

"As you can see, we are comfortably settled."

I bit my lip. "Forgive me—I do not mean to insult you or to criticize the choices you have made. But why would you agree to such an arrangement?"

"I was brought up well, but my father lost his fortune in a bad business deal. When he died, some years after my mother, he had nothing left. I had no skills and therefore no way to earn an income. My only brother is in the navy, and I've no other relatives. I had nowhere to go."

I couldn't imagine the woman sitting before me turning to prostitution. She was so shy she could hardly bring herself to look at me. Could she have been that desperate, with no other options?

"I know what you're thinking," she said, and I had to lean forward in my seat to hear her. "But you're wrong. I was so naïve, I don't think it would have occurred to me. My father's creditors forced me to leave the house, not allowing me to take anything save my clothes, which I sold for enough money to rent a room for some weeks. I tried in vain to find employment and found myself thrown out of my lodgings when I could no longer pay the landlady. I wandered around the city, not knowing where to turn. Eventually, I wound up on a bench in Hyde Park."

"You slept there?"

"No. Mr. Francis found me. He assumed, as had several others before him, that I was a park girl. Of course, I had no idea such people even existed and didn't know that simply by being in the park so late at night, I had, in effect, identified myself as one of them."

"So Mr. Francis…hired…you?"

"No. He admonished me to abandon my evil ways, which shocked me greatly. I told him of my circumstances, and he insisted that I allow him to help me."

"You had no other options," I said.

"Quite true. He set me up in this house, paid for two servants, and saw to it that I never wanted for anything."

"And now?"

"Now…I don't know what shall happen to us." Tears streamed down her face, but she did not bother to wipe them away. "He didn't intend to make me his mistress."

This confused me. "But he kept this house for you?"

"He wanted to prevent me from turning to prostitution, Lady Ashton, not to seduce me into a more comfortable version of it. It was two years before—" She stopped.

"Before you fell in love with him?"

"I fell in love with him almost at once. How could I not have? He saved me from the worst sort of fate. But he never showed any romantic interest in me, and eventually I discovered that he was married and gave up hope."

"So what changed?"

"His wife. Mr. Francis wanted a child, but eventually it became clear that his wife couldn't give him one, so he turned to me. How could I deny him after all he'd done for me?" She sighed. "And I didn't want to deny him. I wanted him to love me."

"I'm sure he did."

"No, it was only for the child. I know that all too well. Forgive me, Lady Ashton, I don't think I've been of any use to you, and I must beg that you leave me now. This has all been a great strain, and I don't think I can stand much more."

"Of course. I'm sorry to have disturbed you."

"I hope his wife is coping."

"She will manage," I said.

"Please do all you can to figure out who killed him," she said. "Whatever he did, he didn't deserve to die." I was about to ask what she thought he might have done, but she left the room before I could open my mouth. I wouldn't have guessed that she could move so quickly.

I f you were married and had a mistress, would you be able to keep your wife from suspecting anything was amiss?" I was once again in Colin's fine library.

He raised his eyebrows. "If I were married, it would be to you, and my fidelity would make you the envy of all of London."

"Really, Colin, I'm not talking about us. Theoretically, do you think a spouse could conceal such a thing?"

"In many marriages, yes, I don't think it would be difficult at all. How many of your friends married because they felt true affection? Even when they're not arranged, marriages are usually entered into because of the status or the financial advantages the match will bring."

"I had no idea you were so cynical."

"I'm not cynical in the least, just realistic. Why do you think I've remained a bachelor for so long?"

"Well, I'd like to believe it was because you hadn't met me," I said, smiling.

"You've no more interest in a society marriage than I do. They're business arrangements, really, and I've no desire to share my house with a business partner."

"Put aside the notion of a society match. Imagine a marriage in which there is genuine affection. Could an affair be concealed in that?"

"Perhaps if there is only genuine affection. Not if there is passionate love."

"Surely if there is passionate love, there would be no need for an affair," I said and swallowed, suddenly finding my breath difficult to control.

"No, there wouldn't be," he said. We both sat very still, neither of us able to tear our eyes away from the other's. The tense pleasure was almost unbearable, and just when I thought I couldn't stand it any longer, Colin leapt to his feet. "Some port?" he asked, heading for a tray on which stood two decanters.

"Please," I replied. He handed me a glass that I accepted with a trembling hand. He poured for himself from the other decanter. "Whiskey?" I asked, noting the color of the beverage.

"Yes."

"You prefer it to port?"

"Sometimes."

"May we return to our marriage discussion? The question of the affair."

"Right. I'll be candid. People can be discreet, very discreet. But I don't believe that it is possible to hide entirely from one's spouse the transfer of affections to another person. Unless, of course, the spouse doesn't care."

"I can't imagine not caring."

"Nor can I."

❋ ❋ ❋

The walk home passed quickly, and back at Berkeley Square Davis opened the door before I had reached it. "There's been another delivery, madam," he said, ushering me inside to the drawing room. "The smell is rather overpowering, so I thought you'd prefer not to have them in the library. I didn't separate them, as I thought you'd want to see the full effect."

The room was crowded with flowers, vases stuffed with lilies, roses, freesia, covering every table. Sitting on the center of the mantel was an envelope, which I opened at once. Davis was right; the scent of the flowers, though lovely, was overwhelming, and I went back into the hall to read the note, which I knew came in response to my notice that had appeared in the *Times* the previous day.

Ἤν μοι συννεφὲς ὄμμα βάλης ποτέ, χεῖμα
δέδορκα, ἢν δ᾽ ἱλαρὸν βλέψης, ἡδὺ τέθηλεν ἔαρ.

...if ever thou dost cast a clouded glance on me, I gaze on winter, and if thou lookest joyously, sweet spring bursts into bloom. Beneath the Greek was a simple statement: *You'll never again receive any but the freshest flowers from me.*

16

❈—❈—❈—❈—❈—❈—❈—❈

IT WAS WITH A CERTAIN DEGREE OF TREPIDATION THAT I CALLED ON
Beatrice the following day. I wanted to learn more about her marriage without making her suspect that her husband had a mistress. Assuming, of course, that she did not already know. She was in the garden when I arrived, filling a basket with cut flowers, their bright colors a perfect contrast to her dull black dress.

"This heat is dreadful," she said when she saw me. "I quite envy you your dress." She looked longingly at my gown, which was fashioned from a pale pink lawn.

"It may look cooler than yours, but I can assure you that it doesn't feel it."

"Black's so oppressive, don't you think? Particularly in the summer." Sweat trickled down the side of her face. "But there's something cleansing about being in mourning. A sort of justice. It wouldn't be right for one to go on as if nothing had happened."

I took the basket from her and followed her down the path to a shaded grove, where we sat on a small stone bench. "I've found one of Léonard's letters," I told her. "And I'm wondering if your husband had the rest of them."

"How can that be possible? We've combed every inch of the house. They are not here."

"I think they may have been stolen, possibly with the snuffbox."

"Does this help Jane?"

"It may," I said. "I'm not sure."

"I cannot bear this, Emily. The poor girl is rotting in prison—"

"Please do not upset yourself. I need your help. Think carefully: Did your husband's manner or mood change at all in the days before his death?"

"No, not that I can remember."

"Did he ever seem withdrawn?"

"David was the most constant man I ever met."

"A perfect husband?"

"As near as one could be."

"Was there never any strife in your marriage?"

"Not really. We argued on occasion, as everyone does."

I thought of my own brief marriage. Philip and I had never argued. We hadn't known each other well enough. "About anything in particular?"

"I sometimes complained that we did not go out much in society, but there is no use in trying to change a husband. I knew when I married David that he preferred a quiet life."

"But he did go out, didn't he? With Mr. Barber? And to his club?"

"Yes, of course. That's very different from going about in society, though. He went to a political meeting every Sunday at his club. I can't think that he ever missed one."

"What sort of politics?"

"Oh, I haven't the slightest idea. He never told me details, but there was an energy about him when he returned. I can't quite describe it."

"And they always met on Sundays?"

"Yes." She laughed. "It was a concession to the wives. When they first started, they met three nights a week. Can you imagine? The wives complained, and eventually they were persuaded that happiness at home required them to curb their enthusiasm for politics."

"Did you complain?"

"Actually, I didn't. I could see that the meetings did him good. He felt useful. And, at the time, I was rather glad to be by myself."

"Why is that?"

"It was a difficult period for me, Emily. David and I had been married for more than seven years, and not once was I with child. It was hard to accept that I would never be a mother."

"I'm sorry."

"There's no need to apologize. I came to terms with it years ago."

"How did Mr. Francis react?"

"He handled it with grace and understanding. Never complained, never made me feel my failure."

"Perhaps it wasn't your failure at all. It could have been his."

"No, Emily, it was mine. I'm sure of that."

D avis could not hide his pleasure as he handed me the mail that afternoon, and when I sorted through my letters, I knew why. "Have we both had letters from France today, Davis?" I asked. "Is Odette glad to be home? Or does she long for England?"

"I'm sure I wouldn't know, madam; she wrote only to inform me of her safe arrival in Paris."

"Hmmmm." His cheeks took on a slight color as he bowed quickly and left the room. I tore open my letter from Cécile.

Ma chère Kallista,

There is no joy more complete than that felt when returning to Paris. London has its diversions, but nothing could compare to the beauty of my own city. Monet and Renoir have both inquired after you; Monet has finished the paintings for the villa, and is shipping them to Madame Katevatis, where she will have them ready for your arrival on Santorini in the fall.

There is sadly little to report to Monsieur Hargreaves, but tell him not to despair. I have made the acquaintance of Monsieur Garnier. He will not be a stranger to me for long. Already I have captured his attention—he is an oddly attractive man—I know I shall enjoy working on him.

How is Davis? I am being subjected to unbearable waves of melo-drama here, Odette mooning about and singing mournful arias from Italian operas. Beware, Kallista, I may be forced to steal your butler, as I can tolerate lovesickness for only so long.

I smiled as I read this, and then looked through the rest of my mail. The next envelope I opened contained a note from Mr. Sinclair, who single-handedly restored my hope that the work I was trying to do for the British Museum was not futile. He'd consulted with the Keeper of Greco-Roman Antiquities at the museum, Mr. Murray, who agreed with my assessment of the Archaic statue I had seen in Richmond. In view of the piece's intrinsic value to scholars, Mr. Sinclair had im-mediately donated it to the museum. It turned out that his wife had never been overly fond of the piece, so the decision did not cause any strife in the house.

I scrawled a quick reply, expressing my gratitude, and then, my confidence bolstered, penned a message to send to the *Times*. Not only did I need to uncover the identity of my admirer, and, of course, thank him for the flowers, I had to confirm that he had more of Léo-nard's correspondence. *You've overwhelmed me with flowers. Care to do the same with L's letters?*

That taken care of, I changed into something suitable for walking and set off for the park, where I was to meet Ivy and Margaret. They were waiting for me in front of the statue of Achilles when I arrived, Ivy a picture of English perfection, her delicate skin shaded by a frilly parasol, Margaret dressed in a modern-looking suit and carrying a stack of books bound together with a leather strap.

"These are for you, but I won't make you carry them," she said. "I've decided to bludgeon you with Latin until you agree to take up the study of it."

"I'm sorry, Margaret, you'll not convert me yet. I'm nowhere near being satisfied with my mastery of Greek, and I think I shall turn to hieroglyphs when I want something new."

"You're both so clever," Ivy said, looking at the ground.

"Perhaps you can convince Ivy to discuss Latin with you," I said.

"No, no, I've no head for that sort of thing."

"I think you do," Margaret said. "You don't give yourself enough credit." Ivy blushed furiously, and her knuckles turned white as she clutched her parasol.

"You're perfectly capable of learning it, but don't let Margaret bully you. She won't be satisfied until she's at Oxford reciting Ovid until all hours of the night."

"I wish the Season was over," Margaret said, slinging the books over her shoulder.

"I think it's unfortunate that Jeremy isn't willing to embrace his classical education. If he were, you might just marry him."

"He'd make a decent husband," she admitted. "He's a brilliant kisser—"

"Margaret!" Ivy cried.

"Well, you knew I'd have to check."

"I rather assumed he would be," I said. "He's very…" I smiled as I considered Jeremy.

"Yes, exactly," Margaret said.

"I haven't the slightest idea what either of you is talking about," Ivy said.

"That, my dear, is because you are too good," I said, squeezing her arm. The park was bursting with the best of society, mothers parading their daughters, gentlemen looking as dapper as possible in the heat, young married women bending their heads together, asking and giving advice, gossip, and encouragement to one another. We had to pause every few feet to nod greetings to acquaintances, but it was impossible not to notice that no one seemed interested in actually speaking with us. Until, that is, we came to Lady Elliott, my mother's bosom friend. She stopped and forced a pained smile onto her face.

"Mrs. Brandon, Miss Seward, how delightful to see you." She did not so much as look at me. "Dreadful heat, don't you agree?"

Ivy managed a sputtered but genteel reply. Margaret glared at Lady Elliott, who walked on without further comment.

"Emily, she deliberately cut you," Ivy said. I felt the unwelcome sting of tears in my eyes.

"Are you all right?" Lady Elinor and Isabelle approached us.

"We're fine," Margaret snapped.

"Thank you, Lady Elinor, for asking," Ivy said.

"I saw Lady Elliott. Dreadful. Pay her no mind, Emily. She's a petty, jealous woman."

"Thank you," I said, pulling my shoulders back. "I hadn't realized I was in such disgrace."

"Oh dear," Lady Elinor said. "You've not heard the rumor then?" I shook my head. "Ivy, will you walk ahead with Isabelle?"

"It must be quite awful if you're unwilling for her to hear it," I said, trying to inject into my voice a light tone as Ivy and Isabelle pulled away from us.

"One would think the fact that the two of you are walking together would put an end to all this, but apparently not." She looked back and forth between Margaret and myself as she spoke. "The story goes that the Duke of Bainbridge had a large quantity of flowers delivered to you as a gesture of thanks after you had...well...you can imagine what they think."

"That is absolutely outrageous!" Margaret cried.

"Do lower your voice, Miss Seward. Any hint of excitement on your part will do nothing but appear to confirm this rumor."

"I received flowers, but they weren't from Jeremy," I said.

"They say that you prominently displayed the card he sent on the center of your mantelpiece."

I could not speak. This was beyond awful, more terrible than I could have imagined. People might talk and criticize me for indulging in a romantic flirtation with no intention of marrying Jeremy, but if they believed that the relationship had progressed to an actual affair, and that we were so foolish as to not be discreet—that could ruin me.

"I won't stand for this," Margaret said. "We have to do something."

"There's very little we can do," Lady Elinor said. Ivy looked back over her shoulder, her face full of questions. "The duke has of course denied it, but no one would expect a gentleman to do anything else."

"So Emily is to sit here and allow this trash to fester? No. Not acceptable."

"You could perhaps go abroad, let the scandal die down."

"That would be tantamount to admitting guilt," I said. "I shan't do that."

"I see your point, but I do hate the thought of your being subjected to all this," Lady Elinor said. "I'm afraid that Lady Frideswide has been particularly vocal about you."

"I suppose that shouldn't come as a surprise," I said.

"This is my fault," Margaret said. "I've taken advantage of your generosity, Emily." She turned to Lady Elinor. "Mrs. Taylor and my mother won't give me a moment of peace. They hover over me mercilessly when Jeremy calls. Emily's kind enough to let me meet him at her house, and this is the thanks she gets."

"Hush, Miss Seward. Telling people that Emily allowed you to have inappropriate interactions with the duke will not help her reputation."

"I didn't say she let us do anything inappropriate."

"No, but that would be implied, wouldn't it, after you say that your chaperones are too severe and that meeting at Emily's house is an improvement?"

"I hadn't considered that," Margaret said, and fell silent.

"Isabelle, come back, dear," Lady Elinor called. "I want the three of you to walk with us for a bit. It will do you good to be seen in company, Emily."

Ivy did not ask what had happened but drew my arm through hers as we walked. No one whom we encountered would meet my eyes.

Following Lady Elinor's advice, we spent three quarters of an hour meandering through the park. Not a single acquaintance offered me more than the most basic courtesy, but at least no one save Lady Elliott cut me. Still, I was thoroughly disheartened when my friends and I returned to the library at Berkeley Square.

"I don't care what Lady Elinor says," Margaret said. "I blame myself entirely for this."

"Don't, Margaret," I said, letting my head fall against the back of my chair, eyes focused on the ceiling.

"How could anyone think such things about you?" Ivy asked. We had waited until we reached my house to tell her the story; she was horrified. "What will you do? What will Colin say?"

"Colin is the last person we need to worry about," Margaret said.

"I don't agree," Ivy said. "Colin matters more than anything."

"Please! I can't have the two of you arguing." I wished I could loosen my corset. "Colin will know it's all nonsense. As for the rest of society, there's nothing to be done. I shall have to sit out until the scandal blows over."

"You can't be serious," Margaret said. "You need to fight back."

"It won't do any good to make a spectacle of yourself, Emily," Ivy said.

"Fine. Then come to Oxford with me. Or go to Bryn Mawr. University life would suit you."

"Thank you, Margaret, but I don't think so. I'd rather stay and face this than run from it."

"You must think carefully about what will be the best way to approach this," Ivy said. "You don't want to lose your position."

"Her position?" Margaret slammed her hand on the table that stood next to her chair. "I hardly think that her position—"

"I don't think you fully understand the situation, Margaret. Emily is in danger of losing everything if she does not carefully consider how to best reconcile herself in society. Perhaps you could host a dinner party, Emily. Your parents would, of course, come, and you can count on Robert and me. A royal guest would work wonders for your reputation. Colin's with Bertie so often these days because of Mr. Berry, and your mother's friends with Princess Alix— "

"You can't be suggesting that hosting the Prince of Wales, a notorious profligate, is going to improve Emily's situation."

"I am well aware of the prince's flaws, Margaret, but you know that people are more than willing to overlook them," Ivy said.

"Can you bear this hypocrisy, Emily? You are falsely accused of having an affair. To save yourself, you should invite to dinner a man with more mistresses than sense."

"There's no need to insult the prince," Ivy said.

"You can't agree with this nonsense!" Margaret exclaimed, turning to me.

"That's quite enough, both of you." I rubbed my temples. "I shall have to figure this out on my own."

"You could marry Colin," Ivy said. "All these problems would disappear."

"Marriage does not make problems disappear," Margaret said.

"I'm not about to marry Colin simply to save my reputation."

"That wouldn't be the only reason for doing it, but perhaps it's the push you need to finally make a decision."

I was appalled to hear my friend say this. "Is that how you feel? That I need to finally make a decision?"

"Oh, Emily, no, I just—" She stopped. "I've never wanted anything but your happiness."

"When will you understand that her happiness does not depend on finding a husband?"

"Margaret, don't," I said.

"I'm not advocating husbands in general, just Colin in particular," Ivy said. Margaret rolled her eyes, and I was too tired to continue the argument. "I'm going home. I'm sorry, Emily, I wasn't trying to upset you."

"I know." I embraced her.

"Send for me if there's anything I can do," she said, then left us. Margaret watched her go, a look of supreme dissatisfaction on her face.

"Does she really consider husbands a panacea?"

"I don't know, Margaret," I said, thinking about the strife in Ivy's marriage.

"I like her very much, Emily, but I can't help but wonder if you've outgrown her friendship."

I'm ashamed to admit that I said nothing in defense of my dear friend.

❋ ❋ ❋

C olin came to me that night, in evening kit, astonishingly hand-some. His eyes were all seriousness as he dispensed with the usual greetings and refused to hand Davis his top hat, silk scarf, and walking stick. "Change your dress. We're going to the opera."

"It's lovely to see you, too," I said.

"We've no time, Emily. I don't want to be late." His voice had taken on the calm tone it always did in situations of extreme gravity. I did not question him. Meg dressed me as quickly as possible, lament-ing all the while that she did not have time to do my hair justice. De-spite her frustrations, she managed to work such a miracle that I do believe Colin's breath caught in his throat as he watched me descend the staircase into the hall.

"'She walks in beauty, like the night/Of cloudless climes and starry skies...'" he said as he watched Davis slip a cape around my shoul-ders.

"Byron. Very nice."

In short order we arrived at Covent Garden. As we entered Colin's box, where Margaret, Jeremy, and Mr. and Mrs. Seward were waiting for us, an uncanny hush fell over the theater. All eyes were on us as the gentlemen shook hands and Margaret and I embraced. Our audience began to chatter once again.

"They will not defeat you," Colin said, handing me a pair of opera glasses. The lights dimmed, the curtain rose, and I did my best to pay attention to the performance, despite being sadly distracted. The music was glorious, but the story of Aïda's doomed love was not the thing to lighten one's mood. This did not trouble me in the least. I was comforted in the knowledge that, no matter how bad things got for me, the odds that I would ever be shut up in an Egyptian tomb, waiting to suffocate, were very, very small.

17

My appearance at the opera saved me from being completely ostracized by society. Margaret and I were both considered eccentric enough to remain friends despite my alleged affair, but the fact that Colin and Jeremy were on good terms cast doubt on the veracity of the rumor. Both gentlemen were highly respected, and it made little sense to believe that a man of Colin's stature would seek out the friendship of someone who was flaunting me, the woman everyone presumed he wanted to marry, as his mistress. Truly, the most infuriating part of all this was that Jeremy suffered not at all for the rumors. Dalliances, after all, were expected of a gentleman, and while he might be criticized for not having been as discreet as he should have been, his social standing was not compromised in the least.

I was also helped by the distraction caused by another theft. This time, it was not an object owned by Marie Antoinette that was stolen but a portrait of her, by Elisabeth Vigée-Lebrun, one of the queen's favorite painters. Charles Berry's outrage over this event captured everyone's attention for almost a week, and I welcomed the respite from being the centerpiece of society gossip. Still, invitations to social events came almost as infrequently as they had when I was in mourning for Philip. This was not an entirely bad thing; it left me plenty of time for my investigations.

I'd had no response from my admirer since my last notice in the *Times*, but imagined that he had been too busy with the planning and execution of this latest theft to tend to romantic matters. After the incident of the flowers in the carriage, Colin had spent a good hour teaching me the best ways to avoid being followed, as well as the techniques he employed when he tailed someone. Although I did my best to persuade him, he would give me no descriptions of the circumstances in which he had used these fascinating skills.

As I thought more about my situation, I decided that I wanted to be followed, to draw out this mysterious man. I was tired of waiting for another note, and I thought if I could at last meet him face-to-face, I could persuade him to give me the rest of Léonard's letters. One thing concerned me, however: He had tailed me the day I went to Oxford Street in search of information about the letters. When I left Oxford Street, I'd had my encounter with Mr. Berry, whose hands had been too forcefully thrust too close to my neck. Surely if the thief cared for me, he would not have stood by and watched another man threaten me. Had he stopped following me before I'd reached the park? Or could it be that Charles Berry was the man for whom I was looking?

It seemed unlikely that he could pull off such a scheme, but I began to consider him more carefully than I had before. His licentious behavior might be deliberately contrived as a cover. Hadn't Cécile and I both ruled him out as a suspect almost immediately because of it? Furthermore, he'd made no secret of the fact that he wanted me for a mistress, and I had rebuffed him at every turn. Could he believe that taking a mysterious approach might endear himself to me? The idea that he would consider such a course of action seemed ridiculous, but I refused to dismiss it out of hand. Certainly he had reason to want all the stolen Marie Antoinette objects. Who, in fact, had better motive?

My butler tapped on the door and entered the room. "I've removed all the flowers, madam."

"Thank you. I've no doubt that you've heard this latest rumor about me?"

"Yes, madam, I'm sorry to say that I have. None of the staff lend it any credence, and I've ordered them not to speak about it to anyone. I will not tolerate gossip coming from this house."

"I'm concerned because I believe the story did come from this house. Only someone who knew where you put the envelope that came with the flowers would have known to include that particular detail."

"Madam, I can assure you that I—"

"I would never, for a moment, suspect that you were involved."

"Thank you."

"But what of the rest of the staff? Have you noticed any discontent belowstairs?"

"I can't say that I have, but let me assure you that I shall look into it at once."

I hated the notion that there was someone in my own household spreading rumors about me, and that, coupled with my recent revelation that the house was not really mine, made me feel horribly unsettled. The feeling was to quickly get worse. That afternoon, Philip's sister, Anne, called on me. I did not see her often—we'd never been close—but we respected each other and had always been on friendly terms.

"The house looks lovely," she said as she sat in the drawing room. She and Philip had grown up here, at least when they weren't in Derbyshire at Ashton Hall. It was Anne who had insisted that I stay here after Philip's death. She and her husband had a fine house in Belgravia and hadn't wanted to see me displaced.

"It's kind of you to call," I said. She refused my offer of tea and played nervously with the trim on her sleeves.

"All of us in the family are…concerned, Emily. It's not that we believe these dreadful stories circulating about you, but…it's awkward, you see. This was Philip's house, and will be Alexander's someday—"

"It's Alexander's now," I said. "I'm fully aware that I am here only because of your own generosity."

"Mother doesn't know what's being said about you, but I'm afraid that if she were to find out, she'd insist that you leave at once."

"But I haven't done anything, Anne."

"Of course you haven't. Yet the house at Berkeley Square is gaining a sort of notoriety. Can you understand that we must do everything we can to avoid having the family name embroiled in scandal?"

"I understand perfectly. I shall start looking for another house."

"No, Emily, I'm not here to evict you from your home. We all know how much Philip loved you and wouldn't dream of asking you to leave unless…" She didn't continue but blushed furiously. I was struck by how much she looked like her brother, the same sandy hair and light eyes. "Perhaps you could just try to fit in better in society. I know that you find it tedious, but it is our lot in life, and we may as well make the best of it."

She didn't stay long, and I felt perfectly awful when she left. It was true that I found much of society tedious, but I had never intended to make my casual acquaintances feel it so keenly. I wanted to be gracious, kind, to put others at ease, not to make them feel as if I were sitting in judgment of them. Clearly, I was not succeeding at any of this, and regardless of Anne's reassurances, I knew the time had come for me to find a house of my own.

❦ ❦ ❦

I did not leap eagerly to the task of looking for a house, but did force myself to discuss the matter with my solicitor. He was shocked that I would consider leaving my current home, which I took as evidence that the story of my downfall was not so well known that it had spread even to the professional classes. Of course, I would need not only a house, but also to furnish it entirely, fill it with books, and hire a staff. I couldn't expect to take all of the Ashton servants with me, but I would fight to the death to keep Davis. Him, I could not do without.

I left the office feeling thoroughly downtrodden, as if my life were being taken apart a piece at a time. I walked aimlessly for a while, wanting to sit in the park but knowing that I would encounter nothing but icy stares there. I might as well return home.

Back at Berkeley Square, I found the stage set for a scene that had been played out too many times in my life: I, tense and worried, would arrive home to find my mother, irritated and ready to lecture, waiting for me. Resigned to go at least one round with her—I hadn't spoken to her since this latest debacle over Jeremy—I greeted her with a sigh and sank into a chair, surprised to find that she was in the library, not the drawing room.

"I will accept none of this, you know," she said, tapping the point of her parasol against the floor. "You have behaved badly—there is no question of that—and after all your father and I have done for you, we deserve better." I could not bring myself to respond; this, however, presented no problem. My mother always preferred soliloquies to dialogue. "Through it all, I have done whatever I can to secure you the best possible position, and I will not abide having my work destroyed by idle gossip."

"Mother, I can assure you that I never—"

"Do not interrupt me. It is intolerable to think that the daughter of an earl could be treated with such absolute contempt, that her reputation could be sullied on the basis of so little fact."

"Mother?" I was aghast.

"Why shouldn't a gentleman send you a roomful of flowers? You're quite possibly the richest girl in England. I shouldn't think you'd have to do more than slightly acknowledge an eligible bachelor to inspire him to such a gesture. The idea that he would have done it only after..." She had no intention of finishing the thought. "I despair for the jealous cow who invented this fiction."

I sat there with my mouth open, completely unable to form a coherent thought. Never did I think I would see the day when my mother, my harshest critic, would come to my defense.

"I won't stand for it, that's all there is to it. You've invited more than your share of trouble, but these stories have gone too far. Even if you were guilty, it would go against all things decent to give away one of our class, and that's what these vicious people are doing. I know of more badly managed affairs than I can count but would never have the bad taste to expose those involved."

She paused for a moment, hoping, I think, that I would press her for details of these affairs. When it became clear I was not going to, she continued.

"I've arranged for us to have tea with the queen on Tuesday next. No one can doubt your innocence after that. Her Majesty would never tolerate being in the presence of a fallen woman. I wonder if you should wear mourning?"

"I've been out of mourning for months."

"Yes, but you haven't seen the queen in all that time. You might endear yourself to her if she thinks that you honor your late husband the way she does poor Prince Albert."

"But surely someone will point out to her that I stopped wearing mourning, and she'll think I'm being insincere."

"Oh, I suppose so. Still, it wouldn't harm you to return to, not mourning, precisely, but maybe some sort of fashionable dress in subdued colors. If only you had been able to get some of the viscount's hair to make into a ring."

"If only," I said, managing not to roll my eyes.

"This would all be much easier if you would just behave like any other rational girl and marry one of your suitors. I don't care whom, though why you haven't accepted Bainbridge is a mystery to me. It's almost as if you don't want to be a duchess, but that, of course, would be absurd."

"What makes you think that he's proposed?"

"Don't toy with me, Emily. If you wanted him you could have him on a platter."

Hearing my mother speak like this made me smile, then laugh, so hard that I had difficulty breathing. She watched me, her lips pursed, not amused in the least.

"Are you quite finished?" she asked. "There is an art to catching a husband, an art to which you have an inexplicable aversion." Her eyes narrowed. "Yet, you still manage to attract gentlemen, primarily because of your pedigree and your fortune. Your…unique…character may draw them in, too, I suppose. But think hard, Emily. Do you really intend to stay alone the rest of your life? The women in our family are known for their longevity. Ninety years is a long time to live by oneself."

I thought it best not to point out that, longevity of the Bromley women aside, I was unlikely to live *another* ninety years from the present, and even if I did, it would be virtually impossible to find a husband who could manage the same thing.

"I will do everything I can to stop these rumors. I'm convinced that Lady Frideswide is behind them. She's furious that Lettice has been thrown over. I'm sorry for the girl, but she wouldn't make much of a duchess. Dull as dishwater. Bainbridge would be much better off with you. His family could use some fresh blood. For all your faults, Emily—and make no mistake, you have many—there has always been a sparkle about you."

"Thank you, Mother." I did not fight the tears that filled my eyes. I couldn't remember a time when she'd ever said something so kind to me.

"You will undoubtedly send me to an early grave, but I'll not let anyone destroy your chances for a good marriage. We must not forget Mr. Hargreaves, either. Another very attractive option. And what a gentleman! I've heard all about him taking you to the opera."

"It was lovely of him."

"Be warned, though. A man like that will not tolerate your games indefinitely. Oh, he finds you entrancing now, but before you know it—"

"Yes, Mother, my looks will fade. I know, I know."

She rose from her chair. "You will have to alter your behavior, Emily, or you will find yourself continually subjected to this sort of gossip. The sooner you accept that, the better off we will all be." She adjusted the collar of my dress and scowled at my waist. "Your corset is practically hanging off you. What is wrong with your maid?"

"It's not hanging off me, I just didn't want it laced tightly. I find that being able to breathe greatly enhances my daily life."

"I really hope we can find a husband who will tolerate you. It's a pity that Charles Berry—"

"There is nothing that could ever induce me to marry such a man."

"A woman could tolerate a great deal to marry into a royal family."

"Forgive me, Mother, but if I am to marry royalty, I want a prince who has an actual throne." Her eyes brightened, and I could see her beginning to silently catalog all the bachelor princes of Europe. Eventually, she would come to the conclusion that none of them would want a widow, but, in the meantime, I would not spoil her fun by pointing out that I would want none of them, either.

When she left, I walked her to the door. As Davis closed it behind her, he smiled, quite unabashedly, at me. "She asked to wait for you in the library, madam."

18

M Y MOTHER'S EFFORTS ON BEHALF OF MY REPUTATION WERE NOT IN vain. Somehow, she managed to broker an uneasy peace between society and me. Although I was still not being invited to many of the best parties, no one dared to openly cut me, and my situation could only improve after the following week's tea with the queen. And so I learned that there are, in fact, benefits to having an absolute dragon for a mother, and I loved her for it. I know not what my mother said to Lady Elliott, but I received from her a gracious note of apology and a belated invitation to a soirée she was hosting. I sent a gracious note of my own, determined to remain above reproach, but declined the invitation. My mother might want me to change my behavior, but she had to have realistic expectations. Although I was not about to embrace all the nonsense required by society, I was going to make a very deliberate effort to make sure that no one ever felt belittled by me for having chosen to play all its games.

I took to spending days when the weather was fine in the park but avoided the fashionable sections. This chagrined my mother, who shuddered at the thought of running into people from Bayswater or, worse, those who rowed boats on the Serpentine, but she managed to keep most of her criticisms to herself.

Relishing the shade provided by a large plane tree, I sat in the same spot each day, hoping that this predictable routine would draw the attention of my admirer, who had remained silent for far too long. I would bring my Greek with me, and work at translating the *Odyssey* while attempting to take note of anyone who seemed to be watching me. Not once, however, either while walking to or from the park, or while I was sitting in it, did I notice anything suspicious. It was a grave disappointment.

One morning, as the sun slipped behind an ominous-looking cloud, I was gathering my books, not wanting to be caught in the rain, when a small, very dirty boy ran up to me.

"Are you Lady Ashton?" he asked.

"I am. Who are you?"

"Johnny. A gent asked me to bring you these." He handed over a thick bundle of letters held together with a blue ribbon. The handwriting was that of Léonard.

"What gentleman?"

"He's right over there." The boy pointed behind me, and I whipped around as fast as I could but saw no one. When I turned back, he had started running away from me in the opposite direction.

"Johnny, wait!" I cried, setting off after him. I was able to keep him in sight for a few minutes, but my heeled boots and fashionable gown made me no match for his speed, and I stopped, out of breath, the letters still in my hand. A quick survey of the area told me that my quest was futile. The boy had disappeared, and the gentleman, too...if he had even been there in the first place. I walked back to the bench, only to find that my books, my notebook, and my pencil were gone.

This took my breath away more than the running had. My copy of the *Odyssey* had been Philip's. It was bound in the finest Moroccan leather and matched his *Iliad*. He had written his name on the front page and made very light pencil marks to highlight his favorite passages. I felt sick. I had taken to copying down those passages in the original Greek, as I had done with the *Iliad* before, but was only halfway through the volume. Now I would never know what he thought of the rest of the book. And his nephew, the new viscount, whom Philip had hoped would share his love of all things classical, had lost another connection to his uncle.

I buried these thoughts as best I could and went home. At least I had the letters. Back in my library, I did not sit at my desk—Philip's desk—but instead took the bundle to the window seat and began to read. I raced through the first three without pausing, grateful that I was fluent in French. But as I started in on the fourth, two things struck me. First, that my admirer, who I assumed had sent them to me, had left no note of his own, and second, that I had not the slightest clue what I hoped to find in them.

I pulled Marie Antoinette's letters out from the desk drawer in which I had placed them—the same drawer in which I kept Philip's journal, and the sight of that familiar book at once warmed my heart. I picked it up for just a moment and opened it but did not read even one sentence. Somehow, the feel of the ink on the pages brought me comfort, as if they had the power to forgive me for having lost the *Odyssey*, and I decided to continue my work at the desk. I took stock of the letters. There were thirty-six altogether: sixteen of them written by the queen, twenty by Léonard. I sorted through both sets, laying them out by date, so that they could be read in the sequence written, but this strategy brought no new illumination. The correspondence provided only a mundane account of the queen's days in prison, with the revelation of not a single significant detail.

Jane Stilleman's trial was to begin before long, and I had let myself run amuck with this foolish notion that reading hundred-year-old letters would somehow help me find David Francis's murderer. I was now hideously short of time and could not afford to squander any more. The letters, my admirer, and Charles Berry were proving to be nothing more than fruitless distractions. Davis rallied me from this unpleasant thought by announcing that Ivy was waiting for me in the drawing room.

"You should have brought her here," I said as I breezed past him into the hallway.

"Your callers seem to have their own opinions about what room they would like to be received in, madam. Who am I to argue?"

Ivy was not sitting when I entered the room. "Good afternoon, Emily," she said, all formal courtesy.

"Heavens, Ivy! What's the matter?"

"I came here to apologize for not having done anything to assist you these past weeks. I've been entirely remiss as a friend." I pulled her down next to me on the settee.

"Why is it always too early for port when we are faced with these sorts of conversations?" My question did not draw even the slightest smile to her face. "I'm perfectly aware that I've put you in far too many awkward situations. If anything, it's I who should be apologizing to you."

"You deserve a friend who understands you better, Emily. Colin brought you to the opera. Margaret and Jeremy persuaded her parents to join you. Your own mother has come to your aid. But all I have done is sit, listen to the gossip, and say nothing more than that I can't believe you would do such a thing."

"Your job is not to disprove these rumors."

"No, but I should have at least tried to offer an impassioned defense of your character."

"I'm not sure that my character would stand up to an impassioned defense."

She still would not smile. "I'm so sorry, Emily. I've just become so embroiled in my own troubles that I've no longer time to manage yours." I was not certain whether she meant this as an explanation or a good-bye. "I need to return this to you." She handed me the book she'd been holding: my copy of *Mount Royal*.

"Did you enjoy it?"

"I never had the chance to finish it."

"What are these troubles, Ivy? Are you and Robert still having difficulties?"

"Yes, but it's more than that. Lord Fortescue is heaping pressure on him, and—"

"And Lord Fortescue doesn't think it becomes the wife of a future cabinet minister to consort with a fallen woman?"

"You always were too clever," she said.

"I have such a low opinion of Lord Fortescue that nothing you could tell me about him would shock me. What has he done now?"

"He wants you off the guest list for my ball and has had very sharp words with Robert over our friendship."

"I'm sorry, Ivy."

"I've insisted on keeping you on the list. Robert was very kind about it."

"I'll stay home if it will make things easier for you."

"No. You must come. I just wish all this would stop, because, Emily, in the end, my loyalty has to lie with Robert."

"Of course," I said. "How are you enjoying your charity work with the Duchess of Petherwick?"

"It's absolutely dreadful. I think I shall scream if I have to embroider one more christening robe. I can hardly stand the sight of baby clothes."

"So you're not..."

"No," she answered quickly, averting her eyes.

"This is not your fault, Ivy."

"How can I ever know that?" she asked.

"Couldn't you tell Robert that you'd prefer to do your good works elsewhere?"

"The Duke of Petherwick is a valuable political ally."

"You are a very good wife, Ivy. Robert is a fortunate man." I didn't like to see her slipping into melancholy. "So tell me about the duchess. Do you think the marriage is a happy one?"

"She's quite content," Ivy said, perking up. "It surprises me. He's so much older than her!"

"And she's the second wife."

"And he has children nearly as old as she."

"Poor woman," I said.

"Best I can tell she has a baby every time her husband so much as glances at her."

"Doubly poor woman."

This made Ivy laugh. "I suppose you're right. Though at the moment, it sounds like perfection to me."

"Not every time he looks at you, my dear. As lovely as you are, you'd be saddled with an inordinate number of children."

She blushed. "I'd be satisfied with two or three."

"Keep *Mount Royal*, will you? Read it at night when you're waiting for Robert to come home. Leave your door open. Call to him when he comes in. Tell him that you can't sleep."

"He doesn't like my reading—"

"Throw the book under your bed when you hear him coming. I know you don't feel right going to him, Ivy, and I understand your hesitation to do so. But surely there's nothing wrong with greeting him when he returns if you're awake?"

"Perhaps, Emily, perhaps. I might need more than one book, though. He stays out terribly late."

"I can happily provide you with as many books as you would like." I took her by the arm and led her to the library. "Why did you insist that Davis put you in the drawing room?"

"No nefarious reason. I've always liked the way the room is decorated and wanted to steal ideas for my own house."

"I was afraid you'd come here prepared to throw me over," I said as I opened the door to the library. "What has happened here?" The letters that I had so carefully laid out on the desk were no longer as I had left them. Instead, they had been placed in two neat stacks, and closer inspection revealed that the two final letters written by Léonard were gone.

19

———————————————

D AVIS WAS CERTAIN THAT NO ONE HAD COME THROUGH THE FRONT door, and I was convinced that the Marie Antoinette thief, who in all likelihood had given me the letters in the first place, was not behind this. Someone in the household must have taken them. Reluctantly, I had my butler round up the staff so that I could speak to each of them individually. No one admitted to having been in the library, nor did any of them behave suspiciously in the least.

There was one servant whose absence from these interviews was glaring: Molly, who, according to my housekeeper, had left the house to visit her ill sister.

"Have you had any problems with her?"

"She's a perfectly adequate girl, although I have noticed that she's rather withdrawn from the rest of the staff." This was hardly surprising, given her experience with Mr. Berry. I asked Mrs. Ockley to send her to me when she returned.

"I wonder about her." Ivy had stayed with me. "Are you quite certain that she's not a friend to Mr. Berry?"

"Of course she's not!" I said. "Think what he did to her."

"I suppose you're right. But it's awfully convenient, don't you think, for him to have a servant whom he knows in your house?"

"I can't imagine that he even is aware that she's here."

"I'd want to find out if I were you."

I watched from the window seat as Ivy left, carrying with her four of the most sensational novels I had on hand. I hoped she could lure back Robert's attention, and I hoped that I would not ever lose her friendship. But I knew that as she was drawn further into the world of the Duchess of Petherwick and her ilk, we would be pulled away from one another. This would trouble me less if I thought it would bring my friend a happy contentment. Though I feared loyalty to her husband might in the end lead her to a life of the worst sort of tedium, I knew that she could never bring herself to choose another path.

These thoughts made me relish my own choices all the more. I might have to tread carefully to keep from alienating society, but I would never have to worry about succumbing to monotony. Quite the opposite.

I find it difficult to believe that you didn't know he had a son," I said to Mr. Barber, whom I had found hard at work on another sculpture in his studio.

"I didn't even know David had a mistress."

"But you did know that he offered financial assistance to those he felt needed it?"

"Yes."

"Did he buy houses for anyone else?"

"I don't know."

"Should I expect to find more of his children flitting about London?"

"I haven't the slightest idea."

"You didn't know him so well as you thought?"

"No, no, I can't believe he left a string of mistresses and children," he said. "He was a devoted husband."

"Only if you apply a rather unusual definition of *devoted*."

"You must not tell Beatrice any of this. It would devastate her."

"Are you quite certain that she doesn't already know?"

"Of course she doesn't! She would have told me."

"Really? That's an awfully private matter to share with your husband's friend."

"If she suspected David of infidelity, she would have bullied me for information."

"Wouldn't she have assumed your loyalty would rest with him?"

"Beatrice and I have been friends for more than twenty years. She knows I would never lie to her."

I stood up and walked over to where he had been working and touched the cool block of half-carved marble. "Were you better friends with her than with him?" He looked away from me. "Were you in love with her?"

"Years ago, but I knew—"

"Did she return the feeling?"

"My income would not allow me to support a wife. At any rate, I can't remember when I last thought of her in romantic terms. It was for the best that we never married; she's not the sort of woman who would make a good artist's wife. I wouldn't have made her happy. Our interests are too different, as are our temperaments. Furthermore..."

The length at which he went on made his feelings for Beatrice perfectly clear. He still loved her.

"How soon did she marry Mr. Francis after she broke off with you?"

"Beatrice and I never had a falling-out. David proposed to her, and she decided to accept him."

"Did you try to stop her?"

"How could I? I wasn't in a position to offer her half what he could."

I thought of Lord Pembroke, who was calmly standing by, watching the woman he loved prepare to marry Charles Berry. Did men not have the same capacity for love as women? How could they react with such tepid indifference to having their passions thwarted?

"Did it never occur to you that perhaps she cared more about you than the money?"

"Maybe she did. But the reality, Lady Ashton, is that I could not have supported her in an adequate way. As romantic as the idea of an abiding love is, it is not something that can overcome every obstacle."

"I think you are too quick in jumping to your doomsday conclusions. You live comfortably."

"What is acceptable for a bachelor is a far cry from what a wife deserves."

"So we women are left to suffer lost love in exchange for a house and an allowance?"

"It is a man's duty to see that the woman he loves has that which she needs. Sometimes that requires graciously stepping aside."

"Oh, Mr. Barber! I do wish men would allow women to make some choices of their own. We'd all be better off."

I headed directly from the studio to Richmond, thinking during the drive about Beatrice and her husband. Mr. Francis had lied to me about his wife's personality. Beatrice, who had come to me accusing me of an affair, presented herself as a devoted wife. As I considered her behavior, which had initially struck me as bold and direct, I began to wonder if she had practiced a deception of her own. Her husband's request that she give me the snuffbox made her believe that he had not been faithful to her. Grief might wreak havoc on one's ability to think rationally, but unless she had already suspected that his affections had strayed from home, why would she immediately leap to such a conclusion?

"I wish you had told me about your feelings for Mr. Barber," I said, sitting with Beatrice in her garden. "I've just come from his studio. You were in love with him."

"Michael is the truest friend I've ever had."

"More so than your husband?"

"Husbands fall into a different category altogether. You know that." She gazed out over the flowers in front of us. "There is always the desire to bring more comfort than distress to one's spouse, and the result is that, on occasion, one chooses to bury painful experiences."

"But I thought that you and Mr. Francis were so close, perfect companions."

"As perfect as husband and wife can be," she said.

"And Mr. Barber was your confidant?"

"In the past few years, yes. He was always on hand to listen to those fears and anxieties with which I did not want to burden David."

"Forgive me for being so direct, but did this have to do with your inability to have a child?"

"What else could cause such pain? I could see the disappointment in David's eyes. I wanted to mourn, to cry, to shout at the injustice of it, but to do so would only have made him feel more helpless."

"Did your husband have a confidant, too?"

"You mean did he have a mistress. He didn't."

"You thought he might when you first came to me."

"I was upset." I watched her as she spoke. "I should never have questioned him. It was disloyal of me." There was a measured tone in her voice, too measured, that made me continue to doubt the veracity of what she said.

"I'm sorry that I brought it up. It was wrong of me," I said. "But

I'm afraid I'm going to continue asking difficult questions. Is your financial situation comfortable?"

"Dear me! I'd no idea you were such a competent detective!" She smiled but did not answer my question.

"You mentioned that the pink diamond was not something that your husband could have afforded to buy anymore. What happened to cause that?"

"David had some capital that, coupled with my dowry, enabled us to live without worrying about money. As the years went by, though, and it became evident we wouldn't have a child, he started spending more. Not on us, but on people he wanted to help. Like Michael. He left enough for me, though. I've no cause for complaint."

20

~~~~~~~~~~~~~~~~~~~~~~~

THIS IS BECOMING A TERRIBLE HABIT," I SAID AS HOSKINS LED ME INTO Colin's library. "Shouldn't you be calling on me?"

"I would if you weren't here so often. Dare I flatter myself by thinking that you are irresistibly drawn to my library?"

I looked at him. He was a bit disheveled, jacket off, shirtsleeves rolled up, hair tousled. The result was devilishly handsome. "Yes, drawn to the library, of course. Which reminds me, I need to peruse your much-lauded fiction collection. I want to find something quite sensational for Ivy."

"I'm just lowbrow enough to have an abundance of that," he said. "What were you thinking? Braddon's your favorite, am I right?"

"I do adore her."

"You just like books where husbands get pushed down wells."

"You've found me out."

"How about Wilkie Collins? *The Woman in White?* That might be good for her."

"I'd nearly forgotten about that. I don't think it's in my library. I read it when I was still at my parents' house."

"I'm surprised your mother allowed it," he said, stepping up a ladder to reach the book in question.

"She didn't. I borrowed it from a maid."

"Here you are." He handed it to me. "Have you something for me?"

"I do." I gave him the letter I'd brought. "Unfortunately, Cécile doesn't have much to report." He leaned against the edge of his large, leather-topped desk so he could read. When he got to the end, he laughed softly.

"I can't believe that I've managed to hide something from you."

"What?" I asked.

He gave the letter back to me. "Read it again." I did but still saw nothing of particular interest.

"I'm pleased, of course, that Cécile's ordered a new dress, and that Caesar is triumphing over Brutus." I frowned. "She makes no mention of Odette continuing to pine for Davis. I do hope he's not going to have his heart broken."

"Is that all you see?"

I leaned next to him, against the desk, so close that my elbow touched his sleeve. "It's perfectly obvious that you're bursting at the seams to reveal that which I have missed, and you know that I'd never want to keep any pleasure from you."

He breathed deeply and crossed his arms. "You will be the death of me." I met his eyes, doing my best to look all innocence. Neither of us spoke until I dropped the letter. He bent over, picked it up, and, leaning against my shoulder, held it in front of me. "The new dress refers to the planned coup. She knows that the plot has been set in motion but must not yet have an idea of the date. The reference to her dogs means that she is winning over Monsieur Garnier."

"It's so obvious now that you've told me."

"Codes generally are once you know how to decipher them."

"Do tell me that Davis and Odette aren't code for anything. I'll be despondent if I find out that what she said in her previous letter had nothing to do with my poor butler."

"You're quite safe. Davis and Odette are not part of the code."

"That's a relief." I loved the feeling of him so close to me and for a moment allowed myself to think of nothing but the warmth of his arm against mine. I was not, however, so carried away as to overlook the implication of what he had just shared with me. When I realized what it meant, I was quite overcome. "I am such a fool!"

"Don't be so hard on yourself. I understand your reluctance to marry."

"You're absolutely terrible," I said, but couldn't help smiling. "I'm talking about the correspondence between Marie Antoinette and Léonard. They must have written in code."

"It's possible."

"How can I tell?"

"Well, if the letters are encoded, it's likely that there's a simple sort of key. The queen wouldn't have been able to hide anything in her cell, so she must have been able to decipher and write without consulting a key."

"Her jailers would have read everything she wrote and received, so it can't have been too simple or obvious."

Colin crossed the room to another bookshelf, ticking off each volume with a finger until he found the one that he sought. After glancing through it, he passed it to me, then returned to his search. "This might be helpful, as well, so long as it doesn't distract you from the matter at hand." He gave me a second book, this one in French, *Les secrets de nos pères: La cryptographie; ou l'Art d'écrire en chiffres.*

I glanced at both of them while he opened a drawer in his desk. "This is a definitive work, though it's more pertinent to military cryptography. Fleissner von Wostrowitz is a master, and it's possible that reading his articles will inspire you, though the more I think about it, I'm inclined to say your letters rely on both steganography and cryptography."

"You've absolutely baffled me. I've not the slightest idea what you're talking about."

"Cryptography is codes. If you pick up a document and see a series of numbers or letters that look like gibberish, you know at once that they need to be deciphered. Steganography, however, provides a way to send a hidden message that does not look like a code."

"Like your letter from Cécile?"

"In a sense, yes, though we're primarily using a jargon code, substituting words—*Brutus* for *Garnier*. Our system is laughably unsophisticated. Were we to employ a null cipher, for example, it would be much more difficult to crack. In such a case, you might need to read only the second letter of every other word in a document to find the imbedded message. It's an elegant method—utterly simple once you know the technique that's been employed—but doesn't necessarily require a complicated key. And, to the untrained eye, the paper looks like an ordinary letter."

"Perfect for our jailed queen," I said, my excitement growing.

"I think so. It will be difficult to figure out their system, but not impossible. You will have to analyze each letter very carefully." He squeezed my hand so hard that it almost hurt. "I rather envy you the task."

"I never expected you were a gentleman who keeps ready references on code breaking in his library. I'm beginning to suspect that your work is more fascinating than you let on."

"Think what you will. My current assignment requires little more than an ability to stay up until all hours of the night drinking in less-than-satisfactory company."

"And a quick mind that can recognize when something of significance occurs."

He smiled. "Yes, I must be careful not to sacrifice any cognitive function."

"It must be exciting to feel that the fate of the empire rests in your hands."

"That's quite a romantic exaggeration. Most of my time is spent waiting, gathering small bits of information that, if I'm lucky, will eventually prove useful."

"Come home with me. We can work on the letters together."

"I'm afraid I'm bound to our friend Berry tonight."

I sighed. "You poor man. But I deserve a share of sympathy, too. I'm forced to return to an empty house and spend another evening alone."

"But not truly alone. It's impossible to have any privacy in these houses. A servant can come in at any moment. Have you ever been really alone?"

I thought about this. "No, not when you put it that way. Have you?"

"Whenever I work on the Continent I try to go to Switzerland after I'm finished. There's a chalet I rent in the Alps. You cannot imagine the quiet, the beauty. The mountains are spectacular, but what I crave most is the solitude. It's intoxicating like nothing else to go into a house and know that it is entirely empty aside from you."

"I can't even imagine it," I said. "But who feeds you? Don't try to tell me you cook for yourself because I'll never believe it."

"There's a village two miles away. I hike down, stock up on bread and cheese, whatever else I can carry."

"So you picnic?"

"Essentially, yes."

"And do whatever you please?"

"Exactly, and it typically amounts to very little. There's something freeing about it. No questions to answer, no etiquette to be obeyed, no obligations to meet."

"It sounds like just the thing for me." I smiled.

"I should very much like to take you there. Do you think you could bear the loss of your maid and your butler and your cook?"

"I do."

He reached up as if he would touch my face, but changed his mind, instead putting his arm around my waist and pulling me to his side. I let my head fall against his shoulder, and stayed there, perfectly content in our silence, until his butler marched into the room.

"Mr. Berry is here, sir."

"Take him to the billiard room. He can occupy himself while I finish here." Hoskins nodded, bowed, and left us.

"I can't imagine what Berry wants." Colin pulled a watch from his vest. "We weren't to meet for dinner for another two hours. I'd better tend to him."

"You're far too rumpled for public consumption," I said as he unrolled his sleeves. "Though I must confess to finding you most appealing this way."

"You'd find me like this much more often if we were married. Think on it, Emily. You could curl up in the library, all these books at your disposal—"

"Yes, but they would still be *your* books, Colin. I want my own."

Hoskins interrupted us again. "I'm very sorry, sir. Mr. Berry is insisting that you come at once."

Colin waited until the butler had gone to turn back to me. "Possessions can be more binding than you think. But I understand how you feel. Know, my dear, that if you did marry me, all that is mine would be yours."

It sounded perfectly lovely but wasn't really true. All of it could be mine only so long as he remained alive. If he died before me, I would find myself once again at the mercy of someone's heir.

"I can see your mind working," he said. "Remember your Austen: 'Let us hope for better things. Let us flatter ourselves that *I* may be the survivor.'"

I raised an eyebrow. "Have you been consulting literature in search of references that might ease the mind of a lady considering the proposal of a gentleman whose estate is entailed? If so, *Pride and Prejudice* is unlikely to provide the desired result."

"I don't see why not. It all ends perfectly well."

"While we are on the subject of marriage, I have a question for you. Several people have suggested to me that all my problems with society would disappear if I were to marry Jeremy. Do you agree?"

"I suppose so, but the entire scenario is ridiculous."

"Yes, well, forget that for the moment. I'm interested in the hypothetical. If I came to you and said that I'd been persuaded to accept him for the good of my reputation, what would you say to me? Would you stand aside?"

He tilted his head slightly to the side and looked at me. "Absolutely not. I'd throw you over my shoulder and carry you to Gretna Green."

I could not help myself. I stood on my toes and kissed his cheek. "You are a dear man."

He smiled, his eyes dancing as he kissed my hand. "I'll come to you soon to see how successful you are at code breaking."

21

CODE BREAKING, IT TURNED OUT, WAS AN EXCRUCIATING, FRUSTRAT-ing endeavor. The books and articles I had from Colin were fascinating studies, but I found in them nothing that helped illuminate the letters strewn across my desk. I was forced to tear myself away from my work, however, as the hour for my tea with the queen approached. I dressed carefully, choosing to wear the gown Mr. Worth designed for me after I gave him a swatch of ice-blue silk Cécile had cut from one of her curtains the first time I'd called on her in Paris. Meg didn't even try to contain her excitement as she assisted me. She tugged on my corset strings with such enthusiasm that I could hardly draw breath, and worked on my hair with complete disregard for the violence her hairpins inflicted upon my scalp.

The result was worth the suffering. I might not be able to breathe, but my tight stays would force me into perfect posture, and my hair was absolutely flawless. Not even a monarch could find fault with my appearance. Meg stood back to admire her work, nodding, with her hands firmly planted on her hips.

"Oh, madam, you are lovely! Your mother will be so proud. I can't even imagine getting to have tea with Her Majesty."

"I'll try to smuggle out a scone for you," I said.

"You wouldn't dare," she said in a hushed tone, her eyes wide. "But will you tell me what it's like? Do you think you might see Prince George?"

"Highly unlikely, Meg. I don't know that the prince is even in Windsor."

"I think he's very handsome. Everything a prince should be."

She looked so eager that I couldn't resist giving her something to feed her daydreams. I leaned towards her and whispered conspiratorially. "I've danced with him, you know. A most courteous gentleman and even handsomer than the pictures you see in the paper."

"Molly knows that gentleman who might be king of France. She's told me all about him."

"Has she?" I asked. "What did she say?"

"Well, he's no Prince George, but he sounds friendly enough. Really great men know how to connect with the common people, I've always thought."

I was stunned that, after discussing Charles Berry with Molly, Meg could have come away with any conclusion except that he was the worst sort of cad. Molly would not want to share the details of her ordeal, but surely neither would she deliberately paint a favorable picture of a man who had harmed her. There was no time for such thoughts at the moment; my mother had arrived.

We spoke very little as we left Berkeley Square, but I could see that she was pleased with my appearance. She had come for me in an open carriage, and ordered her driver to go slowly on the way to Paddington Station so that anyone passing by would have no difficulty in seeing and identifying us. More than one acquaintance appeared surprised to see us together. My mother bestowed on these people her chilliest smile, chatting with me the entire way. Once aboard the train, however, we sat in silence.

I had seen the queen on numerous occasions, but usually only for official events: royal garden parties and my presentation at court. Today, as we approached the palace, I thought about the last time I'd been in Her Majesty's presence, during her Golden Jubilee, when Ivy and I had watched the fireworks from the garden at Buckingham Palace. Neither of us was yet engaged, and she had been flirting shamelessly with a dashing member of the diplomatic corps. Bright flashes filled the sky with color that washed over the crowd below, only to fade and plunge us again into darkness. It was during one of these dark intervals that the gentleman standing next to me took my hand in his. The memory was so faint I questioned its veracity, but it kept tugging at me, until I was able to picture Philip's face, a questioning smile in his eyes as the light returned to bathe us.

"I am certain that I need not remind you to make no mention of your eccentricities when we are with Her Majesty," my mother said, jarring me back to the present. Before I was born, she had served as a lady-in-waiting to the queen, and the two of them had been on friendly terms ever since. It was only because of this that she had been able to arrange for today's meeting. I doubted very much that Queen Victoria made a habit of taking tea for the benefit of repairing ladies' reputations.

"I am grateful to you for doing this, Mother," I said. "There's no need to worry. I shall be graciousness itself."

A servant led us into a large sitting room in the queen's private apartments, where Lady Antrim, a lady-in-waiting, greeted us.

"Catherine, dear, it is so good to see you," she said. "And you, too, Emily. You are looking well." A door opened, and the queen was wheeled into the room. As always when I saw her, I was struck that a person of such small stature could have such a commanding presence. We all curtseyed and observed the formal niceties, then sat down at a heavily laden tea table.

"You are bearing the loss of your husband quite well, Lady Ashton," the queen said, accepting from a footman a plate full of dainty sandwiches.

"Yes, Your Majesty. I manage the best I can." Should I have listened to my mother and worn a dress of a more muted color?

"The pain of a widow stays with her forever."

"Yes, ma'am."

"Your mother has not brought you here for consolation, though your husband was the best sort of man. She tells me you have fallen victim to rumors of a most insidious sort."

"I have, ma'am."

"I do not doubt your virtue. Your mother would never have raised a girl of questionable morality. Yet it is essential that you guard your reputation as if it were your greatest treasure."

"Let me assure you, ma'am, that I do. I have never behaved in a way that should have led to these stories." My mother blanched slightly as I spoke.

"You would not be here, Lady Ashton, if I had any reason to doubt that. As queen, I have been attacked by ill-natured gossips more than once. The reprehensible nature of these people knows no bounds. I hope that news of your meeting with me does something to quell these rumors."

"Thank you, ma'am. I am most obliged." I knew at once that she was referring to the scandalous stories that had circulated about her relationship with Mr. Brown, the Scottish ghillie. Some people had gone so far as to claim that they had been secretly married. My mother assured me that was nonsense, but I always had wondered what the queen's true feelings were. A woman in her position would be so very alone, surrounded by people, but no one who was her equal; who but a spouse could offer her real companionship?

Without another word to me, she directed her attention to my mother. "Now, Catherine, have you given further thought to potential brides for Eddy? I cannot tolerate him remaining unmarried for much longer."

The eldest son of the Prince of Wales, Prince Eddy, had been embroiled in any number of scandals of his own and always suffered in comparisons with his younger brother, Prince George. It came as no surprise that the queen would want to see her grandson married.

"Of all the names we have discussed, my thoughts keep returning to Princess May. She's a sensible girl, well brought up, with a strong sense of duty."

"She's fairly pretty, too," Lady Antrim said.

"What are her interests?" I asked. "I don't know her well."

"Her interests?" Lady Antrim's face was blank.

I was about to question whether the lady's interests were compatible with those of the prince but stopped myself in time. Stopped myself from speaking, that is. I couldn't keep from wondering how the poor girl would feel to be thrust upon the prince.

"As I said," my mother replied. "She's a very sensible girl. No silly romantic ideas."

"I shall invite her to Balmoral in the fall," the queen said. "Your efforts in these matters never go unappreciated, Catherine."

I don't know that I had ever before seen my mother look so pleased. But, then, I suppose that I'd never really seen her in her element. Here her skills as a matchmaker were a valuable commodity, while to me they were anathema. I was glad that she had friends who acknowledged her talent.

"Bainbridge is a decent man," the queen said. "He might do nicely for your daughter."

I sat very still, willing myself to remain silent.

"He might. Although Hargreaves has a better fortune."

"He is invaluable to the palace," the queen said.

"And so handsome!" Lady Antrim exclaimed.

"His work will force his wife to spend much time alone," the queen said.

"Unless she were to travel with him," I said.

"A romantic notion, child, but hardly appropriate. It is best for women to distance themselves from all things political. Of course, there are times when we cannot avoid these matters entirely, but it is a distasteful thing for which we are not made."

How I longed to draw attention to her hypocrisy! How could she, queen and empress, say such a thing? I was thankful for my corset, which prevented me from gasping. My mother sat, frozen, looking at me. I smiled at her.

"I don't know that I've ever had the equal of these cucumbers, Your Majesty," I said, picking up another sandwich from a silver plate. "Are they grown in your garden?"

"I haven't the slightest idea," she replied. "You are a very diplomatic girl. Perhaps you would do well with Hargreaves."

"Thank you, ma'am."

"I expect that you will make your decision soon. I will not host another tea to save you. Do not forget that we women require male protection, and it is that which you need."

Before we left, I removed a scone from the table and, careful that no one should see me, wrapped it in my handkerchief and hid it in my reticule. Meg would have her treat from the palace.

The invitations began pouring in again almost from the moment I left Windsor. My reputation was not entirely restored; mothers of impressionable young ladies still viewed me as dangerous, and the grandes dames of society were not about to suddenly decide that they *liked* me, but no one would dare exclude me from a guest list so long as I had the backing of the ruler of all Britannia. My own parent had manipulated me with the mental dexterity of a genius. I was utterly indebted to her for her assistance, yet now I had been, in effect, commanded by the queen herself to marry. Truly, my mother was brilliant.

I was eager to return to the letters in my study but felt that I owed her something in return for having come to my assistance. For the next week, I played the part of perfect society lady, flitting from the park to luncheon, to tea, back to the park, to garden party, to dinner, to the opera, to ball after ball after ball. It was exhausting, but not without its share of exhilaration. My heart quickened at the mere thought of dancing with Colin, and I relished every waltz I had with him.

On the last day of this whirlwind, I dined at Lady Elinor's, but rather than going on to a ball or party afterwards, I went home, choosing to walk because the night was a fine one. Colin escorted me, and I was reminded of a night in Paris when we had walked along the Seine, before his now dear face was so familiar to me. We cut through the park in the center of Berkeley Square and had just stepped into the street when a closed coach appeared, seemingly from nowhere, the horses running at a full gallop, careening towards us by the curb. Colin yanked me back, and I lost my balance, falling against the hard stone of the sidewalk. He bent over me to see if I was hurt.

"Go! See who it was!" I said, not wanting him to waste a moment. Of course there was no way he could catch up with the horses, but he did try admirably. I, meanwhile, pulled myself to my feet and was met by Davis, who did nothing to hide his horrified expression.

"Madam! You must sit down at once."

I have always secretly suspected Davis of having supernatural powers. The speed with which he situated me in the library, plied me with brandy, and ordered the footmen to secure the house was, without doubt, beyond that of an ordinary human. By the time Colin came in, my butler was tending to a rather nasty abrasion on my cheek. He stepped aside at once, passing the cloth he had been using to clean the cut to Colin, who knelt by my side, his face a mask of calm.

"The coach bore no markings," he said, neatly finishing the job Davis had started. "Are you hurt anywhere else?"

"I don't think so."

He took a bandage from Davis's outstretched hand. "Hold this against your cheek until the bleeding stops. I'm sorry I pulled you so hard."

"I'd rather have a scrape than to have been trampled by those horses," I said, draining the brandy, not keen to admit how shaken I really was.

Davis left us so that he could oversee the footmen, and as soon as we were alone, Colin took me in his arms, pressing my unwounded cheek against his chest. I started to cry, and the tears stung. He was silent until my breathing had slowed, but the moment it did, he started to speak, his voice all calm seriousness.

"There must be something of great significance in those letters, Emily. It is imperative that you decipher them as soon as possible, and I'm more than willing to assist you. Have you made any strides towards figuring out who stole the two from your desk?"

"No," I admitted. My eyes filled with tears again.

"Do not think me cold, but you cannot succumb to emotion right now. You are in danger, and the only way out is to discover whom it is your actions are threatening." I opened my mouth to reply, but he stopped me. "And do not tell me it is Charles Berry. Not unless you have facts, Emily."

"He has threatened me, Colin."

"I know. You're one of his favorite topics of conversation, after Versailles, of course. What he wants from you is not in the least honorable, but it does require that you are..." He cleared his throat. "Suffice it to say that running you down with a coach would be most detrimental to his hopes."

"But I have rejected him."

"He's convinced that he'll be able to bend you to his will once he is king. He has an amazing capacity for self-delusion."

"And he tells you these things despite knowing of your attachment to me?"

"I make a point of not bringing my own emotions into play when I am working."

"So you let him believe that you are not in love with me?"

"I let him believe what he wants."

"I don't much like this," I said.

"Forgive me, but I'm not about to lay bare my own feelings to such a man."

"But everyone knows—" I stopped.

"What everyone in polite society accepts as a given truth often does not entirely correlate with the information circulating amongst gentlemen."

"That's dreadful."

"No more so than ladies taking no offense to being cut when they see a gentleman out with his mistress."

"Another reprehensible habit. If I saw Robert with his mistress, I would never stand aside and pretend that I didn't know him."

"Robert Brandon has a mistress?"

"Doesn't he?" I asked, all innocence.

"Don't try to fish for information, Emily." He poured himself a glass of whiskey. "Where are the letters?" I removed them from the safe, where I had kept them since the theft, and spread them out on my desk.

"I feel as if I'm missing something obvious when I look at them," I said.

"That, my dear, is code breaking. Do you want me to stay and help?"

"No, I'll be all right. I know I can do this."

"Then I'd like to speak to your servants, if you've no objection. Someone must know who came into the library when the letters were taken. They may be more willing to talk to me than to you or Davis."

I let him, of course, pleased that I was to have the more interesting task. Once he had left the room, I picked up the first pair of letters, beginning by looking for words that were repeated in both of them. Nothing. I wrote down the first letter of each word and was left with nonsense. Hardly surprising; that would be too obvious. The second pair of letters offered up nothing, either. The only thing that struck me as notable about any of them was that neither writer ever seemed to refer back to the previous letter he had received. This spurred me on, because one would not expect to find such a thing in an ordinary correspondence.

Colin returned more than an hour later. "You certainly do have devoted servants."

"Of course I do," I said, smiling.

"But a few raise my suspicions. You've an under gardener who's in rather a lot of debt, and a maid who's more sympathetic to Charles Berry than she ought to be."

"Molly!"

"You told me the circumstances under which you hired her, yet she still is in contact with the man."

"How is that possible?"

"It could be nothing more than coincidence, but she told me that she has run into him on more than one occasion since coming to your house."

"Do you think she is spying for him?"

"I don't know, but I would keep a close eye on her."

"And the under gardener?"

"He's a good sort, but inclined to gamble."

"How great are his debts?"

"Enough to tempt him to try to earn some extra."

"But he doesn't have the access to the house that Molly does."

"Quite right. There's another maid, Lizzie, who's new to the household. Have you had any trouble with her?"

"She's not the most efficient girl, but I wouldn't say that she's been a problem. Does she strike you as suspicious?"

"Not particularly, but I think it wise to look closely at anyone who has so recently joined your service." He stood behind my chair. "Any luck with the letters?"

"I'm getting there."

"I'm not surprised." I looked up at him. With his finger, he traced around the cut on my cheek. "I will not let him hurt you again, Emily, whoever he is."

How easy it would have been to throw myself against him at that moment, to beg him to decipher the code, find the thief, protect me from this danger. I resisted, however, and as I did, I realized that it was not so much to satisfy myself as to keep from being diminished in his opinion. He might offer protection, but I knew that he no more wanted a helpless mate than I wanted to be one.

22

I T'S NOT WORKING, EMILY." IVY HANDED THE BOOKS I'D GIVEN HER back to me. "I've tried four nights in a row, and Robert told me to ask the doctor for something to help me sleep."

"He didn't stay with you?"

"He sat on the edge of the bed until I managed to fall asleep."

"Oh dear."

"I don't know what to do."

"What exactly did you say to him?"

"I did just what you said. I left my door open and called to him when he came in. He was concerned to find me still awake, and I explained that although I was dreadfully tired, I couldn't sleep."

"I think he took you at your word. You couldn't very well expect that he would...that...well...he thought you needed rest. Next time look at him wistfully while you speak, make it clear that you've no intention of sleeping but that you want his...company."

"Be serious, Emily."

"I'm quite serious. Colin gave me this for you." I put *The Woman in White* on the table next to her. "It comes highly recommended."

"I don't know how much longer I can keep this up. I'm exhausted."

"I'm sure Robert is just trying to be considerate."

"He's got to know that being considerate is never going to produce an heir."

"Ivy, I'm shocked!"

"Well you shouldn't be. You were married."

"Not shocked like that. Shocked to hear you speak in such a way." I wanted to ask her if she suspected her husband had a mistress, but did not want to give her something else to worry about. "You two always seem perfectly happy when I see you at parties."

"He's all attention when he needs to be."

"Do you want to help me with my investigation?" I asked, hoping to distract her.

"How?"

I showed her the letters and explained the general principles of steganography. For the next hour, we pored over them but found nothing.

"I have an idea, Emily," Ivy said. "It's probably silly—"

"No, tell me."

"Have you stepped away from them? Looked from a distance? I'm thinking of how the paintings of the impressionists look so different close up. You almost can't make sense of them. Of course, you can't exactly read letters from afar, but—"

"Ivy, that's inspired," I said. Taking a step back from my desk enabled me to see more than a single letter at a time, and if it were possible to be enlightened instantaneously, I was at that moment.

Ivy spoke before I could. "It was stupid. There's nothing to see."

"No! Ivy, don't you see it? Of course not. You haven't read the letters a thousand times like I have. But look—look at the numbers."

"Numbers?"

"There is a number written out in every single one of them. *Il y a dix ans que j'ai lui parlé.* Ten. *J'ai quatre livres.* Four."

"Yes, yes, I see."

I reached for a blank piece of paper. "This must be the key." For the rest of the afternoon, we played with the numbers, but still the formula eluded us. Nonetheless, I knew we were on the right track. Eventually, we would hit on a permutation that produced something other than a random string of letters.

"Have you figured out who gave these to you?" Ivy asked.

"I'm assuming the Marie Antoinette thief. I can't imagine who else it could be."

"And you've no idea who he is?"

"No. Unfortunately not." I told her my ideas for drawing him out of hiding.

"It sounds as if he's not the sort of man whom you can goad into revealing himself," she said. "But what if you baited him?"

"Ivy, I'm impressed. Tell me more."

"What if you had something that belonged to the French queen?"

"I don't know how he could possibly break into my house again. It's too well guarded."

"Mine is not. And my husband is rarely home. You could come stay with me to keep me company."

"Robert wouldn't let me into the house with an object certain to lure a thief to his door," I said.

"I suppose you're right."

I knew better than to suggest that we not inform Robert of the scheme. "What if I were to make a production out of it? Let's say I had a necklace of Marie Antoinette's and told everyone that I was not afraid to wear it. He could take it directly from me at a ball. Your ball."

"That sounds more dangerous than luring him into my house. I don't like the idea of your wearing the piece when he comes after it."

"It might work, though, and I don't think he would harm me. How could he in a crowded ballroom?"

"It would be a departure from his normal modus operandi. He always breaks into houses. And at any rate, you don't own anything with a provenance that would attract him."

"No, but I could buy something that does. Or pretend to have bought such a thing. Cécile mentioned that the stones from the notorious diamond-necklace affair still exist. I could find out who owns them."

"And persuade the owner to part with them?"

"I think most people view owning Marie Antoinette objects as a liability at the moment."

"Only people in London. There's no reason to think the diamonds are here."

"You may be right. I could have a copy made, though, and ask the owner of the true necklace to act as if she sold it to me."

"What would you say to this man if you met him?"

"I'm not sure. I'd like to know why he's so fixated on Marie Antoinette."

"Are you absolutely certain that none of the objects he's stolen have come up for sale on the black market?"

"It's difficult to determine these things, but so far as I can tell, yes. He's keeping what he steals."

"Or giving it all to Charles Berry," Ivy said. "Who other than the heir to the House of Bourbon would have such a focused interest?"

"An excellent point, and we mustn't forget the list I found in his room at the Savoy," I said. "I'd like to know more about the evidence Mr. Berry uses to support his claim. He's certainly not the first man who declared himself the direct descendant of Louis XVI and Marie Antoinette. Apparently, early in the century, there were no fewer than forty pretenders vying for the prince's rights."

"Do you believe the dauphin did escape?"

"There are plenty of anecdotes that say he did. Supposedly, one of the women charged with caring for the boy early in his imprisonment grew quite fond of him. He had stayed in her house for a time before his captors moved him to prison. It's said that she smuggled him out of his cell in a basket."

"But a child did die in the jail," Ivy said.

"Yes, but he may well have been a substitute for the dauphin. The doctor, a man called Desault, who treated him after the boy fell ill, died himself under mysterious circumstances soon after coming to the prison. He had assisted him some months earlier and would undoubtedly have recognized the child. Louis Charles's death was announced only a week later."

"Mr. Berry has the support of the Bourbon family. Surely they must be thoroughly satisfied with his story."

"Yes, but think on it, Ivy. The entire Bourbon family stands to see their situation improve should the monarchy be restored in France. Perhaps persuading them to accept Berry wasn't so difficult."

"I'd be more inclined to agree with you if Charles Berry were the sort of man likely to inspire the people of France to embrace a monarch. You'll never convince me that the Bourbons were thrilled to find the heir of the lost dauphin to be such a...well..." She did not finish.

"Regardless, I am convinced there is much we do not know about Mr. Berry. We must not make the mistake of underestimating him, Ivy. He stands to make enormous gains in the immediate future, and with such aspirations comes the risk of failure."

"But does it matter if he never becomes king? He's making an excellent marriage and has the goodwill of society behind him. I don't see that he has anything to lose."

I sighed. "I admit the soundness of your logic but take no pleasure in doing so. Colin's right. I'm too bent on finding Mr. Berry guilty of something."

"He's guilty of being an arrogant, mannerless bore. Isn't that enough?"

"Perhaps it shall have to be."

I'm absolutely delighted that your social troubles seem to be dissipating," Lady Elinor said as we strolled through Hyde Park. "But I must confess that my interest in the matter is somewhat self-serving."

"How so?" I asked.

"Isabelle is very anxious about her wedding, and I think you could ease her mind on the subject. Forgive me, but I worried about letting her spend too much time with you when..." She closed her eyes and sighed. "I never believed the rumors, but you know how awful people can be about such things, and Isabelle's reputation must remain spotless."

"Don't apologize. You were one of the few people who didn't cut me. And though I may be back on guest lists, don't think that in private people aren't still talking about me."

"It's so dreadful, but people's memories are short. In another month they'll have moved on to something else altogether."

"I've been hearing lots of talk about Mr. Berry," I said. "From what I gather, it sounds as if there is a chance that the monarchy will be restored in France."

"Oh, Emily, if only that were true, but I'm afraid that it's too much to hope for."

"When is the wedding to be?"

"Everything will be ready before the end of the month."

"So soon?"

She tilted her head to me and spoke softly. "If these political events to which you refer do take place, I should very much like the marriage finalized before then. Isabelle is not from a royal family, after all."

Lady Elinor was wise in this regard. I had no doubt that Mr. Berry, if he were to become king before the wedding, would throw Isabelle over for a royal bride with a more impressive fortune. To my mind, however, this would be good news for Isabelle. I liked the girl, and hated the thought of her married to such an undesirable man.

"What does Isabelle think of marrying so quickly?"

"She's a good girl, although it's clear that she's terrified. I know this is best for her, but I hate to see her unsettled. Would you be willing to talk to her? I've tried, of course, but sometimes such things are easier to believe coming from a friend than from one's own mother. I'd be so grateful. I don't want to see her consumed with worry."

"Isabelle is fortunate. Most mothers are not so concerned." I remembered the conversation I'd had with my own mother prior to my wedding; it was hardly encouraging. The primary thrust of it had to do with learning to bear the inconveniences required by marriage. *Inconveniences.* "Have her come see me tomorrow. I'll do what I can to allay her fears."

All of a sudden, a gentleman bumped into me, nearly knocking me off my feet. He grabbed my hand to steady me, mumbled a quick apology, and disappeared before I could say a word to him.

"How rude!" Lady Elinor exclaimed. "The park is simply too crowded these days, and so many gentlemen do not have the manners they ought to. I think—"

"Lady Elinor, will you excuse me? I must go home." The man had pressed into my hand a folded piece of paper that opened to reveal a passage written in Greek followed by a single sentence in English: *Am I to get no thanks for my gift?*

At last my admirer had shown his face! If only I'd had the presence of mind to get a good look at him. I had a vague idea that his eyes were blue, but was not certain even of that.

"Are you unwell?"

"Just a bit off balance. Forgive me. Send Isabelle to me tomorrow." I rushed off in the direction the man had taken, not giving her a chance to reply.

The paths in Hyde Park were crammed with the best of society, and it was difficult in the extreme to maneuver along them with any sort of speed. My friend had a decent head start and the advantage of anonymity; I had little chance of finding him. I did try, though, not giving up until I reached the Achilles statue. Ready to admit defeat, I looked around for an empty bench, but there was none in sight. I stood for a moment, wondering if he was watching me, hidden somewhere in the vicinity. How could I know?

Then something caught my eye. Not my admirer but a familiar face: Robert Brandon, walking arm in arm with a lady I recognized from Lady Elinor's ball. They leaned close together as they spoke, laughing at something, their heads nearly touching. I was stunned. Surely Robert would not be so indiscreet as to appear with a mistress in Hyde Park. I managed to make my feet move and started after them. I would not remain a silent party to this.

"Good afternoon, Robert," I called as I approached them.

"Oh, Emily. Delighted to see you." His expression did not match his words.

I smiled at his companion. "How lovely to see you, Mrs. Reynold-Plympton."

"Likewise, Lady Ashton," she replied, scrutinizing every detail of my dress as she spoke.

"Where is Ivy this afternoon, Robert?"

"With the Duchess of Petherwick, I believe."

"Of course." I managed another smile but suspected that he could see me seething behind it. "Are you a friend of Mrs. Brandon's?" I asked his companion.

"I'm not much acquainted with her," the lady replied. This came as no surprise.

"How unfortunate. So nice to see you both. I'll leave you to your walk." I did my best not to spit out the words but cannot vouch for my success. As they walked away from me, I looked at the paper that was still in my hand:

'Οφθαλμοί, τέο μέχρις ἀφύσσετε νέκταρ
'Ερώτων κάλλεος ἀκρήτου ξωροπόται θρασέες;

Although the message was short, the Greek was beyond my sight-reading abilities, so I went home, where, with the aid of my lexicon, I was able to translate the passage: *Eyes, how long are you draining the nectar of the Loves, rash drinkers of the strong unmixed wine of beauty?*

23

I was not sure what to do next. The matter of deciphering the letters was certainly urgent. Finding my admirer was something that might provide answers beyond those that I sought for personal reasons. And then there was the question of what Robert was doing with Mrs. Reynold-Plympton. All this was in addition to the problem of solving the murders in Richmond.

Saving Jane Stilleman from a guilty verdict deserved primary importance, and it could be argued that the letters and my admirer tied in to this. But can I be faulted for wanting to help Ivy first? I penned a note to the one person in London who would be able to provide the most possible information about Robert's friend; I only hoped it would not take long for her to reply.

Next, I wrote a notice for the *Times*:

> *What an exhilarating encounter. I'd prefer that next time you stay long enough for a chat. Many, many thanks for the letters.*

I debated asking to set up a meeting but rejected the idea. I'd do better trying to catch him following me. If only there were some simple way to draw him to me. I would think on this later. For the moment, I needed to apply myself to unlocking the secrets of Marie Antoinette's correspondence with Léonard, but no sooner had I set out the letters than I was interrupted.

"Hard at work?" Colin asked once Davis had closed the door after announcing my visitor.

"Always," I replied as he kissed my hand.

"I've checked up on Berry and am convinced that he had nothing to do with the wayward coach."

"Why is that?"

"Because he went straight from Lady Elinor's to a...er...club of sorts with Bertie."

"You believe him?"

"I believe the Prince of Wales."

"Mr. Berry needn't have been inside the coach himself, you know. He might have hired someone to drive it."

"A valid point, but I don't see how he could have alerted the driver to our departure from the party. The prince collected him at the Routledge house, and they left together more than an hour after we did."

"And was Mr. Berry never out of sight during that hour?"

"Lady Elinor's watching Isabelle like a hawk—didn't let her out of sight the entire evening. She's a chaperone nearly as ferocious as your own mother."

"You've never had to tolerate my mother as a chaperone."

"Ashton told me all about it."

"Oh." A feeling of vague discomfort swept over me, but I forced myself to ignore it. "He could have arranged it ahead of time."

"He might have, but I'm certain that the coach was not following us."

"It could have been on a street out of sight, waiting to see us leave

Lady Elinor's. As soon as we'd passed, it rushed to Berkeley Square ahead of us and was there, ready, when we arrived."

"I shan't discount the possibility," he said. I handed him one of the letters I'd been working on. "Will you help me? I'm close to cracking it."

"I think you're headed in the right direction," he said after I'd told him my theory about the number words being the key. I kept track of each system I'd tried, and the list was growing hideously long.

"Paragraphs—that's what I've ignored," I said, my head bent over the letter before me. "Of course. It's not simply the third letter of each word. The code doesn't begin until the third paragraph." I quickly copied the letters; more nonsense. I threw down my pencil and picked up another note.

"It's incredibly frustrating, isn't it? I've a colleague who refuses to spend more than thirty minutes on any single code. Insists that if he can't break it in that time, he'll never be able to."

"Thirty minutes?"

"Well, he's quite good. There's not much he can't crack that quickly."

"Where is he now?"

"Vienna."

"How unfortunate."

"Have you tried applying the numbers to the next note in the series?"

"Yes, no luck."

"What about the dates?" he asked. "They're the only other place that numbers appear."

"Combine them with the others, you mean?" I asked.

"Yes," he said. I stared at the document in front of me.

"Yes, I think that's it. Look, the number in this one is *vingt*, and the date is the *vingt-trois juillet*. Subtract twenty from that and you're left with three." I scribbled down the pertinent letters. The result appeared to be another random string, so I decided to skip to the third sentence, and when that failed, to try every third letter of every third word. This last attempt didn't result in enough letters, but I was convinced that I needed to look at every third word. Maybe every other letter of every third word?

And this, at last, provided something other than nonsense, which I read aloud to Colin, translating from the French:

Safe house found. B will travel with LC.

"Louis Charles. The dauphin. My dear girl!" He pulled me out of my seat, put his hands around my waist, picked me up, and spun me in a circle.

Truly, it was exhilarating. But we could not afford to bask in the moment and immediately applied the system to the next letter:

S sympathetic. May help with escape. Travel unlikely before fall at earliest. LC in good health, asking after MT.

"You've no need of my help," Colin said, his eyes shining. "Brilliant work, Emily."

"MT" was undoubtedly Marie-Thérèse, the dauphin's sister, but I had no clue who "B" or "S" might be. Perhaps Mr. Wainwright at the British Library would have an idea. Both of the letters I had decoded were from Léonard. Now I turned my attention to one written by the queen.

Longing for mon chou d'amour. I trust B but worry about this S. Promise they will send him where we discussed.

I could hardly wait to read the rest. But I would have to learn patience, for no sooner was I poised to delve into the next note than my mother arrived.

"Mr. Hargreaves! What a pleasant surprise."

"Delighted to see you, Lady Bromley," he said, leaping to his feet and kissing her hand. "You look well. Are you one of those ladies immune to aging?"

This was too much, but I resisted the urge to glare at him. "You are too kind, sir," she said, an expression of smug satisfaction on her face, and sat down. "I must say, I had no idea how much Her Majesty depends upon you. When Emily and I were having tea at Windsor..."

Clearly, this was a dialogue that could go on without me, so I kept at my work, paying only the slightest attention to what they were saying. Colin played my mother flawlessly, in turn flattering her and asking for advice about mundane household matters. He needn't have wasted his time; there was no question but that she would support a marriage between us. Nonetheless, it was amusing to watch him play the part of aspiring son-in-law.

"What are you working on over there, Emily?" she asked, ready to draw me into the conversation.

"Oh, nothing of significance," I said. "Just my Greek, as usual."

"She's a very smart girl, you know." Her voice was a melodramatic whisper.

"Only one of her many charms," Colin replied, and I decided I'd had enough of this nonsense. I walked over to them and sat next to my mother on the settee.

"Did you receive my note?"

"I did and thought discussing it with you in person would be preferable to writing an answer. I don't entirely trust your servants. Discretion is my utmost concern." This last sentence was directed to Colin.

"Quite as it should be, Lady Bromley. Shall I leave you alone with your daughter?"

"It might be best, sir."

"Very good," he said. "May I call on you again tomorrow, Lady Ashton?" His eyes danced with laughter.

"Of course," I replied.

"He is all politeness!" My mother exclaimed as soon as he had left the room. "You'd be hard-pressed to find a man who could better him, although I do wish he were a peer."

"He's rich enough to make up for that," I said. She could not have missed my wry tone but did nothing to acknowledge it.

"His family has been prominent in England since the time of William the Conqueror, and rumor has it that no fewer than two of his ancestors refused offers to become peers. A bit strange, but wealthy men are often eccentric. And as fond as the queen is of him, I shouldn't be surprised at all if she bestowed a title on him."

"I wonder if he would accept it."

"Of course he would! How could you think otherwise?"

"He might follow the lead of his ancestors."

"Hmpf. And tell me, have you seen much of Bainbridge?"

"He's been a bit scarce lately."

"Make sure you encourage him, Emily. There's no need to cast him aside unless you've a settled arrangement with someone else."

I decided to change the subject. "Have you information about Mrs. Reynold-Plympton for me?"

"Your note was most interesting, Emily. Are you at last taking an interest in society?"

"Just Mrs. Reynold-Plympton."

"Her husband is a retired ambassador. They spent years in the farthest reaches of the empire, and she's always been rather...untamed."

"She's much younger than her husband, isn't she?"

"He's at least thirty years her senior. They've eight children; the oldest stands to inherit a most significant fortune. If she is a friend of Mr. Hargreaves, I shouldn't let it trouble you much. She's perfectly discreet. Still, I should insist that he break it off before the wedding."

"Why would you think she's his mistress?"

"Mrs. Reynold-Plympton has been linked with more than one bachelor since her return to England seven years ago. Her husband's health has been in decline for some time. He must be seventy-five years old if he's a day, and it is Mrs. Hamilton—do you know her?— who takes particular care of him. They were attached to each other in their youth, but his parents wouldn't let him marry her. No money in her family."

"So now he forsakes his wife for her?"

"Don't play naïve, Emily. It's most unbecoming. People find a way to cope with arranged marriages. It's a necessity of life."

"Sounds more like sanctioned hypocrisy to me."

"It's very bad of Mr. Hargreaves to have let you find out about this. Perhaps you should take Bainbridge instead. He is discretion itself."

"Colin is not involved with Mrs. Reynold-Plympton. I'm only interested in her because I saw her in the park with another gentleman."

"Really? Who was it?"

"I'd rather not say."

"Don't be tedious."

"I'm not about to start spreading unfounded gossip."

"Fine. I've no interest in playing silly little games with you." She stood. "I do hope you're prepared to make a quick decision about your wedding. The queen will expect to hear news about it before the end of the Season."

"Perhaps I shall have to flee to Greece before then."

"Don't even consider it." She departed without another word. I returned to my desk after watching her carriage pull away and had just picked up my pencil when the window at the front of the room shattered as something flew through it, the missile landing on the side table next to Colin's favorite chair. Tied onto the brick was a note with a simple message:

A little knowledge can be a dangerous thing. Stop now.

24

EVEN BEFORE I COULD RING FOR DAVIS, THE POLICE WATCHING my house mobilized and set off after the person who had thrown the brick. Although none of them had actually seen the act, an instant before he heard the crash of breaking glass, one alert officer had noticed a man run off at top speed, and his cries immediately caught the attention of the plainclothes policeman in the square.

Davis and three footmen appeared in the library almost at once, clearly relieved to find me unhurt. It was lucky that I had not been sitting on the window seat, as was often my habit. The abrasion on my cheek from when the coach tried to run me down had healed, but the anxiety caused by knowing that I'd been targeted for harm had not faded with my wound. This latest incident only increased my feeling of unease.

Unfortunately, the miscreant eluded his pursuers, and the police were baffled as to his identity. There was very little more they could do. Inspector Manning was called to the scene, and he, along with Colin, whom Davis had sent for, examined the note. Not unexpectedly, it bore no identifying features. The only thing we were able to determine was that the handwriting was significantly different from that on the missives I had received from my admirer. Hardly surprising. I wouldn't have expected him to start flinging objects through my windows. It wasn't his style.

"We're taking every precaution we can to ensure your safety, Lady Ashton," Inspector Manning said. "But I would suggest that you perhaps consider heeding the message. There's no point in exposing yourself to further danger."

"The only way for the danger to be averted is to solve the crime, Inspector," Colin said. "And I've come to see that Lady Ashton's contributions in such matters are inestimable. I suspect the culprit knows it, too, or he wouldn't feel so threatened by her."

"So you think this has something to do with the murders in Richmond?" the inspector asked.

"I'm certain of it," I replied.

"I'm not," Colin said. "It may be that the letters you're deciphering are completely unrelated but dangerous in their own right."

"The police are confident in the case against the maid," Inspector Manning said.

"That does not mean they're right," I said.

Perhaps the most baffling thing to me at that moment was the connection between the murders and the thefts. If Beatrice were culpable, then why would the news reports of the pink diamond have correlated with her husband's death? Could learning about the stone have made her want to kill the man she claimed to love?

I looked to Ivy's masquerade ball to provide a much-needed respite in the midst of all this excitement. When at last the night of the party arrived, it seemed as if all of London had descended upon Belgrave Square. The line of carriages crowding the street paralyzed traffic for blocks, and an atmosphere of gaiety permeated the entire neighborhood. Ivy, always the most considerate of hostesses, had some of her footmen bring cider and cakes around to all the coachmen while they waited. I had arrived early to help my friend with any last-minute catastrophes but found I had nothing to do. Ivy was far too organized to allow for emergencies.

She had decided not to impose upon her guests a theme, and the result of this was a house filled with costumes of every sort. I counted at least two queens of Sheba, three Cleopatras, and, not surprising given the current goings-on in town, no fewer than eight Marie Antoinettes. Lord Fortescue had come as Cardinal Richelieu. I was dressed as Helen of Troy, in a long tunic made by Mr. Worth from the finest white silk, artfully held together at the shoulders by gold brooches. Meg had spent nearly an hour arranging my hair in a complicated series of upswept braids and curls to a stunning result. My ensemble was completed with dainty golden sandals.

I had planned my costume before deciding that I would wear something of Marie Antoinette's to the ball, and by the time I had arranged to do so, it was too late to order something different. So my Helen wore an anachronistic choker fashioned of diamonds that came from the infamous diamond-necklace affair. They weren't the actual stones; I was unable to persuade the current owner to part with them. She did, however, agree to pretend that she had sold them to me, and lent me the paste copy that she'd had made years ago for times when she wanted the look of the necklace without having to worry about losing it.

"I don't think I've ever seen you look more lovely," Ivy said, coming to me as soon as the bulk of her guests had arrived.

"I do well so long as I stand away from you," I said, smiling. She was resplendent as Britannia. Her flushed cheeks and sparkling eyes commanded the attention of any gentleman in her immediate vicinity. "No one stands a chance next to you."

"You underestimate yourself," she said. "Have you seen Colin yet?"

"No. Has he arrived?"

"Yes. He's dressed as an Elizabethan courtier and looks devastatingly handsome."

Robert, appearing as the emperor Charles V, came up next to his wife. "Who is devastatingly handsome?"

"You of course, darling," she replied with the sweetest sort of smile. He kissed her lightly on the cheek, and, I'm happy to report, didn't seem distracted in the least. Nonetheless, I couldn't help but wonder if Mrs. Reynold-Plympton was on the guest list.

In the ballroom the dancing had started. Isabelle, as a shepherdess, wore the most sweetly innocent costume in the house. She was positively beaming at the gentleman who guided her across the floor. It was Lord Pembroke. My heart felt heavy for the girl, and I hoped her mother would not notice her choice of partner.

Charles Berry, proving once and for all his complete lack of imagination, appeared as Louis XIV and was hanging lecherously on a very young and very pretty girl whom I did not recognize. I couldn't find Colin but had promised the next dance to Jeremy, who was decked out as a Roman soldier, complete with bronze armor. Although he did not dance so gracefully as Colin, he was a good partner, and we spent a pleasant time together on the floor.

"Will it scandalize everyone if you stand up with me again?" he asked when the music stopped.

"I don't think so," I said. "Three in a row might raise eyebrows, but two surely wouldn't." We accepted champagne from an obliging footman and drank it, catching our breath as we waited for the next dance to begin. When the music started, he led me back to the floor, but almost immediately a gentleman wearing the robes of a Bedouin warrior interrupted us.

"If you'd be so kind, Your Grace, may I steal your partner?"

Jeremy laughed. "I knew I couldn't keep her for two full dances." He bowed and left me with this stranger.

"Are you a friend of the duke?" I asked as he placed his hand on my waist, and we started to dance.

"You could say that," he replied.

"I'm a bit embarrassed to admit that I don't recognize you."

"I didn't think you would, though I must confess to finding that slightly disappointing."

"What is your name?"

"Sebastian Capet." I racked my brain but could think of no acquaintance called Sebastian. My partner laughed, seeing my confusion. "You've no idea who I am, have you?" he asked.

"Not the slightest." I could see nothing of his face except for a pair of bright blue eyes rimmed with thick, dark lashes.

"Perhaps this will refresh your memory." He pulled me closer to him and spoke in a quiet but intense voice, reciting something in ancient Greek.

"I hoped you would come tonight," I said, a pleasant thrill tingling all the way to my toes.

"You were very foolish to announce to anyone who would listen that you'd be wearing diamonds from the queen's necklace. Although, you know, it never precisely belonged to her. She insisted that she'd never ordered it."

"I did worry about that, but obviously the technicality didn't keep you away. Does it mean, though, that you won't steal them from me?"

"That, my darling Kallista, remains to be seen. Are you enjoying Léonard's letters?"

"Very much. From whom did you take them?"

"Why do you assume they're stolen?"

"Really, Mr. Capet, isn't the answer obvious?"

"I admit that my actions are not always precisely legal, but laws do not always lead to justice."

"And what is the justice you seek?"

"I won't be tricked into revealing myself so easily."

"You can't fault me for trying."

"I should never fault you for anything. You're terminally charming. I lost my heart the moment I saw you asleep in your bed."

"I can't say that I particularly like having a gentleman watch me sleeping."

"Then I won't do it again."

"And I want Cécile's earrings back."

He stopped dancing. "Would you come outside with me?" This was no time to hesitate. He could vanish as quickly as he'd appeared. I followed him into the garden, which was filled with couples who had come outside for air and the privacy they could not find in a ballroom. Japanese lanterns hung from every tree, casting a romantic sort of dancing light over the scene. He took my hand rather than my arm, and I did nothing to protest. It was rather exciting to be escorted by such a skilled thief through a society ball. He paused to take two glasses of champagne off a footman's tray, then sat on a bench in a quiet corner.

"Did you kill David Francis?" I asked.

He laughed. "I'm the last person on earth who would have done that."

"I didn't really suspect you. If you were the murderer, you wouldn't have left the snuffbox at the scene."

"No, I certainly would not."

"Although given the cause of death, there's no reason to think the murderer was there when Mr. Francis died."

"I suppose."

"Why didn't you take the snuffbox when you stole the diamond?"

"I didn't know Francis had it."

"So you went back after you read about it in the papers?"

"No, darling, I didn't. Someone else took it."

"Who?"

"Now, don't you think if I knew that, I would get it for myself?"

"How would you go about finding it?"

"I'm not about to reveal professional secrets," he said.

"What do you do with everything you steal? It doesn't appear that you're selling it."

"Investigating me, are you? No, I don't sell what I take."

"Do you give it to anyone?"

"No."

"Do you work with anyone?"

"Do you really think I would tell you? Oh, darling, I would love to confide in you, but I'm afraid you've not yet earned my trust."

A strange, heavy feeling crept up on me, and I found that I could hardly keep my eyes open. "How do I earn your trust?" It took a considerable effort to hold up my head.

"Forgive me, darling," he said. He caught me as I started to slump over, and though my memory of the rest is, at best, hazy, I could swear that he kissed me before laying me on the bench.

I need hardly say that he took the necklace. When I awoke, I was upstairs in a bedroom, Ivy, Robert, Colin, Jeremy, and Margaret hovering around me. I felt like lead and knew at once it would be pointless to try to sit. "What happened?"

"You fainted," Ivy said. "Margaret and Jeremy found you in the garden. They were unable to rouse you so thought it best to bring you inside."

"How did I get here?"

"Bainbridge carried you," Colin said.

"Oh dear," I said. "The gossips must have found that a ripe scene."

"Don't worry about that now," Ivy said.

"I didn't faint. You know that I don't faint. My champagne was drugged." I told them about my conversation with Sebastian.

"Good gad, Emily," Jeremy said. "I should never have turned you over to him. I thought you knew him."

"And I thought you did. It's all right, Jeremy. You're not to blame."

"Shall I send for a doctor?" Robert asked.

"I think so," Jeremy said. "We've no idea what he gave her."

"I'm feeling much better," I said.

"I'm getting a doctor." Robert left the room.

"We found this next to you," Margaret said, handing me a book.

"My *Odyssey*!" A note fell from the pages as I flipped through the book. "He's left me a message: 'You are not being careful enough, Kallista darling. It was too easy for me to take this from you, and too easy to get you to follow me tonight. Think what someone with a more nefarious purpose could do to you.'"

"Emily, I don't think you should continue to pursue this man," Ivy said. "He's a thief and now reveals himself as dangerous."

"Quite the contrary. He reveals himself to be concerned with my well-being. I do wish he'd given back my notebook, too."

"He drugged you," Ivy said. "How can you not see the seriousness of this?"

"I baited him to take the necklace. I should have known better than to drink with him."

"If he didn't get you with the champagne, I'm sure he would have figured out another way. Going into the garden with such a man was not, perhaps, the best decision," Colin said, his eyes darker than usual.

"Easy to say now," I said. "But I didn't think he would divulge any useful information on the dance floor."

"It doesn't sound like he divulged anything useful in the garden, either," Colin said.

I raised myself up on my elbows. "Well, I had to try. And he did reveal one interesting tidbit: His name is Sebastian Capet. Does it seem familiar to any of you?"

"No," Margaret said, but none of the rest replied.

"It was the name given to the French royal family during the revolution. Stripped of his title, the king became Louis Capet."

"Surely you don't suspect—" Ivy began.

"The dauphin would have changed his name," Margaret said.

I shrugged. "Maybe. But it's entirely possible that, later, his heirs adopted it."

25

WHATEVER SUBSTANCE SEBASTIAN SLIPPED INTO MY CHAMPAGNE had been innocuous enough, and we were all relieved when Robert's physician confirmed that there was no cause for alarm. Aside from sleeping extraordinarily late, I felt no ill effects the next day. Lady Elinor sent Isabelle to me in the afternoon, and I did my best to calm the girl's myriad worries about becoming the wife of Charles Berry. Not an easy task. It was obvious that her loyalty was fiercely divided. She wanted to please her mother, but she still loved Lord Pembroke, and the feeling had only intensified at Ivy's ball.

"He's simply the most exquisite dancer," she said. "He wouldn't stand up with me more than twice, but, oh, Emily, I would gladly have given anything to dance with him all night."

"Are you finding Mr. Berry an agreeable companion?"

"He's tolerable. I understand why Mother thinks he's a good catch, and I know that she's always done what's best for me. Do you believe she could be right? Am I too swept up in romance to be practical? Will I be happier with Mr. Berry?"

"Only you know the answer to that, Isabelle. Your mother's intentions are good. There is no doubt of that. But you alone can determine what sort of a marriage you are willing to accept."

"Mother insists that young people often fall in love before they really know what will make them happy."

"That's probably true." I thought about the time, during our first season, that Ivy had come close to being convinced she was in love with a particularly dashing army officer. He turned out to be the worst sort of cad, something her mother had suspected from the beginning. "I don't deny that mothers are sometimes useful for vetting one's admirers. But she never objected to Lord Pembroke, did she?"

"No, but she's certain that I'll be happier in the long run with Mr. Berry. Charles. I should call him Charles." She frowned. "Is it very awful, being married? One hears such dreadful stories."

"No, Isabelle, it's not dreadful in the least. Many people are quite content, even in arranged marriages. I was not in love with Philip when I married him, but the experience was far from unpleasant."

"Perhaps there's hope for me, then."

Had I any courage, I would have convinced the girl to throw over Mr. Berry and run away with Lord Pembroke. I'm ashamed that I didn't. How could I sit here and offer her comfort when I knew her future husband to be an utterly vile man? "I believe Mr. Berry's most-admired quality is his proximity to the French throne. Rumors suggest that he may be made king soon. Does that change his estimation in your eyes?"

"Do I want to be queen? I ought to say yes, but, honestly, the prospect terrifies me."

"An answer that shows more than a modicum of wisdom."

"Well, it didn't work out well for Marie Antoinette, did it?"

We talked for nearly three quarters of an hour, and I will say that, although it was abundantly clear that her heart was still very much with Lord Pembroke, she seemed less nervous about her betrothal by the time she left. I wish I could say the same for myself. If anything, I was more convinced than ever that someone needed to find a way to help her escape.

I sorted through the mail that had come that morning, half expecting to see something from Sebastian, but he had sent nothing. I did have a letter from Cécile, and knew when I read it that I would have to show it to Colin immediately. There was no need for me to go to him, though, for even before I had returned the paper to its envelope, he walked through my door, his eyes sharp, his features marked with a severity I had not before seen on him.

"Have you anything from Cécile?" he asked, not bothering to greet me.

"Yes, I do, I was about to come—"

He took the letter from my outstretched hand. "Good. I'm glad to have a date. We never suspected they planned to act this quickly."

"What will you do?"

"Berry told me not an hour ago that he's arranged for passage to France. He's using falsified papers so that no one will know he's there."

"Can't you stop him?"

"I'm to go with him."

"When do you leave?"

"Tomorrow afternoon."

"I see." I studied his handsome face. "Is there any chance the plot will work? Will the republic fall?"

"Not if I've anything to do with it."

"And Cécile?"

"Her role may be more important than mine, but it's you that I'm worried about. I don't like to leave you in the midst of your own intrigue."

"I'll be perfectly all right."

"No more drinking drugged champagne? Next time it could be laced with something less benign."

"Well, I've won our bet, so you can rest easy knowing that I have every intention of staying alive to collect my prize."

"What do you mean, you've won our bet? You most certainly have not."

"I've identified my admirer: Sebastian Capet."

"Would you recognize him on the street? Do you know where he lives? How to contact him without having to use the *Times*? I don't think you can say that you've really identified him."

"His eyes are an unmistakable shade of blue. Sapphire, really. I'd recognize them."

"A Bedouin with sapphire eyes. Is there any hope for me?"

I was glad to see some light return to his eyes but couldn't help thinking about Sebastian kissing me. Had it really happened? I could almost picture it, a foggy image, but the memory of soft lips was undeniable.

"Are you still with me?" Colin asked.

"Yes, sorry."

"I've spoken with Manning. He's agreed to help you with whatever you might need regarding the situation in Richmond. And should anything happen, telegraph me at once in Paris. I'll be at the Meurice."

Molly entered the room. "Excuse me, Lady Ashton, would you like me to light a fire for you?"

It was far too hot for me to want a fire, and I had never encouraged my maids to make a habit of dropping in, without being asked, to see if I needed their assistance.

"No, Molly, I don't." Her eyes were ringed with dark circles, and her skin was even more pale than usual. "Is something the matter?"

She looked at Colin, then back at me. "Of course not, madam. Just trying to be helpful." She bobbed a curtsey and disappeared from the room before I could utter another word.

"Are you keeping a close eye on her?" Colin asked.

"I've spoken with her multiple times. She insists that she has no idea what happened to the letters that disappeared from the library."

"And you believe her?"

"I do worry that she may still be in contact with Mr. Berry, but surely once he's in France he'll no longer be concerned with me."

"Someone is gravely troubled by those letters. If it's Berry, you might be in more danger now than ever. Just because he's out of the country doesn't mean that he can't harm you."

"But you've been convinced all along that he's not out to hurt me."

"I'm not always right, Emily."

"Do you expect violence in Paris?"

"I very much hope that we shall be able to stop this entire thing before it even begins." He pulled me towards him and bent down, resting his cheek against mine.

"I wouldn't object if you were to kiss me," I said. "You are leaving the country headed for an attempted coup. Who knows when you'll return? I feel almost as if I'm sending you off to battle."

"Very nice try," he said, stepping away from me. "But I won't be so easily seduced. Did I tell you that I've found the perfect engagement ring for you? It's from ancient Crete and is in the shape of a reef knot, gold inlaid with lapis lazuli."

"It sounds lovely."

"I keep it in my pocket at all times on the off chance that you might accept me. It wouldn't do to be unprepared."

"Will you show it to me?"

"Absolutely not. When at last you agree to marry me, I want to know that it's because you can't resist me any longer, not that you want my ring."

"You're a beast," I said. "I'm going to finish the letters this afternoon. I'll send you a message if there's anything of significance in them."

"Take care, Emily. I shall be thoroughly aggravated if I find that you've taken any unnecessary risks."

"But you'll forgive me the necessary ones?"

"How could I do otherwise?" He kissed both of my hands and left without once looking back. With him went all the warmth from the books and the ancient statues in the library, leaving me to a room filled with a conspicuous emptiness.

Continuing my work on the letters proved an excellent distraction from melancholy, and the further I delved into Marie Antoinette's correspondence, the more fascinating it became. Léonard fed her bits of information regarding the plans for the dauphin's escape, and the queen did not hesitate to criticize them. She had deep concerns about the loyalty of S, whom I identified initially as Antoine Simon, a cobbler who took charge of Louis Charles after the boy was taken from his mother's cell in the Temple.

According to the histories I had read, Simon had been notoriously cruel to the child, but some accounts claimed that his wife grew fond of their charge. This led me to suspect that she, not her husband, was S. The identity of B, however, completely eluded me. If B were the person who traveled with the dauphin, he was probably not someone who would have been mentioned in a history. It was unlikely that a recognizable figure could have pulled off the escape.

The queen's fears about S did not abate, but by the end of August 1793, she had accepted that there was no one else in a position to smuggle Louis Charles from his prison. Her concern now focused on the details of where he would go. One thing was abundantly clear: Marie Antoinette stated over and over that he was not to go to America. She did not want him to face such a long journey when his health was already compromised from being jailed. Léonard reassured her again and again that there was no plan to send the boy there; a safe house was already being set up for him in England.

The last two letters from the series were the ones that had been stolen, and I could only assume that they offered more details. Regardless, the information now before me conflicted entirely with the story of the dauphin presented by Charles Berry, who claimed that the plan all along had been to send the boy to the United States. Somehow, I found it much easier to accept these letters as factually correct than the word of a man who stood to gain a kingdom if he could only convince the world that his version of history was the truth.

The next morning, I went back to the letters but found myself distracted by the recollection of an exchange Mr. Berry had with Mr. Francis before the murder. I sifted through the papers in my desk until I came to the letter I'd found in Richmond: *I thank you for alerting me to the situation you mentioned, and assure you that I have the matter well in hand.* Had Mr. Francis known about Léonard's letters? And if so, was he sympathetic to Mr. Berry's position?

I wondered if I had missed anything in Mr. Francis's letters or possessions that pertained to either Marie Antoinette or to Charles Berry, and decided to return to Richmond. But first I scrawled a quick note to Colin to inform him that the code had indeed provided crucial information and left it on the mail tray in the hall, asking Davis to have one of the footmen deliver it to Park Lane before Colin left for France.

Much had changed in the Francis house since my last visit. The curtains in the drawing room were no longer closed, and bright sunlight streamed through the windows. Beatrice was playing the piano, and Mr. Barber sat cozily next to her on the bench, turning pages for her.

"Emily! I had no idea you were coming today." She leapt off the bench as a maid led me into the room. "Betsy, do try to remember to announce visitors *before* they come in." The maid curtseyed halfheartedly and closed the door rather loudly as she left.

"I'm sorry to disturb you," I said.

"Michael had just persuaded me to play."

"There's no need to explain," I said. "I've never believed that one's own life should stop after the death of a loved one."

"I should leave," Mr. Barber said.

"No." Beatrice did not look at him as she spoke.

"I came only to see if it would be possible for me to take another look at your husband's study. I'm hoping to find more of a connection with Charles Berry."

"Could you possibly come back later? Tomorrow perhaps? It's not a good time."

"Of course," I answered automatically, stunned by her response.

"Anything there now will still be there then," she said, her lips pulled thin in a forced smile.

There was nothing I could do but leave. I did not begrudge Beatrice any happiness she might find in Mr. Barber, and I certainly did not believe that the rituals of mourning did much to help a person manage her grief. But in denying me access to the study, she was not behaving in a manner I would expect of a woman desperate to find her husband's killer.

Rather than leaving Richmond, I decided to pay another call on Mrs. Sinclair. Happily, I found her at home, and she welcomed me with all the warmth absent from Beatrice.

"What a lovely surprise, Lady Ashton. I'm so glad you've come. My hall looks so much better without that horrid statue you persuaded Mr. Sinclair to give to the museum. I'll never be able to thank you enough."

"I'm glad to know that you're not suffering from the loss."

"I've heard that you're fond of such things, and please don't think I'm criticizing your taste, but I'd much rather have something more modern in my house."

"No offense taken, Mrs. Sinclair," I said, smiling.

"I've half a mind to bring you through the rest of the house to see if there's anything else the museum would take. Mr. Sinclair's grandfather traveled rather too extensively and collected all sorts of sordid things as he went. I'd love nothing more than to get rid of most of them."

Judging by the quality of art I'd seen in the few places I'd been in the house, this was an exciting prospect indeed. But for the moment, it would have to wait. "I wish I had more time today. Perhaps I could come back next week? At the moment I've more questions for you about Jeanne Dunston. Do you know if she left any personal effects for her son?"

"The housekeeper put aside what was in her room, but I doubt that Joseph will ever return to collect the box."

"Is there any chance you would let me take a look at it?"

"I don't see why not, though I can't imagine you'll find anything of interest. I imagine this has to do with the snuffbox again?" I nodded and smiled but decided not to say anything further. The fewer people who knew what I was doing, the better. Mrs. Sinclair rang the bell, and while we munched on lovely watercress sandwiches, the house-keeper was dispatched to the attic. She appeared a quarter of an hour later, carrying a wooden box that must have been covered with the dust now clinging to her dress.

I opened the container at once. Inside were the humble souve-nirs of a life spent in service: two nicely embroidered handkerchiefs, a carefully mended pair of gloves, a photograph of a small boy, a post-card from the queen's Jubilee, an ivory rosary, and an extremely old Bible. The postcard was from a woman called Sarah and offered in-sight into neither sender nor recipient. The Bible was my only hope. The endpaper in the front cover was inscribed: *To Bernadette Capet, on the occasion of her first Christmas in England, 1794.*

26

My hands trembled as I held the book. "Do you know who Bernadette Capet was?" I asked.

"Let's see...Bernadette...she would have been Jeanne's grandmother."

"And was it she who left France during the revolution? I remember you mentioned something about that during my previous visit."

"Yes."

"Did she come to England alone?"

"Her son was with her, but I've no idea how old he was."

"Did he work here, too?"

"Yes. I don't know much about him, only that he had quite an affinity for horses and worked in the stables all his life. It's such a lovely thing to have the same family in service for multiple generations in the same household, don't you think?"

"Quite. Did Jeanne have any family other than her son?"

"She had two brothers, but they both died long before she did."

"Did Joseph have close ties to anyone in the household? Any friends?"

"I wouldn't know, Lady Ashton. You're welcome to ask the butler, but I'm certain no one knows how to reach him. As I told you, my husband tried."

"Could I borrow this, Mrs. Sinclair?" I asked, holding up the Bible. "I think I might be able to contact Joseph. I'll bring it back, of course."

"I'd be thrilled if you could find him and get the entire box out of the house," Mrs. Sinclair said. "It's very awkward storing legacies for other people, don't you think?"

I could hardly contain my excitement when I was back in my carriage. Sebastian Capet must be Jeanne's wayward son, and if, as I suspected, he was the true heir to the House of Bourbon, his motivation for the thefts was perfectly clear. I could well believe that Mr. Francis knew this. It might even explain his hesitation to report the theft of the pink diamond. Jeanne had confided in him, and he was loath to send her son, a man who in other circumstances might have been a king, to prison. But I still wondered at his letter to Charles Berry. Had he warned Berry of possible exposure? And if so, why?

The road must have been bad, because I was being jostled with such ferocity that it was nearly impossible to keep straight the thoughts in my head. I looked out the window and saw that my driver had moved to the side to let a rider approaching from behind pass us, which it did with most impressive speed. Once it was gone, our ride became smoother but only for a short while. All of a sudden, I heard Waters shouting at the horses. One of them shrieked, and the carriage lurched violently, throwing me against the door. The latch gave way, and I fell out onto the ground.

Waters managed to stop the horses and leapt from his seat. The footmen, who rode standing on the back of the carriage, had jumped clear as we headed off the road and reached me first, helping me up.

"Are you all right, madam?" Waters asked, doing his best to keep his voice steady.

"I think so," I said. "What happened?"

"There was a man on the side of the road. When we got close to him, he drew out a horse whip and struck Aziza across the face. She reared up and startled Hadia. I could hardly control them."

"Where did the man go?" I asked, my heart pounding so violently that I could hardly breathe.

"He had a horse with him, madam. Must've been the gent who passed us just a minute ago. There's no sign of him now. I'd wager that he rode away through the woods."

"You drove magnificently, Waters. I'm amazed that we didn't flip."

While the three men inspected our carriage, I took stock of my injuries. Although I was bruised and dirty, nothing seemed broken, but I could not stop shaking. Waters concluded that everything was in fine working order, and we headed back to London, where, once home, I walked stiffly past Davis as he held the door open for me.

"I can see you want to scold me, Davis," I said. "I assure you that Mr. Hargreaves would find no fault with what I've done." I made my way upstairs and called Meg to help me undress. She was horrified at the condition of my gown and terrified when she heard what had happened, but did not let this get in the way of her efficiency. She sent for tea and prepared a hot bath. I soaked for more than half an hour, knowing that I was likely to feel worse the following day as my bruises developed.

The word of my adventure spread quickly through the household. When the tray arrived from the kitchen, it held not only tea but chicken broth, Cook's panacea for all things dreadful, fresh cut flowers from the garden, a glass of port, and a copy of *Great Expectations*, which I imagine had been randomly selected from the library by some well-intentioned member of my staff. I applied myself at once to the chicken broth, not because I was particularly hungry but because I had no wish to hurt Cook's feelings by sending it back untouched. Meg tapped on the door.

"Mrs. Brandon is here, madam. Would you like her sent up?"

"Please." I had finished the broth and moved from the table to my bed, where I sat on top of the covers, leaning against the pillows. It was obvious from Ivy's expression that someone had told her about the accident. She rushed to me, sitting on the edge of the bed, biting her lip so hard I thought it would bleed.

"What on earth is going on? You must stop, Emily. You must make sure that you are no longer putting yourself in danger."

"It's not so simple, Ivy," I said. "There's too much at stake."

"Well, that needn't be your concern. Tell the police what you've learned, and remove yourself from the investigation."

"I don't yet know enough to set them on the proper course."

"You're going to get yourself killed. And for what?"

"To keep an innocent woman from being hanged. To prevent a liar from causing the overthrow of a peaceful government."

"Leave it to Colin, then. Why must you insist on doing it yourself?"

I looked at her face, which was filled with a tortured confusion. "Because it's important, Ivy, because I like it, and because I think I'm good at it. I'll be perfectly all right."

"It's selfish, Emily. Selfish. Here I am half-crazed with worry over you, and you dismiss my concern. I know you're clever, I know you're good at what you do. But why can't you leave these things to the people who are supposed to take care of them? You'll hate me for saying it, but it...it...it doesn't become a lady."

"I'm sure my reputation as a lady will come as a great comfort to Jane Stilleman in the hours before her execution."

"You're not the only person capable of solving this, Emily. Haven't enough bad things happened to convince you that you're placing yourself in too much danger?"

"I promised Colin that I would take no unnecessary risks. He made no attempt to stop me."

"I suppose I'm just not as smart as the two of you because I don't see why your involvement is so crucial. I understand that you like the adventure of it, but this is no longer a fun sort of game. Someone is trying to kill you."

"I think you're rather exaggerating things, Ivy."

"Maybe I am, but maybe, Emily, I'm right. Not that you'd listen even if I was. I wonder how you would respond if Margaret said the same things."

Now it was I who bit a lip. I wanted to say that Margaret would make no attempt to stop me, that Margaret would buckle down and help me solve the puzzle, even if there was danger involved. But I had no desire to hurt Ivy, especially now, when she hardly even sounded like herself. I could only assume that things between her and Robert were getting no better.

"I'm sorry, Ivy. I don't mean to dismiss your concerns."

"I know that you and Margaret don't take me seriously. I suppose I ought to try to be the sort of friend to you that she is, but I don't want to. I only wish that things would return to how they used to be, before either of us was married, when you were satisfied with being happy. I think that you now prefer challenge to contentedness."

"Is that so wrong?"

"It is when you ask your friends to sit back and watch you throw yourself in harm's way."

"I'm not asking you to sit back."

"You know full well that there's nothing else I can do." She clasped her hands in her lap and fixed her gaze on them. "I apologize for arguing with you after you've had such a frightening experience. It was wrong of me."

"Ivy—"

"I must go. Robert's at Westminster and will expect me to be home when he returns."

"Are things well between you?" I asked.

"Robert's such a considerate husband. I'm fortunate to have him." And with that response, so impersonal, so perfectly appropriate, I knew that Ivy was releasing me as a confidante. She smiled stonily, her lips hardly moving, and wished me well. I couldn't bear to watch her walk away from me, but when I heard the heavy bedroom door close behind her, I started to cry. Our lives may have taken contrary directions, but I had no desire to be adrift in a sea of my own without the comfort of her friendship.

It was dark when I next opened my eyes, so I knew that I must have fallen asleep, and was disappointed to have let so many hours slip away from me. My head was throbbing, but I lit a lamp and rang for tea, asking to have it sent to me in the library. I made my way slowly downstairs, feeling notably stiffer than I had a few hours ago. With effort, I lowered myself into my desk chair and pulled open a drawer in which my husband had kept the blank leather notebooks he used for his journals. There had been five there when Philip died. One I used for my study of Greek. Another, which contained both Greek and notes from my investigation, Sebastian had stolen in the park along with the *Odyssey*. Now I would use a third. I hesitated for an instant, wondering if I should save these remaining volumes for something else, perhaps reserve them only for Greek or to start a journal of my own. When they were gone, I would be left with one fewer remaining tie to Philip, and for some reason this struck me as unreasonably poignant. I liked the idea of the notebooks, sitting where he'd left them, waiting to be used.

"Cook sent tea and a hot toddy, madam," Davis said, placing the tray on my desk.

"She takes good care of me."

"Are you quite certain that you're not in need of medical attention?"

"Quite." I smiled. "The footmen assured me that they suffered no injuries, as did Waters. Is that true?"

"They're all perfectly fine, madam."

"Good." I sipped the toddy. "And the horses?"

"They suffered no lasting injuries. If I may, madam?" Davis was standing at rigid attention.

"Please, go ahead."

"I took the liberty of informing Inspector Manning about the events of the afternoon. Mr. Hargreaves asked me to"—he cleared his throat—"that is—"

"He asked you to make sure the inspector was aware of my activities."

"Yes, madam. I have no doubt that you would have told him yourself were you not recovering from the accident."

"Of course." I couldn't help but smile. "I found the reticule I had with me in the carriage in my room, but I didn't see the Bible that I was holding. Do you know where it was put?"

"A Bible? I don't remember seeing it. I'll check with Baines." He returned a few minutes later with the footman.

"I gave your bag and the Bible to a maid, madam," Baines said. "But I don't know what she did with them."

"Which maid, Baines?" I asked.

"I can't remember her name. She's one of the new girls."

Davis sprang into action at once. A quick search of the servants' quarters revealed that Molly and her few humble possessions had disappeared.

27

❦ ❦ ❦ ❦ ❦ ❦ ❦ ❦

Y ou should never have trusted her," Margaret said the next afternoon. She was pacing but kept well away from the windows in the library.

"I suppose you're right, but I still cannot believe that she would have any ties to Berry after what he did to her."

"I don't like to be cynical, but it's possible that he didn't force himself on her. She might have welcomed the attention and then been upset when she realized she would never be anything to him."

"Theoretically possible, I suppose, but highly unlikely."

"So what now?" she asked.

"It's time to send another message to Sebastian. It's essential that I speak with him." Margaret wanted me to quote Homer to him, but I elected to take a simpler approach:

Sebastian, I've seen your mother's Bible and know your true identity. Please come to me at once.

"Surely he's no reason to hide from you any longer now that you know the truth," Margaret said. "Capet is the Bourbon heir. Francis knew this. Presumably, he told Berry. But how do you reconcile all this with Francis's infidelity? Berry may have had motive to kill him, but so did Beatrice."

"It's entirely possible that the murder had nothing to do with the French throne. If Beatrice knew that her husband had a mistress and a child"—I sighed—"it would be much more satisfactory to know that there was a larger motivation behind Mr. Francis's death."

"Is there a motivation stronger than love betrayed? Although..." Margaret paused. "If Beatrice always loved Mr. Barber, can she really claim to have been betrayed?"

"Think on it: She loves Barber but has given him up for Francis. For years and years she buries her feelings and treats her husband with respect and affection, coming, in the end, to love him. Now, presume she learns that this man, for whom she had walked away from love, has callously tossed her aside for another woman. That is a betrayal that would be keenly felt."

"Maybe. I think she'd take the opportunity to invite Barber back into her life. If her husband took a lover, why shouldn't she? That's exactly what I'd do."

"Really?" I looked at her carefully. "Is this a roundabout way of telling me that you've decided to marry Jeremy?"

"Heavens, no! First off, his mother would never stand for it, and second, I'm convinced that Jeremy is capable of grand passion. Now, I've no illusions about fidelity in many marriages, but I shouldn't like to have a husband with a grand passion for someone else."

"You sell yourself short, Margaret. Perhaps you will be his grand passion."

"There's no chance of that. I thought him to be the most frivolous of gentlemen up until the past couple of weeks. Now there's a change in him, a seriousness in the way that he looks at one woman in particular."

"Tell me it's not Lettice?"

"No, Emily, it's you."

"Jeremy is a dear friend, and I can assure you that he would never consider me anything else."

"Believe what you will. I can only tell you what I see. There's a sort of adoration that's crept into the way he speaks about you. There's no fawning in it, mind you. 'Passion' is the only word that fits."

"Infatuation, more likely," I said, not believing he felt even this. Jeremy and I had been friends so long that any other sort of relationship was inconceivable.

"Think what you like. I am confident, however, that unless your own affections take a remarkable change of course, the Duke of Bainbridge is going to remain a bachelor for a very long time."

"Jeremy has always had a fickle nature. Any apparent devotion he has for me stems entirely from my lack of availability and will soon be replaced with fervor for someone equally inaccessible." Davis entered the room with the mail. "Did Mr. Hargreaves send a reply to my letter yesterday?"

"Not of which I am aware. I shall look into the matter at once, madam."

He returned not half an hour later, deeply apologetic. He had instructed Baines to deliver my letter, but when the footman had gone to collect it, he could not find it. A maid—the same one to whom he'd later given my effects from the carriage—was passing through the foyer and told him that she'd seen me remove a note from the mail tray moments earlier. He assumed I had changed my mind about sending it. There was no doubt in my mind what had happened. Molly had taken it, along with Bernadette Capet's Bible, to Charles Berry.

"I need you to find Molly," I said to my butler. "Do whatever you must, but bring her to me."

❋ ❋ ❋

While I waited for Davis to bring news of my wayward maid and for Sebastian to reply to my latest message, I decided to distract myself by calling on two ladies, each of whom was in a position to provide information significant to friends of mine. I went first to Eaton Place, where I spent a most diverting half hour with the Countess Anders, Lord Pembroke's mother. After discussing the German state visit (there was a feeling of general relief at the kaiser's good behavior), Princess Louise's wedding to Prince Aribert of Anhalt (the countess was convinced the marriage would never last), and the difficulties in finding and keeping a decent cook (I made a mental note to increase Cook's wages), I moved the conversation in a different direction.

"How is your son, Lady Anders? I know that he and Miss Routledge were quite attached before her engagement."

"Oh, poor Tommy was heartbroken when she threw him over, though I must admit that I wasn't entirely disappointed. I'm sympathetic to Elinor wanting Berry for her daughter. Royal blood is always an attractive lure. Charles Berry may have no fortune, but if rumors are correct, that will all change shortly, and Elinor will be lauded for having gambled so well."

"I hope Isabelle finds some happiness."

"Her prospects are as fair with Berry as with anyone, I suppose. She's a sweet girl. She might have done nicely for Tommy if her circumstances were different, but now he's free to find someone who can bring in a sizeable dowry. The Routledges don't have the fortune they used to. Not, mind you, that that would be of particular consequence to us, but"—she smiled winningly—"if one has the chance to better one's financial situation, why not take it?"

"Is Lord Pembroke still in town? I haven't seen him since the Brandons' ball."

"His father sent him to Yorkshire to take care of some business on the estate. The distraction will do him well."

I was satisfied to know that Lord Pembroke was indeed suffering for the loss of Isabelle. He did love her. Someday, she might be very glad to know that. After taking my leave from Lady Anders, I walked up Grosvenor Crescent, across Piccadilly, and back into Mayfair. Now that the initial pain from my carriage accident had begun to subside, I found that walking helped me to feel better, easing the stiffness from my sore body. I could not help but slow down as I reached Park Street, however, fearing that my next call would not be so pleasant as the last.

I felt terrible about my falling-out with Ivy and knew that I bore more guilt for it than she. We might not be able to return to the closeness we shared in the past, but I could at least make an effort to stop the woman I was certain was destroying my friend's marriage. Taking a deep breath, I knocked on the door in front of me.

The Reynold-Plympton residence was an exercise in bad taste. So far as I could tell, anything that could be gilded was, and nearly every surface in the drawing room to which I was admitted had been covered with hideous displays of stuffed birds, mounted in various stages of flight. I believe the goal was to give one the sense of being outside in a garden, but the actual effect was that of being trapped in a bizarre aviary. However, I gave no further consideration to the setting once I realized the lady of the house was already entertaining a caller. Robert snapped to attention when he saw me and quickly collected his hat and walking stick.

"I shan't stand in the way of your conversation," he said, rushing out almost before he'd said hello to me. I made no attempt to reduce his feeling of unease.

"What a pleasure, Lady Ashton," Mrs. Reynold-Plympton purred, eyeing me critically. "To what do I owe the honor of this call?"

"I'll not mince words. I'm concerned about your friendship with Mr. Brandon."

"Concerned? How can it be of any concern to you? Robert is not the most exciting man I've ever known, but he's not so awful."

"My concern is more for him than you."

"Is it?" She laughed, and as she did, I knew at once why she was such a favorite with bored, married gentlemen. The sound was like silver bells, cascading through the most delicious sort of melody, utterly captivating.

"I'm afraid I fail to see the humor in the situation."

"A great loss for you, I'm afraid."

"I can assure you I don't feel it at all," I said.

"So you are here to reprimand me? How tedious."

This woman had no shame! She made no attempt to deny her illicit relationship! I was about to launch into a spirited attack on her morals when I was struck by an unnerving thought: I had no firm proof that she was Robert's mistress. She had danced with him twice in a row, walked with him in the park, and received him as a caller. Not exactly irrefutable evidence of adultery. Was I any better than the gossips who had so savaged my own reputation? I considered another strategy.

"I'm a great friend of Robert's wife," I said.

"So I gathered when we met in the park."

"I want to see her happy."

"You are an impetuous thing, aren't you? Make a habit of leaping to conclusions?"

"I do my best not to."

"You clearly need more practice. I'm not having an affair with your poor, dear Robert." She laughed again. More music. "How naïve you are! Can you really think I'd waste my time on a gentleman who's not even a junior minister? Oh, you have succeeded in diverting me greatly."

I knew not how to respond so remained silent.

"Lady Ashton, I spend time with many of Basil's friends, especially when he's grooming them for future greatness. I know little details about *everyone*—and you can well imagine how useful that is in politics. Basil likes me to pass this knowledge on to his protégés."

"Basil?" I asked. "Lord Fortescue?"

"Is there another? He quite depends upon me."

"Lord Fortescue? I'm...I'm...astonished."

"There is an art to choosing a lover, Lady Ashton. The obvious choice is not always the most...valuable, shall we say?"

"So you are..."

"Providing Robert with an inestimable service. But you have caused me concern. Is there trouble in his private life? Basil won't tolerate that. He insists upon discretion."

"No, I don't know that there is trouble, I just thought that—"

"To have so quickly concluded that he was having an affair means there is indeed trouble. Is his wife in a delicate condition?"

"Oh, I couldn't—"

"This is not the time for false modesty, Lady Ashton. Fortescue wants Robert on track for a position in the next government. He'll need to be guaranteed at least the appearance of a happy home."

"I never said that their home is not—"

"She's not with child, is she?" Mrs. Reynold-Plympton frowned. "I'll have to speak to him about this at once. Do you think there is some sort of medical problem?"

This conversation was decaying with such rapidity that there was no hope of trying to save it. Ivy would die a thousand slow deaths if she ever learned that I had spoken to anyone about this. "No, no I don't."

"Oh dear. You're gone all scarlet. How unattractive. Why do you find this so embarrassing?"

"I should never have said anything."

"Of course you should have. I'll take care of it at once."

"You can't tell Robert—"

Again came the laugh. "My dear girl, is it possible that you are really so naïve? Basil will talk to Robert."

This was even worse.

"I don't think—"

"Basil always keeps up on these things. Robert doesn't have a mistress, nor does he visit—well, best not mention that. For some reason, undoubtedly a result of the long hours he works, he is neglecting his marital duties. A few choice words from his mentor about the benefits of having a cherubic infant around to complete the picture of a perfect English family will do the trick. I'm glad you came to me, Lady Ashton. Basil has great hopes for Robert. It wouldn't do for him to have trouble at home."

"Please, Mrs. Reynold-Plympton, don't think there is trouble—"

"Say not another word. I am the soul of discretion. No one beyond the necessary few will ever hear a word of what we've discussed."

I can't say that I felt altogether confident about her silence. And who did she think were the "necessary few"? As I walked home, I was filled with despondency. My muscles ached, and I regretted not having taken my carriage. Why had I ever thought I could help Ivy by confronting this woman? What right had I to meddle in my friend's marriage? My intentions may have been blameless, but I should have had the sense to say nothing about Ivy's problems to anyone. I would have to tell her what I'd done; I couldn't risk her learning it from someone else, and I knew this would be the absolute end of our friendship. Ivy could never forgive me for having so mortified her.

28

D AVIS, PROVING ONCE AGAIN TO BE NOT ONLY INVALUABLE BUT POS-
sessed of an almost inhuman efficiency, located Molly within a
matter of days. She had taken a position near Fleet Street, folding
newspapers, and was working no fewer than twelve hours a day for
very little money. I decided to wait for her outside her place of employment in the evening and caught her the moment she came out
the door.

"Molly!" I called. She cringed when she saw me. "Don't even consider running from me." I took her by the arm.

"I'm sorry, Lady Ashton. I shouldn't have left the house like that. I
should've given notice. You were so good to me."

"How much did Mr. Berry pay you to steal from me, Molly?"

"What?"

"I know about the letters and the Bible and the note that was to be
sent to Mr. Hargreaves."

The girl burst into tears. "I would never steal, milady, never. Especially not from you. I tried to tell you I was going, but I didn't
know Mr. Hargreaves was with you. I couldn't do it in front of him,
milady."

"Have you had any communication with Mr. Berry since you left the Savoy?"

"Of course not! Why would I want to talk to that horrid man? Not that he even would talk to me." She was sobbing with such ferocity that it was difficult to understand her.

"Why, then, did you leave the house?" Her reply was unintelligible. "You must get control of yourself. Come with me." I sat her down in my carriage and gave her a handkerchief. "What is the matter?"

"I couldn't expect you to keep me on in my...my...condition. But I couldn't bear to have you let me go. I didn't know what to do. Gabby told me they was looking for girls here, so I took a job. They weren't particular about having a character from my previous position, but I suppose they'll get rid of me as soon as they know."

Now I understood. "Is it Mr. Berry's?" She nodded. I wasn't sure if she would want me to offer her comfort, but I couldn't stop myself. I embraced her, then spoke firmly. "I would never have thrown you out of my house for something so completely beyond your control. Do you want to return with me?"

"I...I don't know. It's all so awful. Everyone will think the worst of me."

"More than one person has told me that you speak highly of Mr. Berry. Why would you do that after having been so abominably treated by him?"

"He threatened me, Lady Ashton. Told me that if I ever said a word against him, he'd hurt me again. I saw him from a distance a few times in the park and wondered if he was watching me. I was scared."

I considered a number of scenarios. It would be best, perhaps, to get her out of London, to someplace where no one knew her. I could send her to Ashton Hall, but that might cause problems for her later with Philip's family. It would not, after all, be my home forever. "Would you like to work at Mr. Hargreaves's estate? I'm certain I can arrange for you to have a position there. We'll tell everyone that your husband died. No one need ever know about this, Molly."

"You would do that for me?"

"I only wish I could do more. Clean up your face, then go back inside and give your notice. You're coming home with me." I watched her walk away from me and heard a tap on the carriage window.

"Nice work, Emily. Will you let me in?"

Waters and the footmen dropped down immediately and surrounded my visitor. "It's all right," I said. "He's a friend." I opened the door.

"Rescuing a despondent maid from ruin. It is difficult not to adore you more with every passing moment. You may be nearly as romantic as I."

"Sebastian, I know who you are."

"Congratulations," he said. His hat was pulled so far down that it was difficult to see his face. He handed me a velvet bag. "I've no use for paste." He slipped away before I could even mention his mother's Bible. I followed him as best I could, calling after him to stop. He paid me no heed. My footmen joined in the chase, but he managed to elude all of us. Molly returned in the midst of the confusion, and Waters sat her next to him on his perch above the horses. She seemed content there, so I let her ride with him back to Berkeley Square.

Alone again, I opened Sebastian's bag, finding, as expected, the false diamond necklace along with a note.

> Κῦμα τὸ πικρὸν Ἔρωτος ἀκοίμητοί τε πνέοντες
> Ζῆλοι χαὶ χώμων χειμων χειμέριον πέλαγος,
> Ποῖ φέρομαι;

Bitter waves of Love, and restless gutsy Jealousies and wintry sea of revellings, whither am I borne?

❦ ❦ ❦

I f Molly was innocent of the charges I'd thrown at her—and I did not for a moment doubt her—someone else in my household was to blame. It did not take long for my suspicions to fall upon Lizzie. She was also new, had turned up at odd moments, lingered over her tasks, and had taken more notice of my guests than she ought to have. Mrs. Ockley, my housekeeper, had hired two other girls at the same time as Lizzie, so I questioned each of them, just to be certain. One had been visiting her brother in Brighton the day the letters were stolen from my library, and the other came across as so candid, so straightforward, that I was hard-pressed to think her guilty of any crime.

Lizzie, on the other hand, was belligerent, which took me greatly by surprise. I had always made a point of treating my servants with respect, and I recalled that when she first came to my house she had been rather nervous; I had done my best to calm her nerves. To find her now so rude was quite a shock.

"I don't know why I'm here," she said, looking me straight in the face. "I've heard all about what's happened in the house, but you can't possibly think I've anything to do with it."

"Why is that, Lizzie?"

"Because I know you can't prove I've done anything." Her smile was gratingly confident.

"Careful, are you?"

"I don't need to be. I haven't done anything."

"I should very much like to believe you. It's most unsettling to have a spy in one's midst. A letter was taken from the hall some days ago. Mrs. Ockley tells me that you were cleaning the floor there as well as the stairs at the time it disappeared. Did you see someone take it?"

"I wasn't paying any attention. I was busy with my work."

"Surely another member of the staff would have spoken to you as he passed?"

"Maybe, maybe not."

"I also know that the day the letters were taken from the library, you were dusting in there. Again, you saw nothing?"

"I can't say that I really recall the day."

"Nothing stands out? The house was burgled. Davis questioned the staff immediately. You have no memory of this?"

"I remember it, I guess, but for me it was an ordinary sort of day. I didn't know I should have been looking out for a thief."

"When you were dusting, did you notice the letters on my desk?"

"Of course I did, but how could I know that two of them were missing? I didn't know how many there were to start."

"A keen observation, Lizzie. But unfortunately, Davis made a point of not telling anyone how many had been taken. How could you know it was two if you were not the culprit?" She sucked in her cheeks and stood very still. I sat there, saying nothing for some time. Then, taking a cue from Colin, I continued in the calmest possible voice. "If you did it, Lizzie, it would be best to tell me. I'm more interested in discovering who put you up to it than I am in punishing you."

She did not reply.

"I can, of course, call the police, but I'd much rather keep the matter private. This household has suffered enough scandal in these past months. Surely you would prefer that we settle this between our-selves?"

"So that you can turn me out of the house with no character?"

"You're hardly in a position to make demands, Lizzie."

"I think I am."

It took a great effort to remain calm; I would have to ask Colin how he managed to do it so well. "As you wish, then." I pulled the bell, and Davis entered the room. "I'm afraid we're going to need Inspector Manning."

"Very well, madam." He turned, very slowly, started for the door, and then looked back. "Have you ever visited a jail, Lizzie? Terrible place. You can't imagine what it's like. Not when you're used to a snug room in one of the best houses in London." Her gaze was still fixed on me, and Davis, standing behind her, actually winked at me. I nearly fell out of my chair. "Lady Ashton is generosity itself. I can't imagine she'd want any of her girls to wind up in such a situation. Rats. Lots of rats. Filth everywhere. The smell's unbearable. You'd probably wind up falling ill before long and would welcome an early death."

"Enough!" Lizzie cried. "I admit that I took your letters."

"Why did you do it?" I asked.

"I didn't think I was hurting anyone."

"Did you also pass information about myself and the Duke of Bainbridge?"

Now that she knew she was caught, all her confidence evaporated. She seemed nervous and began talking very quickly. "Not precisely, milady. I just confirmed that he was here a lot, and alone with you. And that he sent the flowers with the note."

"You read the note?"

"Yes, I'm sorry."

"How did you know that Mrs. Francis had come to call on me the day that you offered to bring us tea?"

"I don't remember, milady. Honest, I don't."

"How did you pass along your information?"

"I left notes tacked to a tree in Berkeley Square, milady."

"I don't believe you, Lizzie. Can you read?"

"Yes."

"And you read the note from the Duke of Bainbridge?"

"Yes." She swallowed hard.

"How did he sign it?"

"I don't remember exactly. I...I think he signed it "Bainbridge." Or maybe "Jeremy"?"

"What exactly did your employer ask you to do?"

"At first I was to keep an eye out for signs that you were having an affair with Mr. Berry, but I never saw any, so then he told me it was the duke I should watch for."

"So when you saw the note, you assumed it was from the duke?" She nodded.

"You can't read, can you?" She did not look at me. "The trouble is, Lizzie, the note wasn't from him. It wasn't even signed."

"Oh."

"There's no shame in not being able to read. It's not your fault that you weren't given the opportunity to learn. Why did you steal the letters?"

"I thought they were from the duke, too, but started to worry that the person paying me would begin to figure out that I couldn't read them and stop paying me."

"Who is that person?"

"I don't know."

"Lizzie, do not lie to me now."

"I'm not lying. I don't know who it is."

"You obviously don't leave notes in the square. How do you communicate with this person? How did he contact you in the first place?"

Now the girl turned deadly pale. "I had trouble at my last position and was let go without a character."

"What had you done?" I tried to picture Colin. Calm Colin, able to persuade anyone to admit to anything.

"I...I flirted with my master's son."

"Just flirted?"

"Yes."

"Are you quite certain?" Surely I couldn't wind up with two maids in delicate situations in the course of a single evening.

"Oh, yes, Lady Ashton. His father turned me out of the house the moment he saw his son talking to me."

"What house was this?"

"Please don't make me say."

"You must tell me, Lizzie. I will have to confirm your story."

"It was Lord Grantham, milady."

Lord Grantham, the man whose Limoges box Sebastian had stolen. "So you were expelled from the house?"

"Yes. My mother's in service in Richmond, and got the housekeeper to let me stay with her while I looked for another position, but, as you can imagine, without a character, I couldn't find anything."

"Richmond? Whose house?" My heart was pounding. Was this all to be so easily solved?

"Mrs. Sophie Hargreaves, milady. A very kind mistress."

Not so easily solved. Sophie was married to Colin's brother, William. "So what happened?"

"I had just about given up and was ready to take a job in a button factory, when a man approached me and said he could help. He's in service, too, you see, and had spotted me on my rounds looking for work. Said he could get me a character if I would agree to help out his master and that I'd get extra money for doing it. I didn't see any harm in it. Sounded like a bit of fun."

"A bit of fun that could have destroyed me. And, Lizzie, had you succeeded in doing so, I would no longer be in a position to be able to help you."

"I'm sorry, milady."

"Who wrote the false character?"

"I don't know."

"Surely you know what house it was from? Otherwise how could you have known what to say when Mrs. Ockley interviewed you?"

"I just meant that I didn't know who had actually written it. It was supposed to be a Mrs. David Francis. She lives in Richmond, too."

This was certainly bad news, but I retained my composure. "And this man you spoke to? Who is he?"

"He wouldn't tell me his name. Too risky, you know. If we was to get caught."

"How did you communicate with him?"

"We'd meet on my day off in the park."

"Are you to meet with him this week?"

"I saw him a few days ago, and he said they didn't need me any-more."

"Did you give him the Bible that was in my carriage?"

"I did, milady."

"But you could not have thought that had something to do with the Duke of Bainbridge?"

"No, but after I brought the letters, the next week he said that if I came across anything out of the ordinary, it would be a good idea to bring it to him. When I heard the carriage had been run off the road, I knew that wasn't ordinary, so when Baines gave me your things, I looked through them."

"You went through my reticule?"

"Yes, milady." She no longer was meeting my eyes. "I thought it was odd you was carrying a Bible instead of that funny Greek book, so I figured I'd give it to him."

"Did you also take a letter that was to be delivered to Mr. Har-greaves?"

"I did."

"And you told Baines that I'd removed it from the mail tray?"

"Yes, milady."

"Is there anything else about this you think I should know?"

"I don't think so." She squirmed in front of me, and I knew she wished I'd let her sit.

"As you might imagine, I'm having a rather difficult time trusting you."

"I'm sorry."

"I'm a bit confused as to why you are so repentant now, after having been so contentious when I first began to question you."

"I shouldn't have done it, milady, I know. He told me that if I ever got caught, I should deny everything as strongly as possible. Said that if I stood my ground, there was no way you could ever prove that I'd done anything wrong."

"Lizzie, when a person has done something wrong, it can always be proved somehow."

"Yes, milady." She was beginning to look rather ill. I turned my attention to Davis, who was still standing at the door.

"Take her to Mrs. Ockley and tell her not to let the girl out of her sight until I have this all settled." As soon as they had left, I weighed my options. I could send letters to Sophie Hargreaves and Lord Grantham, but it would be best to speak to Beatrice in person. I wanted to see her reaction to Lizzie's story.

29

Beatrice was not at home when I called. She had gone to visit Jane Stilleman in prison. I spoke to Mrs. Fenwick, who emphatically denied that she'd ever so much as heard Lizzie's name. The girl had never worked in the house. This was not unexpected, of course. The real issue was whether Beatrice had written the false character, but that was not a question for the housekeeper. As I was preparing to leave, I noticed Thomkins in the garden and decided to speak with him.

"I understand Mrs. Francis is visiting Jane today. Have you gone to see her, too?"

"No, madam." He continued trimming the rosebushes.

"I'm afraid that it's becoming more and more likely that she'll be found guilty of murder."

No reply.

"Mr. Thomkins, this is most serious. Jane, the woman you supposedly love, could very well be hanged. Have you nothing to say?"

"What could there be to say? I don't know who did it."

"Have you tried to offer her any comfort?"

"What could I do? Tell her I'm sorry for her?"

"I'm sure she'd appreciate it. You could at least send a letter."

"I'm not much good with writing."

"Can you think of anyone else in the household who would have wanted to see Mr. Francis dead? Has anything out of the ordinary happened in the past few months? Any unusual visitors, any—"

"Do you think I haven't gone over this a thousand times in my head? The police have questioned me from morning to night over and over. It all looked bad for me, too, you know, the nicotine having come from my shed."

"Your shed?"

"I use it for the roses. Kills aphids."

Why had Beatrice not told me this? "So how did you manage to avoid arrest?"

"I was at my sister's the week before the murder. Jane brought the lotion to Mr. Francis while I was gone."

"But you could have put the nicotine in it any time before then."

"I suppose so, but I didn't." He paused. "Look, why would I want Mr. Francis dead? Or Stilleman for that matter? You pointed out yourself that I could have married Jane, and I didn't."

"Here's what I don't understand: If Jane wanted to kill her husband, why would she have killed Mr. Francis first?" I asked. "Are we to believe that she only intended to kill Mr. Francis? He was, after all, the one threatening her position. She had no way of knowing that Mrs. Francis would let Stilleman take the shaving lotion and any other toiletries he wanted."

"I don't know," he said.

"But if Jane knew the lotion was poisoned, wouldn't she have stopped him from using it?"

He stopped trimming the roses and turned to face me. "Not if she wanted him dead."

"If she wanted to be free of her marriage, she could have achieved that by simply killing Stilleman. It would have looked much less suspicious had there been only one death."

"Maybe she never thought of that. Maybe Mr. Francis had already told her he was letting her go and she panicked."

"You sound as if you think she's guilty," I said.

"Maybe I do."

"You think her capable of murdering two men?"

"All I know is that she helped me with the roses more than once. She knew all about the nicotine. Now, I didn't tell the police that, but can you see that I'm not sure what to think?"

I could indeed. Regardless, it seemed to me unlikely that these crimes were simply the result of a servant being caught in an illicit affair. Not when there were so many other things swirling around. Was I to believe that the connection between Mr. Francis and Charles Berry was, in the end, meaningless? Surely the fear of losing the throne to which he aspired was as strong a motive for murder as any Jane Stilleman could have had. Both she and Berry stood to lose everything; in this, at least, the servant and the gentleman were equals. Yet I wanted the more complicated explanation to be the correct one.

I needed to think but found that doing so served only to confuse me. Better that I should detach myself, focus on something else, and let all this simmer in the back of my mind. Back in London, I sought out Mr. Wainwright in the British Library. It took very little effort to find him; he was at his desk in the Reading Room, in danger of being buried by the badly stacked piles of books that surrounded him.

"Lady Ashton!"

"Please do not get up," I said. "I'm afraid something will fall on you if you make a sudden movement." He did not heed my warning and, as he stood, knocked over at least a dozen books.

"I'm terribly sorry," he said, bending over to retrieve them from the floor. I would have liked to help him, but a corset, even one laced loosely, makes bending over nearly impossible.

"There's no need to apologize to me. It's the books that deserve your concern." He finished stacking them, though in no less precarious a way than they'd been before. "I've been pondering for some weeks now the dauphin's escape from France during the revolution and have come to the conclusion that he must have gone to England."

"A popular theory," Mr. Wainwright said. "Certainly supported by legend. There are numerous stories of English families who helped Frenchmen flee the terror."

"Do any of them claim to have assisted the dauphin?"

"None that can prove it, but I've always thought that anyone who had aided the boy would have kept quiet. He would have been in a great deal of danger, even in England, had the revolutionaries known what became of him."

"But what about later? The monarchy was restored after Napoleon's defeat."

"Quite right. But Louis XVIII would never have been king if the dauphin had been around to inherit the throne. Would it have been safe for Louis Charles to reveal himself? If the dauphin survived, he did so anonymously. He had no band of supporters, no army, no court."

"I wonder if, after having witnessed at such a young age the brutality of the revolution, he would even want to be king," I said.

Mr. Wainwright shrugged. "I don't know. Royalty think differently than we do."

"But if he were brought up as an ordinary boy, surely he would think more like us? Do you know the names of any of the English families that aided the aristocrats?"

"William Wickham helped thousands of people escape, but he was based in Switzerland on orders of the Foreign Office. All secret, of course. The Viscount Torrington in Sevenoaks housed refugees, and a number of exiled clergy stayed at the King's House in Winchester."

"Sevenoaks? In Kent?"

"Yes."

"Thank you, Mr. Wainwright. You've been most helpful." I rushed home, not to my library, but to the sitting room that Philip's mother had used when she was mistress of the house. I pulled open every drawer in the room and searched the contents but did not find that which I needed. Davis entered the room as I was in the midst of this tempest, and stood, looking more amused than he ought, waiting for me to speak.

"What is it, Davis?"

"May I help you, madam?"

"*Burke's Peerage*, Davis. I need *Burke's Peerage*."

"I don't believe that the viscount owned it."

"I figured as much. But surely his mother—"

"She took all her things to the dowager house in Derbyshire, madam. But if I may? Our own Mrs. Ockley has a copy."

"Really?"

"She was quite devoted to the viscount, and when his engagement was announced, she took it upon herself to evaluate your ancestry."

"Would she be willing to lend the book to me?" I asked, and sat, astonished, as I waited for him to inquire. He returned shortly, bearing a well-worn volume.

"It's an older edition, madam. Mrs. Ockley bought it used."

I searched through the book until I found the Torringtons and traced my finger along the page, stopping when I came to the children of the fourth viscount: Sarah Elizabeth, Catherine Jane, and Elinor Constance. The estate was in Kent, near Sevenoaks, just where Lady Elinor told me she had spent her childhood.

What, if anything, had the Torringtons known about the dauphin's escape? Had they helped the boy? And if so, what did Lady Elinor know of it? I had to consider my next move very carefully. So much for letting my thoughts simmer.

30

Ever since Sebastian told me that he hadn't stolen the silver snuffbox, I'd intended to see if it had turned up for sale anywhere, but one distraction after another had kept me from this task. Today, at last, I was determined to search for it, and by two o'clock had visited no fewer than seven shops, many of them of dubious reputation. I was not foolish enough to think that I would stumble across it on display. Rather, I hoped that one of the shopkeepers could be convinced to reveal anything he'd heard about such an item appearing for sale on the black market.

So far I'd learned nothing, although I had purchased two red-figure vases, both fifth century, one depicting the myth of Zeus and Io, the other the birth of Apollo and Artemis. And though I wrestled with the ethics of it, I also bought a fragment from a charming frieze of the three Graces dancing, their arms entwined, hair and robes flowing. The dealer selling it was notoriously unscrupulous, and the provenance he offered was laughable. I hated to do business with anyone furthering the illegal trade of antiquities, but the piece was so exquisite that I couldn't bear to leave it behind. If I owned it, it would go to the British Museum; in the hands of someone else, it might be lost forever to scholars. Not a satisfying way to reconcile such a purchase, not when I knew that, in theory, the only way to stop black-market transactions was by eliminating the demand for objects that lacked a verifiable history of acquisition and ownership.

I was musing over whether this was a realistic possibility in my lifetime as I browsed through my eighth shop, and was nearly ready to quietly approach the owner to see if he had anything else in the back, when something caught my eye: a delicate pin in the shape of a bird of paradise, set in gold with sapphires, rubies, and emeralds. I recognized it at once as the one Lady Elinor had been wearing the day Margaret and I first saw Jeremy in the British Museum. My strategy changed at once.

"What an exquisite brooch!" I exclaimed.

The shopkeeper, who had been keeping an eye on me from a distance, gave me a broad smile and walked to the counter in front of me. "Eighteen-carat gold, madam, and the finest-quality stones."

"However did you get it?"

"The same way I get most of my jewelry. If you'll pardon my saying so, you ladies tend to exceed your allowances."

"I should love to buy it, but it's awfully familiar to me. I'm afraid it belonged to a friend of mine, and it would be rather embarrassing to turn up with something of hers. I don't suppose you could check?"

"Can't do that, madam. I offer my clients absolute confidentiality."

Apparently, absolute confidentiality was worth somewhere in the vicinity of six shillings. I left the shop with the pin and confirmation that Lady Elinor had sold not only it, but several other very valuable pieces in the past few months. I may not have been able to locate the snuffbox, but I was beginning to think that I had a fair idea of who might have taken it.

If Colin had been in town, I could have asked him to make discreet inquiries with the Routledge family solicitor to determine just how dire Lady Elinor's financial situation was. His connection to the palace would be invaluable in such a situation. I would have to rely on more imaginative means, and decided to call on Lord Pembroke's mother, the only person I could think of who might have insight into the matter.

"Forgive me for being so direct, Lady Anders, but did you and your husband enter into any sort of negotiations with Lady Elinor when your son wanted to marry Isabelle?"

"Not in any formal sense. I discussed matters with her in a casual sort of way once it had become clear that Tommy was serious about the girl. As I told you before, there's not a lot of money left, so her dowry would have been very small."

"How small?"

"Nonexistent, really. I'll be quite candid with you, Lady Ashton. Lord Pembroke and I would never have allowed Tommy to marry the girl, regardless of how fond he was of her. I hinted as much to Elinor. She's been a friend, you know, and I hated to think her daughter might have her hopes set unreasonably high."

"Is it that bad? I thought Mr. Routledge was quite well off."

"He left Elinor well settled, but somehow the money's gone. Isabelle's lucky she managed to secure Charles Berry. I don't think most gentlemen would consider taking her for so little."

"Why did Berry take her, then? He's no money of his own."

"There must be a very great attachment on his side. Either that or he wants a bride with a good English heritage. Excellent thing for someone with royal blood, you know. There's hardly a monarchy in Europe without a connection to our own dear queen."

That may have been true, but to marry the penniless granddaughter of a viscount was a far cry from allying oneself with even a minor princess in the House of Saxe-Coburg-Gotha. Charles Berry had no money, and he had no throne. He needed a wife who could bring him a fortune. It made no sense at all that he had agreed to marry Isabelle, unless Lady Elinor had something else to entice him. Or a way to prove that he was not who he claimed. Maybe she was blackmailing him.

I thanked Lady Anders and considered my options as I drove back towards Berkeley Square. I needed to talk to Sebastian. He surely had some way of proving that he was the true descendant of Louis XVI and was perfectly capable of stopping Mr. Berry. I would have to go, yet again, to the *Times*, a course of action that was fast becoming infuriating. Why must he make it so difficult for me to contact him? I stuck my head out of the carriage window and called for Waters to stop.

Sebastian had followed me on enough occasions that I thought it reasonable to surmise he was doing so now. I got out of the coach, crossed Knightsbridge, and went into the park, sending the carriage home without me, assuring Waters that I would be safe there on my own. He was not easily convinced, but I eventually managed, pointing out that his loitering outside the park would serve no purpose and refusing to have one of the footmen accompany me. I appreciated my staff's concern, but I needed to be alone.

I walked slowly along the entire length of the Serpentine, all the while watching for signs of being followed. There were none. I continued on, turning into Kensington Gardens, where I sat on a bench in the most secluded spot I could find. There I waited for three quarters of an hour, going over the facts of the case, making lists of questions whose answers I needed to discover, and checking, at far too frequent intervals, the gold watch pinned to my bodice. Finally I gave up, stood, and surveyed the scene before me. It was getting late, and there were few people in the garden. None, in fact, that I could see, but I was certain that Sebastian was there, lurking somewhere out of sight.

"Sebastian?" I called. "I know you're here. Won't you come talk to me?" Leaves rustled in the wind, and I heard the sound of a dog barking far off in the distance, but my admirer did not present himself. "Please! I need your help! Sebastian!" I stamped my foot in frustration and dropped back onto the bench.

"You really shouldn't lose your composure like that, Kallista darling." He came, seemingly from nowhere, and sat next to me.

"Why do you insist upon skulking about like this? It's infuriating."

"You are lovely when you're in a temper."

"Answer the question."

"I'm merely keeping an eye on you. Do you think it's safe to trot about, unescorted, after all that's been happening to you?"

"I'm perfectly capable of taking care of myself."

"Are you? I could do anything I like to you right now. Take you prisoner; carry you off to my den of iniquity. There's no one to see or stop me."

"If I screamed, someone would come. And I imagine that your den is far enough away that it would be difficult to get me there with no one noticing."

He shrugged. "Perhaps. Fear not, though. You're in no danger with me." For the first time, I could see his face. His eyes, as I remembered, were a shocking blue, but the remainder of his features were unremarkable. Although I wouldn't have described him as handsome, there was a vibrancy about him that was most appealing.

"I've lost your mother's Bible. I'm very sorry."

"It's of no consequence to me. If I had wanted it, I would have taken it when she offered it to me."

"I believe that Charles Berry has it."

"Well, I hope it amuses him."

"How can you be so cavalier about all this? Don't you want to stop him?"

"Berry? He's a bloody boor. Why would I care to involve myself with him?"

"He's stealing your heritage." This brought a hearty laugh from my companion.

"Darling, I do adore you. Such drama! Such enthusiasm! *Τῆλε διαθρέζωμεν ὅπη σθένος.*"

"I might be able to sight-read, but I'm afraid that my verbal skills are woefully lacking. Translation?"

"*Let us run far away, as far as we have strength to go.*"

"How did you become so well educated if you were brought up as a servant?"

"I was sent to school by a benefactor."

"I see. I wondered if you had some sort of hidden trust."

He raised his eyebrows. "A hidden trust? Where would you get such an idea? Have I been misled about your character? Tell me you don't read bad fiction. I thought you were devoted to Homer?"

"Don't try to distract me. Surely you're not going to stand aside while Charles Berry ascends to the throne in France?"

"What concern is it of mine? My family has done more than enough."

This simple statement touched my heart. The pain this poor man must have suffered! I could only imagine the horror he felt from the knowledge of the brutality of his relatives' executions. To think that he'd had to live his entire life denying his identity, posing as a servant, when, by birthright, he should have been surrounded by every luxurious comfort. Despite myself, I took his gloved hand in mine and squeezed it.

"You're quite right. But you cannot allow him to claim something that is rightfully yours. Even if the monarchy is never restored, he should not be able to say he is the true heir to the House of Bourbon."

"And you think *I* am? Oh, this is a delight. No, no, darling, I'm no relation to the poor dauphin. If anything, I'm sick to death of hearing about him."

"But the Bible? Bernadette Capet? I know that she came to England with the dauphin."

"Yes."

"And his daughter was your mother."

"No, you've lost the story completely. Bernadette and her son, my grandfather, brought Louis Charles to England, but they did not stay with him. It was of paramount concern that his identity remain a secret, so the boy was given to the guardianship of a childless couple."

"Did they know who he was?"

"Of course, but they never told a soul."

"But Capet was the name given to the royal family."

"And dear Bernadette adopted it for just that reason. There's nothing my family is fonder of than honoring the French monarchy. You can't imagine how tedious it is."

"If that's how you feel, why have you devoted yourself to stealing things that belonged to Marie Antoinette?"

"Yes, it's quite a conundrum, isn't it? My mother was fixated on the Bourbons and the service Bernadette had done for them. From the time I could speak, she taught me the history of France."

"Is that so awful?"

"When it's done to the exclusion of all other things, yes. She had a practiced litany of all the things that had been stolen from the Bourbons. I couldn't stand listening to it. After I'd gone to school, I knew that I did not want to go back to Richmond. She was horrified that I would consider staying away. Insisted that I remain."

"She had no other children?"

"No. Just me."

"Perhaps she wanted your comfort in her old age?"

"No. She believed emphatically that it was necessary for me to stay because that, darling, is what Marie Antoinette would have wanted. Bernadette, you see, swore that she would stay near enough Louis Charles and his heirs to make sure that they were always well. Her son followed her, as did his daughter, and now I am supposed to do the same."

"You were to watch the dauphin's heir?"

"Yes. Can you imagine? It's been a hundred years since the revolution. Surely it's safe for us to move on." He picked up a pebble from the ground and threw it with some force over the flower bed across from us. "We had a terrible argument, and I left. Came to London, changed my name, started anew."

"But you took the name Capet?"

"I've never been able to resist such a fine opportunity for irony," he said. "Before I came to London, she tried to give me that bloody snuffbox, and I wouldn't take it. It was the most precious thing she owned, you see. The dauphin had given it to Bernadette, and it had been passed down since then. My mother used to show it to me when I was a boy but would never let me touch it. She told me that inside was a piece of paper on which the entire story was recorded, written in Bernadette's hand."

"Why did you refuse to take it?"

"Whoever has the snuffbox has tacitly agreed to look out for the dauphin's heir. I had no intention of doing that."

"You didn't return to Richmond, even when she died?"

"No. What would have been the point?"

"I still don't understand why you are now collecting things that belonged to the queen."

"I felt a terrible guilt after my mother died. I'd left her alone and mocked what she viewed as the sacred purpose of her life. Shortly after her death, I overheard a gentleman saying that he owned a Limoges box purported to have belonged to the French queen. I knew that my mother would have loved to own such a thing."

"And you couldn't afford to buy it from him?"

"Not at all. I'd had a difficult time earning a living in London and had discovered that I possess a certain talent for entering houses undiscovered. And that talent, once developed, offers a handy way to supplement one's income. It was simple to get the box from Lord Grantham's house."

"And the rest?"

"It's rather addictive, sneaking about like that, causing a stir. Quite exciting."

"So why did you return the pink diamond?"

"Despite my best efforts, it was impossible for me to completely rid myself of the hereditary awe for the House of Bourbon my family has passed to me. Once I realized that I'd taken the stone from the dauphin's heir, I thought I ought to give it back, particularly as it was he who paid for my schooling."

"David Francis is the true heir?" I wondered if Beatrice was aware of this. "You didn't know this when you took the diamond? Surely your mother would have told you?"

"No. That was something revealed only once a person had agreed to carry on the family business. Absurd, isn't it? So I didn't know it was Francis. Not until I read in the newspapers that he owned the snuff-box. When I'd refused it, my mother made a great show of saying that it would be gone from our family forever, that I'd left her no choice but to return it to the Bourbons."

"Who do you think killed him?"

"I've not the slightest idea. Of course this all proves my mother right. The Bourbons did still need watching."

"It wouldn't have made any difference," I said.

"No, it wouldn't have."

"How did you get Léonard's letters?"

"I'm afraid they were one of the first things I stole. I stumbled on them quite by accident. I'd gone into the library at a country house to get an enameled Fabergé box that was on display. When I removed it, I noticed a bundle of papers behind some books on the same shelf. They were held together with a red ribbon, and I thought they might be love letters. Being the romantic that I am, I pulled them out, hoping for a good read. So far as I know, the gentleman who owned them still has not noticed that they're missing."

"Who is it? I should return them to him."

"You wouldn't dare."

"Of course I would."

"Then I shan't tell you."

"Why didn't you take Marie Antoinette's letters from Mr. Francis when you stole the pink diamond?"

"I had no idea that he had them." He rose from the bench and stood in front of me. "This has been lovely, darling, but I'm afraid I must run."

"No, wait. What about the things you've stolen. Will you give them back?"

"Certainly not."

"Not even Cécile's earrings? For me?"

"Maybe if they were yours." He reached down and turned my head to the side, gently touching my ear. "They would look lovely on you."

"You're not planning to disappear again, are you?"

"I've no reason to stay."

"Can you at least tell me how to reach you?"

"For what? So that you can abandon the dashing Mr. Hargreaves for me? I don't think so, darling. But I'll always come if you need me."

"I don't like being followed, Sebastian."

"You can reach me through the *Times*." He bowed and walked away. I didn't bother to call after him but sighed and looked down at where he had sat next to me. There, on the bench, he had left my notebook.

31

—————————————

THE MOMENT I RETURNED HOME, I PULLED OUT THE LETTER I'D received from Colin the previous week, the first he had sent from France. He'd written it on the ferry and posted it as soon as he'd arrived in Calais, even before boarding the train for Paris. I smiled as I read it; he always managed to make letters sound like his half of a conversation, and I could almost hear him saying the words, picture him sitting across from me, running a hand through his tousled hair, his long legs stretched out in front of him. I did not, however, let this entrancing image distract me from my purpose. I skimmed the rest of the page until I found the sentence for which I was looking. *We've tickets for the opera on the third, seats in the first row of the balcony.*

I composed a cable for him, a clumsy-sounding message, but it would convey its intended meaning when he read the first letter of every third word. This would provide him a brief but incisive update on the situation in London, particularly as it pertained to Charles Berry.

"Did you see that another letter arrived from Paris today, madam?" Davis asked as he took the cable from me, looking not at me, but at the pile of unopened mail on my desk.

"No, I haven't had a chance." I skimmed through the letters until I found one addressed in Colin's familiar handwriting.

"Would you like me to send this cable at once, or shall I wait until after you've read what Mr. Hargreaves has to say?"

"Send it now, Davis. It's quite urgent. If I need to add anything, I can always send another."

Davis bowed and left me to my reading. I was glad for the privacy the moment I opened the envelope. This letter was, if I may be so bold, the most exquisitely written, lyrical declaration of love that had ever been put to paper. It sang from the page. I read it three times through before noticing that my skin had grown hot, and my hands were trembling. So beautiful was it that I longed to read it aloud, to hear its melody spoken, until I remembered Colin's suggestion that in a London town house, one is never truly alone.

And then, all at once, I realized that I'd missed the point entirely. With a sigh, I pulled out a blank piece of paper and copied out the first letter of every third word. His news complemented mine perfectly: Lady Elinor's fortune had been spent funding Garnier and his would-be revolutionaries. That was why there was no money left for Isabelle's dowry. She wouldn't need one if her mother were in the position to arrange for her marriage to a future king. And surely, financing the enterprise gave Lady Elinor the power to choose a queen for Charles Berry.

It was a risky proposition, however. Without a dowry, Isabelle would be in dire straits should the restoration fail. But it was nearly a reasonable gamble. The republic in France was staggeringly unpopular. Monsieur Garnier was loved by all and was too savvy a politician to fall victim to the weaknesses that had caused Boulanger's coup to fail.

Did Lady Elinor know that Berry was a fraud? Had she been willing to risk so much only because she believed he truly had descended from Louis XVI? The knowledge that her family had helped refugees fleeing from the terror nagged at me. Would they have known what became of the dauphin?

I am not particularly proud of what I did next, but my options were limited. I sent a note to Isabelle, inviting her to come with me to the British Museum. I received her reply at breakfast the next morning and went round to collect her at Meadowdown as soon as I'd finished eating.

We walked through two Greco-Roman galleries before, in the Archaic Room, I summoned the courage to turn the conversation in the direction I knew it must go.

"Do you miss Mr. Berry?" I asked as we stood in front of the Strangford Apollo, a marble statue said to be from the Cyclades. Looking at it made me long for Santorini.

"I find that I can bear his absence rather well," Isabelle said.

"I've learned about your family's involvement in assisting refugees from the French Revolution. It seems some sort of poetic justice that you should wind up engaged to the heir of the House of Bourbon."

"That's precisely how my mother views it." She stared blankly at Apollo.

"I understand that the Torringtons helped a most important person," I said. "It must be quite a wonderful story."

This, to my surprise, made Isabelle smile. "I always did like it, especially the bit about the pink diamond. So romantic."

"I don't think I know that part," I said.

"The dauphin offered my family a pink diamond to repay them for their help, but my great-great-grandfather refused to accept it. It was one of the few things the boy had that belonged to his mother, and the Torringtons felt strongly that he should keep it as a memento of her." She laughed. "A lovely gesture but foolish in the end. He obviously had to sell it at some point, probably to pay for his passage to America. If he hadn't, it never would have wound up being stolen by that dreadful thief here in England, would it?"

"No, I suppose not," I said, and realized that I'd been holding my breath while she spoke. Apollo's smile seemed to reproach me.

We walked through the rest of the museum. Isabelle found the mummies most diverting. As for me, I hardly took notice of anything that we saw. I did not for a moment believe that Louis Charles had sold the pink diamond. When the newspapers reported its theft, Lady Elinor must have immediately identified the stone's owner as the one person who could, without fail, bring her plan to ruin.

Did she confront him? Confirm in some way that he was Louis Charles's heir? I felt sick once again, certain that, had I not convinced Mr. Francis to report the theft, he would still be alive. My thoughts turned at once to little Edward. Was there any possibility that Lady Elinor knew about the boy? Sebastian was not the only person who had been following me; could I have unwittingly led her to Edward? And what about Mrs. White? Did she know of her son's royal blood?

I invented a headache and took Isabelle home, then directed Waters to drive me to the Whites' house. The housekeeper admitted me at once but glowered as she brought me to her mistress. I would not have thought it possible, but Mrs. White was even thinner than when I had last seen her.

"I'm so sorry to bother you again, but I have a few more questions about Mr. Francis. Did he ever tell you anything…special…about himself? Perhaps by way of explaining why it was so important for him to have a child?"

"Don't all men want children?"

"Probably," I said. "But he gave you no particular reason for his desire?"

"No, Lady Ashton. He was always very kind to me but kept his thoughts to himself. Took great interest in what I was doing, and, of course, in Edward, but almost never told us anything about the rest of his life. No surprise there, though."

"Have you noticed anything strange around your house since his death?"

"Whatever can you mean?" she asked.

"Has anything or anyone struck you as suspicious?"

"You don't think that someone in my household—"

"No, no. It's just that I have reason to believe that the person who killed Mr. Francis might have an interest in Edward."

"You think my son is in danger?"

"I can't be sure," I said. "But I think it would be best if you and the boy went away for a while."

"We don't have anywhere to go." I had to strain to hear her voice.

"Don't worry. I know of a place where you will be perfectly safe."

"I don't know that I should trust you," she said.

"I can well understand that, and I fear there's little I can do to reassure you. Forgive me, but you and Mrs. Francis held dear the same man. She knows me well enough to trust that I am capable of solving his murder. Please, Mrs. White, I'm only trying to protect your son."

"I'm not sure what to think," she said, and tugged at her already ragged cuticles.

"Inspector Manning of Scotland Yard can vouch for me. Would you like me to send him to you?"

"Mr. Francis would want me to keep the boy from harm."

"Will you go?"

She looked as if she wanted to sigh but that the effort would be too great for her frail body. "Yes. What else can I do? I can't very well stay here if I've been warned of danger, and I wouldn't know where to take him on my own. But I would like to speak to the inspector."

"I'll ask him to come as soon as possible. I shall need you to be ready to depart tomorrow. Tell none of your servants, and don't bother to pack. I'll arrange for clothes and whatever else you need to be purchased for you. If there's anything to which Edward is especially attached, you may bring it, so long as it won't draw attention to the fact that you're leaving."

"You're certain this is necessary?"

"No, I'm not. But if there is danger, and we do nothing, the consequences could be more dreadful than either of us can imagine."

Inspector Manning called on Mrs. White a few hours later and reported that he had little difficulty convincing her that she was doing the right thing by following my advice. After talking to her, he seemed to take my role in the investigations more seriously.

My suspicions regarding Lady Elinor troubled me greatly, particularly because, if they were correct, Isabelle's life would be thrown into turmoil. I hated to think that a woman who had been a family friend for so many years could be guilty of such a crime, but it seemed increasingly likely that she was responsible for the deaths in Richmond. I needed firm evidence, and decided to visit Floris, the store from which the shaving lotion that had killed both men had been purchased. Mr. Floris himself spoke to me. He was, understandably, hesitant at first. But when I explained the nature of the case on which I was working, he agreed to help. Together, we combed through his records. A mere two days after the story of the pink-diamond theft appeared in the papers, someone bought one bottle of lavender shaving lotion. The receipt, unlike the others, did not list the name of the purchaser, so Mr. Floris called for the clerk who had written up the sale.

"Oh yes, I do recall this," he said, smiling. "She ordered a number of items for herself, too, but wanted this to be kept separate. I believe it was a gift for a gentleman."

"Do you remember her name?" I asked.

"I'm afraid I don't."

"Could you describe her?"

"Middle-aged, I think. Fair hair."

"Would you recognize her if you saw her again?"

"I think so. It wasn't the first time I'd helped her."

"There must be a receipt for the other things she bought," I said, and continued to make my way through the stack of sales records, stopping when I found a name I recognized. On the same date, from the same clerk, Lady Elinor Routledge had purchased two bottles of eau de toilette and four combs.

I never would have suspected her!" Margaret exclaimed as we sat in my library that evening. Davis had opened an excellent port for us and, though I know he did not approve, brought what was left of Philip's stock of cigars for my friend.

"I'm not absolutely certain that she did it. What I've got to do now is—" We were interrupted by the arrival of Ivy. I had not spoken to her since our argument and was shocked that she would come to me after things had gone so badly between us. She was dressed in a ball gown fashioned from red silk and would undoubtedly have created a winning impression at whatever party she attended were it not for the fact that her eyes were swollen, and her cheeks streaked with tears. My first thought was that Mrs. Reynold-Plympton had talked to Lord Fortescue, who, in turn, had talked to Robert.

"Ivy! Whatever is the matter?"

"Oh, I'm having a rather difficult evening, that's all." She tried to smile. "You know how the Season can overwhelm one."

"You need port," Margaret said, and handed her a glass. "Are you off to a party this evening? Where's Robert?"

"We were to go to Lansdowne House for a ball. But Robert decided that it would be better for me to stay home."

"Why?" I asked.

"He's afraid my health isn't what it ought to be," she said. "And he was going to have to spend the evening discussing politics, so he thought there was no need for me to come."

"What would make him think that?" Margaret asked, blowing rings of smoke. "You're strong as a horse."

"He just didn't want you to be bored if he was off with Lord Fortescue and his crew all night," I said.

"How could I possibly be bored at a ball? No, I think that there's some other reason." She looked at Margaret, as if weighing whether to continue, then emptied her glass in a single drink. "I think he has a mistress, and she is going to be there tonight. He knew that if I saw him dance with her, I would be able to read the infidelity on his face."

"Dearest, no, that's not it at all," I said.

"And to think that he would keep me at home instead of telling her to stay away. I suppose she's married, too. Maybe her husband was insisting that she go."

"No, Ivy, truly this is wrong. I know—" I stopped.

"Well?" Margaret asked. "Continue, please. What do you know?"

"I know that Robert is not having an affair," I said, and out spilled the details of my own suspicions and my confrontation of Mrs. Reynold-Plympton.

"Emily!" Ivy cried. "How could you?"

"I know. Forgive me, Ivy, I shouldn't have, but I could not bear to think that Robert was neglecting you."

"I know I've been upset with you, but I realized that I've nowhere else to turn. You've always been my dearest friend." She rested her head daintily in her hands. "And though I am horrified at what you've done, how can I fault you for it? I've been worried about this for weeks, and you have eased my mind, Emily."

"I'm glad of that, but I should never have done it without talking to you first."

"I would never have agreed to let you do it."

"I can be very persuasive, Ivy," I said.

"Oh, for heaven's sake!" Margaret said. "Enough! What are we to do about Lady Elinor?"

"Lady Elinor?" Ivy asked. I brought her up to date on all that had transpired since we last spoke. "Oh, how dreadful. Poor Isabelle. Whatever shall happen?"

"Nothing good, I'm afraid," I said. "I've just been trying to determine how I can prove beyond question that she is the one responsible for the deaths in Richmond."

Ivy hesitated for just a moment. "Could the police..."

"I shall, of course, include Inspector Manning. But I don't want the police sprung upon her, nor do I want Isabelle there."

"Where did you send Mrs. White and her boy?" Ivy asked.

"They're to go to Greece and stay at the villa. Meg's going to travel with them." An idea came to me, vaguely at first, and then gradually formed into something approaching coherence. "Lady Elinor believes that there is no surviving heir of the dauphin, correct? What if she learned about Edward? Believed that he, or his mother, could come forward and make a claim to the throne?"

"I like this idea, Emily," Margaret said, still puffing on her cigar.

"But what if the boy were to get hurt?" Ivy asked.

"We couldn't tell her until after he is safely out of the country," I said. "But then, I could call on her, subtly alert her to the situation, and then wait for her to come to the Whites' house."

"But how would you know when to expect her?" Ivy asked.

"I wouldn't, really. Colin once told me that most of the time his work is little more than waiting for something interesting to happen. I'm beginning to understand what he meant."

"You could skulk about the house and sleep in the boy's room," Margaret suggested. "Eventually, she would figure out a way to come to you."

"We might be able to force her hand somehow. Make her think that Edward's identity was going to be revealed on a certain day."

"What a pity Bastille Day's already passed," Ivy said.

"I'm afraid it won't work," I said, my mind racing. "Whoever committed these crimes knows that I've been investigating. That person has had me followed, forced my coach off the road, flung a brick through my window, sent a maid to spy on me. If I tell Lady Elinor about Edward, she will know at once that I'm aware of her guilt, no matter how congenial my guise for delivering the information. What would she have to lose at that moment? I promised Colin I would take no unnecessary risks. I'm afraid this course of action would fall into that category."

"You're right," Margaret said. "It's too dangerous."

"We'll just have to keep thinking," I said. Davis tapped on the door and entered, his face ashen.

"Madam, I'm afraid that someone's attacked Baines. Could you please come right away?"

32

IT WAS HIS DAY OFF," DAVIS EXPLAINED, AS I FOLLOWED HIM, ALONG with Margaret and Ivy, up to the servants' quarters. "He was walking home, and as he approached the back of the house, someone struck him over the head. I've sent for a doctor."

I was greatly relieved to learn from the physician that my footman's injuries were not serious. Less welcome was the response of the police. The officers assigned by Inspector Manning had caught a man they'd seen running from the house and questioned him, but their conclusion was that this had been nothing more than a simple robbery. Baines's money and watch had been stolen, and the culprit had been implicated in more than one other similar crime.

"How can they possibly think this is unrelated to the attacks on me?" I asked. "It makes no sense."

"I begin to see why you feel that you cannot rely wholeheartedly on the police," Ivy said.

The next day was exceedingly hectic. Between getting Mrs. White, Edward, and Meg off to Greece and checking on Baines, I had not a moment to return to the question of how to trap Lady Elinor. Meg was thrilled to be going to Santorini, and I smiled when I thought of how, less than a year ago, she had dreaded traveling. I wished that Cécile could join them, but until she was finished with Monsieur Garnier, she would not be able to leave Paris. Still, they would be in capable hands with my maid, who would manage every detail of the trip with her usual smooth efficiency.

Once the morning mail arrived, I was able to convince Inspector Manning that Baines's attack was not an isolated incident. Someone had sent a letter with a sinister message: *Who will suffer next for your impudence? Abandon your investigation.*

After speaking to the inspector, I was left to consider my options and felt immediately out of my depth. I had not the slightest idea how to trick Lady Elinor into implicating herself. It would have been so easy to turn to Colin, if he weren't in Paris, or Sebastian, if he could be reached without going through the *Times*. Either of them was certain to have insights into the matter beyond mine.

It was a frightening feeling, knowing that so much was at stake, that if I did not handle matters in the best possible way, more people could be hurt than those already affected by Lady Elinor's crimes. I could not allow another member of my staff to be brutalized as Baines had been. If I could resolve all this on my own, it would be a significant accomplishment, and the thought of achieving such a thing filled me with a surge of inspiration that led to a new idea. It was so obvious now that I laughed at myself for not having come to it earlier. Not wanting to waste another instant, I sent for Margaret at once.

"It's inspired!" she cried. "Does it have to happen tonight, though? Jeremy and I've arranged everything for our public falling-out to take place at the lord mayor's ball tonight. I don't see how we can possibly reschedule."

"You don't need to come with me, Margaret. The fewer people on hand the better, and you know that I must have Inspector Manning. What I need you to do is write the letter. Lady Elinor would recognize my handwriting."

"Very well," Margaret said. "But I don't like missing the adventure. You must promise me that the next time you unmask a murderer, you do it at a time when I can help in a more exciting way."

"I'll do my best," I said. "Now, here's what I want you to write." We spent the next half hour crafting our letter. In the end, I was most satisfied with it.

Dear Lady Elinor,

It has come to my attention that your daughter's future happiness depends not only upon the marriage you have arranged for her, but on the success of her fiancé's claim to the French throne. My own dear son, only six years old, is the child of David Francis. I've no doubt that you grasp the implications of this statement. I assure you that I've no interest in seeing him named king; politics is a risky business, and when I consider what happened to his ancestors, I cannot hope that he would ever sit on a throne. But if I am to hold him back, I cannot do so in good faith without asking for some sort of compensation on your part. I will gladly remain silent and hand you the keys to the kingdom, as it were, if you would be so kind as to make it worth my while. You might imagine that our circumstances are no longer quite so comfortable now his father is dead.

If this is agreeable to you, I should like to see you this evening at my house. Call no earlier than nine o'clock, as the boy will be asleep by then and I can guarantee us a reasonable amount of privacy. We will be leaving for Paris in the morning, and I would very much like to have finished with this matter before then.

I am yrs., etc.,

Mrs. Elizabeth White

"I don't see how she could refrain from coming," Margaret said. "I must go if I'm to be ready for my grand performance. Oh, Emily, I do envy you all this excitement!"

"I don't know if 'excitement' is the proper word."

"If I didn't have absolute confidence in you, it wouldn't be. But I'm not worried that you'll come to harm. You're perfectly capable of outwitting Lady Elinor. She doesn't stand a chance."

As I walked her to the door, I saw that Inspector Manning was outside, speaking to the officers stationed in Berkeley Square. It was the perfect opportunity to consult with him and request his assistance. He was concerned that my plan was too dangerous, but I insisted that Lady Elinor was more likely to talk to me than to him. Furthermore, so long as he and his men were near, I would be perfectly safe. He promised to meet me at the Whites' at eight-thirty.

I spent the remainder of the afternoon buried in Homer. I'd woefully neglected my Greek in the past weeks and feared that if I did not keep up, Mr. Moore might make me return to reading Xenophon, the tedious texts he'd forced upon me in the early days of my study. I was captivated by the trials of Odysseus, suffering the wrath of Poseidon, longing for home and Penelope, although I was not entirely sympathetic to the man. There were bits of his adventures that I think he enjoyed rather too much, and I wondered if he really was the equal of his wife. She was a woman to be much admired. Clever, faithful, inventive.

The hours passed quickly, and I was surprised to see that it was nearly seven o'clock. I would have to hurry to prepare myself to meet Inspector Manning, and was halfway up the stairs to change my dress when Davis handed me a note from Lady Elinor:

My dear Emily,

Ivy Brandon called on me late this afternoon and fell ill after taking tea with me. I've tried to reach her husband and her mother but can locate neither of them. Isabelle and I are to dine with the Prince and Princess of Wales this evening, and I hate to leave Ivy alone with only servants. Would you be so good as to come sit with her until Robert can be summoned?

> I am yrs., etc.
> E.R.

A horrible, sickening feeling crashed into my stomach. Surely Lady Elinor would not be so foolish as to harm Ivy, not in her own house? Her guilt would be immediately apparent. I felt compelled to investigate but did not have time to go to Meadowdown before I needed to be at the Whites'. Perhaps this was nothing more than a ruse to distract me from my purpose. If I hurried, I would have just enough time to go by Belgrave Square and leave an urgent message for Robert.

I was shocked to see my friend's husband, looking utterly disheveled, open the door himself. "Is she with you?" he asked, looking around me.

"Ivy? No, I've just received—"

"We're having Lord Fortescue and the prime minister to dine tonight. They'll be at the house by eight. She would have needed to start dressing by now, but she's never returned from making calls this afternoon."

"Read this," I said, thrusting the letter at him.

"She's ill? What can Lady Elinor mean, she couldn't locate me? I've been home all afternoon."

"She never tried," I said, and told him as quickly as possible all that I knew of Lady Elinor's crimes.

"I'll go to Meadowdown at once."

"It's unlikely that she would have done anything to hurt Ivy, but be careful, Robert."

"I'll pretend that nothing's amiss. You found me, and I've come to collect my wife."

"I pray that you find Ivy well. It's unlikely that you'll find Lady Elinor home."

"So help me, I will tear that woman limb from limb if she has so much as looked at my wife in a menacing way."

Robert transformed from an average-looking man into a paragon of the most handsome sort of divine wrath. I hoped that when he found her, Ivy would be in a condition to appreciate the change. I wished him luck and set off on my own errand, my heart heavy with worry for my friend. It took considerable effort to force my attention to my role in this intrigue, but I looked at my watch and knew that I could not afford the luxury of spending even another moment lamenting what might have happened to Ivy.

After sending my letter to Lady Elinor, I had asked Inspector Manning to visit Mrs. White's housekeeper. Knowing that the woman was not a particular admirer of mine, I thought the scheme I was proposing would go over better with her if it came from a policeman. When I arrived at the house, she greeted me with her usual scowl, but this time there was a hint of concern in her eyes.

"They're perfectly safe," I said to her. "They boarded the train this morning and are well on their way to Greece by now."

"I hope you're right," she said. "I don't much like you. You're the sort who brings trouble into a house."

I could hardly argue with her. On this point she was right. I'd certainly brought Ivy trouble, and Isabelle, not to mention David Francis. He had suffered the worst of all of them. It was hardly an encouraging line of thought on which to embark before trying to capture a murderer, but I found myself quite unable to stop thinking about the misery I had brought to those around me.

The housekeeper gave me the reply Lady Elinor had sent to my letter. It stated quite plainly that she had no idea what Mrs. White was talking about and that there clearly had been some sort of confusion. She apologized and said that she was unable to meet that evening, but that if Mrs. White still wanted to speak with her, she was welcome to call at Meadowdown anytime following her return from Paris.

"I didn't expect she would agree to the meeting," I said to Inspector Manning as we went over the details of our plan. "But I hope that this has instilled in her a sense of urgency, that she will decide the boy must be silenced immediately. I do believe she is scared."

As the hour grew late, we set our trap in Edward's room, and I was filled with anxiety. I took my position, hiding behind the armoire, wondering if I should have gone with Robert, chastising myself for not even considering it until now. She was my friend, and I'd left her to...to what? The darkness was claustrophobic and I began to feel chilled, unable to steady myself. Robert was perfectly capable of looking after his wife. It was right that he be the one to go to her.

I wondered what time it was and hoped that Inspector Manning, who was watching the house from the outside, was still awake. My own eyelids had grown heavier than I would have thought possible. I wished I could have stretched my legs.

After what seemed like an eternity, the floorboards creaked and the door to the nursery opened. The effect of the sound on me was more intense than that of smelling salts. I strained to listen, and heard someone walking with steps lighter than a child's, crossing the room to the small bed. I could see the intruder's form in silhouette against the moonlight that struggled through the curtains on the window. With a swift movement, she tipped a bottle against a piece of cloth she held in her hand, then pressed it over what she thought was the child's mouth. I had piled pillows under the blankets to make it look as if someone were sleeping, and her hand recoiled as she realized the boy was not there. She spun around as she heard me step out from where I'd hidden behind the armoire.

"Emily?" She stepped away from the bed. "What is this?"

"What are you doing?" I asked. There was an awful look in her eyes: scared, dazed, almost as if she were in a trance, but at the same time fiery with a deep anger.

"I can't let him live, Emily. He'll ruin everything I've done for Isabelle. And now you will, too. Why didn't you stop? You've forced me to make everything worse."

"I'm sure it's not so bad as you think."

"You've no idea how very bad it is. You haven't seen your good friend Ivy, have you? I never guessed you would abandon her so easily."

"What did you do to her?"

She laughed. "Maybe you should go see."

I knew she was trying to distract me. "Why did you kill David Francis?"

"We both know why he had to die. It was you, after all, who led me to him."

"The pink diamond was the key?" I asked.

"As soon as I learned he had it, I knew I couldn't let him live. The dauphin swore to my family that he would never part with the diamond. I let Isabelle believe otherwise, of course. It wouldn't do for her to know the sordid details of these affairs. They would only upset her."

"You didn't have to kill him."

"I most certainly did. The letter in the snuffbox only confirmed that."

"You stole the snuffbox? How?"

"My dear child, you've no idea how easy it is to break into most houses."

"Had Mr. Francis threatened to expose Mr. Berry?"

"I don't know, but I could not risk his doing so. Do you not understand what I've sacrificed to get Isabelle where she is? I've spent my entire fortune to ensure that she will be queen of France."

"But what if the coup fails?"

"It won't. Garnier is unstoppable. And even if he weren't, Isabelle will always command a position of respect so long as she is married to the head of a royal family, even one without a throne."

"Mr. Francis never told anyone his true identity. Why did you think he would suddenly reveal himself?"

"People change when there is an actual crown at stake. And if Berry were cast aside, Isabelle would be left with nothing. She has no dowry and would be able to get no other husband. She would be left a spinster, doomed to a life of poverty and discomfort. No mother could stand by and watch her daughter come to such ruin."

"You've been living quite comfortably. Surely it's not as bad as all that."

"The creditors cannot be put off indefinitely." She stepped towards me. "Why did you have to interfere?"

"I could not stand by and watch someone cause such injustice in the world."

"Your ideals are amusing, Emily. You should have heeded my warnings. I tried to stop you."

"You were following me."

"Oh, that wasn't me. It was quite simple to get Mr. Berry to take care of that. All I had to do was plant the idea in his head that you were bent on proving him a fraud. As soon as I learned you weren't interested in him romantically and that you were investigating for Mrs. Francis, I knew I had to do something. I never thought it would come to this, but you're rather stubborn. You ought to have taken my advice and gone on a trip."

"Is that why you made such a point of keeping me as a friend? To try to influence me to leave?"

"Once I knew you weren't going to do as I suggested, I had to come up with a way to distract you from your purpose. Sinking you in scandal was an obvious solution."

"You started the rumors about the Duke of Bainbridge and me," I said.

"You couldn't have made it easier for me. Your eccentric habits cry out for the gossips' attention."

"And you sent Lizzie to my house?"

"You have figured it all out, haven't you? When I first hired her, it was to make sure you weren't involved with Mr. Berry. Later, as I figured out what you were really up to, she became more important to me. She's a stupid girl but did manage to get me some useful information. I hadn't expected your mother would come to your rescue."

"A foolish error, Lady Elinor, considering the lengths to which you were willing to go to protect your own daughter."

"It didn't matter. Berry was perfectly willing to step things up once your reputation had been saved. I only wish the fools he'd hired had been more efficient. You should never have made it across Berkeley Square the night the coach nearly hit you. It would have saved me the trouble of having to take care of you tonight."

I took a step back. "How did you know that nicotine was such an effective poison?"

"I use it on my roses. It helps keep everything beautiful. I only wish I had some with me now. But I think you'll prefer this. It's more pleasant." She lunged at me, forcing against my face the damp, sweet-smelling cloth she still clutched in her hand. I pushed back with all my weight, flinging her across the room.

Inspector Manning stepped out of the shadows and picked Lady Elinor up from the floor.

"I didn't hear you come in," I said.

"I followed her inside. Waited right outside the door while you talked with her. Mr. Hargreaves was right. You are decent at this sort of thing. I've heard all I need. My men should be coming up any time now. I've already signaled for them."

They arrived shortly and escorted their prisoner from the house.

I kicked at the cloth Lady Elinor had dropped. "What's on this?" I asked.

Inspector Manning reached for it and sniffed. "Chloroform."

"Hardly would have had the same effect as nicotine," I said.

"It would have if she'd been able to finish her plan. She left a large quantity of lamp oil in the hall outside the room. Looks like she planned to set the house on fire to cover up what she'd done."

"I see," I said, willing my body to stop shaking.

"You've done good work here, Lady Ashton. Mr. Hargreaves will be pleased."

"I promised him I would take no unnecessary risks."

The policeman shrugged. "I'd say you kept that promise. I would never have gone along with your scheme if I wasn't certain that I could've protected you. Mr. Hargreaves would throttle me himself if I'd let anything happen to you."

33

THE INSPECTOR BROUGHT ME HOME, WHERE DAVIS, TIRED BUT CLEARLY pleased, met me at the door.

"Madam!" he exclaimed. "Are you all right?"

"Fine," I said. "Exhausted, but fine. Any word from Mr. Brandon?"

"Not from him, but from Mrs. Brandon herself, madam." He handed me a note that contained only one sentence: *All is well*. A bit more detail would have been welcome, but this would suffice for the moment. I collapsed into my bed, where, despite my weariness, I found I could not sleep. Pleased though I was to have solved the crime, I took no joy in knowing that I was sending someone I'd known for most of my life to prison, and possibly to her death. I ached at the thought of Isabelle learning the truth about her mother and worried that her own life would now be ruined, too.

Added to this angst was Colin's absence. His actions during the past months had surprised me at every turn. He had not tried to keep me from pursuing my investigations and had offered assistance without taking charge on his own. And now, in the aftermath of it all, I wanted nothing more than to sit with him, in quiet triumph, discussing what had transpired.

I loved to flirt with him, to tease him, to discuss Greek with him. But I had not expected to find that, as a partner, he could offer more than that. He challenged me, stimulated my thinking, and offered both comfort and support when I succumbed to frustration. Was it possible that, as his wife, I might grow more than if I remained alone? The idea was an appealing one, and I could not recall him having done anything that suggested he would keep me from pursuing my interests and ideals. I wondered when he would propose again. If he would propose again. Surely he would? I let my mind wander, remembering the last time he'd kissed me, the feeling of his arms around me, and then, at last, I was able to fall asleep.

The next morning, Ivy stormed into my breakfast room at an indecent hour, embraced me, and began apologizing.

"I was very foolish, Emily. I wanted to help you. I thought the plan you'd mentioned was a good one, and that my own reputation was such that I would never be suspected of being an accomplice in this sort of thing. So I went to Lady Elinor bent on telling her this long, convoluted story about how I'd been barraged with rumors of people's infidelities and that I was shocked to see how low the moral fiber of the empire was sinking."

"You told her about Mr. Francis's child?"

"I meant to, Emily, truly I did, but I found that I could not bring myself to do it."

"So what happened? Why were you at her house for so long?"

"While we were taking tea, a letter came for her. It was urgent, so she read it at once. She said that there was a matter of business to which she needed to attend and excused herself, promising that she would return shortly, and she did. When she came back, we drank more tea, and I was overcome with the most dreadful fatigue."

"She must have drugged your tea," I said.

"I believe so. She called for a servant and had me put into a bedroom, where I fell asleep immediately. The next thing I knew, Robert had come for me."

"Did he encounter any difficulties in reaching you?"

"No, none at all. He was quite upset, though, worried that I had put myself in harm's way. Carried me out of the house, Emily, can you imagine? It was magnificent."

The glow on her face made it perfectly clear that it would no longer be necessary for Lord Fortescue to have that conversation with his protégé. Robert would not make the mistake of being an overly considerate husband any time in the immediate future.

"And you, Emily? What happened with you?" I told her the entire story, and she was duly horrified. "You could have been killed."

"No, I was perfectly safe. Inspector Manning was never far away."

"It's all so dreadful. Poor Isabelle. To know that her own mother is capable of such terrible things."

"And all in the name of protecting her daughter," I said. "It's ghastly."

"I do wish there was something we could do for her."

"I've sent her a note this morning, but I don't expect she'll reply." Poor Isabelle was in a precarious situation, but I understood completely that she would not want my help. All the papers would be full of the story of her mother's downfall, and there could be little doubt what the outcome of her trial would be. I only hoped that, as she was a woman, Lady Elinor would be spared from execution. "I wonder if anyone's sent for her brother?"

Inspector Manning called soon after Ivy left, and found me still at breakfast. He knew better this time than to resist my offers of food. He filled a plate and sat across from me.

"She's made a full confession," he said. "She believed your letter was indeed from Mrs. White. Gave Mrs. Brandon laudanum in an attempt to distract you, because she'd started to worry that you were

onto the scheme. I don't think there was ever any intention of harm-
ing her."

"So Stilleman's death was an accident?" I asked.

"Yes. Lady Elinor only intended to kill Mr. Francis. Stilleman was
allowed to take what he wanted from the toiletries in the dressing
room, and made the bad choice of selecting the shaving lotion. Jane
Stilleman was released from prison this morning. Would you like to
go to Richmond and bring Mrs. Francis the news?"

"I would," I said, and for a second time, left the inspector breakfasting at my table.

Beatrice wept when I told her the story. "I had no idea. No idea at
all who he was."

"I wish I could offer you some comfort."

"Why didn't he tell me?"

"I don't know. To protect you, I suppose."

"Foolish man!" Her handkerchief already soaked, I gave her mine,
which she used to wipe the tears from her face.

"There is something else you must know," I said. "Something that
will be difficult to hear." Beatrice took the news of her husband's illegitimate son better than I would have expected. She cried, but softly,
no gasping sobs.

"Is there any point to being angry with him now?" she asked.
"That child is all that is left of him. Can I regret what he did? He so
desperately wanted a son."

I left her but, instead of going home, went to Mr. Barber's studio to
ask him to go to Richmond at once. He would be more capable than
anyone of offering comfort to Beatrice.

Within a few days, Monsieur Garnier's coup had been abandoned.
Word that Charles Berry was a fraud scandalized his supporters,

and Garnier was too savvy a politician to ally himself with such a man. Cécile was disappointed never to have had the chance to lure Garnier away from his plans but remained convinced that she, like Boulanger's mistress before, would have been more attractive to a man than the idea of ruling a nation.

As for Mr. Berry, he disappeared from Paris as soon as the news broke that David Francis was the true heir of the dauphin. Although we were not able to keep from the press the news that Francis had a son, we did manage to persuade them not to identify the boy. It was rumored that Berry had returned to America, and I hoped that to be true, preferring to have the vile man as far from me as possible. I'd written Colin to inquire about the list of stolen objects I'd found in the Savoy; he believed that Berry kept it because he planned to ask that everything belonging to the queen be given to him once he was named king of France.

Once the case was fully settled, I began to make plans to travel to Santorini. I was eager to see Mrs. White and relieved that I would not have to tell her that Lady Elinor had burnt down her house. Meg's absence meant that I had to rely on another maid to pack for me, and she required more direction than I was used to having to give. I had just sent her back upstairs after her third trip to the library to inquire about the specifics of what I would need when my mother burst through the door, Davis close on her heels.

"Lady Bromley to see you, madam," he called out over my mother's shoulder.

"Again you have embroiled yourself in controversy," she said. "I am most displeased. The newspapers are full of the role you had in bringing down Lady Elinor. It is disgraceful, unladylike, outrageous."

"Mother—"

"It is of no consequence, however. I am here on the queen's business. She asked that I inquire whether you had yet made a decision about the matter we discussed with her at Windsor."

"A decision?" I asked.

"Don't play dumb with me, child. You know perfectly well that Her Majesty expects you to marry. Who is the lucky gentleman to be?"

"Colin isn't even in England."

"Then Bainbridge. Excellent. I do like the idea of your being a duchess. And I heard all about the falling-out he and your American friend had." Margaret had expertly staged the event. She cried, he stormed off, and somehow everyone felt sorry for her before the end of the evening. Even the lord mayor of London himself consoled her. Her parents felt particularly bad and were convinced she had been ill used and was heartily disappointed. So convinced, in fact, that they agreed to let her take up residence in Oxford a full three weeks before they'd intended. Her only disappointment, she insisted to me, was that she hadn't been there to confront Lady Elinor with me. That, she said, would have made her Season complete.

"Jeremy hasn't proposed to me, Mother." I shook my head. "Haven't we already had this conversation?"

"Let me assure you, Emily, that it is a conversation that will be repeated at regular intervals until you have an answer for the queen."

"Perhaps when I return from Greece—"

"Greece? Good heavens, you can't intend to go back there! What will you do? Mr. Hargreaves isn't there, is he? It wouldn't be proper without a chaperone, although if you were engaged..."

I let her prattle on and gave her very little trouble. I felt I owed it to her after all she'd done to save my reputation. I listened to her well enough only to know when to give the right meaningless answers and wondered what she would do with herself if ever I did remarry. Hound me for an heir, I suppose. I shuddered at the thought.

With Lady Elinor in prison, I'd been able to persuade Colin that my house no longer needed to be guarded. I insisted that Sebastian, should he ever come back, would not harm me. On my last night in London, I awoke to find that, once again, an intruder had come into my bedroom. This occasion, however, brought me no fear. Sebastian had been perfectly quiet, disturbed no one in the house, and had not had to cut through my window; I'd left it open, an invitation of sorts, I suppose, though not one I had consciously made. On the pillow next to me, I found a bundle of letters, a rose, and a small box. An oddly familiar scene.

I opened the letters first. One was from him; the other two were those that Lizzie had stolen from my library. His note was, as always, short:

> I've kept some things for myself: Mother's Bible and the snuffbox. Yes, I realize what this means. You may tell the boy that he'll always be looked after. I hope you enjoy the rest. We will meet again, my darling Kallista. Δακρύει φιλέραστον ἰδοὺ ῥόδον, οὕνεχα κείναν ἄλλοθι χοὺ κόλποις ἡμετέροις ἐσορᾶ.

I could read the Greek with little difficulty: *Lo, the lovers' rose sheds tears to see her away, and not on my bosom.* It came as no surprise to find that the box contained Cécile's Marie Antoinette earrings.

34

━━━━━━━━━━━━━━━━━━━

I WAS IN GREECE BY THE END OF THE FOLLOWING WEEK, HAVING TRAV-
eled through Paris to give Cécile her earrings and to collect her,
Caesar, and Brutus. I wanted her in Greece with me and knew that I
could not have her without her dogs. Colin was no longer in France,
having been summoned by Buckingham Palace to Vienna to work on I
knew not what. I missed him but was content to be back on Santorini,
basking in the warm sun, unable to get enough of the salty air.

Mrs. White had been quite altered by her stay at the villa; I hardly
recognized her when I arrived. Mrs. Katevatis, my cook, had been horrified when she first saw the woman and immediately took her under
wing. She fed her all the wonderful Greek food I had come to love,
and before long Mrs. White had started to gain weight and eventually
lost altogether the gaunt, pained expression that I had seen when I
first met her. Edward thrived on the island, chasing Cécile's dogs and
following Adelphos, Mrs. Katevatis's son, everywhere. Edward idol-
ized the older boy. The trip had done both mother and son immeasur-
able good.

I let Mrs. White explain to the child who his father had been,
and after she had finished, I presented him with a gift from Beatrice:

Marie Antoinette's pink diamond. He was too young to understand the significance of the stone and its history, but someday he would, and I hoped it would bring him some measure of happiness.

We fell into a happy routine at the villa, and as always when I was in Greece, I thought that I should never want to leave. Cécile and Mr. Papadakos, the village woodworker, had completed the miniature rendering of Pericles' Athens they had started on in the spring and were now working on a re-creation of the temple of Artemis at Ephesus. I studied my Greek, dividing my time between reading Homer and practicing the modern language by conversing with the villagers.

We ate breakfast outside whenever the weather was fine, and on this day the sky was bluer than ever, and the Aegean Sea spread below us like a great swathe of sapphire silk. I was reading the mail and nearly jumped out of my seat when I opened the first letter in the pile.

"I cannot believe it!"

"What is it?" Cécile asked.

"Mr. Bingham has donated the silver libation bowl to the British Museum."

"I am most impressed. You have mastered the art of persuasion."

"Don't get too excited. He says that he did it only because he could no longer stand being bothered by me with such astounding regularity. Excellent phrase, don't you think? Astounding regularity. 'It is as if, Lady Ashton, you are the tide, banging away at a delicate seashore, oblivious to the effect of your battery on the sand.'" I laughed. "I'd far prefer to be the ocean than the sand."

"Kallista, you have a visitor," Mrs. Katevatis called to me from the kitchen window. "He's said he would wait for you on the cliff path."

Now I did jump from my seat, knowing instantly that there was only one gentleman who would come all the way to Imerovigli to call on me. The village, perched high atop a cliff on the island, was connected to the city of Thíra by a path that offered spectacular views. I walked along it nearly every day, and it was here, months ago, that

Colin had proposed to me. Today when I found him, he was looking over the caldera at the remains of the ancient volcano, but he turned to face me as soon as he heard me approaching.

"I have to admit that, in the end, you did win our bet," Colin said, taking my hands. "So I've come to Greece as you demanded."

"Here only out of duty?" I asked, smiling, wondering how I could have forgot how perfectly handsome he was.

"There are some duties a gentleman prefers to others."

"How was Vienna?"

"I've actually come from London. I had some business there."

"Anything that would interest me?" I asked, fully expecting his usual reply to this question.

"Yes, actually. I hope it will all interest you. But first, I've some gossip I think you'll be pleased to hear."

"What?"

"Lord Pembroke has caused a scandal that has shaken the aristocracy to its core."

"Dare I even hope? What did he do?"

"He eloped to Gretna Green with Isabelle Routledge."

"He didn't!"

"He did."

"That is most welcome news," I said. "My faith in the English gentleman is restored."

"I'm glad to hear it. Now for the rest." He pulled some papers out of the pocket of his white flannel jacket. "Your solicitor sent this. It's a list of houses he thinks might suit you in London."

"Oh." I took the paper from him and glanced at it, hating the thought of having to set up an entire house, dreading the emptiness of it, and feeling a piercing disappointment that such impersonal business had brought him to me.

"Anne confirmed that there is no need for you to feel that you can't stay at Berkeley Square."

"That's kind of her."

"I hope that the rest of these will change your mind about purchasing a house altogether. I cannot leave my estate to you, Emily, and I am aware of the difficult position in which that could place you. I can't break the entail, but I can do this." He handed me two pieces of paper.

I gasped as I looked at the one on top. "A deed for the books in your library?"

"All of them. They're yours, whether you marry me or not. I've settled them irrevocably on you."

The next paper made me laugh out loud. "Your port? You're giving me all of your port?"

"I do hope you won't object to my keeping the whiskey." Our eyes met, and I thought I could stand there forever drinking in his love for me. He brought his hand to my cheek, gently, barely touching it, but the sensation was completely overwhelming; it had been so long that I could hardly remember the feeling of his skin on mine.

"Colin—"

"Emily, will you have me?" he whispered.

"I've done an excellent job resisting you up to now, but when faced with your books and your port…" I took his hand. "You were quite right when you told me a person could find in *The Greek Anthology* a passage appropriate for nearly any situation. 'I am armed against Love with a breastplate of Reason, neither shall he conquer me, one against one; yes, I a mortal will contend with him the immortal: but if he have Bacchus to second him, what can I do alone against the two?'"

"I knew you wouldn't be able to pass up the port," he said.

"Does this mean I get my kiss?"

He bent down and brought his lips to mine, but not before he had slipped the ancient band of gold and lapis lazuli onto my finger. I can say without hesitation that all the time I'd waited had served only to heighten the moment; never before had there been such a kiss.

ACKNOWLEDGMENTS

Myriad thanks to...

Jennifer Civiletto and Anne Hawkins, my two favorite people in the world of publishing: editor and agent extraordinaire.

Danielle Bartlett and Tom Robinson, tireless publicists who work miracles.

Laura Klynstra, for the stunning cover design. Nobody does it better.

Kristy Kiernan and Elizabeth Letts, who read, edit, neurote, comfort, celebrate, and still manage to write their own books. What's wrong with talking on the phone three times a day?

Marcus Sakey, who not only found a title for this book (a seemingly impossible task) but also led me to the wonderful poem by W. H. Auden that so perfectly frames the story.

Jon Clinch, Rachel Cole, Zarina Docken, Melanie Lynne Hauser, Renee Rosen, and Sachin Waikar, for keeping writing from becoming an isolating endeavor.

Bente Gallagher, for reading an early version of this manuscript in record time and providing almost instantaneous feedback.

Shiloh D'Orazio and the crew at the Five Points Starbucks, for keeping me well supplied with chai and letting me sit for hours on end. Jon Allen, we all miss you!

Christina Chen, Tammy Humphries, Carrie Medders, and Missy Rightley, for being the most steadfast friends a person could have.

B.S.R.: Yes, I could have finished the book without your mountain retreat, but the experience wouldn't have been nearly so idyllic.

Gary and Stacie Gutting, who consistently go above and beyond the call of parental duty, even volunteering to read for me in the middle of the night.

Anastasia Sertl, for constant inspiration.

Matt and Xander, who are forced to tolerate substandard meals and a house full of dust buffaloes, not bunnies, while I'm writing. You deserve far more than thanks.

THE HISTORY

BEHIND

THE STORY

The London Season

* * *

A CYNIC ONCE CALLED ENGLISH HIGH SOCIETY "THE BORES AND THE bored," and though there may be a certain measure of truth in the description, particularly to those with modern sensibilities, it's difficult to deny that, particularly during the Season, society was hard at work. The precise dates varied from year to year, but families came from their country estates to their spectacular London townhouses once Parliament was in session, most not arriving until late spring, ready to embark on a dizzying whirl of activites.

There were numerous sporting events, including Ascot, the Derby at Epsom Downs, and the Henley Regatta. The finest horses in the country raced at Ascot and the Derby, while at Henley, oarsmen competed against one another for three days, crowds lining the bank of the Thames, watching two boats vying in each heat. The races themselves were of great importance to the spectators, but equally captivating were the elaborate picnics set up on the grounds, because regardless of the specific occasion, the Season was a Marriage Market designed to provide ample opportunity for matches to be made.

Every activity, from races to the annual Summer Exhibition at the Royal Academy of Arts, provided young ladies a chance to spend chaperoned time with eligible bachelors. Whether at the opera at Covent Garden or at any of an obscene number of luncheons, teas, dinner parties, and balls, there was no time to be wasted. Days started early, often with a ride in the Park, and ended late, many balls only beginning to wind down at three o'clock in the morning.

Doing a Season took no small amount of money; it was a game open only to the wealthy. Aside from the costs incurred from simply having a house in London, there were enormous wardrobe expenses. Moderately well-to-do families might scrimp and save so that their daughters could have a single Season—a time in which girls faced enormous pressures to find a suitable husband quickly or be faced with the possibility of lonely spinsterhood. The weeks were limited— as soon as grouse season opened, the *ton* disappeared from town in a great rush, headed to the country to shoot birds.

Charles Frederick Worth

━━━━━━━━━━━━━━━

Dressing for the Season was serious business, and no one turned out better-looking gowns than Charles Frederick Worth. Worth, an Englishman from Bourne, Lincolnshire, went to Paris in 1845. After some years working for Gagelin, a textile company, he opened The House of Worth at 7 rue de la Paix, and was soon designing gowns for the wealthiest and most influential ladies in Europe and the United States. The French Empress Eugénie, wife of Napoleon III, the Austrian Empress Elisabeth, and Queen Victoria were clients of his, as were numerous members of the Rothschild and Vanderbilt families.

Worth was known for using the finest fabrics available and insisting that his gowns fit flawlessly. His autocratic personality may have occasionally inspired fear in ladies, but none would be disappointed with his creations. Perfection, however, came at a steep price. In today's dollars, his dresses could cost nearly $10,000, and the number of gowns required for a Season could lead to a staggering bill.

Marie Antoinette and the Dauphin

⁕⁕⁕⁕⁕⁕⁕⁕⁕⁕⁕⁕⁕⁕⁕

The much-maligned French queen had at her disposal an impressive collection of jewelry. She wore some of the most famous gemstones in history: the Hope Diamond, the Hortensia Diamond (which is pink), the yellow Sancy Diamond, and the 140-carat Regent Diamond. The Crown Jewels were not her own, but her personal collection was extensive—and when she tried to escape from France during the Revolution, she handed them over in a box to her trusted hairdresser, Léonard, who kept them safe, eventually giving them to her daughter.

Sotheby's recently auctioned one of these jewels—a pink diamond—along with a small leather trunk owned by Jackie Kennedy Onassis that had once belonged to the queen. The Smithsonian displays the diamond earrings I've given to Cécile in the novel—the ones Marie Antoinette was wearing when she was arrested. They're pear-shaped drops, one 14.25 carats, the other 20.34 carats, and are no longer in their original silver settings, but instead in platinum reproductions meticulously made by Harry Winston. And although I'd already conceived of Sebastian and his thefts, a locket stolen from a house in London's Notting Hill in 2004 could have inspired the story.

The piece, which had belonged to the French queen, had been in its current owner's family for more than two hundred years.

The dauphin, Louis Charles, son of Louis XVI and Marie Antoinette, spent his final years in prison, dying at the age of ten. Stories that he had escaped flew across the continent, and many people believed that the child who died was an imposter, sympathetic jailers having smuggled out the true dauphin. By the time the monarchy was restored in France in 1814, there was no shortage of men claiming to be the Lost Dauphin. Among the more eccentric claimants was Eleazer Williams, a soldier, spy, and Episcopal missionary, who settled in Wisconsin. In fact, he was the great-grandson of a captured colonist and an Indian chief.

Another man, Karl Wilhelm Naundorff, received the blessing of Louis Charles's nurse and one of Louis XVI's ministers. The one person who might have actually been able to confirm his identity, the dauphin's sister, Marie Thérèse, would not see him. And just as well— she would have been disappointed. In 2000, DNA testing to compare the heart taken from the body of the boy who died in prison with Marie Antoinette's hair proved the child was in fact Louis Charles. Not all stories have romantic ends.

Suggestions for Further Reading

The Party That Lasted 100 Days: The Late Victorian Season, Hilary Evans

Sex Scandal: The Private Parts of Victorian Fiction, William A. Cohen

The Art of Dress: Clothes and Society 1500–1914, Jane Ashelford

Nineteenth-Century Fashion in Detail, Lucy Johnston

The Opulent Era: Fashions of Worth, Doucet, and Pingat,
Elizabeth A. Coleman

Select Epigrams from the Greek Anthology, J.W. Mackail (editor)

TURN THE PAGE FOR A PREVIEW OF
TASHA ALEXANDER'S NEXT NOVEL

FATAL
WALTZ

AVAILABLE IN SUMMER 2008 FROM

wm

WILLIAM MORROW
An Imprint of HarperCollins*Publishers*

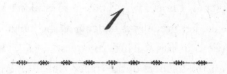

1

I HAD NOT NOTICED IT WHEN SHE FIRST ARRIVED: THE WAY SHE LEANED too far towards him as he kissed her hand, the hint of surprised recognition in his eyes. But having spent an afternoon in the same room as them, watching the effortless manner in which they fell into familiar conversation—two striking individuals against an equally spectacular backdrop—I could not deny that they were more than casual acquaintances. Never had I suspected my fiancé was so close to another woman.

I was accustomed to and often amused by the parade of young ladies who flirted with Colin Hargreaves at every opportunity. The fact that he looked something like a Greek statue of ideal man—by Praxiteles, of course—made him irresistible to debutantes. His enormous fortune, family lineage that could be traced to the time of William the Conqueror, and a well-tended estate ensured that he was equally attractive to their parents. But until today, I'd never seen him react to a woman the way he did to the Countess von Lange.

"And you know, *Schatz*, the Baroness Meinz thought that Tintoretto had done the doors of the Duomo in Florence. Can you imagine?" she asked. *Schatz?* I was shocked to hear her use a term of endearment in such an intimate tone of voice.

"Well, perhaps she's no scholar of art, but—" Colin began.

"Scholar? Darling, she's absolutely hopeless. Why even you know who Tintoretto is, don't you Lady Ashton?"

"Of course," I said, my lack of knowledge of Renaissance art making it impossible for me to add anything more.

"You understand, I hope, why Tintoretto couldn't have done the doors?" she asked, her green eyes dancing as she looked at me.

"My expertise is in classical art, countess," I said. "I'm afraid I'm unable to discuss the nuances of the Italian Renaissance."

"Nuance has nothing to do with it. Tintoretto was a painter. Ghiberti was a sculptor. He did the doors—Michelangelo called them *gates of paradise*." She pushed against Colin's arm playfully. "You are going to have to educate her. I can't have you married to someone who's as foolish as the baroness. It would be unconscionable."

"You've nothing to fear on that count," he said. "Emily's brilliant."

"Spoken like a man in love." She had turned so that her back was almost to me, cutting me out of the conversation.

"Will you excuse me?" I asked. There are moments when one is overwhelmed with a feeling of awkwardness, when grace and sophistication and even coherence are goals more remote than that of a woman in evening dress climbing Mount Kilimanjaro or of my mother convincing me to adopt her definition of a successful life. This was one of those moments, and I had no desire to prolong it. As I stood up, my heel caught the silk hem of my gown and I tripped. Not daring to look at the countess, I mustered as much dignity as possible following what was a decidedly inelegant recovery and headed for the tea table.

Every inch of the mahogany surface was covered by dainty china platters heaped with sandwiches, biscuits, and cakes. Although I did not doubt for an instant that it was all delectable, none of it appealed to a stomach seared by embarrassment. I poured myself a cup of tea, my unsteady hands sloshing the golden liquid onto the saucer, and took a seat on the other side of the parlor.

"Stunning woman, the countess, wouldn't you say, Lady Ashton?" Lord Fortescue dropped onto the chair across from me, its delicate frame bowing under his weight. "Great friend of Hargreaves's. They've known each other for years. Inseparable when he's on the continent."

I'd had the misfortune in the past year of drawing the attention and ire of Lord Fortescue, confidante of Queen Victoria and broadly considered to be the most powerful man in the empire. I despised him as much as he despised me, and wondered how I would survive for days on end trapped at Beaumont Towers, his extravagant estate in Yorkshire. Ignoring his question, I looked across the drawing room at a gentleman sprawled on a moss green velvet settee. "Is Sir Thomas asleep? That can't bode well for this party."

"So unfortunate that you had to postpone your wedding," Fortescue drawled. "But we needed Hargreaves in Russia. Couldn't be avoided." Colin and I had planned to be married as soon as possible after I'd accepted his proposal, but he was called away just two days before the wedding—no doubt by Lord Fortescue—to assist with a delicate situation in St. Petersburg. This had caused a considerable amount of gossip, as we'd bowed to family pressure to invite several hundred guests.

"Mrs. Brandon tells me that Sir Thomas has a terrible habit of dozing in Parliament. I marvel that his constituents continue to reelect him." I turned my head to stare out the window across the moors.

"I wouldn't expect Hargreaves to be in a hurry to marry you now that he's renewing his acquaintance with the countess." He tapped on the side of his empty glass, which a footman immediately refilled with scotch. As soon as the servant had stepped away, my adversary resumed his offensive. "I've no interest in protecting your feelings, Lady Ashton. You will never make an appropriate wife for him, an

I shall do everything in my power to make sure that he never marries you."

"I wonder if I could fall asleep in Parliament," I said, refusing to engage him. "I shouldn't think the benches are that comfortable, though it's not difficult to believe many of the speeches are tedious enough to induce even the heartiest soul to slumber. But I'd wager the House of Commons is more lively than Lords." Across the room, the countess had pulled her chair closer to Colin's, her hand draped elegantly over his armrest.

"You will not avoid conversation on this topic," Lord Fortescue said, his voice sharp, his already ruddy complexion taking on an even brighter hue.

"You're quite mistaken." At last I allowed my eyes to meet his. "Let me assure you that I have every intention of avoiding it entirely. My private life is exactly that: private." I was resolved to let this man see me as nothing but unflappable. "It's rather cold in here, isn't it? It can be so difficult to heat large houses."

"The sooner you learn your place the better," he said.

"Lord Fortescue, there is little less appealing to me than having to pass even an hour in close quarters with you. But we're both here and rather than spending the duration of this party bickering, I shall do all I can to be pleasant." I gave him my most charming smile. "Let's begin again. I was surprised to receive your invitation. It was good of you to acquiesce to Mr. Brandon's request." Robert Brandon, who was married to one of my dearest friends, Ivy, had recently decided to enter politics. His quick mind and steady character appealed to Lord Fortescue, who decided to groom the younger man for greatness. It was Ivy who had wanted me at this

you really think I agreed to invite you to amuse Brandon's woman who claims an above-average intelligence, you are ted."

There was no point in replying to this. Unfortunately the only thing I could focus on other than Lord Fortescue was not a welcome distraction: the intent look on Colin's face as he listened to his beautifully sophisticated companion. Thick, dark lashes framed eyes that sparkled when she spoke with lips more red than should be found in nature. I bit my own, hoping to deepen their hue, then applied myself to my rapidly cooling tea. I was thankful when Flora Clavell sat next to me.

"Emily, Gerald decided to give the British Museum that Etruscan statue you found in our house." I had met Flora soon after her marriage to Sir Thomas's son and, though we were not much in each other's company, had always enjoyed speaking with her. She and my friend Margaret Seward had attended the same school in New York when they were girls, but unlike Margaret, who had gone on to graduate from Bryn Mawr, Flora did not continue her education. Nonetheless, she was enlightened enough to have invited me to search her husband's estate when she'd heard about the project on which I'd embarked, a quest to locate and catalog significant works of art buried in country houses.

"How wonderful," I said. "Your family does a great service by making this permanently accessible to scholars. And I'm grateful beyond measure that you allowed me to record the rest of the objects in your collection."

"I've heard of your efforts regarding this." Mr. Harrison, whom I had not met before he joined us that morning, approached us. Tall and wiry, he was all angles and bent down to give Lord Fortescue's hand a sharp shake before sitting next to him. "They are much to be commended."

"Thank you," I said.

"I can't imagine your meddling in private estates is much appreciated," Lord Fortescue said, finishing his scotch with a loud gulp and shooting Flora a strange sort of too-long look. The footman refilled the glass the moment it was drained. "Why must you harass people, Lady Ashton? Aloysius Bingham still rages about your inappropriate behavior."

"He may rage all he likes. I did nothing inappropriate. And he did, as I'm sure you well know, donate the silver libation bowl to the museum." I was still pleased with this triumph, which had taken more than an entire London season to achieve. Mr. Bingham had refused to part with the bowl, not because he admired it but because he did not approve of a lady pursuing any sort of academic agenda. I had no difficulty picturing him and Lord Fortescue as the closest of friends. If, that is, Lord Fortescue bothered to have friends.

"I didn't know. I shall have words with him."

"I'm sure he would welcome that," I said. The strained look on Flora's face reminded me that I ought to at least attempt to get along with this odious man, though I confess to being surprised that she showed such concern for Lord Fortescue. The expression on his face while he looked at her gave me further pause. He nodded almost imperceptibly, an admiring shine in his eyes as they met hers.

"Brilliant." Mr. Harrison said, giving me a broad smile. "It's been far too long since I've seen someone spar openly with you, Fortescue. Wouldn't have thought a lady could do it."

"Watch yourself, Harrison. I've no need for your nonsense."

"Gentlemen, please!" Flora said. "This is to be a sporting party, not a weekend of argument." Mr. Harrison apologized at once; Lord Fortescue held up his glass for still more scotch. At that moment, Ivy, cutting an elegant figure in a gown of dark green brocade, entered the room. As always, she was dressed in the latest fashion, her waist impossibly small, the sleeves of her dress fuller than what had been popular the previous year. I was relieved at the opportunity to remove myself from the conversation and nearly knocked over my chair as I leapt out of it to rush to my friend, who greeted me with the warmest embrace.

"You look as if you've narrowly escaped from Lord Fortescue," she said in a low voice. We retreated to a window seat far across the room, away from the other guests. Had the weather been better, the view would have been spectacular: the estate overlooked the moors, and was considered by many to have the most sweepingly romantic location in England. As it was, a heavy mist had settled above the ground, limiting the distance one could see. This was not an entirely bad thing; I half expected to see Heathcliff striding purposely towards the house.

Like the rest of Beaumont Towers, the drawing room was an exercise in ostentation, every piece of furniture upholstered in the finest silk or velvet, the parquet floor covered with an Axminster carpet. But quality and extravagance do not guarantee comfort. It was more like a state reception hall than a place to entertain friends. Rumor had it that Mrs. Reynold-Plympton, Lord Fortescue's longtime mistress, had overseen extensive redecoration of the house and that she considered this, the drawing room, her greatest triumph. The ceiling, all mauve, green, and gold, was at least twenty feet high, its plaster molded in an intricate pattern of entwined rosettes. The gilding continued in a diamond pattern against a taupe background down the top two-thirds of the walls, below which was paneling too dark for the room. On this, at regular intervals, characters from Shakespeare's *Merchant of Venice* had been painted.

"If only it were possible to escape," I said. "I wouldn't have agreed to come here for anyone but you, Ivy." The party was not to be a large one, populated by a select group of politicians and their wives. When the men were not buried in meetings, they would be out hunting the estate's birds, the ladies left with very little to do inside. A typical shooting weekend.

"I know he's awful, but he's so good to Robert. We owe him everything." Robert's ascent in politics had been hastened by Lord Fortescue's support, and in return, Robert was expected to give his mentor absolute loyalty.

"I wonder which is less pleasant: being Lord Fortescue's protégé or his enemy?" I asked. "At least his enemies don't have to spend as much time with him."

"But they do. Lord Fortescue makes a point of keeping his enemies near. That's why Mr. Harrison is here this weekend."

"You mean I'm not the only unwelcome guest?"

"Oh, Emily, let's not talk politics. What do you know about the Countess von Lange? I'm told the attachés in Vienna speak of nothing but her. Her parties are infamous."

"Her existence had entirely escaped my notice until today," I said, frowning. "A statement Colin clearly could not make."

"They do look rather cozy. He must know her from his work on the continent."

"Yes, Lord Fortescue was kind enough to let me know that."

"Oh dear. We shan't talk about it," Ivy said, and dropped her voice to a whisper. "Lord Fortescue seems awfully friendly with Flora Clavell."

"I noticed the same thing. I thought he was devoted to Mrs. Reynold-Plympton?" For years she had acted almost as a wife and offered considerable assistance to him in political matters, particularly when he required personal information concerning his rivals. He was on his third marriage—his first wife had succumbed to fever when they were visiting the West Indies, the second to the rigors of childbirth. Like her predecessors, the current Lady Fortescue did not seem troubled in the least by her husband's mistress.

"*Devoted* is perhaps not the right word, but he certainly hasn't dropped her. I saw them together last weekend at Lady Ketterbaugh's in Kent. There was perhaps a coldness between them, but it was obvious that they're still very much attached. Have you been to the Ketterbaugh's estate? The house is gorgeous beyond belief."

"No, I haven't—"

"Her conservatory is absolutely unrivaled. I don't know when I've seen such an array of plants and—"

I could see that Ivy was about to launch into a full description of the estate, and though no one could help being charmed when she waxed enthusiastic on any subject, I stopped her, not wanting to lose the thread of our conversation. "Surely Flora couldn't be . . . wouldn't . . . Lord Fortescue is so . . ."

"I couldn't agree more," Ivy said. "But I don't think the Clavell fortune is what it used to be. I've heard that at least half of his country house is shut and all the rooms are in dire need of refurbishing. I think she's hoping to improve her husband's position. When Sir Thomas dies, there may not be much left for his son."

"I don't see how allying herself with Lord Fortescue is going to help her husband. Gerald isn't in politics."

"Perhaps he wishes to be," Ivy said, raising her delicate eyebrows.

I smiled. "You are enjoying the role of politician's wife, aren't you?"

"I am, Emily. Very much."

We both looked up at the sound of someone clearing his throat. A gentleman wearing the ribbon of some knightly order I did not recognize stood before us. "Lady Ashton, Mrs. Brandon, may I be so bold as to introduce myself? I've been waiting for our hostess, but she is blind to my plight, and I cannot bear to be kept from conversing with such beauties for even one moment longer. Surely at a party as intimate as this, formalities may be overlooked?"

"I don't see why not," I said, offering him my hand. He took it and raised it to his lips as he bowed deeply and clicked his heels together in a flawless Austrian *handküss.* "*Küss die Hand, gnädige Frau.* Or do you prefer English? I kiss your hand, gracious lady." He repeated this routine on Ivy, then stood still, perfectly erect, a shockingly tall man. "I am the Count von Lange, but I insist that you both call me Karl. I am not a sportsman, I'm afraid, so Lady Fortescue has given me the task of entertaining the ladies while the gentlemen shoot."

"I can assure you we'll be in dire need of entertainment," I said. His earnest manner made me warm to him at once, as did the fact that he was willing to dispense with social formalities. His smile could have charmed the coldest soul, but his eyes revealed nothing. He was more guarded than he wanted to appear.

"Nothing would give me greater pleasure than to provide it," he said, looking as if he were about to twirl the ends of his enormous dark moustache.

"What news have you from Vienna?" Ivy asked. "It was one of my favorite stops on my wedding trip." She blushed slightly as she said this and glanced across the room at her husband, who was speaking with Lord Fortescue.

"The city is as beautiful as ever. So far as I am concerned, nothing in Europe can match the Ringstrasse. And you English know nothing about waltzing."

"Is that so?" I asked. "Then I shall have to visit."

"You are fond of the waltz?" he asked.

"Immensely," I said. As if he could hear what I was saying, Colin looked towards me and I felt bathed in warmth.

"Your fiancé is a lucky man," the count said.

"Well spoken." Ivy's eyes sparkled. "Do you know Mr. Hargreaves?"

"Very well. He's a frequent visitor when his work brings him to Austria."

I was about to ask the count how he and his distressingly elegant wife wound up at Beaumont Towers on a dreary English weekend when I was distracted by Sir Thomas, who, upon awakening rather violently from his nap, managed to knock a towering vase off the table in front of him. His son grimaced, embarrassed on his father's behalf. I had always liked Gerald Clavell. He was well intentioned, if more than a little too eager, but even I had to admit that the prospect of spending more than two days in a row with him was exhausting. It was as if his father's lethargy had spurred him to become the polar opposite.

"I'm absolutely depending on you this weekend, Lady Ashton," he said, coming to my side in a poorly disguised effort to divert my attention from his father. "Will you help me put together a theatrical entertainment? It will give you ladies something to do while we shoot. I can't bear the thought of you all sitting around wasting away."

"I—"

"You simply must. Perhaps something from the Greeks? You can choose whatever you'd like. I'm sure Lord Fortescue's library is at your disposal."

"If I may," the count interrupted. "I would be honored to assist you in finding an appropriate piece."

"How about something from *The Trojan Women*? We've more ladies than gentleman who could be persuaded to take part," I said.

"I beg you, not a tragedy. Not a tragedy!" Gerald was turning beet red. "You must find something that will put us in a festive mood."

"Aristophanes?" I suggested.

"You know your Greek literature quite well, don't you Lady Ashton?" I had not heard Mr. Harrison come up behind me and startled at the sound of his voice. "Not a woman to be underestimated, eh?" He looked at me carefully as he spoke.

"I find *Lysistrata* vastly diverting," I said.

"*Lysistrata*?" Gerald sounded a bit panicked. Rightly so, I suppose. The story of women joining together to withhold physical pleasures from their husbands in an attempt to thwart a war was, perhaps, not appropriate for our current gathering.

"Not to worry, Gerald," I said. "I'll find something that will delight us all."

"Right." The wrinkles between his eyebrows smoothed. "Please don't wait too long to get started. We should plan to be ready no later than Saturday, don't you think? Do you know where the library is?

I could bring you there now." He took my arm and nodded at Ivy. "Mrs. Brandon, why don't you organize some cards while I'm delivering Lady Ashton. Whist? Yes? We could all meet in the game room in half an hour?"

Ivy stammered a reply as he steered me towards the door. Colin stood up to follow me, but was intercepted by Lord Fortescue. The countess watched all this, a glittering smile on her face, barely nodding at her husband as he rushed to join me.

She is an enchanting thing, Colin, but so young!"
I had gone to my bedroom after leaving the library and was about to return downstairs when I heard the countess's voice floating up from the main hall. I ducked behind a pillar.

"I will not discuss this with you," Colin said.

"Don't be silly. You can't expect that I—"

"Kristiana!" He spoke firmly, and I wished I could see them. The hall was an atrium, gothic arches lining the second floor balcony. If I were to stand two or three arches from where I was, I would be able to look down on them from behind a pillar. But if I moved, they might notice me.

"So you're abandoning your lifelong role as confirmed bachelor?" she asked.

"Yes, and I'm looking forward to it more than you can imagine."

"You underestimate my imagination, *Schatz*."

"Kristiana—"

"You had to know I'd be disappointed."

"I wrote you. This does not come as a surprise," he said.

"I confess that I did not take you seriously when you threw me over, though you were very stubborn about it."

"I've nothing more to say on the subject."

"I believed you when you said you'd fallen in love. It's an easy enough thing to do. But I never thought you'd marry her."

"She is everything to me."

"For the moment, perhaps. But I think we both know . . . well, best not to consider that now."

"You're terrible," he said, and I could hear a smile creeping into his voice.

"That's why you've always adored me."

Stunned? Horrified? Frozen? If there were a word that might have captured my emotion at that moment, it was one I did not know. I realized I had been holding my breath, and when at last I drew air, it felt like icy knives in my throat.

"I may have held you in the highest esteem, Kristiana, but I never loved you, nor did you love me."

"We both know that's not true. But it was never your love that I wanted, *mein Schatz*. Wasn't that always our problem?" She was moving away from him, her heels clicking on the marble floor as she stepped into the hall under the balcony. Once her footsteps had faded, I tentatively peeked over the railing and saw Colin leaning against a pillar, arms crossed, countenance imperturbable. I counted to one hundred in Greek before speaking.

"There is a deplorable lack of fires in this house, don't you think?" I asked, calling down from above. "I've not been warm since I arrived."

"Don't move," he said, and crossed the hall to the Elizabethan staircase. When he reached the top, he took me by the arms and in one swift motion pressed me to the wall and kissed me with an urgent passion. Delicious though the moment should have been, I found myself distracted. Was he, in his usual charming manner, doing his best to keep me warm? Or was this display fuelled by his encounter with Kristiana? *Kristiana*. Already I hated the name.

He pulled back and straightened his jacket, turning his head towards the stairs.

"Is something wrong?" I asked.

"Wait," he said. An instant later, I heard heavy, slow footsteps coming from the direction of the bedrooms.

"Hargreaves, let's go." Lord Fortescue, clutching a thick stack of papers to his chest, nodded sharply at him but ignored me. "I want to speak with you privately before Harrison and the rest descend upon us."

"I'm not quite done here," Colin said. Fortescue grunted and gave me a disparaging look before going back downstairs.

"You're not afraid of him?" I asked. "Everyone else in England is."

"I'm not afraid of anyone. And there's no one in Britain or elsewhere who is going to keep me away when I want to be with you." He kissed me again, and this time I did not think of the countess at all.

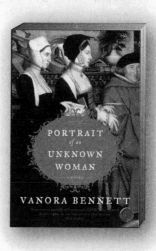

PORTRAIT OF AN UNKNOWN WOMAN
A Novel

by Vanora Bennett
978-0-06-125256-3 (paperback)

Meg, adopted daughter of Sir Thomas More, narrates the tale of a famous Holbein painting and the secrets it holds.

THE SIXTH WIFE
She Survived Henry VIII to be Betrayed by Love...

by Suzannah Dunn
978-0-06-143156-2 (paperback)

Kate Parr survived four years of marriage to King Henry VIII, but a new love may undo a lifetime of caution.

A POISONED SEASON
A Novel of Suspense

by Tasha Alexander   978-0-06-117421-6 (paperback)

As a cat-burglar torments Victorian London, a mysterious gentleman fascinates high society.

THE KING'S GOLD
A Novel

by Yxta Maya Murray   978-0-06-089108-4 (paperback)

A journey through Renaissance Italy, ripe with ancient maps, riddles, and treasure hunters. Book Two of the Red Lion Series.

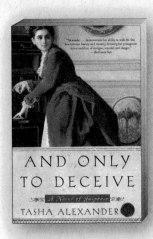

AND ONLY TO DECEIVE
A Novel of Suspense
by Tasha Alexander
978-0-06-114844-6 (paperback)
Discover the dangerous secrets kept by the strait-laced English of the Victorian era.

TO THE TOWER BORN
A Novel of the Lost Princes
by Robin Maxwell
978-0-06-058052-0 (paperback)

Join Nell Caxton in the search for the lost heirs to the throne of Tudor England.

CROSSED
A Tale of the Fourth Crusade
by Nicole Galland   978-0-06-084180-5 (paperback)
Under the banner of the Crusades, a pious knight and a British vagabond attempt a daring rescue.

THE SCROLL OF SEDUCTION
A Novel of Power, Madness, and Royalty
by Gioconda Belli   978-0-06-083313-8 (paperback)
A dual narrative of love, obsession, madness, and betrayal surrounding one of history's most controversial monarchs, Juana the Mad.

PILATE'S WIFE
A Novel of the Roman Empire
by Antoinette May   978-0-06-112866-0 (paperback)
Claudia foresaw the Romans' persecution of Christians, but even she could not stop the crucifixion.

ELIZABETH: THE GOLDEN AGE
by Tasha Alexander   978-0-06-143123-4 (paperback)
This novelization of the film starring Cate Blanchett is an eloquent exploration of the relationship between Queen Elizabeth I and Sir Walter Raleigh at the height of her power.

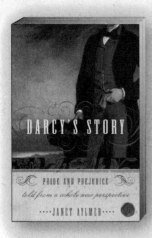

DARCY'S STORY
by Janet Aylmer
978-0-06-114870-5 (paperback)
Read Mr. Darcy's side of the story—*Pride and Prejudice* from a new perspective.

THE CANTERBURY PAPERS
A Novel
by Judith Healey
978-0-06-077332-8 (paperback)
Follow Princess Alais on a secret mission as she unlocks a long-held and dangerous secret.

THE FOOL'S TALE
A Novel
by Nicole Galland   978-0-06-072151-0 (paperback)
Travel back to Wales, 1198, a time of treachery, political unrest...and passion.

THE QUEEN OF SUBTLETIES
A Novel of Anne Boleyn
by Suzannah Dunn   978-0-06-059158-8 (paperback)
Untangle the web of fate surrounding Anne Boleyn in a tale narrated by the King's Confectioner.

REBECCA
The Classic Tale of Romantic Suspense
by Daphne Du Maurier   978-0-380-73040-7 (paperback)
Follow the second Mrs. Maxim de Winter down the lonely drive to Manderley, where Rebecca once ruled.

REBECCA'S TALE
A Novel
by Sally Beauman   978-0-06-117467-4 (paperback)
Unlock the dark secrets and old worlds of Rebecca de Winter's life with investigator Colonel Julyan.

REVENGE OF THE ROSE
A Novel
by Nicole Galland
978-0-06-084179-9 (paperback)
In the court of the Holy Roman Emperor, not even a knight is safe from gossip, schemes, and secrets.

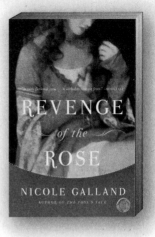

A SUNDIAL IN A GRAVE: 1610
A Novel of Intrigue, Secret Societies, and the Race to Save History
by Mary Gentle
978-0-380-82041-2 (paperback)
Renaissance Europe comes alive in this dazzling tale of love, murder, and blackmail.

THORNFIELD HALL
Jane Eyre's Hidden Story
by Emma Tennant   978-0-06-000455-2 (paperback)
Watch the romance of Jane Eyre and Mr. Rochester unfold in this breathtaking sequel.

THE WIDOW'S WAR
A Novel
by Sally Gunning   978-0-06-079158-2 (paperback)
Tread the shores of colonial Cape Cod with a lonely whaler's widow as she tries to build a new life.

THE WILD IRISH
A Novel of Elizabeth I & the Pirate O'Malley
by Robin Maxwell   978-0-06-009143-9 (paperback)
Hoist a sail with the Irish pirate and clan chief Grace O'Malley.